Living Things

The boy was utterly terrified to be in the cemetery, a few feet away from the exact spot where the bokor and his evil disciples were buried. Glancing nervously at the long mound of dirt, he jumped when he thought he saw the ground move, ever so slightly. Clenching the crucifix so tightly his fingers hurt, he blinked his eyes rapidly. Nothing had moved, he told himself. It must have been a shadow.

"Be brave and patient," Silvo admonished. "It won't be much longer." He wiped sweat from his brow, then resumed digging, much more exhausted now, and breathing hard.

Jean look intently at the cypress casting a moon shadow over the mass grave, and the branches did not seem to be rustling. There wasn't even a faint breeze to cool the perspiration on the nape of the boy's neck. Not enough wind to make a shifting shadow. It must have been a trick of his mind that had made the earth quiver.

But, in unison with the sound of Silvo's spade throcking into the ground, the mounded dirt shook again. Jean's eyes widened, and he almost dropped the ebony crucifix. As his grandfather had done, he kissed the face of Christ, speechlessly hoping for some kind of help from the martyred savior.

The spade throcked again.

And again the grave mound trembled.

Books by John A. Russo published by
BURNING BULB PUBLISHING.

The Academy
The Awakening
Black Cat
The Booby Hatch
Dealey Plaza
Limb to Limb
Living Things
Night of the Living Dead

Most Burning Bulb Publishing books are available at special quantity discounts for bulk purchases for sales promotions, premiums or fund raising. Special books or book excerpts can also be created to fit specific needs.

For details, write to our marketing department at info@burningbulbpublishing.com or via standard post at Burning Bulb Publishing, P.O. Box 4721, Bridgeport, WV 26431

LIVING THINGS

JOHN A. RUSSO

Burning Bulb
PUBLISHING

Living Things
by **John A. Russo**

Burning Bulb Publishing
P.O. Box 4721
Bridgeport, WV 26330-4721
www.BurningBulbPublishing.com

Cover designed by Gary Lee Vincent with the following licensed elements from Fotolia:
– Black witch © Arman Zhenikeyev
– Thunder © Galyna Andrushko

First Burning Bulb Publishing printing.

Edition ISBN Paperback 978-0692252499

Printed in the United States of America

Library of Congress Control Number: 2014945117

Chango – The ultimate master of voodoo's blackest secrets, his lust for power is matched only by his desire for horrifying vengeance . . .

Vince Dawson – A burned-out ex-detective, he's got one desperate chance to destroy the sorcerer forever – but possibly at the cost of his immortal soul. . .

"Sal the Strap" Stropoli – He spattered the Miami streets with blood to build his massive drug empire – only to confront an evil far beyond his most hideous reckonings . . .

Dr. Martha Lewis – An expert in voodoo, she's determined to finish Chango – even if the price is her life and the lives of the ones she loves . . .

"RUSSO CARRIES HIS TALENT FOR THE HORRIFIC NEATLY OVER INTO THE NOVEL FORM. In fact, reading this book is rather like watching a horror film being shown in your head: the scenes are short, tightly written and graphic in their visualization of violence, terror and death. . . if you like the movies, you'll love the book."

– West Coast Review of Books on Voodoo Dawn

Author's Note

Some of the events depicted in Part One of this book were previously described from a different perspective in my novella, *Voodoo Dawn*, published in a limited edition by Imagine, Inc.

"The Effigy may be made of clay, wood, cloth, soap, filth, snow, or any material the bokor wishes. But in this as in all other diabolic practices, there is no substitute for the required blood."

– Dr. Martha Lewis
Voodoo in Modern Haiti

PROLOGUE

From Haiti the terror came to America, its voyage hastened by the arrest of a demonic little girl with the face of an angel. Like the creatures of Hades, who assume innocent shapes but still stink of sulphur and brimstone, Lucia Suerte had a foul odor that gave her away and caused her to get caught.

Awakened by a bad smell, Chantal Midi jumped when she spied a prowler in the shadows of her bedroom. Chantal's husband was a leader of the *Tontons Macoutes*, the private militia maintained by the president of Haiti, so there was an authorized pistol in her home, and she knew how to use it. Pulling it out of a drawer, she ordered the smelly little thief to lay the bundle of household goods on the bed. Then the bundle cried, and Chantal realized how close she had come to losing her baby boy.

She wanted to pull the trigger, killing the intruder on the spot, but loud shots might rupture the baby's eardrums. Holding the gun steady, Chantal bent toward the tall, narrow window where the screen had been removed by the would-be kidnapper, and yelled for the police.

Handcuffed in the back of a Jeep, the cuffs tightened to the last notch so they wouldn't slip from her frail wrists, Lucia Suerte offered to perform oral sex on the two arresting officers if they would just set her free. Smiling sweetly, she admitted that she was a *loup-garou*, a werewolf, stealing infants and selling them for their flesh.

Captain Armando Raphael, the tough middle-aged chief of police in the capital city of Port-au-Prince, was afraid of the innocent-looking little waif. His nose twitched when he came near her. She stank of poverty, of disease, of the decay and squalor that permeated the rat-infested slum where she was spawned. Fourteen years old, she looked nine. Common sense told the captain that nutritional deprivation had forestalled puberty, making her eerily youthful and sexless. Yet her thin, breastless chest and narrow, bony hips seemed purposefully designed to enable her to wriggle through narrow window openings.

Instead of taking Lucia to an interrogation room, Captain Raphael questioned her from outside her cell, mopping sweat from his broad, swarthy brow, stifling the urge to make the sign of the cross over and over, his bowels turning to water with the feeling that she might suddenly slither her small frame between the bars and sink her *loup-garou* teeth into his neck.

"I work for Chango," she said proudly. "He is my lord and master, the prince of the loas of darkness. I supply him with sustenance for his earthly reign."

Captain Raphael shuddered. Within his jurisdiction many small children had disappeared, never to be seen or heard of again. The people whispered that this was the work of Chango, a *bokor*, a voodoo sorcerer, who had named himself after the god of thunder, lightning, fire, and death. It was rumored that Chango not only murdered the children on his sacrificial altar, but also cannibalized them, eating the flesh and stirring the powdered bones into diabolic potions that he and his followers drank. That was why the remains of his victims would never be found.

Chango could not be found either. He was as elusive as his myth. Fear of him was as pervasive as the fear of the god whose name he had assumed. Captain Raphael yearned to capture him and yet dreaded to meet him face to face.

His fear of pagan spells was more powerful and more immediate than his faith in Catholic prayers. Maybe the Christian saints could help him get into heaven, but an evil god like Chango could make his life a hell right here on earth.

Lucia Suerte confessed to kidnapping ten children over a period of three months. Bragging of her prowess, she said she stole babies from homes, stores, and cars. Half hoping that her claims were just the ranting of a deranged mind, the captain pretended not to believe her – but she was able to fill in substantial details that proved she was telling the truth. On one occasion she had actually plucked an infant from a mother's arms on a busy street.

"Three hundred dollars for each victim," she said wistfully. "More money than I ever dreamed of."

It was indeed a shocking sum. Doing the arithmetic in his head, ten babies times three hundred dollars, Captain Raphael came up with a total of three thousand dollars earned by Lucia Suerte in three months, in a country so poor that the average citizen made less than a hundred and fifty dollars per year.

"What did you do with your fortune?" the captain asked.

The cherub smiled slyly. "It is hidden where you will never find it. And if you do find it, you will wish you hadn't. Lord Chango protects it with a powerful curse."

Sweating profusely, Captain Raphael backed away from the *loup-garou*, trying to maintain his composure. His mind was blank, paralyzed by terror and confusion. He had ho idea how to proceed further, and he would have been reluctant to latch on to a strategy, had one presented itself. Whatever step he took, it might lead to his own destruction. He had no wish to incur the wrath of the evil loas.

A young corporal slinked into the cell block, cast Lucia Suerte a wary, frightened glance, and informed the captain that a telephone call had just come, summoning him to the National Palace. He sighed inwardly with relief that his interrogation was interrupted. Perhaps this scary little prisoner would be taken out of his hands. Maybe the President-for-Life would turn her over to the Tontons Macoutes. Let *them* pursue the leads to Chango, if they dared, like mice following a trail of crumbs toward the fangs of the cat.

As his aide drove him down the wide, palm-lined boulevard to the Palace, Captain Raphael told himself that Chango was a powerful loa, more formidable than Baron Samedi, the loa that had possessed the former President-for-Life, Dr. Francois Duvalier, known as "Papa Doc." Baron Samedi was the spirit of death, but Chango was the Prime Mover of Baron Samedi and all the other loas of the dark realm, wielding their powers and attributes in an infinitely amplified ferocity. Chango encompassed the loas of horror and destruction the way that God the Father, the Son, and the Holy Ghost were encompassed within the Blessed Trinity. If God could send his only begotten Son to earth, Chango could assume the corporeal form of the bokor bearing his name; he was death in the flesh, its raw essence loose in the land, stalking earthly prey.

Escorted by two armed and helmeted guards down the wide, pastel-colored, creamily carpeted corridors of the National Palace, Captain Armando Raphael could discern no visible evidence of the thirty million dollars recently spent by Madam Michele, the wife of Jean-Claude ("Baby Doc") Duvalier, for "renovation and redecorating." A pragmatic, if superstitious man, the captain knew that most of this money had probably been deposited in the

President-for-Life's Swiss bank account. The six million peasants from whom the tax appropriation had been squeezed had never been inside the Palace and were never going to be allowed in to see whether or not their cash had made the least little improvement in the decor.

The two guards ushered Captain Raphael into the exalted presence of the President-for-Life. The captain saluted and then bowed before Jean-Claude, who was seated behind a huge mahogany desk that had once belonged to his father. Above Baby Doc's head hung a huge oil painting of Papa Doc in the black clothes of Baron Samedi being embraced by Jesus Christ, who was crying bloody tears into a crimson pool at the bottom of the portrait, ripples in the pool forming the words, "I have chosen Him." Knowing that he was old and ready to join the loas, in 1970 Papa Doc rewrote the Constitution, lowering the minimum age for president to twenty to ensure his son's succession. But the loas called him sooner than he thought – within less than a year – and Jean-Claude was only nineteen when his father died. No matter. The Legislature passed a special bill declaring him to be twenty-one, magnanimously granting him one year of maturity more than the Constitution required.

Secretly, Captain Raphael did not revere the handsome, mild-mannered Jean-Claude as much as he had feared and respected Francois Duvalier. From his father, Baby Doc had learned how to rape the Haitian treasury, but he had not learned how to rule the peasants. He was trying to reform and subdue the practice of voodooism in favor of Roman Catholicism. He failed to understand that voodoo was the mainstay of Papa Doc's iron reign. When the people saw their President-for-Life always in black suits, their belief that he was the incarnation of Baron Samedi was enhanced.

He magnified this image by designing the Haitian flag in red and black, the colors of the voodoo secret societies. He claimed to be able to read the future in the entrails of goats, and to commune with dead friends by sleeping in their tombs. Tales of his ferocity toward his political enemies were not based merely on rumor and legend. With his own eyes, Captain Raphael had seen Papa Doc torture and kill prisoners in the blood-spattered basement of the palace, and had seen the President-for-Life drinking wine from mugs made out of the dead prisoners' skulls.

One of these mugs used to be on the desk, but it was gone now. Jean-Claude liked to think of himself as a more subtle and civilized ruler, and was often embarrassed when wealthy North American businessmen and politicians derided him for ruling a country that was "ninety percent Catholic and one hundred percent voodoo." Lately, because international human-rights groups were raising a fuss with him, he had officially changed the name of the militia, the Tontons Macoutes, to the Volunteers for National Security. But the people still called them the Tontons Macoutes and still feared and hated them as much as before. Old habits are not quickly changed, old fears not easily erased. Luckily, this was so, or else Baby Doc might have unwisely weakened his presidency beyond the margin of safety. A rebellion might take place, and the government might be overthrown. In such a cataclysm, Captain Raphael could lose his rank, his privileges, his hard earned right to scrape off his share of the governmental graft. He might even lose his life. Better for him that the populace should continue to see no real change in the Tontons Macoutes, and to dread them as much as ever. Instead of being restrained like panthers on a leash, maybe the enforcers needed to be turned loose just a bit, to extinguish the murmurings of dissent that were growing much too noticeable lately. Not that they would need to be quite so ferocious as they were under Papa Doc. In those days, they were like bloodthirsty beasts in their dark, steel-rimmed glasses, ravaging the countryside, raping, pillaging, burning, and slitting the throats of all who dared to disagree with the regime.

One of the veterans of that carnage, the blood of thousands on his hands, was at this moment in the office of the President-for-Life, offering a warm, smiling greeting to Captain Armando Raphael. "I wish to thank you personally, Captain, for the way that your men came promptly to the aid of my beautiful wife and my infant son. You run an admirably disciplined and efficient police force, which as we all know is not an easy task in a country that does not exactly worship the modern ideals of precision and punctuality."

Those charming words were spoken by Franz Midi, the Tonton Macoute husband of Chantal Midi, who had captured the evil waif Lucia Suerte. Franz was fifty-two and Chantal was only nineteen, a lovely maiden wed to an old, baldheaded warrior whose savagery was masked by a kindly face and a refined, soft-spoken vocabulary. He looked very much the prosperous businessman in his dark blue suit, his thick black wrists protruding from crisp white French cuffs, displaying a glittering gold bracelet and a thin platinum watch encrusted with diamonds. Of course, he always was primarily a businessman; even his butchering of peasants was all business. He had to help the regime stay in power so he could continue to land government contracts for roads and schools and other public projects built, torn down, and rebuilt over and over with inferior grades of concrete and asphalt that crumbled after a couple of rainy seasons.

"Mr. Midi, I deeply appreciate your kind words," Captain Raphael said. "I am honored to be at your service."

The President-for-Life asked the police chief to report all that he had learned from his interrogation of Lucia Suerte. Despite his reluctance to openly admit that he believed in the ancient loas as much as anyone else, Baby Doc crossed himself several times at the mention of the name Chango. At the end of the chief 's report, he said, "I have decided, Captain Raphael, that the Volunteers for National Security will take over custody of your prisoner, under the leadership of Franz Midi. If Lucia Suerte will lead us to Chango, we will destroy him, and the Volunteers will get the credit, giving them a new image in the people's eyes. The common citizens long to see this baby killer, this supposed cannibal, brought to justice. "They believe that no force on earth can do it, and we must disabuse them of that notion, showing not only that we have their best interests at heart in preserving the lives of their children, but that we are truly more powerful than their voodoo gods."

PART ONE

THE BOKOR

Maybe this world is some other planet's hell.
– Aldous Huxley

CHAPTER 1

The frail, gray-headed old man trudged the white sand, a small boy at his side. The long, curved instrument in his hand still felt strange, even though he had used it a couple of times before. Its flat metallic head caressing the sand, as slowly he swept it back and forth, back and forth, like a forked stick in the hands of a *houngan*, a voodoo priest, back home in Haiti.

On this balmy January morning in Braxton Beach, Florida, Silvio Narbonne and his grandson had worked their way down to a section of beach that wasn't safe for swimming because of its beds of coral and unpredictable eddies of current. This stretch was used by sunbathers who wished to avoid the crowds. However, there weren't any crowds as yet; it was a couple of hours too early. The lifeguards wouldn't come on duty till noon, patrolling the roped-off section of ocean shore that Silvio and Jean had already swept with their metal detector.

So far the treasure hunt was a disappointment for the seven-year-old boy. He had envisioned finding a chest full of pirate swag, rubies and diamonds and gold doubloons, not just a few coins and a rusty token for renting a beach umbrella. He carried his pitiful amount of loot in the brown bag that had formerly held his snack; an apple and a stick of chewing gum. He finished chomping on the apple and tossed away the core to watch it being snatched up by a gull. That excitement over, he unwrapped his gum and stuck it in his mouth. Despairing of finding any genuine treasure on the beach, he began hunting for shells, even though he realized that it would be a miracle if he found any large, unbroken ones, because the shore was so thoroughly scavenged by tourists.

Wearing only a skimpy yellow bathing suit, the skinny dark-skinned boy walked along with his head down, energetically chewing gum and kicking up sand with his bare feet. The old man stepped up his pace, forcing his arthritic bones to persevere with the metal detector, wondering how much longer he'd be able to keep up, much less be the leader, in these enterprises designed to entertain his grandson.

Under his breath, Silvio muttered his usual prayer, that the loas be kind enough to allow him to live till Jean could fend for himself. The boy's father and mother had both died in prison in Haiti, tortured and killed for their political views. Silvio had little doubt that if he and Jean had not left their home country, they would be dead, too.

The metal detector buzzed loudly, causing the boy to drop a shell fragment and come running back to his grandfather. Silvio chuckled, more amazed than Jean by this modern magic. Leaning on the handle of the implement that allowed him to uncover unseen things, he let the boy dig for the find, hoping it would be something to widen his eyes with wonder. It turned out to be only a keychain buried in the sand. Wiping it off, Jean stuffed it in the pocket of his bathing suit.

A little while later, the buzzer went off again. This time Silvio knelt and started digging while Jean ran ahead. The boy disappeared behind a long, rocky jetty, out of sight of his grandfather. Silvio hustled to finish digging and catch up, lest something bad should happen. He was always worried that the loas who had decided to make Jean an orphan would return to wreak worse havoc.

Rounding the jetty, Jean stopped in his tracks as he spotted something bobbing in the shallow water close to shore. He dropped his paper bag, squinting and using his hand to shade his eyes as the object drifted closer.

Kneeling in the sand, Silvio finished digging up the spot where his metal detector had sounded. He found two quarters and a dime, and smiled joyously as he rubbed them clean. Then he looked around for Jean. His heart skipped a beat when he didn't spy the boy anywhere. Calling out, "Jean! Where are you, Jean?" The old man got to his feet, peering toward the jetty and the bright sun.

Wading into the water, Jean saw that the bobbing object was a drum with ceremonial markings on it. Trying to get nearer to it, he couldn't hear his grandfather's distant hollering because of the soughing of the surf. The drum threatened to bob out of reach. Jean risked going out till the waves were lapping at his chest. Suddenly the drum, open at one end, filled with so much water that it almost sank. But the boy grabbed it just in time, swallowing saltwater as his head almost went under, coming up coughing and spluttering. He couldn't stop choking till he spit out the wad of chewing gum, which had lodged in his throat. He splashed toward shallower water, staggering with the increasing weight of his burden. He dragged the large, heavy drum through wet, furrowed sand, then rolled it over and over, breathing hard, examining all the markings and taking much pleasure in his great find. It was made of hollowed-out wood with animal skin stretched over one end, secured with rawhide thongs. The designs were voodoo symbols that Jean vaguely recognized. He peered into the open end of the drum, spotted something, and jumped back. Then he dared to look again. Reaching inside the drum, he pulled out what at first had scared him, a long, thick bullwhip that had appeared to be a coiled-up blacksnake.

Jean stood up, wiggling the whip by its handle, trying to make it flick and crack, his slender arms lacking the strength to make the trick succeed. Suddenly he froze. He squinted, staring out toward the glistening tide. Dropping the whip beside the drum, he ran back around the jetty, almost colliding into his grandfather.

"Come quickly!" Jean shouted "Some men are sleeping in the ocean!"

The boy tugged his grandfather's hand, and they ventured beyond the jetty, past the drum and whip lying in the sand. At the far end of the beach, they approached seven bodies lying face down in shallow water. Five males and two females, motionless except for movement imparted by the current. None was white. Silvio assumed from the color of their skin that they must be Haitian "boat people" who had failed to make it alive to America, and instead had drowned and washed ashore. He motioned for Jean to stay back, and gave the boy the metal detector to hold. Then he tugged the nearest body farther out of the water, and searched the dead man's pockets. One trouser pocket was empty, but the other was stuffed with soggy greenbacks. Making the sign of the cross to protect himself from the consequences of his greed, Silvio blotted the money on his jeans, then put it into his own pocket.

Jean looked on in awe. He crossed himself in imitation of his grandfather. Even though in Haiti there had been many terrible taboos against stealing from dead people, poverty was so extreme that everyone knew that the taboos would take second place to practicality. It helped that these corpses were all floating face down; if they had been able to look into the eyes of Silvio and Jean, they could have implanted a curse so awesome that it would have instantly frightened the old man and the boy away.

Shakily, Silvio moved on to the next corpse, which was that of a huge, powerfully built, coal-black man in denim cutoffs, nude from the waist up. This dead man's hair was done up in numerous cornrows and pigtails ornamented with little dangling figurines. He was wearing a machete in a sheathe on a thick leather belt. Around his neck was a leather thong. On the thong was a pouch, which Silvio spotted floating in the water.

Silvio shakily untied the necklace and opened the pouch. Suddenly his fingers jerked back as though they were burned, and he emitted a barely stifled scream as something fell out of the pouch into the water. It was a severed human finger. A tiny finger, that of a child. Silvio and Jean both stared at it in wide-eyed horror as it swirled and sank. Silvio gasped out one blood-curdling word, which he now knew was the dead man's name:

"Chango!"

Trembling violently, Silvio forced himself to fish and grope underwater till he seized onto the severed finger and brought it up all covered with sand. The old man whimpered as he washed the finger off and put it back inside the pouch. Then he dropped the necklace onto the beach, wiping his fingers on his clothes as though they had been horribly contaminated. Still shaking, he backed toward his grandson, putting his skinny arms around the boy's frail shoulders.

Silvio mumbled half incoherently. "It is Chango. . . the evil bokor. . . the son of the devil. The witch doctor will not remain dead . . . unless I kill his spirit. God has put it up to me to do so."

Calling on Saint Joseph to make him brave, Silvio left Jean standing alone and took a few halting steps towards Chango's corpse. He mumbled again to himself and made the sign of the cross. He kept talking to urge himself on. "Chango . . . the bokor. . . the evil witch doctor . . . I must kill his spirit."

Trembling, Silvio slid Chango's machete out of its sheathe, the long sharp blade glinting in the sunlight. Jean watched, his mouth gaping open, his teeth chattering.

"Jean!" Silvio shouted. "Do not gaze upon the evil one!"

The little boy squeezed his eyes tightly shut. Mastering all his courage, the old man raised the machete, intending to behead Chango's corpse. He clenched his teeth, tightened his feeble muscles. Just then a command rang out.

"Stop or I'll shoot!"

Silvio froze, the machete poised to strike downward. He turned his head slowly to see a uniformed policeman tightening his finger on the trigger of a service revolver. With his free hand, the policeman was restraining a German shepherd police dog tugging and snarling on a leash. The dog growled ferociously and lunged savagely against its heavy leather collar. Afraid the gun might go off accidentally, Silvio glanced down at the thick, corded muscles at the back of Chango's neck, fighting with his belief that it was absolutely necessary to behead the bokor.

"Drop it!" the policeman snapped. "I don't want to have to shoot you, old man!"

Jean burst into tears. "Please . . . sir . . . please don't hurt my grandfather!"

The policeman's eyes flicked toward the whimpering little boy. At that moment, the dog made another lunge, threatening to break the leash and tear out Silvio's throat.

The policeman dug his heels in and leaned way back, pulling with all his might to avoid being thrown off balance. Snapping some commands, he got control of his dog and once more aimed his gun steadily at Silvio. Glancing helplessly at Jean, Silvio let his breath out in a trembling sigh and dropped the machete to the sand.

The policeman said, "I don't have to shoot him now, son, but I'll guarantee you he's got a lot of explaining to do."

CHAPTER 2

Chango rolled over, his wide eyes seeming to stare up at the two morgue attendants as they dragged him out of the water and stretched him out on the sand, flat on his back, at the end of the row of dead bodies.

A police photographer continued snapping pictures of the corpses, making sure to get good facial close-ups from various angles, to aid in identification. At the same time, a medical examiner was taking fingerprints from each corpse.

Beyond the jetty, three uniformed cops were pacing back and forth, making sure that crowds of people in bathing suits stayed out of the cordoned-off area. It was noon, the sun high in the sky, and the part of the beach safe for swimming was crowded and noisy. But the usual high-pitched gaiety seemed subdued, skewed toward an ominous murmur because word had spread about the drownings.

Nothing like a few deaths on the beach to titillate the tourists, Lieutenant Vince Dawson thought to himself as he glanced over his shoulder at the crowd of gawkers, then leveled a hard stare at Silvio Narbonne, who was sitting handcuffed at the end of the jetty, his grandson cowering beside him. Lieutenant Dawson felt sorry for the boy. But he couldn't let up on the old man till he scared the truth out of him.

Dawson was used to scaring people. He was a tall, balding, sour-looking man with dark, heavy pouches under his beady blue eyes. At age forty-eight he had seen enough cruelty, enough senseless tragedy, to build a thick-skinned layer of cynicism over his innate kindliness, his deep sensitivity toward the human condition. The soft parts of himself were almost always kept hidden. Exposure was too risky. In his experience, it was an almost sure way to get hurt.

Dawson's partner, Lieutenant Clinton Jones, was also staring hard at Silvio Narbonne, doing his best to contribute to the scare tactic. But he didn't possess – and did not necessarily envy – Dawson's natural ability to look like an insensitive bully. For one thing, he was younger, only thirty-five, with a smooth, unwrinkled, cafe au lait complexion. On certain days, when he managed to get enough sleep, he looked almost callowly handsome. This was his blessing and his curse. It helped him land women, but made it hard to intimidate witnesses.

The drum, the bullwhip, the machete, the leather necklace and pouch were laid out on the sand by Silvio's feet. Grunting with the pressure of his beer belly against his belt buckle, Lieutenant Dawson bent over, picked up the pouch, and fiddled with it. Silvio raised his eyes in a plea for sympathy that was not directed at Lieutenant Dawson, but at Lieutenant Jones and the arresting officer, Patrolman Rudez, because those two policemen happened to be black. Rudez was standing by with his huge police dog, which was now sitting docilely in the sand, panting from the heat and occasionally wagging its tail very slowly, as if to exhibit a mild degree of friendliness without wasting much energy. To the two detectives, Rudez said, "The old man says his name is Silvio Narbonne, and this is his grandson, Jean."

"They speak English?" Jones asked Rudez.

"With a Haitian accent, but you can understand them well enough."

Jones spoke sternly to Silvio, his voice surprisingly deep and gruff for his youthful appearance. "My name is Lieutenant Jones, and this is my partner, Lieutenant Dawson. We can toss you in jail if we want to. You understand me?"

Dawson continued fiddling with the pouch, twining the thong around his fingers, purposely handling the so-called "evil charm" irreverently so the superstitious prisoner would fear him all the more.

"Yes. . .yes, sir. . .I understand," Silvio said tremblingly. Afraid to see the severed finger fall once more out of the pouch, he lowered his eyes, then averted them sideways from his handcuffed wrists. He was ashamed to be like this, like a shackled dog, in front of his grandson. He felt older and more frail than usual. He was unable to sense a trace of pity from any of the three policemen. He couldn't believe that the pock-faced, barrel-chested Rudez had actually refrained from killing him earlier, and he knew he must have been saved only by the presence of Jean. He had been told that here in America he was supposed to be safe from the sort of persecution that was the rule in his homeland. But out of a lifetime of habitual dread of what those in authority might do to him, he couldn't help equating these American cops with the Haitian ones who had tortured and killed his son and daughter-in-law.

Jones said, "Lieutenant Dawson and I want you to explain what you were up to when Patrolman Rudez arrested you. It's against the law to disfigure a corpse. You realize that, Mr. Narbonne?"

Rudez growled, "There's no doubt what he was going to do with that machete, Lieutenant. He was fixing to behead that dead man."

Jones and Dawson exchanged dour, steely-eyed glances. Dawson held the leather pouch in front of his face and let it swing back and forth, back and forth, on its rawhide thong. Out of the corner of his eye he saw the old man looking even more scared than before, and he hated the kind of mumbo-jumbo that could rattle people's brains this way. Ever since the boat people had begun arriving in Florida, there had been a spate of weird occurrences ascribed to the practice of voodoo. The more sensationalistic newspapers were having a ball, playing up stories of animal sacrifices and grave robbery. Voodoo priests were supposed to be using stolen human skulls in their ceremonies. Up till now, as far as Jones and Dawson knew, nothing of this nature had taken place in Braxton Beach. But now this harmless-looking old man had apparently tried to take a dead man's head.

Before the detectives could ask another question, Silvio started babbling in a weak, husky voice. "Sirs. . .where I come from, in Port-au-Prince, we all knew of Chango, the bokor, the evil priest, who stole small children from our towns and villages and killed them on his altar. I never saw Chango till this very day, but like everyone else I knew that the bokor always wore a charm of a child's finger in a pouch to prove that he is the reincarnation of the God of Death, whose name he has taken for himself. He has the power to come back to life in an even more terrible form. The only way this can be prevented is to decapitate the bokor and sew the lips of his followers shut so they won't be able to answer him when he calls them to come out of their graves."

Lieutenant Clint Jones shook his head in amazement. "Weird! You figure he really believes this crap? Or does he want us to think he's senile so we'll turn him loose?"

"Damned if I know," said Lieutenant Dawson, dropping his hand to let the leather pouch dangle at his side. "Tell me the truth, Silvio – are you in this country illegally?"

The old man raised his voice indignantly. "No – no, sir! I have papers, sir. My grandson and I . . .we are not – we are not boat people."

Patrolman Rudez spoke up. "There *are* some papers in his billfold, Lieutenant Dawson. Want to check them out?"

"Let me see," said Jones. He took the billfold from Rudez and fished out the documents.

Silvio stammered, "Sir. . .I have a. . . a visa. I am caretaker for tourist cottages owned by Dr. Martha Lewis, a professor at the college. She helped me obtain the visa, and brought me over here to work for her."

"Nice of her," Dawson snapped. "Saved you from trying to make it in a leaky boat." Maintaining his outward look of hardness, of skepticism, he winced inwardly at the pain that his sarcastic remark brought to the faces of the old man and the little boy. Sorry, but it's the way the cookie crumbles, he told himself. I'm only doing my damn job.

Jones took a note pad from the inside pocket of his suit jacket and started writing. "His papers seem to be in order, Vince. I'll copy down addresses and phone numbers."

Dawson almost cracked a smile. It amused him that his partner always carried the thinnest possible pad to take notes on, and wore his gun in a thin holster clipped under his waistband, for fear that anything bulky would spoil the look of his expensive, impeccably tailored suits. Fine apparel was one luxury that Jones wasn't about to deny himself, even with the recent burden of alimony payments eating away at his cop salary.

While Jones did his scribbling, Dawson told Rudez he'd like a few words with him, and led him a few steps away, where they could talk without being overheard by Silvio and Jean. Dawson patted Rudez's dog, which kept up a low, ominous growl while it was having its head scratched. Under his breath, the patrolman asked, "Are we gonna book the old man for anything?"

Dawson stopped petting the German shepherd and shook his head, grimacing wryly. "Attempted mutilation of a corpse? Sounds a bit ridiculous, doesn't it? I think it'd be a shame to make Mr. Narbonne lose his visa just because he happens to be a superstitious immigrant."

Rudez snorted. "Yeah, I guess you're right, Lieutenant. Better let him go. No arrest report, right?"

"That's what I was going to suggest."

"Okay. I'll take the cuffs off him. But before I do, I'll chew his ass out good, so he won't try anything this goofy anymore."

Lieutenant Jones came over, tucking his notepad away. "Gonna let him go, huh?"

Dawson nodded. To Rudez, he said, "Make sure Narbonne knows to stay where we can find him in case we come up with some additional questions."

"Gotcha," said the patrolman as he and his dog strode toward the frail, frightened prisoner.

Sounding almost cheerful, Jones said to Dawson. "Let's go have a look at this Chango. Which one is he?"

Rudez turned and shouted over his shoulder. "You can't miss him, Lieutenant. He's the biggest, ugliest one. Must be damn near seven feet tall."

"The man wasted his potential, then." Jones snickered. "Can't be as much money in voodoo as there is in pro basketball."

The two detectives walked over to where Chango's huge, powerfully built body was being photographed and fingerprinted. Dawson absently fiddled with the thong and pouch as he stared at the dead man they once belonged to.

It almost seemed impossible that Chango's thick slabs and ridges of sculpted muscle, so apparently strong and useful, weren't actually able to move anymore. About him, even in death, there was an aura of pride, of forcefulness. Each of his massive pectorals bore scars in the shape of lightning bolts. His cheeks were tattooed with small serpents. Other tattoos and scars representing skulls, claws, and daggers dotted his thighs, forearms, and biceps. His ebony face was very handsome in a sinister way, with an unusually large, broad nose and angrily flaring nostrils. His wide lips were slightly parted, revealing extraordinarily white and even teeth that had supposedly bitten into human flesh.

Dawson found himself muttering almost reverently, "So this is Chango, the self-styled God of Death. I admit it, Clint – if he were still alive I'd hate like hell to have to chase him into a blind alley."

"Well, you might have to yet," Jones said with a thin smile. "If Silvio Narbonne is giving us the straight poop, the bokor will come back to life unless we chop his head off. Maybe Rudez shouldn't have stopped the old man."

They scanned the row of corpses. Now that the bodies were lying on their backs, it could be seen that all of them had voodoo symbols burned, carved, or tattooed all over their flesh.

Dawson said, "I think we can be thankful that these particular boat people didn't get here alive. We have a surplus of crazies to deal with already. We don't need any nuts butchering children in the name of some kind of African god. Voodoo did originate in Africa, didn't it, Clint?"

"Yeah, but don't rub it in. Anyway, there's supposed to be good voodoo and bad voodoo. It's not like all my ancestors were bloodthirsty."

"No, they were just cannibals," Dawson said.

Jones was trying to think of a comeback when Rudez interrupted. "Excuse me, Lieutenant Jones, Lieutenant Dawson. What are we going to do with the drum, machete, and whip? Silvio Narbonne wants to take them. He's all shook up, pleading with me. He claims that if the bokor can't be beheaded, then the only thing that might keep him in his grave would be if somebody buries and prays over his most sacred possessions."

Chuckling, Jones said, "I told you there was good voodoo and bad voodoo."

Dawson said, "Let the old man take the damn stuff. We have photos and fingerprints of Chango and the others, so we don't need anything else for ID." He handed Rudez the leather thong and pouch. "Here – take this godawful thing, too. Let the old man bury the whole mess if it'll make him feel any better."

Rudez took the necklace and walked back over to Jean and Silvio. The old man was rubbing his wrists. The handcuffs had already been removed.

"You sure it won't make you feel better too, Vince?" Lieutenant Jones kidded.

"What?"

"Burying the stuff."

"No, Clint, I'm no sucker for superstition. My forefathers didn't live in a jungle, like yours did. They were civilized. They didn't boil missionaries in big pots."

"I know," said Jones. "All they did was burn guys like Copernicus at the stake for coming up with the sacrilegious idea that the earth revolves around the sun."

"How can it revolve when it's flat?" Dawson said.

The two detectives watched the seven corpses being loaded into the morgue van. The deceased weren't going to be taken to the morgue, though. They were destined for a mass grave in the paupers' section of a Braxton Beach cemetery. The money confiscated from them – including the wad that Silvio Narbonne had tried to pocket – would be partly used to defray administrative expenses, and the rest would go into the police pension fund.

Since the early 1980s, when the boat people had begun arriving illegally on American shores, the state of Florida and the United States Immigration and Naturalization Service had not gotten much cooperation from the government of Haiti. Whether the would-be immigrants were alive or dead when they landed in Florida, they were personae non grata. Dealing with them was a costly, time-consuming bureaucratic quagmire. The United States did not wish them to come, and Haiti did not wish them to return once they had embarked. Officials in the Duvalier government did not seem especially alarmed over the fact that large numbers of their former citizens were being lost at sea.

Watching the morgue wagon depart, Dawson said to Jones, "You know, Clint, I was damned tempted to order autopsies on them."

"Why?"

"I don't know. A funny feeling."

"The mumbo-jumbo's workin' on you, man."

Dawson and Jones both laughed. But underneath their laughter they didn't feel quite right about disposing of this case so easily. They were going according to an official protocol that bothered them, even though they understood why it had to be done that way.

American citizens found dead were usually autopsied, to make sure they hadn't died of unnatural causes, but because of the expense and the overload on the system, this practice did not extend to the boat people. If authorities could be reasonably sure that drowning victims washed up on American shores *were* illegal aliens, then the next step was to quietly bury and forget them. Neither the United States nor Haiti would pay to have the corpses shipped back to where they had come from.

"The chief wouldn't have authorized any autopsies," Jones said. "Just the other day he sang the old, tired song telling us to concentrate our resources on crimes rather than suspected crimes, and ones we're reasonably sure we might solve. The ME didn't find any bullet or stab wounds, man. Those people had to have drowned – and from what Silvio Narbonne had to say, it's good riddance."

"I bet it would've made the old man feel better," Dawson said, "if I could've told him that the pathologist was going to go to work on Chango and his cohorts. Cutting the cadavers open, taking out the brains and internal organs, would've been just as good as beheading them, right?"

"I don't know, man," Jones said, as tongue-in-cheek as his partner. "If God can make folks who've been rotting in their graves for hundreds of years rise up whole on Judgment Day, maybe some kind of voodoo spell could animate those suckers even if they were all cut up in little pieces."

CHAPTER 3

By the light of the full moon in the night sky, Silvio and Jean Narbonne entered St. Matthew's Cemetery, passing under a shadowy stone arch. They started picking their way between tombstones and monuments. Silvio carried a burlap sack and a long-handled shovel. Jean carried a crucifix his grandfather had brought with him from Haiti, a gracefully elongated body of Christ depicted in delicately carved ebony.

Earlier today, in late afternoon, Silvio and Jean had come by taxi to the cemetery. Pretending to pray over a grave in the paupers' section, out of the corners of their eyes they had watched the last few shovelfuls of dirt being heaped upon the mound of earth that was intended to be a mass grave for Chango and his followers. The gravedigger was an emaciated, stringily muscled Haitian with a large gold front tooth. Tossing his shovel aside, he staggered toward Silvio, called out a few words in slurred, drunken Creole, and smiled when Silvio answered in the same tongue. He said his name was Jacques Carnot. Swigging cheap vodka from a pint bottle, he kept rubbing Jean's nubbly hair with his knuckles, trying to be friendly but making the boy's head hurt. "Jacques Carnot is no fool," he babbled slyly. "I have done something to help the bokor so he will not put a curse on me for shoveling dirt in his face."

Silvio's heart sank. He was pretty sure he knew what the gravedigger had done.

The elderly priest from St. Matthew's Roman Catholic Church came into the paupers' section of the cemetery.

Opening his prayer book, he stood at the side of the long, mounded trench. Silvio, Jean, and the drunken Jacques Carnot were the only witnesses to the sacred text that the priest read.

"So death is holy, a part of the gift of life. It is God's way of gathering His family unto Himself. Only death in sin is to be feared. Death in grace is to be desired, for death is only the end of probation, not of life. Those who believe in God and honor His commandments will be resurrected. They will enjoy eternal life."

The unintentional irony of the liturgy was not lost on Silvio, but he kept his head bowed and listened respectfully. Chango and his disciples had lived in terrible sin. They had not honored God's commandments, but had defiled them. The resurrection they were hoping for was not the kind referred to by the priest. It was more like a resurrection of the Antichrist.

"Ashes to ashes, dust to dust," the old priest pronounced solemnly, picking up a handful of dirt from the edge of the mass grave and sprinkling it on top of the mound. "Eternal life grant unto them, O Lord. And let perpetual light shine upon them. May they rest in peace. May their souls and the souls of all the faithful departed through the mercy of God rest in peace. Forever and ever. Amen."

Silvio pronounced the "amen" in unison with the priest. But he felt strongly that the Catholic prayers would need some help, in fact would need in a sense to be contradicted, if the bokor and his evil disciples were to be prevented from coming out of their grave prematurely, before they could be called on Judgment Day to answer to Almighty God.

31

Because of his belief, Silvio and his grandson were in the cemetery now, roughly eight hours after Chango and his disciples had been buried. The old man knew that it wasn't enough to pray to Jehovah. The ancient loas also had to be appeased. He hoped to perform a ritual that might be powerful enough to combat Chango's black magic. Much as he hated to include Jean in his mission, he also realized that he couldn't leave the boy out of it, for they both had been tainted by the bokor and his artifacts, so they both needed to be purified. Jean was too young to fully understand what his grandfather was up to. But he knew enough to be scared. In a hushed, tremulous voice, he said, in Creole, "I am very frightened to be here, Grandfather. Why can't we go home?"

Pausing in the moon shadow of a huge, ornately carved monument, Silvio bent toward his grandson and spoke in a kindly whisper. "Now is the time for you and I to be as brave as we can possibly be. All the saints in heaven are watching over us. Chango, the bokor, is dead only in the flesh. Almighty God has given us the task of killing the bokor's evil spirit."

One of Silvio's most intense fears was that his soul or the souls of his loved ones might be captured by a bokor, a voodoo sorcerer. He dreaded the possibility that he or anyone close to him could be turned into a zombie, a soulless slave. For this reason, back in Haiti he had lowered himself to plead with the hated prison officials who had murdered his son and daughter-in-law. He had even ended up bribing the officials to release the bodies of his loved ones into his care so they could be buried in a Catholic cemetery, with Catholic rituals to safeguard them, and with the additional protection of long, sharp daggers in their dead hands so they could fight off any witch doctor who might try to resurrect them.

At present, Silvio knew that both he and his grandson were especially vulnerable, for he had tried to behead Chango and had failed. Thus he had made a powerful enemy in the domain of the supernatural. Even if Chango did not arise from his grave, the bokor could send the spirits of the dead against Silvio and Jean, and they would both fall terribly ill. No medicine would be able to help them. They would grow weak and thin as stick figures, and would cough black blood, and die a slow death.

The old man and his grandson made their way to the paupers' section of the cemetery, where the tablets and markers were small or nonexistent. By moonlight they approached the mounded dirt of the long trench where the boat people were buried. It looked like a thick brown scar on the green earth. There were voodoo charms placed around and on top of the mass grave. Even though the charms had not been there this afternoon, Silvio was not surprised to find them there now. Shivering at the sight of them, he put his arm around his grandson who was also trembling. They stared at the evil omens.

On top of the grave, in sprinkled cornmeal, was the outline of a church, symbolizing Legba, the patron loa, or god, of sorcerers, without whose presence no magic could ever be effective. On a piece of yellowish rag hanging from a tree was a lipstick drawing of Damballah the serpent god, flanked by the twin lightning bolts of Chango, the god of lightning, fire, and death. And dangling from a length of twine tied at the top of a stick stuck in the ground was a carved wooden image of a cross surmounted by a skull and crossbones – the emblem of Guede Nimbo, the loa of eroticism and the keeper of graves.

33

To Jean, Silvio explained, "The bokor has followers and willing servants, even here in America. Jacques Carnot, the gravedigger, must be one of them. He secretly prays for the bokor to come back to life. He placed the sorcerer's charms here. And no doubt he has dug a quite shallow grave to help Chango to arise. It is what I suspected when the drunkard was boasting to us."

For a moment longer, Silvio and Jean stood in awe, looking at the mass grave, terrified to be in such an unholy place. Then Silvio laid down his burlap sack and shovel. He went to the mounded trench and pulled down the voodoo symbols. Bringing them back to where Jean was standing, he flung them onto the ground as if they might burn his fingers. He left intact the cornmeal crutch of Legba, the patron of all magic, in hopes that this powerful loa might facilitate and enhance his own ritual.

Jean shuddered, staring at the horrid artifacts Silvio had cast down. The old man picked up the shovel and leaned on it, panting a bit, more from emotion than exertion. His eyes on the evil-looking mass grave, he made the sign of the cross. "Lord Jesus, protect us. Blessed Virgin Mary, protect us. May the saints and martyrs be with us always. Stay here by my side, Jean. Don't drop the crucifix."

Silvio helped his grandson hold the crucifix up high with his frail arms, as altar boys were trained to do. Jean wasn't an altar boy yet, but he soon would be old enough. Silvio bent and kissed the face of Christ as the boy held it to his lips. Then he backed up and started to dig a hole. He intended to bury not only the hateful items he had cast to the ground but also those in the burlap sack: Chango's necklace, drum, machete, and whip.

In a shaky whisper, Jean said, "Please hurry, Grandfather. I do not like this place."

Silvio needed no urging to make speed. As he worked the shovel to the best of his ability, his pace impeded by the toughness of the sod and the feebleness of old age, his mind drifted back to his childhood in an impoverished Haitian village. There, when he was twelve years old, a strange and fearful incident had transpired. Maria Chastain, a pretty seventeen-year-old who helped nuns at the missionary school that Silvio attended, rejected the amorous intentions of a crude, ugly middle-aged man named Joseph Fornier. Maria had been warned by the elders of the village that to spurn this man was dangerously unwise, for he was a member of the Tontons Macoutes, the Haitian equivalent of the Gestapo, which coupled the use of voodoo sorcery with its iron-fisted, terroristic tactics. In a fit of blind rage when the object of his desire told him she could never love him, Joseph Fornier stormed out of her house, but before he left he told Maria he would put a curse on her so that no one but he would ever have her.

Soon she took sick, falling into a kind of trance, and a few days later she died at the missionary school, despite the best efforts of the nuns who were trying to heal her with prayers and modern medicine. Silvio Narbonne stood at the grave site praying with the rest of the villagers when Maria Chastain was laid in her coffin and buried.

But one day, three years later, Maria's mother found her wandering on the outskirts of the village. Shocked and horrified to see that her beloved daughter was alive, now a mute, hollow-eyed zombie, the mother nevertheless had the presence of mind to lead her, stumbling and faltering, to the houngan, a local practitioner of "white magic." The houngan gave Maria a glass of seawater to drink in an attempt to counteract the spell she was under. .

Maria collapsed onto the floor of the houngan's hut, but instead of disintegrating to a rotting corpse, she slowly recovered her faculties. She claimed that she had never really been dead, although she remembered the day she died and was buried. She said she had heard the nails being driven into her coffin, and all the people crying and praying. She had lain under the earth for what seemed like hours, unable to move or cry out. Then she had heard sounds of someone digging, and in a while her coffin was opened. She was still dazed and totally helpless. Two big, strong men in the uniform of the Tontons Macoutes led her out of the cemetery. By Jeep they brought her to a plantation in the jungle, where her rejected suitor, Joseph Fornier, was smugly waiting for her. He ripped her burial gown off her and raped her. Then he forced a bittersweet liquid down her throat, and she fell into a trance similar to the one that had caused her to "die"– except this time she had enough life left in her to be able to move around half aimlessly, perform simple tasks, and mumble a few words. She was kept at the plantation as a slave, cutting sugarcane most of the time, except for the days when Joseph Fornier would show up to rape her.

She did not remember how or why she had stopped being a zombie. She had no idea how she had managed to come back to her village. As a young boy, Silvio Narbonne was afraid of her – and so was everyone else, even her own family. One day she disappeared and never came back again. Everyone believed that she had once more been captured and enslaved as a zombie by the Tontons Macoutes.

It was the Tontons Macoutes who had arrested Silvio's son and daughter-in-law for publishing newspaper articles critical of the Haitian government. As he labored to make a hole deep enough to receive the voodoo implements belonging to Chango, the old man thought that it was perhaps better that his loved ones had been killed outright in prison instead of meeting the same fate as Maria Chastain. Silvio prayed that the daggers he had placed in their hands would be sufficient protection.

Even at his tender age, Jean Narbonne had heard many zombie legends. The scary stories were told to Haitian children by their parents, or by other children who enjoyed making their playmates get goose bumps. Holding the crucifix while his grandfather had continued to dig, Jean shivered as he recalled the story of the dead boy who had come back to his parents, his neck unnaturally bent to one side and his toes scarred. At the boy's funeral, one of the mourners had accidentally touched his foot with a lit cigarette, and when his coffin had been found to be too short for him, his head had been twisted and tucked into the tight wooden box. Since his burial, he had grown older by three years, but he could not tell his relatives what had happened to him after he had been put in his grave, because he was now unable to talk at all. It was said that this boy had been enslaved by a cannibalistic bokor, who released him when he grew older and his flesh was not tender enough for eating, but first cut his tongue out so he could not give full information to the authorities. Everyone who heard this story, including Jean, suspected that the bokor's name was Chango.

The boy was utterly terrified to be in the cemetery, a few feet away from the exact spot where the bokor and his evil disciples were buried. Glancing nervously at the long mound of dirt, he jumped when he thought he saw the ground move, ever so slightly. Clenching the crucifix so tightly his fingers hurt, he blinked his eyes rapidly. Nothing had moved, he told himself. It must have been a shadow.

"Be brave and patient," Silvio admonished. "It won't be much longer now." He wiped sweat from his brow, then resumed digging, much more exhausted now, and breathing very hard.

Jean looked intently at the cypress tree casting a moon shadow over the mass grave, and the branches did not seem to be rustling. There wasn't even a faint breeze to cool the perspiration on the nape of the boy's neck. Not enough wind to make a shifting shadow. It must have been a trick of his mind that had made the earth quiver.

But, in unison with the sound of Silvio's spade thocking into the ground, the mounded dirt shook again. Jean's eyes widened, and he almost dropped the ebony crucifix. As his grandfather had done, he kissed the face of Christ, speechlessly hoping for some kind of help from the martyred Savior.

The spade thocked again.

And again the grave mound trembled.

Jean froze, paralyzed by fright. He wanted desperately to cry out to his grandfather, but his voice stuck in his throat, as if his tongue had been plucked out. He wondered vaguely if perhaps the spade was striking part of a large rock that might go back all the way to the edge of the grave underground, so that the reverberations of the shovel strokes would cause the loose earth to be disrupted. Trying to be as brave as his grandfather wanted him to be, he silently said a prayer to the Blessed Virgin Mary. He bowed his head so he wouldn't see the earth shake, while his tired arms and shoulders struggled to hold the crucifix on high. But as the icon slowly sank with the weariness of his boyish muscles, his eyes were once more drawn, inexorably, toward the dark brown scar of mounded earth.

The spade thocked and the mound shook worse than before.

Suddenly a hand popped up out of the grave.

Jean shrieked, his bulging eyes riveted on the horrid spectacle.

The hand's long, thick fingers clenched and unclenched.

Silvio dropped his shovel with a loud clang and whirled around, facing the trench. Now there were two grasping hands, clenching and unclenching, pushing away dirt.

Chango's scowling tattooed head come up out of the grave. A wild, ferocious look in his eyes, he sat up farther, shaking his dirt-encrusted, ornamental braids as clods of clay fell away from his massive body. He climbed out of the pit and started moving toward Jean and Silvio. The old man dived for his shovel, managed to grab it, and tried to swing it. But the seven-foot-tall heavily muscled bokor effortlessly thwarted the intended blow, seizing the shaft of the shovel in mid-swing and wrenching it away. With brute strength he swung the blade at the old man, cleaving him nearly in half. Blood spurted from Silvio's gashed torso as he screamed and fell.

Jean dropped the crucifix and ran. Chango came after him in quick, strong strides. The boy darted and zigzagged among some tombstones.

Chango glowered at the dropped crucifix, then kicked it and stomped on it as he went after his quarry.

Ducking behind a large monument, Jean found a dead tree limb lying on the ground. He snatched at it. He could hear Chango's hoarse breathing and heavy, relentless stride coming closer . . .and closer. It was like hearing the living breath, the living footsteps of the Devil. Jean waited till the last moment, then he stuck out the tree branch. But the big scowling beast of a man did not go down, all he did was stumble a bit as the boy took off running, backtracking toward the outskirts of the cemetery.

Jean put some distance between himself and his pursuer. He vaulted over a stone bench, dashed to his left, and squeezed his slight body between a clump of forsythia bushes. He kept going, past rows of tombstones. Then, looking back over his shoulder, he suddenly felt the ground disappear beneath him. Shrieking, he fell into an open grave. He tried to scramble out, then decided to hide there. He cowered down sweating and panting, trying to muffle his hard breathing so he wouldn't give himself away.

Outside of his own ragged breath, he heard nothing, and he hoped against hope that the bokor had gone. Through his mind tumbled the horror of all the zombie stories he had heard, overridden by the horror of his grandfather's murder. He whimpered softly, despite his efforts not to. Biting on his own arm so hard that he drew warm, salty blood, he tried to stop his own whimpering. Curled in a fetal position, he thought of trying to scrape loose dirt over himself so he couldn't be seen.

But before he had a chance, he was snatched at and dragged out of the grave by the scruff of his neck. Chango held him in the air with his feet off the ground, choking him. His whole head was splitting apart, and he was blacking out. Then he kicked the bokor in the groin.

Chango groaned and doubled over. Jean fell and rolled on the ground, scurrying away from his attacker. He plunged headlong into the cemetery, his head still aching terribly, his legs weak and staggering. Feeling that he could not go on much longer, even to save his own life, he hid behind a huge stone mausoleum. Then he noticed a large cypress tree and shinnied up it.

As Chango approached, maddened by the pain in his groin, his view of Jean's hiding place was blocked by the mausoleum. He stopped in his tracks, peering this way and that.

Jean clung to the branches and tried to be invisible deep in the foliage. He held his breath as much as possible, but when he let it go it was even louder than before because of the increased urgency for oxygen. He hoped that his life sounds would be masked by Chango's movements and heavy, raspy breathing. He prayed silently, invoking voodoo gods as well as Catholic saints, which to him were all equal in the supernatural hierarchy.

He saw Chango go off in one direction, then another, searching methodically among the tombstones and monuments. The beast tugged at the door of the mausoleum, and it did not open. He yanked at it hard, only to find that it was securely locked and would not yield, even to his mighty strength. He backed off a few paces, till he was standing directly under the tree where Jean was perched. But he did not look up. Jean prayed fervently that he wouldn't.

The boy's perspiration dripped on Chango's shoulder.

With a burst of demonic laughter and a sudden grasping leap, Chango reached up and plucked the boy by the ankle, as if he were picking live fruit from the cypress tree. He yanked the screaming, thrashing prize down, out of the branches. Hanging upside down in the bokor's grip, Jean flailed and twisted. He tried to kick Chango in the face or punch him in the groin, but the bokor held him straight out to thc side so that his blows rent the air, and he could not free his ankle from the viselike fist that held him suspended.

Chango amused himself this way for a minute or so, then finally delivered a hard chop to the back of the little boy's neck. Still holding the limp body by one ankle, he carried it through the graveyard to the site of the mass grave, where Silvio Narbonne was lying in a pool of his own blood.

The bokor dropped Jean to the ground. Then he picked up the burlap sack and emptied it of its contents – the bullwhip, necklace, drum, and machete. He slipped the thong and pouch over his head. Then he unsheathed the machete and, bending over Silvio, lifted the old man's right arm by the wrist. With a vicious blow of the machete, he chopped the frail arm off at the shoulder.

CHAPTER 4

Clint Jones blamed his divorce on the horrendous crime wave that started in the late seventies and was still going strong. Old, stable marriages on the Braxton Beach police force had cracked up along with relatively young ones like Jones's. He and his partner were both part of this unfortunate trend. Jones's marriage had lasted seven years, Dawson's twenty-two. It was hard for married couples on the force to stand up to the increased pressure – the crazy hours, the danger, and the constant worry that at just about any moment the kids might not have a father because of some thug, madman, or junkie.

Policemen and their families used to be able to live almost like normal people in the laid-back tourist towns like Braxton Beach. But that was before the drug wars and the Cuban boatlift.

Of 125,000 Cubans who landed on Florida's shores in 1980, roughly 25,000 were hardened criminals and psychotics sucked out of Castro's prisons and insane asylums like slime siphoned from a cesspool. In fact, that's exactly what they were called by decent, hardworking Cubans: *escoria*, slime. The escoria loved the Sunshine State the way disease loves the human body that hasn't been vaccinated. Banding together in vicious gangs, they preyed upon innocent citizens with a sadistic ferocity unmatched by the worst American gangsters of the past. Braxton Beach was one of the many towns and cities that lacked the tax money, expertise, and law enforcement personnel to adequately defend against the sudden siege of unprecedented terror. Its small police force was stretched pitifully thin, and the toll on the policemen and their families was devastating.

Even during ordinary times, cops found it hard to stay married, but although Clint Jones had always known this, he had never thought his own marriage would become one of the unfortunate statistics. He and Collette used to be so incredibly close, so tight and in tune. He still believed she would have been able to withstand the normal blows, the regular demands of the job, and would have stuck with him, but too much was put on her too quickly, too much on both of them. Even though he understood her suffering, it was a tremendous shock when Collette left him. The worst part was knowing that her love had left first; he had felt it die little by little. Yet he still cared about her, still lost sleep over her. He tried hating her because she wouldn't let him see his kids, but he could never make the hatred last from midnight till morning. Instead it would turn into guilt. He would start thinking that maybe she was right, maybe he didn't deserve to have the kids call him their daddy because he had barely been around to see them grow up.

On Friday morning, the day after the discovery of the seven bodies on the beach, Clint drove toward the slum section of town, nicknamed by the police "El Escoria." With him was Patrolman Rudez, minus his German shepherd. Rudez was of Cuban descent and was fluent in Spanish. Since he was also black, like Jones, they were going to visit a murder witness who had clammed up when Dawson tried to talk with her, possibly because Dawson was white and often gave Hispanics the impression that he was prejudiced against them. Although Jones didn't really think this was so, sometimes he wondered. One of the things that he noticed happening to himself was an increasing tendency to view Cubans and Haitians with automatic wariness and suspicion. It was because so many of the horrible crimes he had had to deal with in recent years had been committed by the worst element among the new immigrants. He had to keep reminding himself that the vast majority of Hispanics were ashamed of the escoria and despised and feared them as much as he did.

Huge, colorful tourist hotels, snazzy bars, glitzy restaurants, and boutiques lined the broad, smoothly paved thoroughfare, gleaming in early morning sunshine as Jones and Rudez cruised down the main drag of Braxton Beach. Right now, there weren't many pedestrians about. Most of the tourists liked to sleep in, especially if they had done some late carousing. When they woke up they would go to the shore to lie in the hot sun and sweat out their hangovers.

With no people around, no potential victims or villains to look out for, this part of Braxton Beach had a pristine, unspoiled look about it, as the town had in Jones's memory, and he wished it could have stayed that way forever. So what if some of the grandest establishments were owned by Salvatore "Sal the Strap" Stropoli, a Mafia kingpin. Strap was battling the escoria as hard as the city fathers were, maybe even harder. Not too long ago, he was considered public enemy number one, but now he could almost affectionately be called a "gentleman of crime." His operations seemed nostalgically desirable compared to what was going on now. Old time gangsters like Sal the Strap seldom used to hurt women and children on purpose, but the escoria had no such compunction. In the interest of teaching a man a lesson, they would rape and sodomize his whole family, butchering the adults and smothering the little babies in their cribs.

LIVING THINGS

Braxton Beach slowly lost its sheen, the buildings becoming dingier and uglier as the main drag petered out. Year by year the seedy section seemed to be spreading, like an infestation. In a stretch of a few blocks, the ambience went from chic to tacky to outright deterioration – an urban slum of abandoned storefronts, porno shops, massage parlors, dope dens, and gambling joints.

Jones hated to go into El Escoria. Ten years ago, this part of Braxton Beach had been several rungs below middle class in terms of per capita income, but Jones had been born and raised here, and hadn't been ashamed of it. The streets had been clean, the stores and houses attractively painted and maintained. But now the place was a dump. Garbage on the sidewalks. Sickly, half-clothed kids peeping out of windows. Winos vomiting or urinating in front of the bars because they were scared to go into the alleys. If the blight kept spreading uptown at its present rate, the tourist trade would soon dry up and the escoria would be left crawling all over each other like maggots. Cannibalistic maggots at that, Jones thought, thinking back to what had been discovered in the cemetery yesterday.

He parked his black unmarked police sedan in front of a three-story tenement. He and Rudez got out. From a bench in front of a dilapidated pool hall next door, a pack of tattooed, ear-ringed teenage toughs sneered at Jones's tan summer-weight suit and Rudez's J. C. Penney three-piece plaid, and made a couple of "oinks" under their breath to prove they weren't fooled by two cops in civilian clothes. "Probably won't have any hubcaps when we get back," Jones said as he and Rudez climbed three flights of dirty, smelly stairs in dank, sepia shadows, their feet crunching on glass from smashed light bulbs, the empty sockets dangling from long black wires on the landings. They

46

rapped on a flimsy door with a corroded brass number 3 hanging upside down and backwards on its one remaining screw. It was really apartment 13 but the 1 was missing entirely. They had to pound several times before the door creaked open.

"Good morning, Mrs. Carano," Jones said. "Remember me?"

Alicia Carano nodded imperceptibly, her eyes darting nervously from Jones to Rudez. She was a twenty-seven-year-old black woman who must have been beautiful once but was now worn down by poverty and despair. A ratty beige robe was pulled tightly around her stooped, sagging body. She scratched a sore on her face, cowering in the presence of the two cops who wanted her to risk what little she had in life by telling about the crime she had witnessed. According to Dawson, her husband had run away and left her to raise six children by herself. Some of them were squalling in the shabby depths of her two-room hovel.

Lieutenant Jones was sure that she could put the finger on the gang of punks who had raped and strangled the thirteen-year-old girl who had lived in the apartment across the hall. But Alicia Carano knew as well as he did that the escoria would gleefully butcher an entire family in retribution against one stool pigeon. Jones and Rudez were endangering her and her children merely by coming here. But if they wanted to have a shot at catching the murderers, they'd have to keep coming back, keep hammering on her until she cracked. They had to make her feel so threatened, whether she talked or didn't talk, that she might as well talk – and take them up on their offer of protection, which they may or may not be able to back up, even if they moved her to another part of the state. So Jones and Rudez were Judas goats. Their role did not cause them to esteem themselves, but it was the way the job had to be done.

"Mrs. Carano," Jones said, "please let us in. We're hoping, now that you've had a couple of days to think about it, that you may be remembering a bit more. Maybe you can put some names to those shapes you saw running down the stairs."

"I didn't see nothing. I only heard. I didn't look out. Didn't even push the door open. I was busy feeding my kids. I don't know nothing."

"That's not what you said in your initial statement. You said you slammed the door open and ran out into the hall. What if it was your own little girl that was raped and choked to death? Would you want them to get away with it?"

She pulled her ratty robe tighter and started to cry. It was a soundless cry, not much energy in it, containing all the pity she had left to give for the murdered child and for herself. The tears trickled down her cheeks, and she made no effort to wipe them.

"Let us in," Jones said. "Tell us the truth, and we can protect you. You know they'll come back to shut you up anyway, don't you?"

Two hours later, at police headquarters, Vince Dawson was talking on the phone as Clint Jones walked into the office. Jones and Rudez had stopped for coffee before Rudez changed into uniform and went back to walking his beat with his dog, and Jones had bought a couple of takeout containers. He set one of the large coffees in front of Dawson, then stood by, tuning in on Vince's end of the telephone conversation.

Dawson was writing on a pad, scowling, but making his gruff voice sound deceptively pleasant. "All right, Captain

Raphael. I'll expedite the photos and fingerprints to you, and you should have them in a day or so."

Setting down his coffee, Jones picked up the stack of glossy eight-by-tens of the seven dead boat people and shuffled through them.

Into the receiver, Dawson said, "Captain it sounds to me as if you'll be able to write 'solved' to quite a few kidnappings and homicides, and call off an expensive manhunt." He listened for half a minute. "I see what you mean, but at least this way it saves the expense of a trial . . ." He listened again, raising his eyebrows at Jones to convey his annoyance with the party on the other end of the line. "Listen, Captain Raphael, all I can say is you can certainly publish the photos if you want to – they ought to convince your citizens that Chango and his henchmen are as dead as they're ever going to get." He listened for another half a minute, flashing another grimace of annoyance at Jones. "Captain, I'll wait to hear from you after you look at the material we're sending you. Then we can discuss an exhumation order, if you're still interested." Dawson listened again, briefly. Then he said, with studied politeness, "Thank you, Captain. I'll look forward to hearing from you." He hung up, opened his carton of black coffee and took a sip, a sardonic gleam in his baggy blue eyes.

Jones sat behind his gray steel desk, his container of coffee in his hand. "Well? You going to hog all the good news?"

Dawson snorted. "That was his Excellency Captain Armando Raphael of the Haitian police in Port-au-Prince. Speaks three languages – English, Spanish, and Creole. An educated man, but an odd sort of police officer. I described the corpse we think is Chango's, and the honorable captain agrees it sounds like the right man. I didn't know how to read him at first, though. I think he's superstitious himself, maybe just as much as the old man on the beach yesterday."

"Why?" Jones asked, swirling his coffee.

"Right off the bat he kind of stammered that it couldn't be Chango, before he even heard me out. It was like he could hardly believe that Chango isn't immortal and could actually be drowned."

"What was that bit about an exhumation order?"

"Hmph! Captain Raphael turns out to be something of an ingrate, Clint. He isn't exactly jumping with joy that we helped solve a string of disappearances for him. He had the nerve to tell me he'd rather have captured Chango on Haitian shores. That way he could display the body – not only to reap the glory, apparently, but also to prove to the populace that the bokor is really dead."

Jones snickered. "Probably have to publicly behead him, too, so everybody'd know he wasn't coming back as a zombie."

"I don't doubt it," Dawson said. "This Chango had everybody in Haiti absolutely terrified. Captain Raphael said some of the same things we've already heard. He claimed that he wasn't only using children as voodoo sacrifices – he and his sidekicks were also into cannibalism."

"Nice." Jones sighed.

The phone rang and Dawson picked it up. "Homicide, Lieutenant Dawson speaking." His normally somber expression grew a shade darker as he listened intently. "In the cemetery, by the mass grave that was dug yesterday? It figures." He shook his head in disgust. "Okay. Don't disturb anything. We'll be there in twenty minutes." He hung up, flashing a look of angry disbelief at Clint Jones. "Silvio Narbonne has been murdered."

"Shit!" Jones smacked his desktop hard with the flat of his hand. "I bet it's our fault. We should've never let him take that voodoo stuff yesterday."

***

Captain Armando Raphael decided not to telephone the National Palace. He wasn't going to phone Franz Midi at his construction office, either. Let the President-for-Life and the leader of the Tontons Macoutes enjoy a pleasant weekend without worrying about whether Chango was alive or dead. No use crying wolf. If the good news panned out, only then would the captain pass it on to his superiors. He would wait till he got the photographs and the fingerprints and examined them minutely.

Baby Doc had ordered Captain Raphael to work jointly with Franz Midi to capture and kill Chango after Lucia Suerte had been made to tell where the bokor could be trapped. But the Tontons Macoutes' torture methods had not worked on the demon in the little girl's flesh. For three days, Midi and his accomplices questioned her in the basement dungeon of the National Palace, applying exquisite devices to make her screams reverberate off the thick, white, blood-spattered walls. In between the screaming, all she did was curse the souls of her torturers. She did not spit out anything that would hurt her master or turn him against *her*.

In the end, Captain Raphael had to teach the Tontons Macoutes the truth of the old adage, that more flies can be captured with honey than with vinegar. He went to see Lucia by himself. With no guards around, he talked to her as she lay in her own blood and sweat and excrement, chained to a whitewashed pillar. Knowing that money had always been her primary motivation, he offered her a $10,000 reward. He also promised that he could have her turned back over to him right away, in his own jail, where she would no longer be so badly treated.

It turned out that the little girl did not really know how to find Chango. As new confessions poured out of her, it became clear that she had never dealt face-to-face with the bokor. Instead she had always delivered the stolen babies to an innocent-seeming man who was not known as a sorcerer or even a houngan, but only as the owner of a grocery stand. He was the one who would pay Lucia and then presumably turn her "deliveries" over to the cannibals.

Greedy for the $10,000 and the promise of kindness that Captain Raphael never intended to keep, Lucia gave out the name of the grocer who dealt in human flesh. He was Charles Laquinne, and his stand was at the edge of the shantytown slum in Cap Haitien, twelve miles from Port-au-Prince. Now that she was cooperating, Lucia was set free, but under police surveillance. She was allowed to make an appointment with Laquinne, by promising to sell him another baby. Then a squad of men led by Captain Raphael and Franz Midi pounced on the evil grocer, and he took Lucia Suerte's place in the torture chamber. Electricity applied to his genitals made him talk, and he gave in too easily, way before his gonads were appreciably seared.

He could still walk – in a staggering shuffle – when he led the police and the Tontons Macoutes to Chango's hideout. To her great surprise, Lucia Suerte was handcuffed to him, to help him along to the scene of the raid. They were hauled in an open Jeep through Cap Haitien, mobs of people throwing stones at them all the way. Then they were forced to limp along the jungle trail, leading the way to Chango's lair – two mean, miserable wretches bleeding and bent from the effects of the stones and the torture implements that had been applied to their bodies.

With a force of two hundred men, Captain Raphael and Franz Midi surrounded the house in the jungle, at the mouth of a river, where the bokor had established his secret lair. The police and the Tontons Macoutes were armed with grenades, rocket launchers, and rifles that fired incendiary bullets as well as conventional ammunition. They were all given the command to commence firing and to continue to fire, showing no mercy. Some people inside the house tried to shoot back, but going against the immense firepower of the police and the Tontons Macoutes, they were like bees trying to sting a tank. In the ensuing holocaust, the house was burned to the ground.

But none of the charred, shrunken bodies found in the smoking ruins appeared to be Chango. Nine of his disciples had died putting up a feeble fight whose sole purpose was to cover his escape. His boat had already gone down the river to the ocean – on its way to Florida, if what Captain Raphael had been told today by the American policeman turned out to be true.

When Chango wasn't captured on the day of the shootout, Franz Midi was so disappointed that he ordered Lucia Suerte and Charles Lauqinne to be set free on the return trip of the military convoy through Cap Haitien. The grocer and the little girl screamed and howled as the handcuffs were unlocked, for now they did not wish their freedom. Not in the muddy main street of the shantytown, where the jeering citizens stood waiting with stones in their hands.

"Loup-garou! Loup-garou!" the people chanted. "Werewolves! Eaters of baby flesh!"

Suerte and Laquinne did not last long. They were so wounded from torture that they couldn't have gotten far, even if they had tried to run. They merely cringed, covering their faces with their hands. Dozens of stones pelted them, and as soon as they fell their heads were hacked off with machetes. Then all the parts of their bodies were cut into little pieces. The chunks of bone and flesh were heaped up and drenched in kerosene, then set on fire. All Haitians knew this was the way that werewolves had to be disposed of, so the supernatural beasts could never put themselves together again and come back to life.

Captain Raphael shuddered with his remembrance of how the burning flesh had smelled. Then he opened the bottom drawer of his desk, pulled out a half bottle of vodka, and took a big, burning gulp. His eyes watering, he capped the bottle and put it back. He thought about the horror that was about to be unleashed in America, if Chango was truly one of the persons drowned there. The Americans did not know enough to chop him up and burn him; they acted as if they did not even believe in werewolves or sorcerers. Well, let them find out. Let their smugness be punished by Almighty God.

"In the name of the Father and the Son and the Holy Spirit," Captain Raphael said, crossing himself, and making up his mind that under no circumstances would he ask for the seven corpses to be exhumed and shipped back to Haiti.

***

On the way to the cemetery, Jones told Dawson what had gone on in Alicia Carano's tenement apartment. A big fat zero. The poor frightened woman had continued to be uncooperative, even though at one point Jones thought she was cracking. But after a wasted hour, he and Rudez hadn't succeeded in getting anything more out of her than had Dawson. "She's too afraid of what might happen to her and her kids," Jones said.

"It's going to happen anyway," said Dawson, lighting a cigarette and offering one to Jones, who was driving. "Better get some good nicotine in your lungs now, Clint. We won't be able to drop butts on the crime scene."

Jones pulled a Kool out of the pack Dawson tipped toward him and pushed in the lighter on the dash. "I had a weird thought," he said, "that dear old Alicia might be protecting someone besides herself and her kids."

"One of the killers?"

"Yeah. She could be tight with one of them, maybe even shacking up. She might not be in as much danger of getting snuffed as we think."

"Escoria don't think twice about snuffing their wenches," said Dawson. "In fact, they like to do it every now and then just to show how macho they are."

"Maybe we should've treated our wives like that," Jones said, but neither he nor Dawson laughed. He took a deep drag of menthol-flavored smoke, then said, "I think we should put a surveillance on Alicia Carano and see what happens."

"Good idea," Dawson said. "Only problem is the chief will never approve it. He'll say we can't afford to have the men tied up. Besides, you and I both know he doesn't really give a damn if the Cubans kill each other off."

"Especially the black Cubans."

"Now Clint," Dawson needled, "just because the chief is always talking about how his great-grandpap owned slaves is no reason to think he's prejudiced."

"I'd like to own *him* for about a week," Jones said.

Dawson considered suggesting that he and Jones try to run a surveillance on their own. It would give Dawson something to do with his free time, which was weighing on him pretty heavily lately. Sometimes he wondered what would've happened if he'd have done what his ex-wife wanted; maybe he and Peg would still be married, living under one roof with their teenage son and daughter. Peg kept pushing him to get out of law enforcement. When she found out that he had turned down a chance to head up security in one of the big tourist hotels and didn't even tell her about it, it was all downhill between the two of them from then on. Now she was living in South Carolina, the kids both in college up there with Vince footing part of the bill. They never came to visit or invited him to come see them. Timmy and Janie both told him they hated him. They blamed him for the divorce because they knew he'd been cheating on their mother – she had used it to turn them against him. But it was already way too late to save his marriage by the time he started keeping company with another woman. He lost his mistress soon after the divorce papers came through – treated her so badly she had to go. For the past two years, he had lived by himself. He just needed to be left alone most of the time, except when he started climbing the walls of his cheap three-room apartment. Then he went out and gambled and got drunk, letting the racetrack and the booze take the last dribbles of his paycheck.

Sometimes he wondered if Clint was getting along any better than he was as a divorced man. They weren't in the habit of opening up to each other about stuff that didn't concern the job. Even when they confronted sad or horrible things in the line of duty, most of what they felt stayed locked inside. Instead of letting it out, they cracked jokes, never unmasking their feelings. For two guys who had a great deal of rapport as detectives and partners, they sure didn't have much of a slant on each other's personal lives. But Dawson knew that Jones had a steady girlfriend at the moment, so he probably wouldn't dig the idea of putting in any off-duty time watching the Carano family. Might as well let the suggestion slide.

Jones parked behind a black and white patrol car by the stone arch of St. Matthew's Cemetery. He and Dawson took a last drag, then snuffed out their cigarettes. Slamming the car doors, they looked around for Sergeant Bruce Meltzer or his partner, Sergeant Richard Joyce, since it had been Meltzer who had reported the murder to Dawson over the telephone. Sergeant Joyce, his face so fair and smooth that he looked boyish, almost too young to be a cop, met Jones and Dawson just inside the stone arch and told them that Meltzer was scouring the area and doing a preliminary search for evidence. The uniformed cop led the two detectives to the scene of the crime. It was in the rear of the cemetery. On the way back there, Jones and Dawson scoped out a scrawny black man with a gleaming gold tooth. The man was busy digging a grave, but he looked up with shifty, darting eyes before turning his head and continuing to shovel.

"Who's that?" Dawson asked.

"His name is Jacques Carnot," said Sergeant Joyce. "Claims he doesn't know anything about anything."

There was a tractor mower parked about thirty yards from the corpse of Silvio Narbonne, and an obese redheaded fellow in faded overalls was standing about halfway between the tractor and the corpse. "This is George Philips, the cemetery caretaker," Sergeant Joyce said. The two detectives introduced themselves. Then they went over and looked down at Silvio Narbonne, whose torso was cleaved nearly in half. Nothing was left of the right arm but a blood-caked stump.

"Meltzer's over that direction," said Joyce, pointing. "I'll go find him, see if he needs a hand." He threaded his way back among some thickly clustered tombstones.

Wiping sweat from his face to his sleeve, George Philips started to run at the mouth. "I found him like this when I worked my way back here about an hour ago, mowing the grass. I was half expecting to find a grave desecrated, cause I'd already seen that some of the ornaments and candles and so on that were on some of the graves were missing this morning - so somebody must've swiped them."

Jones asked, "Does that happen often, Mr. Philips?"

"No, not often, Lieutenant. Sometimes the college boys do some pretty weird things when they're havin' fraternity initiations, but most of 'em have cleared out for the semester break, so you wouldn't be expecting too many of their kinda pranks. If you ask me, the same maniac who butchered this poor old man probably stole the grave ornaments."

Nodding noncommittally, Jones and Dawson prowled carefully around the murder scene. The mass grave appeared undisturbed, the mounded scar of brown earth intact and unblemished. In the immediate vicinity of the dead body the detectives didn't spot any murder weapon. They knew that the old man had probably come here to bury a machete – plus a drum, a whip, and a leather necklace – but none of those things were in sight. Just about the only evidence of what had taken place last night, other than Silvio's mutilated corpse, was a three-foot-deep-hole in the ground. But the hole was empty. And whatever had been used to dig it was now gone.

They wondered about the old man's little grandson, Jean. Could he have been here when this terrible thing happened? If so, where was he now?

Jones said, "Okay, we can assume that Mr. Narbonne was digging that hole to bury Chango's paraphernalia. I didn't imagine he was going to do it m the cemetery, Vince, but I guess 1t makes sense."

"How?"

"Ritualistically. Casting the spell as near as the person it's supposed to work on."

"Listen to the voodoo expert," Dawson said.

Hanging close to the two detectives, George Philips furrowed his brow and blinked his eyes, befuddled over what to him was a bunch of crazy talk coming from two supposedly sane public servants. Jones and Dawson paced back toward the mass grave and scrutinized it again. "Seems like the old man would've dug his hole here," said Jones, "instead of over there, unless he was scared to mess around too close to Chango."

Good place to hide a little boy's body," said Dawson. "We might have to dig it up and look."

Jones was off on another tack. "Maybe all of Chango's people didn't drown. There may have been more than seven of them. Some could've possibly made it to shore alive."

"Yeah," said Dawson, "I see what you mean. They might have seen what the old man was up to, and they sure wouldn't want anybody casting spells aimed at keeping their bokor in his grave. But if they killed Silvio to stop him, why would they have chopped off his arm?"

"I don't know," said Jones. "Pure devilment? Cannibalism?"

Eavesdropping from behind the detectives' backs, George Philips still couldn't make head or tails out of their conversation. He cleared his throat loudly to stop their babble, and when they turned around he said, "We never had any incidents of grave robbery like you hear has been going on in other parts of the county. Just the college pranks I told you fellows about. But I keep my eyes peeled, try to keep that freaky stuff from happenin' here at St. Matthew's. Not that I want to be a tattletale, but I figure it's my duty to tell you we got a Haitian gravedigger who spouts off some pretty weird stuff when he gets drunk. I don't trust him as far as I can throw him."

"We noticed him when we first came in," said Jones. "We intend to talk to him before we leave."

"We might have to borrow his shovel," said Dawson "Send it to the lab, on the chance somebody used it for the murder weapon."

"There must be other tools around here, too," said Jones. "A sickle . . . an ax, maybe. Where are the tools kept, Mr. Philips?"

"In the shed back by the fence," he said, pointing. "We got sickles and axes, if you want to take a look at them." Just then, Sergeant Meltzer started shouting. "Lieutenant Jones! Lieutenant Dawson! Over here! We found something!"

The two detectives pivoted toward Meltzer, and George Philips started to tag along. Meltzer called out sternly, "Better stay back, Mr. Philips. It isn't a pretty sight to look at!"

"Hmph!" the fat caretaker scoffed. "You fellows think anything's gonna shake me up after I worked in this bone orchard for fifteen years?" He kept on waddling after the two detectives.

Jones told him, "You don't usually have to scope out anything more gruesome than a closed coffin. Hey, watch where you're walking, man! Don't track through those bloodstains!"

Philips juked clumsily to one side to avoid the reddish stains, which had gotten more noticeable all of a sudden. Sergeant Meltzer, a short, stocky, tough-looking cop, led the way to where little seven-year-old Jean Narbonne was laid out flat on his back, nude, right on top of a grave. Flies were buzzing around. The boy's corpse had been eviscerated, the way a hunter would dress a deer. The mounded top of the grave formed a crude altar, around which had been arranged, in a roughly symmetrical fashion, some of the stolen grave ornaments and candles. Overnight, the candles had burned down to shapeless, hardened globs of wax. The crucifix that Jean had been carrying had been driven into the ground upside down, so that the head of the Savior was buried and His legs were protruding obscenely into the air. The bloody shovel lay nearby, and might have been used to pound the crucifix into the earth.

"Oh, my God!" gasped Lieutenant Jones, who thought of seeing one of his own little boys stretched out like that. He normally was more successful at blocking out those sorts of visions. But then, he and Dawson were more used to dealing with man's inhumanity to man and woman than with man's inhumanity to children.

Dawson blinked his eyes and shook his head, trying to force himself to examine the scene objectively and dispassionately, as a criminal investigator must. He had to pretend to himself and anybody who happened to look at his face that his stomach wasn't flipping over, tossing sour coffee-and-cigarette bile up into the back of his throat.

Long strips of flesh had been carved from the dead boy's arms and thighs, exposing slender white bones. Next to the grave where he was laid out were the still-smoldering embers of a small cooking-size fire, and in the ashes lay a wooden spit with chunks of charred meat still skewered.

George Philips's bravado deserted him, and he backed away and started retching. Sergeant Joyce, who had been squeamishly standing back a few steps, took the cemetery caretaker by the arm and led him into the weeds.

Jones spoke over the sounds of the caretaker's vomiting. "That poor little boy. I wasn't expecting anything like this, Vince. I was trying to believe that the old man would've come here by himself to work his magic."

"It sure didn't work in his favor, did it?" said Dawson.

The comment sounded coarse, but Jones knew his partner didn't mean it that way. One thing he had found out about Dawson was that his hard shell covered more sensitivity than he liked to admit.

Sergeant Meltzer said, "There's flesh still in the fire, Lieutenant. Look at the strips cut from the boy. I hate to say it, but it looks like we're dealing with . . . cannibals."

Dawson wished that Meltzer would have kept his mouth shut. He didn't need the awfulness of what he was seeing put into words. Sometimes he wished he had the luxury to put his emotions ahead of his intellect, but the job he had to do wouldn't allow it. The job made him always keep his emotions under tight control. The fewer words the better in a situation like this, because words expressed feelings. Yet he realized that Meltzer was using words as a shield against shock, and it was wrong to blame him for that. The man had to use whatever it took to preserve his sanity, or else he wouldn't stay in uniform very long; either he'd turn in his badge or he'd end up swallowing too much booze, too many pills, or even swallowing his gun - a major occupational hazard for cops nowadays.

Jones said, "Some of Chango's followers must've been lurking in the graveyard, waiting for him to arise from the dead. Silvio and Jean probably walked right into it, and never had a chance. Find whoever has Chango's weird playthings, and we find the killer."

"Easier said than done," said Dawson.

"You know what I was thinking this morning?" Jones went on. "I was driving past a couple of Sal the Strap's places, the Beachview Hotel and the Golden Pier restaurant, you know? And I thought, hey, we didn't know how good we had it when he was leaving us a couple bodies stuffed in car trunks now and then. Most of the time he took them out and fed them to the sharks. The man was neat; he cleaned up after himself. Stuff he did was almost tasteful compared to what we're looking at now, Vince."

"Yeah, Sal the Strap's such a sweetheart I wish it was him lying over there instead of Silvio Narbonne," Dawson said, snarling. Turning to Sergeant Meltzer, he said, "You notified the coroner, didn't you?"

"Joyce did," said Meltzer. "Coroner's supposed to be on his way here, along with a couple of guys from the crime lab. They were tied up with something when Joyce called. Can't be anything worse than this, can it?"

Dawson shook his head no. He didn't want to talk about how horrible the crime was. He only wished to talk about solving it. Averting his eyes from the little boy's body, he slowly scanned the area once again. Later there would be glossy eight-by-ten photographs to study, but photos often obscured things that would register in the human mind.

Jones said, "The lab guys might be able to lift fingerprints from a shovel and some of this other stuff. Maybe we'll get a lucky break, Vince."

"If the killer is Haitian, I'm pretty sure his prints won't even be on file over there," said Dawson. "From talking with his Excellency Captain Armando Raphael on the phone, I got the distinct impression that he doesn't believe in modern police methods as much as he believes in voodoo."

CHAPTER 5

In the bright morning sun, Chango trudged through the sand on a stretch of barren, unpopulated beach. He looked at the burlap sack he was carrying in his left hand, then he looked back at his trail of deep footprints. There were no blood drops in the white sand. Caked brownish red, the sack was no longer dripping.

In Chango's right hand was a ring of keys taken from the body of Silvio Narbonne and a map of Braxton Beach snatched late last night from a tourist information kiosk. The keys were conveniently tagged; by means of addresses on the tags and some papers in Silvio's wallet, Chango had figured out that the ring of keys would enable him to get into the cottage where Silvio and Jean had lived and four more cottages of which the old man had been caretaker.

As Chango made his way along the beach, seeking out the cottage that the map told him he should encounter first as he headed into the rising sun, he was keenly alert, darting his eyes all around, lest he be spied by some enemy or stumble unwittingly into harm's way. He did not like to be out in the open, taking chances. However, there were things he needed that he could not obtain by staying in the woods, where he had stolen a few hours of sleep during the night.

He took heart in the firm knowledge that Damballah, Guede Nimbo, and all the other loas were protecting him with their immortality because he was one of them, as immortal as they. This had been proven when his *vevers*, his symbols of unearthly power – his drum, whip, machete, and omen pouch – were returned to him so promptly, along with his corporeal embodiment. Chango was an omnipotent god! This spiritual truth was confirmed by the miracle of his resurrection from a watery grave. The humans sacrificed to appease himself and his kindred loas had been magically compelled to deliver themselves to his place of interment, and to bring his vevers as an offering, along with their own mortal flesh. But now additional human sacrifices must be made, to give new life to Chango's disciples.

He remembered with satisfaction and pride how he had become a god, a loa, in the pantheon of holy loas that had to be worshipped and appeased. His sanctification had been preordained, for he was of the blood lineage of Hector Chanfray, the first Chango, who led the bloody revolt of black slaves against their French masters two centuries ago, when the island of Haiti was called Saint Dominique. His great and famous ancestor struck terror into the hearts of the rich and arrogant plantation owners by stealing and eating their infants, till he and his small band of renegades were forced to flee to the deepest part of the jungle to live with Yoruba Indians, the pitiful remnants of the tribes that had been slaughtered by the Spanish who ruled before the French came.

Chango's father was named Hector Chanfray after *his* father, and was also known as Chango. He was the bokor of the village of Les Cayes when he was assassinated by the Tontons Macoutes, who feared he might pattern himself after his ancestor and lead the peasants in a revolt against Papa Doc.

Chango was growing in his mother's womb when, at the ceremony for the Reclamation of the Dead, his mother fell into a trance and rode the spirit of her murdered husband to the Kingdom of Guede Nimbo, who told her that the child soon to be born would be the reincarnation of the first and mightiest Hector Chanfray and would avenge his father's death.

That day, three months before his birth, his mother pledged to apprentice him to the bokor who presided over the ceremony for the Reclamation of the Dead. And so, soon after he came into the world, he was given over to his mentor to be raised as a *hunsi*, a spouse of the gods. During his apprenticeship he dedicated all his thoughts, words, and deeds to his namesake, Chango, his ancestor who had become a loa.

Then, when he was twelve years old, he was deemed ready for the rite of *Kanzo*, or spiritual maturization, which invites a hunsi's patron loa to possess him entirely, so that the hunsi and the loa may become one in body and soul. Kanzo was a symbolic enactment of death and resurrection. Chango had to purify and anoint himself, covering his head with a salve of herbs, rice, bread, syrup, and blood, and then he was wrapped in a shroud, like a corpse. Locks of his hair and nail clippings from his left hand were put in a pot and buried so that the earth had custody of his soul till it could be replaced by the loa. For seven days and nights he stayed in a locked room, imbibing no food but only potions prepared by the bokor who was his mentor. During this period of silence, self-flagellation, and prayers to Guede Nimbo, all the other hunsis chanted, beat their drums, and invoked their patron loas to aid in the spiritual transaction. Thus Hector Chanfray's past life died, went into the ground with the locks of his hair and the nail clippings from his left hand, and a new self emerged into being. The eternal essence of his ancestor melded into him, fusing him with the gods, making him one of them, their equal. He was transformed into the true Chango, alive still, and immortal down through the ages. Only humans had to die, and he was their Lord of Death.

He required the flesh of babes to sustain his immortality. The first human flesh he ever tasted came from the children of the three members of the Tontons Macoutes who had assassinated his father. After that he thrived on the practice of cannibalism, which was no sin for him because he was a loa. He was aloof from mortal laws and constraints, immune to the earthly forces arrayed against him. Time and time again he had defeated or eluded his enemies, even his archenemy, the one his mother should have smothered in the cradle. The one whose very image mocked him. That wretched excess of creation who had threatened to usurp the name Chango and rob him of his place among the loas.

Now that the bright sunlight of Damballah was shining upon him in one more moment of supreme triumph, he desired to have his disciples gathered about him, to worship and glorify him and assist him in his earthly rite of passage. He intended to call them forth from their premature interment.

Trudging through the sand, he skirted an outcropping of palm trees and tall, sparse grass, and then he spotted a beach cottage, a large frame bungalow, white trimmed in green. For an instant he thought it was unoccupied: all the windows were shut and there was no light behind the filmy curtains. But he noticed a red Mustang parked under the carport.

Moving swiftly and stealthfully, he crept toward the side of the cottage opposite the carport. He barely got himself hidden, ducking around the corner, when the front door popped open. He drew his machete out of its sheathe.

Peeping out from behind the cottage, he spied a young man and a young woman coming down off the porch. Both were wearing cutoff jeans, sneakers, and colorful T-shirts.

"You have the shopping list in your purse, Susan?" the young man said.

"Yep. You've got the money?" Susan asked.

"Sure do. But let's try not to spend too much before the rest of the gang gets here. That way they can pitch in."

"Smart thinking, Barry!" Susan said, laughing.

"I hope while we're gone Silvio comes and fixes the sail on the boat, like he promised," said Barry.

"He will. Mother says he's very dependable."

Chango kept himself hidden, refraining from attacking the young couple. There were things he needed to do first. He would take care of them in his own good time. Machete in hand, he peeked around the corner of the cottage as the little red Mustang backed out, made a U-turn, and drove away. He came into the open, jingling his keys, but when he was about to mount the porch he spied an outbuilding about fifty yards away: a large shed, white with green trim, with a tar-paper roof.

He went to the shed and found the double doors padlocked. He expected to have a key to the lock on his ring, but for some reason there wasn't one; Silvio must have kept it separately somewhere. Each door had a big, shiny steel handle. Sticking the machete back in its sheathe and setting down his burlap sack, he got a grip on the door handles and pulled hard, quite easily extracting the bolts and nuts from the wood frame so that the hasp came free in a shower of splinters. He opened the double doors wide, allowing sunlight to stream into the shed. He saw that it was built on a concrete slab, which suited him fine. Inside there was a small sailboat with its mast and sails disassembled. Against the back wall was a workbench, and above it a pegboard full of tools. Chango set his blood-caked burlap sack on the concrete floor. Then he shut the doors.

He went up onto the porch of the cottage and used one of the labeled keys to let himself in. Swiftly scouting through the place, he noticed that two of the bedrooms appeared unused, even though the beds were made, and the third bedroom had a messed-up bed with open suitcases on top – obviously the one used by the young couple named Barry and Susan. Deciding not to search for valuables at this moment, Chango went to the kitchen, where he looked in the pantry and found a box of cornmeal. Taking it with him, he let himself out through the front door, twisting the knob so it would relock itself once it was shut.

He returned to the boat shed and flipped on the single overhead bulb that drew power from a line strung from the cottage. Then he closed the double doors. He opened the box of cornmeal and set it on the concrete floor. Then he opened his burlap sack and took out his *petra* drum, his holy drum, which had been blessed and bequeathed to him by his mentor, and some grave ornaments with candles, which he had stolen from the cemetery. He laid aside his bullwhip.

He withdrew the severed arm of Silvio Narbonne, which was wrapped in Silvio's stiff, blood-caked denim jacket. Unfolding the denim and tossing it aside, he laid the arm in the center of the concrete floor, a few feet from the hull of the sailboat. Chanting to himself in Creole, he cupped his hand and poured it full of cornmeal, and used the yellowish grain to draw a full-sized outline of a man on the floor. The severed arm formed one of the figure's arms, and Chango went on from there to complete the effigy.

He placed fat red cemetery candles all around the outline, and lit the wicks, chanting all the while. Then he sat cross-legged on the floor at the head of his cornmeal drawing and began playing his petra drum, beating the tight skin in a rhythmic frenzy and wailing in a Creole-African dialect – a high, keening, primitive invocation.

The orange candlelight flickered on his savagely tattooed face in the blackness of the windowless shed that had become his *humfo*, his voodoo temple. He willed himself to enter a trancelike state, giving himself up to the loas, so that he might relive the joyous miracle of his resurrection.

When the boat had sunk, only a half mile from America, the ocean became his womb, a womb for him alone, where no enemies, no usurpers could intrude. A womb that would give birth to him anew, and in a purer, more godlike presence than before. The powerful waves tossed and pummeled him and sucked him down into the watery depths. He did not fight it, for he knew that he was a loa, under the protection of other loas like himself. He allowed his body to keep turning, over and over, down and down, a helpless fetus peacefully adrift in a sac of amniotic fluid.

Then he left his body, as the fetus leaves the womb, and was able to look down upon himself from above the glittering surface of the sea. He saw a school of deadly sharks swim by him without striking, for they knew that he was not to be violated. He was like a part of the sun, embodied by the sun's rays, the rays of Damballah, as he gazed at himself from a great height.

He understood that he had died, that his soul had risen high above the water, far beyond worldly concerns. He was an ethereal presence, omnipotent and omnipresent. All knowledge was his. And he was fulfilled.

His corporeal self was enveloped in a plasma of death, a watery membrane of darkness. But for his other self, his immortal spirit, everything was growing brighter... and still brighter. He was being whisked toward a vibrant, radiant realm, flooded with light, escorted by choirs of chanting loas; who like himself had once been human. They brought him into the fantastically glorious presence of Legba, Damballah, and Guede Nimbo. He wanted to stay forever in this Kingdom of the Loas, reunited with his supernatural peers, but he knew that he must not remain. His earthly tasks were not yet done.

With great reluctance, he separated himself from the other loas and allowed his spirit to be drawn away from them to reenter his terrestrial body. After a while, he became aware of the rough, heavy soil weighing oppressively on his bones and muscles, his lungs bereft of air. He came fully awake and began to claw his way out of the grave.

It was a joyous task, for he was emerging alone, in sole glory, unlike that long-ago time when his *ti-bon-ange* was there to mock him. This time his resurrection was satisfyingly complete. He was the undisputed *gros-bon-ange*, the ruling spirit.

Now he must help his six disciples to join him, by performing the sacred ceremonies and sacrifices for the Reclamation of the Dead.

CHAPTER 6

At her ranch-style home on a pleasant residential avenue just off the Braxton State College campus, Dr. Martha Lewis, a handsome ash-blonde in her middle forties, was trying to squeeze in a few hours of work on her new book, entitled *Voodoo in Modern Haiti*. She had a card table set up in the spacious, brightly sunlit living room, where she could spread her notes out around the typewriter and try to get her mind in gear, in the midst of the myriad of anthropological artifacts collected by her and her deceased husband. The wall, bookcases, and mantel were adorned with primitive sculpture, tribal masks, jade and ivory carvings, and ornaments made from furs, feathers, ebony, and leather, producing an ambience that she hoped would put her in a suitable mood to devote herself to the task at hand.

She was having a hard time concentrating, because her daughter and son-in-law were in town on a two-week vacation, and she was excited to have them so near. It did no good reminding herself that she ought to be satisfied because she had already gotten to spend three days with them. She was bubbling over with the anticipation of having lunch with them today, as if she hadn't seen them for a month.

Barry and Susan had flown in on Tuesday and had stayed with Martha till this weekend. But today they were being joined by two other couples, friends of theirs from New York City with whom they would share one of the four beach cottages that Martha usually rented out to tourists.

The day before yesterday, Martha had driven Barry and Susan out to the cottage, and they had all helped Silvio Narbonne clean the place up after the departure of the previous tenants, who had been a bunch of slobs. Little Jean had chipped in, too. Even after they were done, the cottage still smelled faintly of mildew and sour milk, for the tenants had left damp beach towels wadded up on the beds and food spoiling on the table. "They had the nerve to ask me if they could rent this cottage next year," Martha had complained to Silvio. "They wanted to pay a deposit and reserve it in advance, but I told them it was booked solid."

After the cleanup job, Silvio had left to buy some stuff for fixing the sailboat. Martha hadn't stuck around much longer either, because she felt that the young people probably wanted to be alone. All the rest of the day, she stifled the urge to phone and ask if they needed anything. She berated herself for being a bit jealous that Barry and Susan hadn't come to Florida by themselves, and so she wasn't going to see as much of them as she had on previous vacations. This morning they were going to knock around town, doing some shopping and sightseeing, using the Mustang she had loaned them. Then they'd pick her up. And after lunch they'd head out to the cottage to await the arrival of their friends.

Martha was lonely, but she didn't want her daughter to guess it. During a shopping spree with Susan earlier in the week, she had spoken blithely about her breakup nine months ago with Albert Scanlon, an English professor she had dated for two years with vague expectations of marriage. Gradually she had decided that Albert wasn't exactly what she wanted, and tried to let him down tactfully, only to realize that she needn't have worried about hurting his feelings – he was clearly relieved to be off the hook. They were still friends, but they didn't date each other anymore. The sad truth was that Martha hadn't dated anyone since, despite the difficulty of wiggling out of some of the offers. The funny thing was that she missed Albert Scanlon, even though she didn't wish to go back to being deeply involved with him. Sometimes she wondered whether, rather than disciplining herself with solitude, she ought to try having a fling. But she had never been seriously or even frivolously attached to more than one man at a time. She had married young, at age twenty-two, and Dr. Morgan Lewis was the only man she had ever been completely in love with. Yet she knew that if she kept comparing everyone she met with him, she would never fall in love again.

Martha's publisher was uptight about the deadline for her book manuscript, which was less than half finished and due to be completed, according to the contract, in just three more months. This wouldn't be such a problem if Martha could work on it full-time, instead of teaching at the college. She told herself she had to stop her mind from wandering and get down to business. The seven-day semester break that she was on now should be the perfect time for her to write her head off and pile up some solid progress. But she hadn't been staunch enough to tell Barry and Susan to come visit some other time, and she hadn't wanted to shut herself away from them once they were here, so she had pretended that the book deadline wasn't urgent.

Putting on her reading glasses, it occurred to her that she found it much easier to work in solitude, when Barry and Susan were far away in New York. Knowing they were just across town, soon to be on their way here, filled her with a tingly feeling that she almost wanted to call "childish." On Tuesday, when Susan had told her over lunch that she had something important to talk over, her heart had filled with the anticipatory glow of being told that her daughter was pregnant. To her surprise, even though she had always been strong and independent and what one might call a career woman, she found herself almost wishing to become a grandmother. But it had turned out that what Susan wanted to divulge was that she and Barry were planning to start their own advertising agency. If they got into *that* kind of struggle, it would probably mean they'd continue to put off having children. But Martha still wished them every success, and didn't mind helping them with the $25,000 loan they had hit her up for.

She tried not to be depressed over the realization that once they launched themselves into such a heavy commitment in New York, they would be unable to come down to Florida to work and live, which had been her vague, unexpressed hope. She had kept on living in this house that was too large for her, because it felt right to keep it for Susan to come home to. And besides, it would be nice if someday there were grandchildren who from these surroundings would sense a little bit of what their grandfather must have been like, even though they were never going to get to know him personally. Maybe these kinds of sentiments were silly, and maybe Martha might just as well move into an apartment. But she believed that she would be even lonelier and more discontented in a place devoid of memories.

She knew all too well that she wasn't really over the loss of her husband, even though three years had passed since his death from multiple sclerosis. One good thing about Susan's living in New York was that she hadn't had to witness, day in and day out, the slow wasting away of her father's vitality. Martha had gone it alone. When she had first fallen for Dr. Morgan Lewis, she was one of his graduate students; he was fourteen years her senior. But it had proven to be much more than a college-girl crush on a mature, intellectual, older man. Martha and Morgan had been intimately compatible as man and wife and as colleagues. They had shared anthropological insights, research, and field trips. They had written all their articles and books together. Their lives had been inextricably intertwined.

Martha hoped she would someday get over not wanting anyone else. She had tried with Albert Scanlon, and missed Albert, but she didn't love him. Yet he had filled gaps in her life that needed filled. Ironically, she had been able to get more writing done when she didn't have so much time on her hands; she had been primed to make full use of her spare moments when there weren't going to be so many of them because she was dating Albert. Since breaking up with him, instead of concentrating more on her work she was letting her head fill up with restless thoughts that would not allow themselves to be stifled when she sat in front of the typewriter.

Today, as on most other days, even though she was under pressure to crank some ideas out onto paper, she kept shuffling through her notes and leafing through her research texts. She was in the middle of a chapter on zombie lore, which had always intrigued and excited her; yet she couldn't drum up any fresh approaches or insights. She wanted to lead up to a discussion of some startling modern discoveries about zombies, but to do so she had to rehash some of the older, better-known legends. She debated whether to quote from her sources or put the stuff into her own words. Finally, deciding that it would be more authoritative to quote, she wrote a crisp, clever lead-in paragraph, then recounted an anecdote told by the French anthropologist George De Rouquet, of a strange incident that had happened to him on a field trip to Haiti in 1930.

"Toward evening," De Rouquet wrote in his journal, "we encountered a group of four male figures coming from the nearby cotton field where they had been toiling. I was struck by their peculiar shambling gait, most unlike the lithe walk of other natives. Their overseer stopped their progress, enabling me to observe them closely for some minutes. They were clothed in rags made from sacking. Their arms hung down by their sides, dangling in a curiously lifeless fashion. Their faces and hands appeared devoid of flesh, the skin adhering to the bones like wrinkled brown parchment. I also noticed that they did not sweat, although they had been working and the sun was still very hot. I was unable to judge even their approximate ages. They may have been young men or quite elderly. The most arresting feature about them was their gaze. They all stared straight ahead, their eyes dull and unfocused as if blind. They did not show a spark of awareness of my presence, even when I approached them closely. To test the reflexes of one, I made a stabbing gesture toward his eyes with my pointed fingers. He did not blink or shrink back. But when I attempted to touch his hand the overseer prevented me, saying that this was not permitted. My immediate impression was that these creatures were imbeciles made to work for their keep. My guide, however, assured me that they were indeed the *zombies*; that is, dead persons resurrected by sorcery and employed as unpaid laborers. I watched as they were locked up by the overseer in a tiny, windowless shed. And I suggested to Baptiste, my guide, that we should investigate this affair. But he, who up until this moment had shown a cool detachment, suddenly became very frightened and insisted that we depart immediately, telling me that our guns would be useless against the zombies, should the overseer send them to attack us."

Finished inserting the quote into her manuscript, Dr. Martha Lewis felt a bit guilty, like a sophomore padding out a research paper. She considered rewriting it in her own style, but she didn't really see the point of doing so. As she was deliberating, the telephone rang. It crossed her mind that it might be Albert Scanlon. Glancing at her wristwatch, she saw that there was still a half hour to go before Barry and Susan were due to arrive. With a pang of anxiety, she hoped they weren't calling to cancel the lunch date.

Reluctant to pick up the receiver, she uttered a tentative hello, and a coarse male voice that she didn't recognize said, "May I speak with Dr. Martha Lewis, please?"

It was an ordinary question, but something about the way it was asked made it feel ominous. "Speaking," Martha said warily, her throat dry and husky all of a sudden.

The man with the coarse voice said that his name was Lieutenant Vincent Dawson of the Braxton Beach Police Department, and he was sorry that he had some very bad news.

CHAPTER 7

"Have you and Susan had a chance to get together?" Albert Scanlon asked his daughter. They were sharing a late lunch on the patio of his Tudor-style home, a few blocks from where Martha Lewis lived.

"No, I've been pretty busy," said nineteen-year-old Mary Ann, a winsome redhead in tight, faded jeans and a red T-shirt with the word *Honda* written across her jutting breasts in fancy white calligraphy. Actually, she was hurt that Susan hadn't phoned her. She figured that even though her father and Susan's mother were no longer romantically involved, it was no reason for her and Susan not to remain close.

"You should give her a call," said Albert. "I'm sure she'll be delighted to hear from you." He sipped his coffee delicately, then blotted his neat white mustache with his napkin. His appearance and mannerisms were extremely refined. An Anglophile who taught college courses in Chaucer and Shakespeare, he strove to model himself after an image of gentility esteemed in past ages. Sometimes the effect was impressive, and sometimes comic. To eat with his daughter at home at a picnic table, he was impeccably shaved and groomed, in a white silk shirt and sharply creased dark-blue trousers with a matching blue ascot.

"Martha and I parted amiably," he said with a mild, unperturbed smile. "There shouldn't be any animosity between you and Susan. Don't be reluctant to get in touch with her."

"I wouldn't want to horn in on her New York friends," said Mary Ann.

"Oh, now, you know you're perfectly welcome at the beach cottage. Susan has said as much, many times. She's never treated you as though you were horning in."

"Then why didn't she call and invite me?"

"I would suspect it's because she's so sure you understand that you don't need an invitation."

After her father left the house, on his way to a meeting of the English Department faculty, Mary Ann went to her bedroom phone and dialed the number of the beach cottage. She got no answer, which didn't surprise her – Susan and her gang were probably romping on the shore. Mary Ann decided to take a run out there on her motor scooter. She could say she just happened to be in the area and thought of dropping by, and if she sensed any bad vibes she could come up with an excuse to split.

Spinning down the highway on her little red Honda scooter, wearing her matching red helmet, she told herself she was foolish to worry about barging in on an old friend like Susan. She remembered how they had joked they were going to be sisters when it looked like their parents were blundering half willingly toward matrimony.

She seemed to get to the beach cottage in no time at all, zipping down the private road and pulling up onto the crushed-shell driveway. To her disappointment, now that she was already here with her excuses ready, it didn't seem as if anybody was home. The place was all shut up, and no air conditioners were humming. No car under the carport. But she killed the scooter engine and took off her helmet. Then she went up onto the porch and knocked. Nobody came to the door.

LIVING THINGS

Shielding her eyes from the sun, she gazed down toward the ocean. No one was on the private beach, not even trespassers. She glanced toward the boat shed. The doors were shut. If Susan and her friends were off on a walk, Mary Ann couldn't hear their voices in the distance – only the soughing of the surf. It was inviting enough that she decided to stay for a while. She would wait and see if the vacationers came back from town or wherever. In the meantime, she could relax and enjoy herself.

She thought of doing some seascape sketches. She always carried her sketchbook and charcoals in her scooter saddlebag. She got to be friends with Susan, even though Susan was five years older, when as a high-school freshman she had audited a summer art course that Susan was taking as a college sophomore. Now Mary Ann was an art major at Braxton State College, and she hoped that, like Susan, she would one day work at a commercial art studio. Being down on the beach drawing when her friend got here would add to the aura of nonchalance she wanted to create about her "unplanned" visit. She got out her sketchbook and charcoals and her flowery plastic satchel full of beach gear. Kicking off her sockless sneakers and leaving them at the edge of the driveway, she strode down toward the shore, enjoying the hot sand oozing between her toes.

Holding the double doors of the boat shed slightly ajar, Chango spied on the young redhead, knowing that Guede Nimbo had delivered her to him. He ran his tongue over his lips as he watched her pert buttocks undulating seductively with her lithe, long-legged stride.

She picked a spot about fifty feet from the lapping water and spread out her beach towel. Then she stripped. Under her skin-tight jeans and red T-shirt, she was wearing an emerald green bikini. Her figure was youthfully firm and trim, yet fully mature and voluptuous. She sat on her towel and gazed pensively out to sea, watching the sunlight glinting off the dying whitecaps of the incoming tide.

Chango started to sneak out of the shed, but then hung back, more carefully considering what his next move should be. Nobody was around. Just he and the lovely young morsel. She was his for the taking. He could toy with her, prolonging the delicious adventure if he chose to do so.

Mary Ann turned around, and Chango jumped back, even though he was sure she couldn't see him through the thin crack between the doors of the dark shed. Her eyes swept past him.

She was looking at the cottage in its setting of cypress and palm trees, thinking it would make a nice sketch to give to Susan as a token of their friendship. But she didn't want to start working just yet. All she felt like doing was soaking up sun.

She didn't like being a redhead, because she had the exceptionally fair and delicate skin that often went along with it. A light sprinkling of freckles, too. She often joked that people like her, with skin that burned easily but refused to tan, weren't meant to live in Florida. She sometimes claimed it was her whole reason for wanting to go to work in New York, like Susan.

She squeezed creamy yellow suntan lotion out of a tube and smoothed it over her legs, arms, belly, and shoulders. Removing her sunglasses, she applied lotion to her face and neck. Then, after glancing all around to make sure she was really alone, she untied her bikini halter and set it aside. She figured she'd be able to hear tires on the crunchy driveway and put the halter back on before anybody saw her. She massaged suntan lotion into her ample breasts, enjoying the subtle erotic feeling of the blazing heat of the sun on her hardening nipples. Guiltily, she looked back toward the cottage again, not wanting to get caught giving herself this pleasure.

She gasped.

A huge black man was standing by her motor scooter. She jumped and scrambled for her T-shirt, almost ripping it in her haste to pull it over her head and plunge her arms through the sleeves. The huge man laughed at her – a loud, nasty chortle that carried over the surf sounds. She let out another angry, frightened gasp as she finished tugging the T-shirt down.

The man picked up her motor scooter as easily as if it were a toy and held it straight up over his head. Then he started to walk toward Mary Ann.

On her feet, staring at him, she yelled, "Put that down! It's mine!" She was terribly frightened of him, but she had no choice but to act brave.

He laughed at her bravado and kept coming. She thought of running, but to where? He'd chase her down – she was sure of it – he was such an awesome brute. In her panicky frame of mind, she hoped desperately that his "showing off" with the motor scooter would somehow satisfy his ego and he would leave her unharmed.

He stopped a few feet away from her, grinning, and she saw the evil-looking brands and tattoos on his face and body, the strange ornaments dangling on his braids. He had a machete strapped to his hip, and something else – something coiled – hanging on the machete's handle.

She trembled, thinking he was going to throw the motor scooter down on her, battering and crushing her. But he chortled and walked past her, a behemoth with a heavy weight overhead, going down to the sea. This was her chance to run, and she did. She dashed toward the cottage. Looking back in her chugging, pumping struggle through the impeding sand, she saw the huge black man wading into the ocean, the scooter over his head, till the waves were crashing around his chest.

Mary Ann threw herself against the cottage door, but it didn't budge. She had seized on the idea of getting in to use the phone – but she also thought that before the police could arrive she'd be dead. She had better try to make it out to the road – and hope that some traffic was on it for her to flag down. Vaulting over the porch railing, she saw the big beast of a man tossing her motor scooter into the ocean. Then he was turning and coming out of the water toward her. In her terror, she forgot herself and ran onto the crushed-shell driveway, lacerating her bare feet, falling and sprawling, cutting up her hands, arms, and knees.

Chango chuckled as he broke into a run, ready to chase down his prey. He was not desperate. He knew he would win the game. There was no chance that she could get away, for she had been bequeathed to him by Guede Nimbo.

Struggling to keep running on her bloody feet, Mary Ann almost made it to the private road, a one-lane blacktop, before Chango caught up with her. He allowed her to keep going for a few yards while he effortlessly matched her pace, enjoying her futile gasps and whimpers. Then he used his whip, flicking it out, coiling it around her ankle. She shrieked and went down in a flailing heap. He yanked her toward him, unsheathing his machete. But he liked her sobs so much that he decided to let them go on for a while. Using the whip and machete to goad and guide her the way a matador works a bull under the power of his cape and sword, he drove her back, toward the ocean. Her lacerated feet made tracks in the sand. When she stumbled to one side or the other, he hemmed her in with a flick of the whip or a jab of the machete. Thus he reduced her to a babbling, simpering wretch, so contemptible to him that he no longer desired her sexually.

"Please," she snuffled, her face and hair streaked with blood, mucus, and sand. "Please . . . let me go . . ."

He laughed at her. But he didn't tell her yes or no. He let her go on begging. Her groveling proved his superiority. He was divine, she was mortal.

He made her keep backing away from his awesome power till the dying waves were lapping at her ankles. She continued to sniffle and plead, not realizing that it was foolish to try to deny the gods when they needed to be appeased. It enraged Chango that she didn't know that she ought to act more dignified in the presence of a loa. He kept coming at her, driving her back, into the deeper water. When she was in it up to her breasts, a huge wave struck her from behind and she went under.

Chango sneered, effortlessly keeping up with her as the current spun and carried her on an angle parallel to him. She came up spluttering, let out a loud sob, and dove under again, as if she could swim away. When she surfaced, he snapped his bullwhip at her and it snaked out, inches from her face. She screamed, splashing more furiously. In long, easy strides he stayed with her, chuckling at her valiant but foredoomed effort, appreciating her gameness. She was now not so boring as she was when it seemed she was giving up.

Finally, when this amusement had run its course, he snaked the whip out with a loud crack, coiling the lash around her throat. Choking, she tore at the coils. She couldn't stay afloat anymore. She went under in a spray of foam.

Pulling viciously on the handle of the whip, Chango towed Mary Ann toward shore. In shallower water, her wildly thrashing body spragged bottom, the coils of the whip tightening harder around her neck. Her final screams were muted because of the choking leathery noose, her body plowing thick furrows in the wet sand as he hauled her toward him like a hooked fish, his machete upraised. He seized one of her thrashing arms, grasping it tightly around its slender wrist. With a flash and a loud thunk, the blade of the machete hacked clean through the shoulder joint. He seized her other arm and chopped again. He kept on chopping and tossing parts of her aside till he had left the part that he needed.

Once more he let himself into the cottage. From the pantry he took two large heavy-duty garbage bags and slipped one inside the other for double strength. Into this plastic sack he put the parts of the girl that he did not need and weighted them down with a heavy stone. After returning to the beach, he waded into the ocean till the waves struck as high as his chin, then tossed the sack as far as he could and watched it sink.

He raked up the crushed-shell driveway and the dry sand where the girl had left bloody footprints. He didn't need to worry about the place where he had butchered her. In his infallible wisdom he had done it close enough to the ocean that the signs of his holy work were already being washed away by the incoming tide.

Satisfied with the pristine appearance of the cottage and its environs, he went into the boat shed to continue the ritual for the Reclamation of the Dead. He shut the double doors and lit his candles. Then he knelt on the concrete floor and unwrapped a bulky, bloody package – the part of the girl that he had saved, wrapped up in her beach towel.

Chanting to himself, he gazed upon the dismembered torso. It would be the centerpiece for his ritual. Speaking the names of Legba, Damballah, and Guede Nimbo, he touched in turn each of her nipples and her navel. Then, still chanting, he placed the torso gently into its appropriate spot within the cornmeal outline of a human figure that he had drawn earlier on the floor of the shed.

Near the fingertips of the severed arm of Silvio Narbonne, there was a sail-patching kit, complete with large darning needles and balls of tough twine. Using the needle, Chango began sewing, stitching Silvio's arm to Mary Ann's torso. As he chanted ever more fervently, his mind dwelt upon glorious visions of the Kingdom of Loas, from which he had been sent forth to bring his disciples up from the earth.

CHAPTER 8

Sitting in front of Vince Dawson's desk, Martha Lewis dabbed at her red, puffy eyes with a balled-up tissue, then took a sip of scalding black coffee. The container was so hot to hold that she set it on the front edge of the desk, her hand trembling so that she almost spilled it in her lap. She still wasn't over the horror of her visit to the morgue, and she doubted that she could have gotten through it without Barry and Susan at her side. Thankfully, they had arrived at her house about fifteen minutes after she learned of the murders. Their day, like hers, had degenerated from gaiety to grief. Instead of taking her to lunch, they had been obliged to drive her to the morgue, and now they were waiting in the reception area of the police station because the two detectives wanted to question her alone.

In order to spare her the pain of seeing Jean and Silvio's death wounds, Lieutenant Dawson had instructed the morgue attendant to unzip the body bags only enough for her to view the faces. But that had been bad enough. Even though she hadn't been able to see any direct evidence of how death had been inflicted, she had been struck by the agonized facial expressions frozen into their silent tale of suffering.

"I'm sorry for what we had to put you through," Lieutenant Dawson said, trying to make his gruff voice sound gentle, "but it's necessary for the next of kin or the next closest associate of the deceased to make the formal identification."

"I understand," said Martha. It was about the third time that he had apologized. His sensitivity amazed her; it was a quality she had imagined would be absent from the typical policeman. She guessed he was about her own age, maybe a little older. His thinning brown hair was streaked with gray. His face was square and rather chunky, dark puffy bags under his small blue eyes. She didn't know if the slight bulge under his left arm was caused by a gun in a shoulder holster or by the store-bought shapelessness of his rumpled blue suit.

"Ready?" asked Lieutenant Jones.

Martha nodded, then forced herself to swallow another sip of scalding coffee.

Jones was sitting to Martha's right, in front of Dawson's desk, punching the buttons of a tape recorder. He had not been at the morgue, but had been introduced to Martha here in the office. Unlike Dawson, Jones apparently was fond of dressing well. He was younger, taller, and slimmer than Dawson, so broad-shouldered and narrow-hipped that his well-tailored tan suit actually made him look dashing – an effect that Dawson probably couldn't achieve even if he were to lose thirty pounds.

Leaning toward the tape recorder, Jones said, "Interview with Dr. Martha Lewis of 18 Macon Drive, employer and sponsor of murder victims Silvio and Jean Narbonne."

Though the two ashtrays on the desk were full of butts and the small, dirty office smelled of stale smoke, neither of the two detectives was bothering with cigarettes at the moment. As Jones slated the tape, Dawson leaned forward and said, "Dr. Lewis . . . I know it must be painful for you to talk about this . . .but Lieutenant Jones and I need to know whatever you can tell us to shed any light at all on who may have killed Silvio and Jean."

Martha's chin trembled and fresh tears rolled from her eyes. Full of self-blame, she said, "I thought I was bringing them to a safer country, and it turned out just the opposite." She wiped her checks with the balled-up tissue.

"I'm sure you did what you believed was for the best," Dawson said. "Jean and Silvio surely must've appreciated all that you did for them."

He wondered if Jones was going to ride him later for taking an obvious shine to this witness, failing to preserve a cool professional distance. He found her much prettier than what he had expected a college professor to be, especially one in her forties. He had been looking for the green suit and white blouse she said she'd be wearing when she met him at the morgue, but he hadn't anticipated how good she'd look in it. Her ash-blond hair appeared natural, even if she might be doing something to it to hide gray. She had a good figure, too. What in the hell was happening to him? Usually he didn't find middle-aged women attractive even though he was middle-aged himself. Like many men in the Florida resort towns, he was spoiled by looking at all the young stuff running around in bikinis – even when it was unattainable, it was still there, making everything else look bad by comparison. Maybe he knew he wasn't ever going to have any of that young stuff again, except by paying for it. Maybe his chromosomes, his stifled yearnings, were making a subtle adjustment toward something more in reach, more attainable, more compatible with his flagging, worn-out mating instincts. But was Dr. Martha Lewis really on his plane of endeavor? He doubted it. They were more likely on two parallel lines pinched closer together by tragedy, but doomed to never quite intersect.

"Why was Haiti unsafe for the Narbonnes?" Jones asked. "I mean, the official line I've been hearing nowadays is that the boat people really weren't in mortal danger back in their native land. All that stuff about political persecution and human rights violations – they're just making that up so they can come here for economic opportunities."

Martha vehemently shook her head no. "Conditions on the island are much more horrible than the politicians want us to believe. The Haitians have a so-called President-for-Life who's really nothing but a ruthless dictator. He has his own private army, called the Tontons Macoutes – which means 'voodoo sorcerers' if you translate figuratively. The Tontons Macoutes are a legalized gang of torturers and murderers, feared by everyone in Haiti for their brutality and their supernatural powers."

"What supernatural powers?" Dawson asked, his eyebrows raised in disbelief.

Martha answered matter-of-factly. "They can command the spirits to tell them who is conspiring against the President-for-Life. And then they can order the spirits to inflict terrible curses upon the President's enemies."

Dawson blinked. "Haitians actually believe what you're saying? In this day and age? You've gotta be kidding."

"Not at all," said Martha. "The former President-for-Life, known as 'Papa Doc,' used to stick pins in a voodoo doll made in the likeness of John F. Kennedy. After Kennedy was assassinated, Papa Doc sent a secret agent to Arlington Cemetery to get a pinch of earth from Kennedy's grave. He wanted to imprison Kennedy's soul to influence Johnson to give Haiti billions of dollars in foreign aid."

"That's what I call voodoo economics," Jones quipped.

A wry look on his face, Dawson pointed at the tape recorder to remind Jones that all lack of seriousness was being logged for posterity, and for the chief, if he should ever decide to take a listen.

Martha said, "Virtually everyone in Haiti believes in voodoo to some extent, even the educated, even the intellectuals. Its influence pervades their society, and affects them as strongly as our religions affect us. When people believe something implicitly enough, it might as well be true, because it takes on a life of its own; it acquires de facto power over them. Some Haitians have been known to go into convulsions and die after being cursed by a bokor – a witch doctor. Their belief in black magic is so strong that it literally *scares* them to death. For centuries we had no logical explanation for this phenomenon. But now modern pathologists know the reason behind it. They've found that extreme fright can paralyze the vagus nerve, the main component of the central nervous system, stopping all bodily functions, including heartbeat."

Dawson cleared his throat and sat back in his chair. "All right, Dr. Lewis, I can understand what you're driving at, even though it requires a stretch of the imagination. But you still haven't told us why you thought there was particular danger in Haiti for Silvio Narbonne and his grandson."

"Did they have enemies who could've followed them here?" Jones asked.

"No, it wasn't that," said Martha. "At least, I don't believe so. I wanted them to get off the island because the boy's parents – Silvio's son and daughter-in-law – had already been arrested for trumped-up political crimes. They both died in prison about a year ago. No autopsy report was ever issued, and although Silvio was able to get their bodies released for what he deemed proper burial, members of the

Tontons Macoutes kept an eye on everything that happened from the prison morgue to the civilian cemetery."

Jones asked, "How did you come to know the Narbonne family, Dr. Lewis?"

"Well . . . you know I'm an anthropologist. So was my late husband. We both taught at Braxton State College, went on field trips together, and published jointly. Now I'm carrying on by myself, in some of the areas that interested both of us. I've been studying the historical and cultural aspects of voodoo, which is really a fairly sophisticated African religion transported to the Western hemisphere by slaves. I'm in the midst of writing a book about what I've learned. I spent two summers in Port-au-Prince, Haiti's capital city. Martin and Estelle Narbonne, Jean's father and mother, were newspaper columnists who helped me in my research, lining up interviews and so forth. They even got permission for me to observe various voodoo ceremonies."

"Sounds dangerous," said Dawson. "Meddling with primitive superstition. Weren't you afraid that some of these people's weird beliefs might cause them to turn on you? What if they had got started thinking you were in control of evil spirits or something?" Dawson cracked a faint smile because the notion sounded so incredible, even though it definitely had its serious side.

Martha answered him quite soberly. "You have to understand, Lieutenant Dawson, that voodoo is like all other religions in that it has its benign aspects as well as its harmful ones – the dichotomy of good versus evil. An ordinary voodoo priest is called a houngan, and is devoted to helping people with his knowledge of herbs and potions and white magic. But a bokor – a voodoo sorcerer – practices all the darkest arts. He tries his best to incite criminal acts, to convince people to worship the devil, and to command the spirits of the dead to commit atrocities."

"Sounds delightful," said Jones.

"What about Chango?" Dawson asked. "Did you learn anything about him while you were in Haiti?"

"Yes, everybody knew about Chango," said Martha. "He was sort of the Haitian equivalent of the boogeyman, but at the same time he was an all too real menace – a vicious killer and cannibal. His real name was Hector Chanfray, but he took the name of Chango – god of lightning, fire, and death – because he believed himself to be the reincarnation of that god. As you know, I wasn't surprised when you told me what Silvio tried to do. Encountering Chango's corpse the way he did must have terrified him beyond all reason."

"Apparently he believed that the bokor could come back from the dead," said Jones. "I suppose most other Haitians believe the same thing?"

"They not only believe it," Martha said flatly. "They *know* it's possible. Zombies are not entirely creatures of myth, Lieutenant. They are a real, verifiable phenomenon."

This statement achieved the shocking effect that she intended. Both detectives raised their eyebrows and stared at her probingly, as if trying to discern vestiges of a mind unhinged by grief. In a gruff, skeptical tone, Dawson said, "Surely you're not telling us that you also believe that people can come back from the dead?"

Unperturbed, Martha answered, "Not exactly, but almost. You see, there's a substance nicknamed 'Zombie Cucumber' that apparently was brought over from Africa in olden times. Only the bokors know how to prepare and use it, supposedly. The potion is a deep, dark secret handed down from generation to generation, from the sorcerers to their apprentices."

"Then how do you know for sure that this potion exists?" Jones asked.

"In recent years," said Martha, "there have been several instances of people being brought to Haitian hospitals in an unexplained coma. Some of them continued to weaken and die, no matter what the doctors tried to do for them – life support systems and so on. But others eventually recovered, after days and days of unconsciousness or semi-consciousness. Some of them came out of their ordeal with their faculties intact, but some suffered brain damage and motor impairment. At first, no one was able to find out what was really wrong with these patients, or why the lucky ones got better. But recently, in a few of the cases, the doctors have hit on something, by analyzing blood and urine specimens. They've found traces of hallucinogenic compounds, anesthetics, and a chemical called tetrodotoxin."

"Tetro who?" said Jones.

"I know," said Martha. "It sounds like the name of a voodoo god. But it's actually a nerve poison."

"Nerve poison?" said Dawson. "You mean like curare?"

"Well, sort of," Martha said. "Curare comes from a tropical vine, and so does tetrodotoxin, but it's a different vine, called the Datura. The same poison is also secreted by a jungle toad that lives on the vine's flowers."

"So Zombie Cucumber is a misnomer," said Dawson.

"Probably an intentional misnomer propagated by the bokors," Martha said, "so people would be less likely to get wise to their secret. In any event, we now have evidence indicating that Datura is the main ingredient of their nasty little potion – no doubt doctored up with additional goodies, like bat's blood and corpse powder, and aided by magic rituals and incantations. It can produce a semblance of death – a deathlike trance scarcely distinguishable from the real thing. Those kinds of zombies *can* come back to life when the drug wears off."

CHAPTER 9

Barry and Susan Crandall were sitting on a long, low sofa in a bright, spacious reception area, waiting for the detectives to get done talking with Susan's mother. It amused Barry that the police station was purposely designed not to look like one. So far he hadn't seen a single uniformed cop; the ones not in plain clothes were probably required to use a rear entrance. In an atmosphere like this, the tourists could almost believe that no serious crime ever happened in Braxton Beach. There must have been a cell block somewhere, maybe at the end of one of the long corridors, but the areas that visitors were likely to see consisted of lots of tinted glass, open spaces, and tall potted plants flourishing between clusters of furniture made of chrome, glass, and bright blue fabric.

Barry was sipping black coffee, and Susan was leafing back and forth through a popular women's magazine, the kind she never bothered to read any other time and wasn't really reading now. Her green eyes were unfocused and there was a blank expression on her smooth, oval face. By nervously running her fingers through her long brown hair, she had made it so greasy and kinky that it was hanging behind her ears in a clump. Barry was annoyed that she wasn't the kind of wife who could manage to always look her charming best, whether hosting a cocktail party or coping with a tragedy. If she couldn't do better, how was she going to help him rise to the top of the business world?

Barry Crandall prided himself on his ability to remain calm and analytical in every situation. He had straight sandy hair neatly parted and cropped, and a narrow, angular face that caused people to peg him for a bookworm when he was wearing his eyeglasses; that was why he had switched to contacts twelve years ago, during his sophomore year in college. Without glasses he was rather good-looking, his bony jutting cheekbones and sharp probing nose not so striking, not so prominent, when they weren't starkly framed in dark plastic. With his contacts he could closely observe and scrutinize people without making them edgy. Susan was the only one who ever got mad and told him, "Stop looking at me that way!" Nobody else ever seemed to notice when he sized them up and doped them out, precisely calculating their weak points and their strong points, their talents and their shortcomings.

Over the past five years, Dan and Lisa Morelli and Paul and Shelly Beck, one white couple and one black couple, had passed his requirements without becoming aware that they were being tested. Then he had befriended them, drawing them into his circle. The main reason that he and Susan had invited them to share their winter vacation was to pitch them on going partners in the new ad agency for which Barry had borrowed some start-up capital from Susan's mother.

The murders couldn't have happened at a worse time, as far as Barry was concerned. The fuss was likely to hang up the business proposition. He'd have to hang back, least until tomorrow, maybe till the day after. He didn't think he was being callous or selfish to still be concerned with his future. After all, life had to go on. But he might as well be tactful. He could wait a day or two before pushing everybody for a commitment, in the meantime earning their respect for his patience and self-restraint.

Luckily, one of the couples driving down from New York, Dan and Lisa Morelli, had a key to the beach cottage. They weren't on a tight schedule; they were traveling by car instead of plane so they could do some sightseeing. Shelly Beck had grown up in the South, but neither Dan nor Lisa nor Shelly's husband Paul had seen much of it before. After poking down through Georgia and the Carolinas, they were aiming to arrive at the cottage sometime today, but they weren't sure exactly when. That was why Dan and Lisa were given the spare key last week when they drove Barry and Susan to La Guardia Airport.

Each of the three times that Barry had gone to the coffee machine down the hall, he had used his cell phone to dial the cottage, but nobody had answered. He got up to try again, and Susan said, "If you reach them, tell them we probably won't be out there tonight. We're going to have to stay with Mother, I think. She's taking this pretty hard."

"I don't think it's necessary to tell them about the murders, either," said Barry. "They can get the details tomorrow. Let them get a good night's sleep first."

"Just tell them Mother's not feeling well."

"Sure. That's what I had in mind."

"I think Mother will be okay after today. She's not fond of being coddled. She'll want us to get on with our vacation. I wish her romance with Dr. Scanlon had worked out. She's pretending that she's over it, but I can tell she's still pretty broken up, and now this has to happen."

"Albert is too prissy for her. She needs someone more manly."

"Like my father. She's looking for someone like my father, and she's probably not going to find him. I feel guilty for living so far away from her. I mean, I'd like to be sure she's happy, instead of picturing her all alone most of the time with nobody to look after her."

"I don't think you have to worry so much. She's a very strong woman."

"Still . . ."

Susan's voice trailed off as Barry bent and kissed her on the forehead. Then he pivoted and headed for a quiet area to try his cell phone again, his head brimming with plans for joining up with his carefully selected group of friends, giving them the glad tidings about the $25,000 loan he had landed from his mother-in-law, and persuading them to risk their futures and work their butts off to help him launch Crandall, Inc. At first, in order to butter his friends up, he was going to have to call the new agency Beck, Morelli and Crandall. Later, after he had time to wheel and deal and buy them out, he'd drop their names from the letterhead. Then it would be Crandall, Inc., the way he envisioned it all along.

***

"Come on, Shelly, cheer up!" Paul Beck said to his wife. "Your mood's been deteriorating ever since we crossed the Mason-Dixon Line three days ago. Now it seems to have hit rock bottom."

From behind the wheel of his blue Buick station wagon, Paul turned sideways to smile at Shelly and glance at Dan and Lisa Morelli in the back seat, hoping they would join in his forced joviality. They were cruising on the Coastal Highway that ran all the way from New Jersey down through Florida. In about a half hour they should be at Canaveral. Maybe visiting the Kennedy Space Center would get Shelley's mind off of what was bugging her.

She said, "Hey, I can't help it. I'm having a lot of trouble handling the fact that here we are in Florida, the land of my quote happy unquote childhood. Back there at the gas station I still half expected the restrooms and water fountains to be labeled 'white' and 'colored.' You know, I warned you guys that I might not be able to rise above some very unpleasant memories even if I gave it my best shot."

"You sure that's what you're doing?" said Paul, angrily tugging at his drooping mustache.

"That's not fair, Paul," said Lisa. She was a slim, sloe-eyed brunette who exuded so much unconditional empathy that her husband sometimes called her a born-again flower child. "I can understand what Shelly is feeling. Really! We all ought to have sense not to push her. Give her a chance to deal with it in her own way."

Shelly grimaced but held her tongue.

"I hear you, Lisa," Paul said. "But what I'm saying is that Shelly's spoiling everything for you and Dan, and if she keeps it up she's not going to seem very grateful to Barry and Susan either, after they went out of their way to invite us down here."

"Paul," Lisa admonished, "your wife still has scars in her arm where a police dog bit her when she was only eight years old. That kind of trauma isn't easy to bury."

Shelly's eyes smarted with tears, but she held them in as she stared through the windshield at Florida scenery that barely registered in her mind: blue sky, palm trees, and flat marshland on either side of the smooth white four-lane highway. She truly doubted that white people could understand what she was feeling in the present circumstances. And it disturbed her more that her husband, a black man, apparently didn't have any keener insights – probably because he was a northerner.

"Let's not forget," said Paul, "that the North is no paradise of racial equality. I've had some pretty ugly experiences in New York, too, but I still live there without letting the negatives get me down so much that I can't ever enjoy myself. Anyway, the civil rights demonstration that Shelly got hurt in happened over twenty years ago. Black people nowadays aren't in any worse danger down here than up north. You can get shot, stabbed, or O.D.'d in Manhattan easier than you can get lynched in Tallahassee."

"I think it's true that the South has changed," said Lisa. "And the way Barry and Susan described the cottage, it's pretty secluded. It's not as though we're going to have daily run-ins with rednecks."

Shelly hated this discussion and wished it would end. "Hey, I didn't mean to bum everybody out," she said with forced cheerfulness. "I'll get my act together, I promise." Reminding herself that she was among close friends, she tried not to feel as though she was playing the role of a good little darkie conjuring up soothing, insincere things to say to the white folks.

"Attaway, Shelly!" Dan Morelli said, chuckling good-naturedly and combing his fingers through his curly black hair. "It's not just you – we've all been in kind of a surly mood. Sometimes it takes a few days to work yourself into a vacation and start to unwind."

"Yeah," Lisa agreed. "Even when Dan and I go away by ourselves, we fight a lot at first. We finally figured out it's because our nerves are so jangled by the pressure of wrapping up things at work, getting packed and trying not to forget anything, and taking care of a jillion little mind-boggling details."

"I guess you're right," said Shelly. She reached out, touched Paul's arm, and managed a faint smile, trying to convey her wish to please him and help him have a good time on this trip. But she couldn't shake her deep-seated fear that something dreadful was going to happen now that she had returned to the South.

She glanced down at the cruel, ugly scar left by the police dog's fangs. It was a mark of evil that she had to carry around with her all her life. When she touched it, she got a chill, as if the evil was looking over her shoulder, ready to pounce.

***

Dr. Albert Scanlon heard about the murders of Silvio and Jean Narbonne on his car radio. As soon as he got home from his faculty meeting, he dialed Martha Lewis's number and Susan answered. "I just learned about what happened," he told her. "Such a terrible, shocking thing. How is your mother taking it?"

"I made her take a sedative, and she's lying down, trying to sleep. Barry and I are just sitting around. Mother hasn't eaten anything all day, and we were debating about trying to coax her out to a restaurant later. But I don't know if she'll come."

"I'll tell you what," Albert said conspiratorially. "I can go ahead and make a reservation at the Golden Pier. I think your mother will just go along with it once it's done. After all, she has to eat something. It's for her own good even if we have to drag her out of the house."

"Will you bring Mary Ann?"

"I don't know where she is at the moment. This afternoon I thought she mentioned heading out to the cottage to see you, but obviously you wouldn't have been there. She's probably at one of the public beaches where the kids hang out when they're on semester break."

"We've been on the go just about all day," said Susan. "I really have been intending to get in touch with Mary Ann, but so much is going on. Why don't you make a late dinner reservation, say seven o'clock? It'll give Mary Ann a chance to get home. Even if she doesn't show up before you leave, you can write her a note telling her where we'll be."

"I'll do that," said Albert. "I know she'd love to see you and Barry, even though these are sad circumstances."

As she got off the line, Susan couldn't help entertaining a slim hope that perhaps tragedy would help get her mother and her friend's father back together.

When she told Barry about the arrangements, he was more pleased than he let on, since it immediately occurred to him that Albert might end up taking his mother-in-law off his hands for the rest of the evening. Then he and Susan could split for the cottage right after dinner. He had tried phoning there several more times, and had gotten no answer. But it was getting late in the day now, so the Becks and Morellis were bound to arrive sometime soon.

***

Shelly had tried hard to lighten her mood, and Paul had turned out to be right – her apparently uplifted spirits had served as a catalyst for the others. A Lionel Ritchie tune playing on the car stereo, they were all presentably cheerful by the time they pulled into the visitors' parking lot at the Kennedy Space Center, a low, metallic L-shaped building surrounded by white and silver rockets towering into the clear blue sky like gigantic Lone Ranger bullets stood on their rear ends. For a peaceful, meandering hour they gave themselves up to being nosy, idle tourists, wandering around gazing at space suits, orbiters, and lunar modules. There was also a wildlife refuge at the Center, featuring herons, pelicans, and alligators. Paul made somewhat of a pest of himself trying to force the animals and the humans into poses for his camera. Then the humans piled into the scorching hot station wagon while Paul got the air conditioning going.

"Unbelievable that it's still so stinking hot at six in the evening!" Dan said.

"Don't complain – it's snowing in New York," said Paul.

"How do you know?" asked Shelly, who would almost rather be in a snowstorm anyway, instead of down here suffering from "Florida phobia."

"I read about the snow in a newspaper on the counter in the photo shop," said Paul. "Looks like the papers down here carry capsule reports on the weather in all the major northern cities, just to let people know how smart they are for vacationing in the Sunshine State."

"To let them know how to dress for going home, too," said Lisa. "How much snow is New York supposed to get?"

"About three inches."

"I won't miss it," said Dan. "Matter of fact, I almost think I could live without it permanently."

"You mean you could move down here?" said Lisa, amazed.

"Oh, I don't know, maybe I'm a country boy at heart," Dan joked. "Maybe I feel a deep-seated urge to go back to my roots."

"Well, I feel a deep-seated urge to get *away* from mine," said Shelly. "Anyway, Dan, you're not from down here, you're from Ohio."

"But not from a big city in Ohio. I started out as a farm boy. But then I got hay fever. I was afraid of all the exotic kinds of pollen I might encounter down here, but so far it hasn't bothered me. My nose isn't running."

"Don't tell Barry you're thinking of moving down here," Paul said, with the air of someone about to reveal a secret. "Barry has big plans for you in New York."

"You mean his pipe dream about starting his own agency," Dan said, lightly laughing it off.

"He told you about it?"

"Just idle talk, little hints and nudges. Why? Is he getting more serious about it all of a sudden?"

"I might as well tell all of you," Paul said, glancing warily at Shelly. "Barry didn't invite us down here purely out of the goodness of his heart. He's committing himself to setting up his own thing, and he's gonna pitch us on throwing in with him."

"He's crazy!" Shelly said. "We all have darn good jobs and we'd be fools to give them up! For sure I wouldn't have made this trip if I had known what he was up to."

"He's got it worked out better than you think," Paul said placatingly. "He's one of the best detail men I've ever known. I feel flattered that he'd think of asking me to be his partner. Matter of fact, he wants to call the new agency Beck, Morelli & Crandall."

"I can see why you think it has a nice ring to it," Dan teased, "since your name is first."

"Pretty decent of Barry to put his name last," said Lisa.

"Oh, that's just to help sucker us in!" Shelly snapped. "I like Barry, don't get me wrong. But he is extremely ambitious. He's a good friend when nothing's at stake, but I think you'd see some big changes in him if he was running the show."

"He doesn't want to run the whole shebang, honey," Paul said. "He wants us all to be equal partners. I'm not saying we have to go along with him, but it'd be foolish not to give him a fair listen."

"Oh, I'm sure he'll make his scheme sound perfectly marvelous!" Shelly said. "Just remember, if something sounds too good to be true, it usually is. That's what my grandmother always said."

"Well, my mama tol' me not to look a gif' hoss in de mouf," Paul drawled.

Everybody laughed except Shelly. She hated to hear Paul talking in dialect, like Amos 'n' Andy, even though he was doing it for fun. In college she had taken numerous speech courses, ones that didn't count toward graduation, in order to remove all traces of her southern accent. To her, this was not snobbish but pragmatic. She had wanted to acquire the diction of an educated woman, not only for reasons of self-respect, but because she had believed it would help her get ahead. As an upwardly mobile young black woman, shrewd and talented enough to take advantage of brand-new opportunities in a white world – opportunities won in the civil rights movement that had given her battle scars – she had wanted to marry a black man with drives and ambitions similar to her own. The thought of her and Paul making a foolish mistake and falling from their present status appalled and frightened her. It was worse than the fear of never making it that had plagued her when she first fled the South as a teenager with nothing to her name but a scholarship to NYU, a promise of a job in a student cafeteria, and forty-three wrinkled-up one-dollar bills pressed into her hand by her grandmother, who hadn't even lived to see her graduate.

"Nothing in life is ever absolutely clear-cut and safe," Paul said. "That includes our present jobs. We don't know when some kind of shake-up might put us out on our butts. It happens all the time. Companies fold or have cutbacks, and people find themselves out on the street when they're too young to go on pension and too old to be wanted in the job market. At least if we had our own agency, *we'd* be the ones doing the hiring and firing."

"You sound like you're on a power trip already," Dan kidded.

"Mista Ebenezer Bojangles Scrooge, das me," Paul said in a grossly exaggerated drawl, once more giving everybody a big chuckle. Except Shelly.

"What time will we hit Braxton Beach?" Lisa asked.

"About an hour," said Dan.

For a while after that, there wasn't much conversation. They all seemed lost in their private thoughts as they zipped along in the approaching twilight, cruising past occasional fishing villages, resort towns, and acres of orange groves asterisked by gaudy billboards advertising snake and alligator farms and dolphin circuses.

***

At seven o'clock, Vince Dawson and Clint Jones were in St. Matthew's Cemetery, at the site of the mass grave. It had taken them a couple of hours to secure an exhumation order and get it signed by the magistrate. Now they were forcing Jacques Carnot, the skinny Haitian gravedigger, to dig up the end of the mounded trench where Chango ostensibly had been buried.

Earlier today, when Dr. Martha Lewis had given the two detectives anthropological details about voodoo and Zombie Cucumber, Clint Jones had started thinking some weird, implausible thoughts. Telling himself he must be losing his sanity, he had sent the fingerprints taken from Chango's corpse over to the Crime Lab to be compared with bloody fingerprints found at the murder scene.

Even though it had been his own whim, his own fluky long shot, he was stunned that it had panned out. The Crime Lab had reported that the two sets of prints were a match. This had led to the decision to exhume the bokor's grave. As Dawson had put it, "This is crazy, but we've got to dig it up. We've gotta try to get some idea of what the hell is going on." Jones had agreed that his partner was correct; Chango's final resting place might not have been so final.

They had been keeping Jacques Carnot in custody as a material witness, even though they could only hold him for twenty-four hours without filing formal charges of some kind. They didn't think the gravedigger was their murderer. But he was an unsavory character by any stretch of the imagination, and under interrogation he had already admitted to purposely digging the mass grave very shallow. At first, he had claimed to have done a halfhearted job because he was too lazy and hung over to work in the hot sun, but a tough grilling had made him break down and admit that he had wanted to help Chango arise.

Now that the detectives had brought him back to the cemetery, Carnot was a nervous wreck, his bulging yellowish eyeballs and his gold tooth gleaming in his sweaty black face. Each downward stroke of his shovel made him likely to bolt and run. To discourage this,

Dawson and Jones had their suit jackets unbuttoned just enough to show the butts of their revolvers.

Shaking from his desperate need for a slug of whiskey as much as from raw primitive fear, the gravedigger kept working with excruciating slowness, like a man unearthing his own doom. Every once in a while one of the detectives would curse him and order him to hurry up. But it didn't do any good. At a snail's pace he toiled at lowering the mound of earth at one end of the grave and raising a new mound a few feet away from his broken, mud-caked boots. When crumbs of dirt rolled toward him from either slope, he jumped back as if he might be struck dead.

By eight o'clock, when it was almost dark, he succeeded in making a large hole the size of a reclining man, but not very deep, exposing hard clay that had never been penetrated by pick or shovel.

This section of the mass grave was empty.

Dawson and Jones could see that Chango was gone.

***

He was watching the cottage. It appeared almost luminescent under the moonlit, starry sky. The ocean breeze fluttered the filmy curtains. Moving as silently as only a loa can move, he crept toward a side window, around the left corner of the front porch. The TV was on. He could hear a newscaster's voice filtering through the open window as he got closer. Clothed in the invisibility of Guede Nimbo, he crouched and peeked past the fluttering curtains.

Chango had watched the two couples arriving in the station wagon a half hour ago. Cunningly, he had kept himself concealed in the boat shed, glad that he had turned it into a humfo, a place of sanctity. He had given the people time to unpack and settle in. Then he had sneaked closer. By now he had heard enough of their foolish prattle to know them by name. This pleased him. A degree of intimacy with the chosen ones always made their sacrifice sweeter.

Dan and Lisa were sitting on the sofa. Paul was on the recliner chair. They were drinking beer and munching pretzels, fairly relaxed in spite of some concern over where Barry and Susan might be and how soon they might arrive. They didn't seem to be paying much attention to the newscaster – but of course they had no idea that the murders he was talking about had hit so close to their vacation home.

"In recent months there has been mounting evidence that voodoo practitioners in Florida have indulged in animal sacrifices, but now two homicides are apparently linked to the primitive religion. Police aren't releasing official details regarding the murders of an aged immigrant and his grandson, but according to a reliable source the case has ritualistic overtones. Speculation revolves around the possible connection of the two victims with the cult of Hector Chanfray, alias Chango, a self-styled voodoo sorcerer who was accused of a string of brutal, cannibalistic slayings in Haiti. Chanfray and six of his followers were fleeing from Haitian authorities but were found drowned yesterday in a failed attempt to land illegally upon these shores. A spokesman for the Immigration and Naturalization Service stated that—"

Click. Dan clicked the TV set off. "Enough bad news," he growled. "We came here to get away from that kind of crap."

"Yeah," said Paul. "Right on." He glanced uncomfortably at Shelly, who was coming down the hall from the bathroom, and the look on her face told him that she had heard enough of the broadcast to upset her. But she forced a smile. Anxious to keep her mood light, he said, "C'mon, babe, let's go for a walk on the beach." She didn't object, so he took her hand and pulled her toward the door. To Dan and Lisa he said, "Hey, *both* the guest rooms have water beds. Don't do anything we wouldn't do, now." He winked and laughed.

Chango drew back from the window and flattened himself against the side of the cottage. From the shadows he watched Paul and Shelly kicking off their beach sandals and walking hand in hand toward the ocean. Under his breath he murmured a prayer, thanking Guede Nimbo for providing the sacrificial lambs that he needed in order to reclaim his disciples from their grave.

The couple walked barefoot through wet sand, down to where the receding water could lap at their ankles. They stood for a while, embracing, gazing at the stars and the moon, letting the surf sounds envelop them in a silence that was more profound than an absolute absence of sound. Paul spoke to her tenderly. "Honey, maybe I made a big mistake by talking you into coming here. I can see how hard it is for you. If you can try to muddle through, I promise I'll make it up to you when we get back to New York."

She told him, "All I want is for you not to go jumping into this deal with Barry. It scares me too much. I don't want to lose everything you and I have worked so hard for."

"But you shouldn't let fear stand in the way of opportunity. I have faith in you, even if you don't. I don't blame Barry for wanting you in his new company. Once you get your confidence, you have what it takes to be the best damned account lady in New York."

"Tell me more. I love your flattery."

"Look," he said, "let's agree between the two of us to hear it out, but not make any firm decision till we get back to the city. If you still have strong reservations by then, I won't buck you. I won't try to force you to go along with anything that goes against your gut feelings."

"Cross your heart?"

"Hey, I love you, babe, remember? We're in this together, all the way."

He took her in his arms and kissed her.

***

As Dan got up from the sofa, Lisa said, "Poor Shelly. . . we promised her she'd have such a good time."

Shuffling through a stack of CDs, Dan said, "Well, she will yet, if she gets over her childhood hang-ups."

"Childhood hang-ups?" Lisa eyed him piercingly. "I wouldn't exactly call them that, Dan."

"Well, you know what I mean," he said, taking a CD out of its jewel box. "True enough she encountered some terrible bigotry, but it was a long time ago and she shouldn't let it fester inside her."

"Easier said than done. Especially when you're not the one who lived through it and you're not carrying any ugly scars on your arm."

He put the CD into the player and fiddled with the buttons. The recording started to play softly. To Lisa's relief, he had chosen an album of Mozart concertos instead of some loud, funky rock-and-roll. She was getting sleepy. "I'm more road weary than I realized," she said. "Think it'd be criminal to get ready for bed before Barry and Susan show up?"

He glanced at his watch. "It's only nine o'clock."

"I don't mean that I'm going to turn in right away, just get ready. I want to be fresh for an early morning on the beach, don't you?"

"Yeah, but I might stay up a bit anyway. I still need to unwind."

Dan sat on the sofa and listened to Mozart while Lisa puttered around in their guest room. When he heard her go into the bathroom, he went to the kitchen, got himself another cold beer, and took it out onto the front porch. He sipped at it, gazing at the stars, the moon and the ocean.

Just then he heard a scuffling sound that seemed to come from the porch roof. Startled, he looked upward. For a long moment he heard nothing more. Then he thought there was another slight noise. Puzzled, he came down off the steps to get a better vantage point.

A whip cracked, and the lash coiled around Dan's throat. He dropped his can of beer, the foam gurgling out like the soft gurgle of his breath, his scream choked short. By his neck he was lifted bodily and pulled straight up. He kicked and flailed and clawed at the coils of the whip but his efforts were entirely futile. Chango hauled him up onto the roof and in one swift stroke impaled him with the machete.

Lisa popped out of the bathroom, toothbrush in hand. "Dan!" she called. "What was that noise?"

Getting no reply, she went to the front door, pushed it open, and saw that there was no one on the porch.

"Dan? Where are you?"

Crouching on the roof, Dan's body at his feet, Chango watched a thick stream of blood running from the gaping wound in the torso, across the slate, and down to a corner where there was a gap in the gutter. The blood welled up, stopped at first by the unbroken part of the rusted metal, but then it began to drip. Plop, plop, it went, falling in a soft rhythm on the grass at the side of the porch.

Figuring that Dan had decided to go for a walk, maybe join Paul and Shelly, Lisa closed the door and went back into the house.

Chango gave her a few minutes. Then he dropped down from the roof, making scarcely a sound, moving with awesome silence, the way that a loa can. He crept up onto the porch, opened the front door, and entered the cottage. He let the door close very quietly behind him.

Done brushing her teeth, Lisa came out of the bathroom, and just as she turned to go down the hall she saw the bedroom door closing. Dan playing tricks. Smiling to herself, she turned the doorknob, pushed the door open. She had left the light on, but now it was dark.

"Dan, don't be cute. Why weren't you on the porch? I thought I heard a—"

All her words ended as Chango's powerful hands clamped around her slender throat. He dragged her all the way into the bedroom and kicked the door shut. He laughed softly into her face as he turned the light on to watch the light going out of her eyes.

***

Returning from their moonlight walk along the beach, Paul and Shelly were in a mellow mood as they approached the cottage. They stopped to brush sand from their feet and put on their sandals. Mounting the porch steps, Paul said,

"What's that?" He listened, peering into the night. "Something dripping?"

"Dew from the palm trees?" Shelly said with a yawn.

Shrugging, Paul led the way into the cottage. Noticing that the stereo was lit up but the CD was done playing, he turned off the machine.

"I noticed some hot chocolate mix in the pantry," said Shelly. "I'm going to make some. Do you think Dan and Lisa would take a cup?"

Paul winked and whispered, "Seems like they've turned in. Too early to go to sleep, so they must be otherwise occupied."

Shelly whispered back. "You have a one-track mind. I can see from here that their door is open and light is spilling out into the hall. I'll go and ask them." Starting down the hallway, she called out cheerfully, "Dan? Lisa? Are you decent?"

Smiling, suddenly she froze, and her smile changed to a sick, stricken expression. Paralyzed by terror, she felt her eyes bulging, her stomach churning, her throat constricting almost as if she was standing outside of herself, and when her scream burst out it seemed to come from someone else. Lisa? But Lisa couldn't have screamed because Lisa was dead, spread-eagled naked on the bed with one of her legs hacked off.

Shelly bolted down the hall. But before she reached the living room Chango charged in a great roaring leap from out of the kitchen, and with a swift two-handed swing of his machete he decapitated Paul. Shelly stopped in her tracks, overpowered by the nightmarish vision of her husband's head rolling and spurting, banging against the CD player nearby.

The murderer lunged at her, but she managed somehow to get her legs going, and she ripped open the front door and ran out of the house. As she was about to leap off of the porch, Dan's body fell off the porch roof right on top of her, pummeling her to the earth. Trying to scramble to her feet, she got struck again and again by the half dangling, half swaying corpse, which was suspended by the whip coiled around its throat, twisting and dripping gobbets of blood on Shelly from the hip with the missing leg.

She screamed, dazed and horrified. Chango was upon her. He judo chopped her to the ground. Then he seized one of her wrists, yanked her arm straight out from its socket, and with a single vicious blow of the machete he chopped her arm off at the shoulder.

He stood up, chuckling gleefully, watching the twisting one-legged corpse of Dan Morelli and holding Shelly's arm upside down to let some of the blood drain out.

***

At the Golden Pier, at a table by a window overlooking the starlit ocean, Barry and Susan Crandall, Martha Lewis and Albert Scanlon had just finished with the main part of their meal. Everybody declined dessert except Albert, who went to work on a huge slice of key lime pie.

At this stage of her grief, Martha found herself yearning to be alone. Earlier she had needed Barry and Susan for close support, but as the day had dragged on she had gotten wearier and wearier of everything, including overly solicitous people. She had agreed to come to the restaurant to show them that she was rallying – and to put a final punctuation on the day. After dinner would be a proper time for her to disengage herself from everyone and go home to do her private mourning.

Susan eyed Martha worriedly over the brim of her coffee cup. Setting the cup down, she said, "You barely touched your dinner, Mother. Are you going to be all right?"

"Yes, Susan, it's just going to take me a while. You and Barry have done enough for now. You've been very kind and supportive. I think I'm ready to be alone."

"Are you sure?" asked Barry. "We're perfectly willing to stay overnight with you, if you'd like us to." Even as he was making the offer for the sake of politeness, it occurred to him that his mother-in-law might be trying to get rid of him and Susan so she could be alone with Albert Scanlon.

Albert looked up from his key lime pie. "Don't worry, Susan, I can drive your mother home. What are ex-fiancés for if they can't help out in a crisis?"

"You've been wonderful, Albert," said Martha, reaching out and touching his hand. Turning to Barry, she said, "You belong with your friends. After all, they came down here to have a nice vacation, and there's no reason for them to suffer on my account."

"I tried phoning the cottage again when I went to the men's room," Barry said. "Nobody's there yet. I hope they don't get lost now that it's dark. I suppose we should be there to greet them if at all possible."

"I had hoped that Mary Ann would show up here," said Albert. "But, this being a Friday night, I expect she got herself invited to a spur-of-the-moment party or something."

"Please tell her to make sure and give me a call tomorrow," said Susan. "I honestly meant to get in touch with her right away, but . . ."

119

"Yes, I understand," Albert said, smiling. "You and Barry have had a lot to think about, what with your plans of getting a new business underway. It sounds very exciting. I wish both of you all the success in the world. You deserve it."

"We owe a lot to Mother," Susan said. "She's helping to make it all possible."

"I'm just doing what any mother would," said Martha. "I'm pleased to be in a position to do what your father would have wanted me to do."

Barry tried to pick the bill up, but Albert beat him to it, which was fine with him. He wished the $25,000 from his mother-in-law would have been a gift instead of a loan. She had explained that she was requiring them to repay the money on easy terms, but on terms strict enough to encourage them not to forgo the kind of discipline they would need to make their venture a success. But Barry didn't think he needed that kind of incentive. He had the ability and drive to take him to the top. All he needed was the right chance.

Albert said, "You two don't have to wait till I finish my pie. Martha is in good hands."

"Yes, it's awfully late," said Martha. "Don't hang around on my account."

Barry and Susan kissed Martha on the cheek and said their polite farewells. While they were waiting for the Mustang at the valet parking station, Susan said with a grin, "Did you have the feeling they were both trying to get rid of us?"

"Yep," Barry said, winking.

"A tragedy like this might bring them back together – don't you think so, Barry? I was glad Albert called. He may be sort of prissy, as you say, but still he's utterly charming.

My father used to refer to him as a 'gentleman of the old school.' He thought some of his ways were funny, but he liked him anyway. I think that's why I do, too."

"Umhmm," Barry said. As far as he was concerned, it was better for him that Martha had remained single, or else he might not have succeeded in hitting her up for a loan. A new husband, even a Milquetoast like Albert, might have tightened the strings on Martha's money.

"Let's stop and buy some of the groceries on our list on the way to the cottage," Susan said, "in case the gang is hungry when they pull in."

"Everything will be closed."

"Not the Speedy Mart. We can at least grab stuff like bread and lunch meat."

***

In the boat shed, Chango was shrieking and chanting in an outburst of primitive ecstasy, his rudely sculpted face shimmeringly contorted in the flickering candlelight. He was kneeling over his cornmeal outline of a human figure. The likeness was now complete, "filled in" by body parts severed from six sacrificial victims. The torso of Mary Ann Scanlon was already joined to the right arm of Silvio Narbonne. Now the other limbs and the head needed to be attached.

Chango wailed and shrieked ever more fervently, praying to Legba, Damballah, and Guede Nimbo. He punctuated his prayers with wild riffs on his petra drum. He invited all the loas to gaze down upon his holy work and share in his glory as he stitched the body parts together with needle and twine.

CHAPTER 10

Albert Scanlon and Martha Lewis left the Golden Pier ten minutes after Barry and Susan. Albert tipped the valet parking attendant and he and Martha climbed into his silver Jaguar. It always amused her that he should own an English sports car, because she realized it was a manifestation of his Anglophilia, not a sign of a daredevil personality.

They drove in silence for a few minutes. Then she cleared her throat and said, "How are you, Albert? Really?" She was surprised to find herself so worried about him, especially since at the moment she was supposed to be the one most in need of a shoulder to cry on. But his shoulders seemed so much frailer than her late husband's.

"Oh, I'm doing all right," he said with a light chuckle as he steered the Jaguar at a conservative speed through streets full of lit-up night spots and strolling tourists. "Everybody always seems to fret over me, as if I'm too abstruse, too much of an anachronism to cope with today's world. But I manage to survive." He laughed again. "Although at times I confess I'm as surprised as anyone else by my ability to muddle along. My own daughter still treats me like a babe in the wilderness. She remains terribly disappointed that you and I didn't succumb to matrimony."

"Susan, too," said Martha.

"How about you, dear?" Albert said, grinning mischievously. "Have you gotten over me?"

"You're a good man, Albert. I value our friendship."

"So do I."

When they got to her home, he walked her to the front door. "Should I stay the night?" he asked. They both understood that he only meant to keep her company, not to be her bed partner.

"I don't think so," she said, kissing him on the cheek. "I really meant it when I told Barry and Susan I'm ready to be alone." She smiled. "I'm sure they imagined we had something else in mind."

"Well," he said, "I suppose I'll just go home and fix myself a drink, watch some drivel on TV, and wait for Mary Ann to come home."

After he had gone, it crossed Martha's mind that perhaps one reason she hadn't married Albert was that he was too accommodating, too safe, and therefore too unexciting. She wondered if by being so choosy she might shrivel and dry up waiting for the right man to come along and enliven her golden years.

Albert's mention of a drink made her want one too. She also wanted noise in the house, as if she had a need to drive away ghosts. She turned on the stereo, already tuned to some "easy listening." After taking off her suit and getting into a lounging robe, she made herself a manhattan. Sipping it, she sat at the card table, in front of her typewriter, and found herself rereading the passage she had completed just before the phone call from Lieutenant Dawson. In a way it seemed like eons had passed since she had gotten the bad news, yet the horror of it remained fresh. She began to doubt the wisdom of coming home to be alone. She realized she wouldn't be able to fall asleep easily – even if she drank more alcohol than she wanted to.

She found herself thumbing through her notes. Then she started typing, keeping her mind numb to everything except what she was doing, letting the manuscript write itself. She told the story of a supposed "zombie" she had interviewed personally, last summer in Haiti. His name was Clairvius Narcisse, and Martha was introduced to him by Dr. Felix Metraux, director of the Psychiatric Center of the Albert Schweitzer Memorial Hospital in Deschabelle. Dr. Metraux had been a friend of Martin Narbonne, Silvio's son. He had taken a hand in Clairvius Narcisse's case, which was particularly well documented, since photos and fingerprints of him were available, dating from before and after his mysterious "rebirth."

In 1962, Narcisse, a big strapping man in superb health, suddenly fell desperately ill. He worked as a security guard for a wealthy family, and they brought him to the Albert Schweitzer Memorial Hospital, but he did not respond to any sort of medical treatment. As he told Dr. Martha Lewis years later, "I could not get any air. My heart was fluttering and my stomach was burning up. My flesh was turning to ice. I heard the doctor say I was dead, and I felt his thumbs on my eyelids, the sheet dropping over my face. I tried to scream out – I'm alive! – but I could not utter a word. I even remember the clip-clop of the horse pulling my hearse to the cemetery, and the sound of dirt falling on the coffin."

The next thing he recalled was standing next to his own grave in a trance. Two men smoked cigarettes and drank whiskey as they filled the hole, tied a rope around his neck, and led him to a sugarcane plantation, where he was kept groggy and docile, forced to chop cane alongside many other workers in the same pitiful condition.

Narcisse believed that he had been enslaved for about two years when one day the overseer must have made a mistake with the dosage of the narcotic put into the food. Some of the zombies came to their senses, killed the overseer, and ran into the jungle. Narcisse was lucky enough to make it out of there alive, but he was scared to go back to his village because he believed that a rival for his security guard job had made the arrangement to have him "killed" and then "resurrected" by a bokor. In 1980, when he heard that his enemy had died, he approached his former employers and told them what had happened to him. Needless to say, they were quite stunned. Eighteen years after he was buried, Clairvius Narcisse had walked back into the lives of the people who had paid for his funeral.

Martha was not only able to interview Narcisse in 1983, but to visit his empty grave. She also closely examined the photographic evidence and the fingerprints, and interviewed the doctor who had signed the death certificate. She believed that she had conclusive proof that Narcisse must have been drugged, buried, and later disinterred. In the course of her investigation, she had talked to a hateful, toothless old man named Pierre Francine who had the audacity to claim credit for what Narcisse had suffered. Francine was a bokor in Deschabelle, and apparently the local authorities were too powerless or scared to move against him. Martha met with him at his humfo, a rickety shack filled with herbs, potions, and animal skulls. "Clairvius Narcisse is a chosen one," Pierre Francine said, cackling and slobbering. "I called his name and took the spirit from his body. No one ever truly escapes the realm of the undead. He is a zombie and will remain one until I grant him the blessing of eternal sleep."

Remembering the toothless old bokor made Martha shudder. She reached for her manhattan, which had gone watery. She went to the sink and dumped it out, then sat down to proofread what she had just written. The doorbell rang. It made her jump – she couldn't help thinking that anything ringing today, especially at this hour, was bound to mean more bad news.

Her anxiety worsened when she looked through the peephole. It was Lieutenant Dawson, on her front porch. She opened the door and let him in. "Relax, Martha," he said in that gruff voice of his. "I'm not going to clobber you with anything. I had to see you. I'm sorry for barging in. Can we talk?"

She nodded, peering at him perplexedly. He looked tired and nervous. He was wearing the same rumpled blue suit she had seen him in earlier. The bags under his eyes seemed puffier. She said, "I was just trying to immerse myself in my writing . . . to blot out what happened today. I wasn't having total success. You look pretty harried yourself. May I fix you a drink?"

He managed a fleeting, grateful smile. "Scotch. Neat. I guess I could've phoned, but . . ." He didn't finish his explanation. The truth was that he had wanted to see her again and latched on to an excuse. But now that he was here the excuse didn't seem so plausible, and he was reluctant to start spouting it off. He watched her going to the small slate-topped liquor cabinet that served as a bar, noting how gracefully she moved in her beige satin robe. Not wishing to get caught staring at her, he sat on the sofa, but he couldn't relax. His eyes darted as he took in the decor, tastefully modern but cluttered with primitive artifacts. "Nice place you have here," he managed. "Uniquely attractive."

Pouring his scotch, she said, "I have too much stuff on the walls, I know, but my husband and I acquired it on various field trips and I hate to part with any of it, so . . ."

Her voice trailed off. She made herself another manhattan, then carried the two drinks over to the sofa and gave Dawson his. She sat opposite him, kicked her slippers off, pulled her shapely legs up under her, and sipped her drink.

Dawson thought she looked both sensuous and vulnerable. He look a long sip of his scotch, then hunched forward, nervously fingering the misted tumbler. He avoided looking her in the eyes. At last he cleared his throat and said, "We didn't let you see what was done to Silvio and Jean, and we didn't release it to the reporters. We only let you see their faces."

He stopped talking. In the silence she could hear her ice cubes jiggling as her hand shook. She knew he was trying to ask her permission to tell her something extremely unpleasant. "Go on," she told him. "I can take it." But she wasn't really sure that she could. She wondered why she felt the need to impress this policeman with her fortitude.

Dawson spewed his words out quickly, like lancing a boil. "The boy was eviscerated, cannibalized. The old man had an arm missing." He looked up and saw the stricken look on Martha's face. He shut up. Grimacing, he dropped his gaze, eyeing the scotch tumbler between his hands as if wishing it could turn into a crystal ball and give him some badly needed answers.

Martha gulped her manhattan.

Dawson turned back toward her. "I'm sorry. I should have my head examined for telling you all the ugly details. I guess I was hoping . . ."

"Hoping what?"

"Well. . . you're an anthropologist. You've been making a special study of Haiti and Haitian voodoo. I was hoping you might be able to tell me something – anything – that could point me in the right direction. You see, something you mentioned this afternoon gave Lieutenant Jones an idea, an off-the-wall hunch, and it panned out – but it's so weird we don't know exactly how to follow it up. This case just keeps getting crazier and crazier."

"What exactly do you mean, Lieutenant?"

He cleared his throat again, louder this time. "Well, I might as well say it, goofy as it sounds. Chango's fingerprints were on Silvio's shovel. A couple hours ago we had Chango's grave dug up, and it was empty. It was a shallow grave, too, and when we questioned the gravedigger – a Haitian – he admitted he had dug it shallow to help the bokor to rise from the dead."

"Zombie Cucumber," Martha murmured.

"Well, maybe," said Dawson. "When you told us there's supposed to be such a substance that can produce a deathlike trance, it gave Clint the notion of checking Chango's fingerprints. He could've drugged himself if he realized that the boat he and his followers were on was going to sink. Because I don't believe for one moment that he was—"

"That he was dead and came back to life. No."

"So he must've drugged himself . . . .Unless . . ." Dawson took a slug of scotch, swirled it in his mouth, and let it warm the back of his throat going down. "Suppose somebody unearthed Chango's corpse and purposely left his fingerprints at the murder scene. A macabre joke – or a voodoo practice of some kind. I suppose that's where I thought you might be able to help us dope this thing out."

Martha blinked her eyes skeptically. "How would somebody else be leaving Chango's fingerprints?"

"Dismemberment," Dawson said. "Some nut could be carrying around one of Chango's hands."

Martha stifled a gasp. Then, calming herself, she said, "No, I don't think so."

"Why not?"

"If you're asking me to use my expertise as an anthropologist, I must tell you that not all voodoo is the same. The various cults have widely diverging beliefs and rituals. Different cults advocate different methods for raising the dead, but most have to do with substitution. The bokor must substitute the soul of an insect or a sheep or another human being for the soul of the person he wants to resurrect. Sometimes a spell is cast so that the substitute soul enters a voodoo doll. Then the doll is buried to take the place of a dead person so he can arise from his grave."

Dawson shook his head over the weirdness of the line of reasoning prompted by Martha's convoluted explanation. "*If* Chango is somehow alive," he said, "he has six followers he wants to resurrect, and so . . ."

"And so," said Martha, "he may be assembling a life size voodoo doll from body parts severed from six murder victims." She shuddered inwardly with the realization of what may have become of Silvio's amputated arm.

Dawson said, "We can't be sure of how many he may have murdered so far. He may have hidden some of the bodies. We might not have found them yet. He could be further along than we think." The detective eyed Martha piercingly. "What you've just told me is anthropologically sound? In your research in Haiti, you've actually encountered people who believe that kind of thing works?"

"Oh, yes," Martha assured him. "Most of the stories told about the bokors tend to make even a strong stomach a bit queasy. They go around making potions out of cemetery dirt and ground-up cadavers. They're said to even use drops taken from a corpse's nose. Little kids are brought up believing in this kind of stuff. Haitians are so afraid of being turned into zombies that when they die they want to be buried with silver daggers in their hands to defend themselves. Rich people have themselves interred inside thick concrete vaults and set aside funds to pay armed guards to stand watch so nobody can dig them up."

"Weird!" Dawson said. He swallowed some more scotch and mulled over all that he had been told. Then he asked, "Assuming that Chango *is* still alive and that he's making the sort of voodoo doll you described, where would he want to bury it?"

"As close as possible to the souls he is substituting for."

"The cemetery?"

"Yes. If he's already killed his six victims, that's where I'd expect him to perform the final ritual to call his six followers out of their grave."

***

Clint Jones had figured he'd stay at the police station no later than ten o'clock, but it was a half hour later than that now, and he was just wrapping up another interrogation of Jacques Carnot. Dawson had taken first go at the gravedigger, coming on hard and mean. Then he had cutout, giving Jones his turn with the "nice guy" approach. Total score: Dawson, zero; Jones, zero.

Jones's girlfriend had a ballet class on Friday nights, but she ought to be home by now, and he was impatient to see her, even if they didn't do anything special, just watch TV, have a couple of drinks, and unwind. As he was about to punch the intercom to call the turnkey to take the handcuffed Carnot back to his cell, the telephone rang.

"Homicide. Lieutenant Jones here."

"This is Dawson. I'm at Dr. Lewis's place."

"Must be nice. You score yet?"

130

"Cool it. I found out some interesting things. What're you into at the moment?"

"Well, I didn't get anything more than you did out of the gravedigger." Jones glanced disgustedly at Carnot, who was slumped in a stiff-backed chair against the wall. "He says that he didn't see Chango come out of his grave on his own power, but he's convinced that it happened. He considers himself an uninitiated follower of the bokor, but he swears he never helped commit any murders. He admits attending voodoo services and making animal sacrifices – but no two-legged animals, except chickens."

Dawson briefed Jones on what he had just learned from Martha Lewis. "I want to put a stakeout on the cemetery, and I think it should start tonight."

"Well, you go right ahead, but count me out. I don't think Chango is coming, Zombie Cucumber or not. My bet is that this gravedigger or somebody like him unearthed the body. Chango is dead, Vince. If anybody comes to that cemetery, it won't be him."

"That's irrelevant. If Chango's body was stolen, whoever stole it probably killed the old man and the boy. We know the killer is into voodoo, so even if he and Chango aren't one and the same, there's a good chance he'll be coming back to the cemetery to perform more rituals and dig up the other six bodies."

"But maybe not tonight," said Jones. "I've had enough for one day. I'm gonna hang around here and wrap up a few things, then I'm splitting. Good luck with chasing zombies, Vince."

"Thanks for being a real trouper," Dawson said, and hung up.

Jones punched the intercom button to have the gravedigger hauled back to his cell.

* * *

Dawson swallowed the last of his scotch.

Martha Lewis said, "If you're going to the cemetery, I'm going with you. I'll get dressed." She pivoted and hurried down the hall to her bedroom, not giving him a chance to object. On the way she called out, "Fix yourself another drink if you want."

He followed after her and shouted through her closed bedroom door. "Martha, a stakeout isn't fun and games! It could be dangerous!"

"I know!" she called back.

He could hear her scurrying around pulling on clothes. She certainly wasn't wasting any time. Even though a large part of him didn't want her to go with him, he was puzzled, surprised, and flattered that she'd want to. All his ex-wife ever had done was sit around and worry while he was off on something dangerous, then bitch and nag at him as soon as she saw him again. He thought of Martha sharing field trips with her late husband, a sign of her enthusiasm and spunk.

Tumbling through Martha's mind were all the reasons why she was jumping into this. She wanted to have a hand in helping to catch whoever had killed Silvio and Jean. Because she had loved them and brought them into her care, she felt partially responsible for their deaths. She also wanted to satisfy her curiosity as an anthropologist: to have actual close experience with some of the more malignant aspects of voodoo. And maybe she had a desire to purposely expose herself to danger – alongside a man like Vince Dawson, who had obviously seen much of it and was therefore an antidote to dull, safe, fastidious Albert Scanlon.

Dawson bellowed, "I can't allow you to come with me on official police business! I'm not permitted to jeopardize—"

The door opened, and he was shouting in her face. He lowered his voice to finish his sentence. "Jeopardize a civilian."

Smiling, she said, "You won't be jeopardizing me. I'll be jeopardizing myself."

"I should've cut out while you were changing clothes."

"I would've just taken a taxi. You can't stop me from visiting a cemetery, even if it *is* an odd hour. Besides, you have to admire my choice of getup, don't you?" She stepped back, posing in her black slacks and black blouse. "I'm a smart deputy, Lieutenant. I know enough to wear dark garments for a job like this."

He grinned. "I still think you should stay here. If you get killed, I'll lose my job."

Knowing that his kidding must mean that he was giving in, she said, "Is that all you're worried about, just your job?"

"No. I like you, Martha. I don't want to see anything bad happen to you."

"This is something I want to do very badly, even though it scares me. I want to do it for Silvio and Jean. You can understand that, can't you?"

He nodded. "But," he said sternly, "after tonight you have to promise me you'll stay away. Whatever happens or doesn't happen, this is your last shot."

"Okay. That sounds reasonable. Let's get going."

On the way to the cemetery in Dawson's unmarked sedan, Martha told him about Clairvius Narcisse – the anecdote she had written into the manuscript of *Voodoo in Modern Haiti.* "Fascinating," said Dawson. "It reinforces the notion that Chango could still be alive. We might not be on a wild-goose chase."

"I know," said Martha. "Dr. Metraux's colleagues told me that Narcisse appeared clinically dead when the death certificate was signed at the Albert Schweitzer Memorial Hospital. He must've been given Datura, or some drug like it, that reduced his vital signs to a level the doctors couldn't detect."

"Here's what I'm wondering about, though," Said Dawson. "If Chango drugged himself like that, why didn't he do the same for his followers? Or did he? And if he did, why didn't they come out of the ground when he did?"

"Maybe the bokor only drugged himself," said Martha. "His disciples may truly be dead. He may be relying solely on sorcery to bring them back to life. Or perhaps he gave them a stronger dose of the drug, to keep them in a coma longer. That way, he gets to see his black magic working in a powerful and dramatic way when he resurrects them, which reinforces his belief in his own divinity."

"Yeah, I see what you're driving at," said Dawson. "A few years ago I took a couple of night courses at Braxton State College – criminology and abnormal psychology." He chuckled. "I did ok – an A and a B."

"Are those the only two college courses you've ever taken."

"Well, when I was in the army in Germany I did some studying under the Educational Development Program. I earned enough equivalency certificates to make me just about a college sophomore. Maybe I would've gone for my diploma if I hadn't knocked up the first American girl I dated when I got back to the States."

"You got married then?"

"Yeah, when I was only twenty-two. Marriage lasted the same number of years. If my rites of passage keep following that basic rhythm, I'll die when I'm sixty-six."

"I don't think so," Martha said, amused. "I think that's how old you'll be when you get your college degree."

Dawson laughed. "You know, you might have something there – if I go back to college when I retire, like a lot of old duffers do nowadays. I can wheel around campus in one of those big tricycles with my books in a basket on the handlebars."

"In the meantime, why don't you audit one of my anthropology courses? It'd help you as a criminal investigator. Anthropology is as useful as psychology as far as gaining insights into what makes people tick."

"I might just do that," he said, pleased that she had suggested an opportunity of being close to her that he hadn't even thought of. But he truly doubted that anthropology would help him understand the scum in El Escoria.

He parked across the street from the cemetery arch. "Well, here we are. Are you sure you don't want to back out?"

"I'm sure. You can't scare me off now. I'm in this all the way."

He took a flashlight from the glove compartment and handed it to her as they got out of the car. "Don't turn it on unless you really have to. The beam would give us away. It might be more useful as a weapon – to conk somebody with. I think there's plenty of moonlight for us to see where we're going. In fact, we'll have to stick to the shadows so we don't get spotted too easily."

Brave as she had tried to make herself sound, her apprehension deepened to dread as they passed under the cemetery arch and worked their way back among the tombstones. She was all too aware that she was following in the final footsteps of Silvio and Jean, who had met their horrible fate for trying to carry out a mission related to her own. Their approach had been superstitious, whereas hers was a supposedly more rational way of dealing with the same facts. But her intellectual enlightenment didn't make her immune to the atavistic fear felt by savages in the jungle worshipping thunder and lightning.

Following Vince Dawson around the outskirts of the cemetery, trying to move as stealthfully as possible in the shadows of the fence and the trees, Martha almost bumped into him when he stopped all of a sudden. "We're getting close," he whispered. "Try to be even quieter now."

"Shhh! I thought I heard something – a faint scraping sound."

He drew his revolver. "Likely some kind of animal. Stay close but a little behind me, like you've been doing. I told you you shouldn't have come here."

"I wasn't about to stay home. Like I said, I feel like I'm part of this because of Silvio and Jean."

They flashed tense looks at each other, then continued working their way toward the paupers' section. The full moon cast long, looming shadows among the monuments and tombstones. Dawson led the way around a huge mausoleum not far from the mass grave.

Suddenly there was a loud crack. Martha jumped – and was proud of herself for not shrieking. It was Dawson. He had inadvertently stepped on a grave ornament, a candle in red glass. In another type of situation the blunder might have been humorous. But not now. He and Martha froze and listened. They heard nothing but ordinary night sounds. Then they started walking again, very softly. Because of the shadowy shapes all around, it almost seemed to Martha as if something might leap out at them at any moment. She clutched the flashlight, remembering what he had said about using it as a weapon.

From behind a large monument of carved cherubims and seraphims, they peeked out at the mass grave. They spotted nothing unusual. Nobody was around. Nothing appeared to have been disturbed. The mound of earth over the trench looked like a long dark scar in the moonlight.

Dawson whispered, "I doubt if tonight is going to be the night. It's probably too soon, after all. Are you prepared to spend five or six hours staring at every moving shadow and jumping every time you hear a sound? That's what a police stakeout is usually like. Boring and generally futile."

Martha whispered back with annoyance. "I keep telling you I'm here for the duration. If he's coming tonight, we must've gotten here ahead of him." She didn't know whether or not she actually hoped Chango would show. Now that she was on the scene, that possibility was even more awful than it had seemed before. To think that Jean and Silvio had been butchered on this very ground.

Dawson muttered, "Tomorrow Clint Jones can take his turn here, if I can talk him—"

Crash! Shattering glass. A loud, evil chortle. Dawson whirled, pointing his revolver. Martha stifled a scream. Fifty feet away from them, a kerosene lamp that was part of a grave ornament spread a puddle of fire on top of a grave, the headstone shimmering white in the flickering flames.

Another ornament shattered in another part of the cemetery. And another. Someone was tossing them all around.

Martha grabbed onto Vince. He flattened himself against the monument, his revolver at the ready – but he could find no clear-cut target to aim at. He yelled into the night:

"Chango!"

In answer he got only an eerie maniacal laugh.

He told Martha, "Stay back!" Then he set off in the direction of the laughter, but it immediately ceased. It was like trying to pursue a ghost. He spied what looked like the silhouette of a big man running, and he fired twice – but he hit nothing. The silhouette evaporated. There was no thudding sound as a man would make if dropped by a bullet. Just silence. Surprised at his own jumpiness, Dawson told himself he must've fired at a shadow.

Blinking, he peered this way and that into the forest of stark white tombstones and monuments. His quarry was here somewhere. Here for the taking. He knew it was Chango. This time he would see to it that the bokor was really dead. He whirled around to make sure Martha was still okay. Just then there was a loud *crack*! – and Chango's bullwhip snaked out, coiling itself in a split second around Vince's wrist. He dropped his revolver as he was savagely yanked and spun – sprawled on his face.

Martha screamed and dropped the flashlight. Seeing the seven-foot bokor in front of her in the moonlight – his teeth flashing, his slab-like muscles rippling with scars and tattoos of voodoo creatures that flexed and slithered – was like seeing the devil materialize out of hell. Nothing she had heard or read about him prepared her for the sheer awe and horror she felt in his sinister presence. He glowered at her as if she were an insignificant thing, weak and mortal, that he would swat like a flea in his own good time. And for a long paralyzing moment she had no doubt that he was right. He would soon finish her.

Chango's insane laugh split the night as he dragged Vince's prone body rapidly over the ground by pulling on the whip coiled around Vince's right wrist. The detective tried to stop his brutal bouncing slide over the cemetery turf. He clawed for a handhold. But to no avail. When he managed to grab on to a tombstone, his grip was effortlessly pulled loose, tearing flesh from his fingers. Then Chango stopped pulling and kicked Vince in the stomach. The air whooshed out of the detective's lungs and he emitted a sick groan. A blade flashed. The bokor stabbed downward – but Vince managed to roll, barely eluding the thrust of the machete.

Chango reared back to chop at Vince's head. But a shot rang out and the machete went flying.

Vince's revolver shook in Martha's hand. She fired another shot that went wild.

Chango came at her, bleeding from his shoulder.

Martha tried to steady herself. She clutched the revolver in both hands, out of desperation trying to emulate cops she had seen on TV. She waited till her target was as close as she dared, then she squeezed the trigger twice, stunned by the recoil and the loud explosion in her ears. But the bokor stayed on his feet. He kept coming at Martha. He was grinning at her, less than ten feet away.

She squeezed the trigger twice more and got two empty clicks.

Chango lunged at her, seizing her by the throat in his big, powerful hands. He lifted her bodily off the ground as he choked her. She could feel herself blacking out, but she tried to kick and scratch. She managed to rake his eyes. He roared and choked her even harder. She knew she was done for. The world was swimming and turning from black to red.

On the verge of losing consciousness for good, she heard a crack – and the coils of the bullrope wrapped around her assailant's thick, corded throat. Blurrily, she saw that Vince Dawson was wielding the whip. Chango relinquished his grip on her throat and dropped her to the ground. On the way down she hit something hard – a tombstone – and she crumbled in an aching, moaning heap.

From behind Chango, Vince Dawson yanked on the bullwhip with all his might – but with only one hand, since the other one was hanging limp from when the whip had been used against him. He managed to pull Chango backward several staggering steps – then the bokor whirled, grabbing the lash with both hands and turning himself once more into the aggressor by pulling Dawson relentlessly toward him. Vince tried with every last ounce of strength to hang on with his one good hand, but was losing the battle. Chango chuckled, toying with the puny mortal, effortlessly hauling him in for the kill. Then, when he got to within a foot of Chango, Vince let go suddenly and punched the bokor as hard as he could in the face. He succeeded in knocking Chango back only slightly. But the whip dropped to the ground.

Her throat and back hurting terribly, Martha crawled toward something gleaming in the moonlight. She hoped it was Chango's machete, but it turned out to be a long-handled shovel. She got her hands on it just as Chango lifted Dawson over his head and, with a great screaming roar, hurled him against a granite monument. To her horror, Martha saw that Vince did not move or make the slightest sound after hitting the ground. She crept up behind Chango, raising the shovel. He sensed her presence and started to turn toward her. With a ferocious scream, she swung the shovel with all her might, hitting the bokor hard across his upper body. But he didn't flinch. She gasped, gaping at him. How could he not be affected by such a blow? Trembling with primal fear, and wondering if she was indeed facing a loa, a supernatural being, she made herself swing the shovel again. Chango laughed as he seized the shaft in mid-flight and twisted it out of her hands. He then reared back to chop the blade down on top of her head.

"Stop!" a voice cried out.

Chango hesitated for the briefest of moments. Then his muscles tightened. Martha tried to make herself dive and roll. But she couldn't move. Like a mouse paralyzed by a striking snake, she was now resigned to her fate.

She heard a loud gunshot. Then she saw blood spurting from Chango's stomach. But he scarcely acknowledged the wound – just a glance at it and a slight pause of the sharp shovel blade in its downward flight.

But Clint Jones had used Chango's moment of hesitation to run up closer. Out of breath from his run into the cemetery, he resumed a firing crouch and tried to control his huffs and puffs so they wouldn't throw his aim off.

Chango changed the impetus and direction of the shovel and flung it at Jones. The detective dived, rolled, and came up firing. His first shot missed, and he scrambled to take aim again as Chango came for him. He squeezed the trigger again.

The bokor's massive head spurted blood as he sagged and fell, smacking the earth with a dull, heavy thud.

CHAPTER 11

Martha Lewis rode in an ambulance with Vince Dawson, holding his hand as two paramedics gave him intravenous and treated him for shock. Her body was battered and bruised, and she was hoarse from having her larynx nearly crushed, but she figured she could live with the pain for now. She was scared that Vince wasn't going to make it. He was still unconscious. He had lost a lot of blood. His right arm was almost torn completely from the socket, and the paramedics had ripped his suit jacket and shirt off and applied compresses to try to stop the bleeding.

Martha's daughter and son-in-law rode with Clint Jones. They had barged into the police station just when Clint was ready to leave. Babbling and crying, they had told him about finding their friends killed and dismembered at the beach cottage. Jones had tied it in with what he and Dawson had already figured out, and had headed for the cemetery. But he damn near hadn't gotten there in time.

He stepped on the gas to keep up with the two screaming ambulances. The second one contained Chango. Jones had already told the ambulance guys to work on his partner first, rather than the bokor, but he was going to the hospital to make sure the doctors didn't get their priorities mixed up. He was amazed that Chango was still alive, even though he did not give him much of a chance of pulling through. Martha Lewis's bullets had hit the bokor in the shoulder and chest. Clint had shot him in the stomach and head. Even if he didn't die from loss of blood, he couldn't survive a .38 slug blasting its way into his brain.

The two ambulances and the unmarked police car pulled up outside the emergency room of Braxton Beach Hospital. Like the police station, it was an attractive modern building of gleaming aluminum and tinted glass, with an ambience that might enable tourists to believe that just as there could be no serious crime here, neither could there be any serious illness. As if to second the motion, the ambulance lights and sirens stopped whirring and strobing before they were even parked.

Martha jumped out as soon as the door was opened. The two paramedics unloaded Dawson and wheeled him on his gurney into the emergency room. Martha had to move quickly to keep up. Clint Jones, Barry Crandall, and Susan Crandall followed behind her. But the gurney was wheeled down a corridor and through a set of double doors painted bright orange, where Martha, Clint, Barry, and Susan weren't permitted to follow.

Jones said, "Vince'll be all right. He's too mule-headed to die and miss out on his share of the credit for solving this big case."

The second gurney came wheeling through the emergency room – the one containing Chango. The paramedics already were administering oxygen and intravenous. Chango's head and torso were swathed in bloody bandages. Martha, Clint, Barry, and Susan stared at Chango's face. He still looked evil and impervious somehow, even in his present state of apparent helplessness. They watched the bokor being whisked past them, flat on his back, going down the same corridor and through the same doors where Vince Dawson had been taken a few seconds ago.

Martha hated to see the bokor being taken anywhere near where Vince Dawson would be. Irrationally, she feared that Chango might yet get up from his gurney and renew his attack. As if sensing her thoughts, Clint Jones said, "I should have finished him off. Saved the doctors the trouble of trying to pull him through."

"What if he lives?" Martha asked. She couldn't bear to think of it. To her the only true justice would be if this inhuman beast would die.

"If he lives, which I doubt," said Jones, "then he'll be what they call a 'living vegetable.' A *real* zombie. A .38-caliber bullet demolished his brain. He probably won't make it."

"But what if he does?"

"He'll have to stand trial. Cost the state thousands of dollars to prosecute. Try to get him the death penalty. If the Haitians don't try to extradite him."

"I hope he dies," Martha said with totally unaccustomed bitterness. "He seems so damned indestructible."

To further reassure her, Jones said, "No way he can escape a murder conviction. The body parts he buried tie him to six homicides."

"You have to. . .to dig. . .dig it up?" Susan Crandall stammered. She was clinging to Barry, crying. Barry was glowering at Jones for mentioning the body parts. He had vomited after finding Paul Beck beheaded, Shelly and Dan and Lisa with limbs missing. Scared to even stay around to try the phone, he and Susan had bolted and jumped into the Mustang. It was a miracle they hadn't wrecked it on the way to the police station.

"Well," said Jones, "he must've buried . . . uh . . . it . . . where he was buried. That's where he made the cornmeal drawings, and the candles and drum were stashed nearby. The coroner will have some men do some digging in that spot."

Jones had noticed the cornmeal drawings just before the ambulances arrived. Then he did a quick look around and found the candles and drum behind a bush, where Chango must have hidden them when he heard Vince and Martha coming.

"We didn't spot the cornmeal from where we were hiding," Martha said. "We were too far away. We thought Chango hadn't shown up yet, and instead his work was almost done."

Susan stopped sobbing and just stared into space, her eyes widening in abject fear. Martha tried to hug and comfort her, but Susan pushed her mother away. "Please. . . why can't they . . . their . . . why can't they be left in the ground?"

Trying vainly to reason with the distraught young woman, Jones said, "It's evidence, don't you see? You want Chango convicted, don't you?"

Susan babbled, "A voodoo doll . . . if you stab it with a pin . . . it hurts the person it represents. If you remove the pin . . . the person stops hurting."

"Honey," Martha pleaded, patting her daughter's shoulder, "you don't believe in those superstitions. You're an educated person. It's just that you're in shock right now."

"Stop talking about it!" Barry exploded. His outburst was directed mainly at Martha, as if she were to blame for all that had gone wrong in his life. She still had her money, while he no longer had his handpicked friends and his dream of a business enterprise.

Susan kept babbling. "What if . . . what if removing the doll from the earth completes Chango's voodoo ritual? What if his disciples will arise when the doll does?"

CHAPTER 12

A camera flashed again and again as a police photographer snapped pictures of the life-size voodoo doll made from body parts of six murdered humans. The grotesque assemblage was lying on a morgue stretcher on top of an unzipped body bag. The photographer kept hopping around, moving in tight and then far away, obtaining wide shots, mediums, and close-ups of the thing made from the stitched-together torso of Mary Ann Scanlon, the right arm of Silvio Narbonne, the left arm of Shelly Beck, the left leg of Lisa Morelli, the right leg of Dan Morelli, and the head of Paul Beck.

Finally the photographer put his camera away and the body bag was zipped shut. Two men loaded the stretcher into the morgue wagon and slammed the doors. Meanwhile, two other men from the morgue finished filling in the part of the mass grave they had had to exhume. They patted down the mound of earth.

More doors slammed, and the morgue wagon drove off.

The gravediggers tossed their shovels into the back of a pickup truck. They wiped their hands off with balled-up rags. Then they climbed into the pickup, slamming the doors. They struck matches, lit up cigarettes, as the engine turned over. Then they pulled forward, backed up, pulled forward again, and drove away, toward the back gate of the cemetery.

The photographer put his camera gear into his car. As he was about to get behind the wheel, he thought he heard something. He turned and looked at the mass grave.

The mound of earth seemed to quiver slightly.

The photographer told himself that it must be the fresh dirt settling. Or maybe just a moon shadow cast by the rustling branches over the long brown trench.

PART TWO

THE CAPO

Every madman has his agenda.
　　　　　　　　　　　　　　　 – Russian proverb

CHAPTER 13

At night the hospital room seemed even more threatening. Why did they always shut the door but not lock it – not that the lock would have been any real protection against his fear. The only light was the thin crack under the door, the dirty-orange glow of a plastic night lamp, and the glowing plastic speck of the nurse's call button looped through the side rails of his bed, lying near the fingers of his right hand, the hand that still worked, the fingers still capable of pressing buttons. In the scanty illumination he could but dimly make out the metallic sheen of the IV pole and the shadow of the bottle and tubing on the white wall.

The stillness was so complete, so eerie, he thought he could hear the intravenous solution dripping slowly into his veins. Then he was sure he could hear it, because it got louder – or was it just his heartbeat, booming rhythmically inside his own head?

He strained his ears, wishing to hear other, more reassuring, sounds. Somehow there was nothing reassuring about hearing his own heart beat so prominently, even though he knew that if the beating ever stopped his suffering as well as his fear would at last be over.

He couldn't move much, couldn't lift himself up or turn himself over without help. His right leg was in traction, his neck in a thick collar, his left arm in a heavy plaster cast that went from shoulder to wrist. The other arm was almost better, but he had to keep it still, palm up, because it was taking the intravenous.

He thought he heard the nurse's medication cart squeaking outside in the hall, but his heart was pounding so loudly he couldn't be sure. He hoped it was the nurse, and he hoped she'd come in. With a sedative for him. If she didn't, he'd press the call button and ask.

To his relief, his door swung open, letting in a shaft of light from the hall. No one was in the doorway yet. He told himself the nurse must have stepped back to handle the cart, wheeling it closer. But the squeak was gone. There were only some tinkling, scraping noises.

A huge black shadow loomed in the doorway.

Dawson's heart pounded so hard it threatened to burst through his chest. Adrenaline shot through him, preparing him to deal with his mortal enemy, but he might as well have been in shackles – the traction apparatus, the plaster cast, and all the impediments of surgery and rehabilitation made him helpless, completely unable to get up and run. All he could do was tremble, his IV pole, bottle, and tubing shaking and vibrating, threatening to topple.

Somehow he could still hear the tinkling, scraping noises, and he saw that they were made by the tubes and needles hanging from various parts of Chango's body. The bokor was stark naked, not wearing any hospital gown. Drainage tubes dangled from his head and from his groin, splashing blood and pus onto the tile floor. Drip! Drip! Drip! *Drip*! Louder than the dripping of Dawson's IV and the pounding of his heart.

He tried to scream, but nothing would come. He reached for the call button and tried to press it, but it turned into a thin writhing snake in his half-numb hand, a snake that he could not subdue, could not turn to his purpose.

Chango laughed his maniacally evil laugh. The pressure of laughing made his head split open where the draining

152

bullet hole was, and maggots crawled down the side of his face. He picked one of the fat squirmy things off, pried Dawson's mouth open, and dropped it onto his tongue.

Dawson gagged. And at last he was able to scream.

Spitting clumps of maggots, he sat up screaming, and the short fat nurse came waddling into the room. Not in any particular hurry, either.

He cut his scream short. He saw that it was morning, slashes of sunlight through the blind. The nurse was staring at him strangely, almost smirking – she seemed to get satisfaction when men proved they were just as vulnerable as women to fear and pain. Dawson was soaked with sweat. He wasn't in traction. There was no IV pole. He had no neck brace or shoulder cast. It slowly dawned on him that he wasn't still fighting Chango. That had happened three years ago. Dawson was all right now. Except for his left arm. He was only in the hospital for tests to see if a new kind of operation could make the arm whole.

"Are you all right, Mr. Dawson?" the nurse asked.

He nodded. Embarrassed, he couldn't find words to apologize or even mumble that he had been having a bad dream. It wasn't the first one and wouldn't be the last. In every one of them, Chango was coming after him again. Always he was helpless to fight or to run.

"We'll have the results on your tests back today," the fat nurse said. "If we're lucky, you'll be staying with us for a while."

She meant if they were lucky with his test results.

Dawson almost hoped he wouldn't be staying. He hated hospitals. He had no doubt that being in a hospital had made his latest nightmare especially powerful and real.

He asked the nurse to bring him a damp washcloth to mop his brow. When she left, he told himself over and over how foolish he was to keep dreaming of Chango. Chango was dead.

CHAPTER 14

Ernest "Ernie Bones" Bonino and Jeff "Bow Left" Stout were getting drunk together in a Braxton Beach nightclub when Bow Left told Bones how easy it would be to put the Root Doctor on waivers and skate away with $8,000,000 worth of coke. When Bones and Bow Left talked about putting someone "on waivers" they meant what CIA agents mean when they say that someone should be "terminated with extreme prejudice." Bones had spent eight years with the Pittsburgh Penguins and Bow Left had played a total of six years with the Islanders, Oilers, and New Jersey Devils, both their careers ending two years ago when they were put on waivers that nobody picked up, which had felt almost the same to them as having their throats slit.

Neither one had ever been a star player; neither had ever scored more than eight goals in a season. They were both known as "diggers": tough, brutal, half-out-of-control skaters who would go in and slam and punch and dig the puck away from the boards even if it meant putting opposing players in the hospital. Ernie Bones got his nickname from the fans who loved to see him thud into people so hard it made their bones rattle. Bow Left got his nickname from a coach who told him he was so bowlegged and left-handed he'd never be able to skate fast enough or swing straight enough to last in the pros. Bones and Bow Left had never played for the same team, so it was a natural for them to hate each other, even after their careers came to a rather inglorious end. On the rink they had tried often to knock each other's teeth out, and they tried the same thing the first time they bumped into each other at a Florida beach party – but they were both too stoned to land any solid punches. They ended up shaking hands, sharing dope and bitterness over how they both had felt compelled to head south to get away from any reminder of the ice that they were no longer playing on, and hatching schemes that would soon enable them to make a smooth transition from the violence of professional hockey to the violence of professional crime.

Both were now working as bodyguards and enforcers, Bow Left's boss was the Root Doctor, whose farm twenty-five miles north of Braxton Beach was a place where rich people came to shell out big bucks for voodoo spells and folk medicine they thought would help them live longer and get richer. Bones's boss was Salvatore "Sal the Strap" Stropoli, who used to control all of the South Florida drug business and now controlled only the portion of it that wasn't being ripped away from him by the Cubans, Colombians, and Haitians.

"This thing'll be our own score, man," Bow Left said. "It'll make us independent. We won't have to kiss anybody's ass anymore."

"I'll be wearing concrete shoes if The Strap finds out I didn't cut him in," said Bones.

"It's up to you what you do with your half," said Bow Left. "My half will be all mine. We've got to put the Root Doctor on waivers, although I hate to do it. I've got nothing basically against him. The plane is coming in just after midnight – gonna land in one of the Root Doctor's fields. We drill the flyboys when they jump out of the cockpit, and we got ourselves eight hundred pounds of coke."

Bones smiled, noticing that Bow Left's green eyes were gleaming as if he had just snorted all that coke all by himself. He looked fully alive for the first time in months, almost like he used to look when he was still playing hockey. He still wore his blond hair the same, all in wild, curly ringlets, but his face was puffy and grizzled. He had a big belly on him, too. He must have weighed 240. Bones knew he didn't look like a rink demon anymore either, with his bent nose, bald head, and pot gut. He and Bow Left were both bigger and stronger than they had been in their NHL days, but unfortunately they were also slower. Their reflexes had deteriorated; what they had gained in size and power, they had lost in finesse. The past two years of soft living and hard, angry drinking and brawling had made them physically resemble ex-boxers or wrestlers more than hockey players. Bones even sported a cauliflower ear, thanks to a puny little cokehead who had smashed the ear with a cue stick just before Bones killed him by bare-handedly ripping his chin away from his jaw.

Taking a long sip of bourbon, Bones toyed with the temptation of not telling his boss about Bow Left's proposed caper. First he pictured himself lounging on the Riviera with $4,000,000 in a Swiss bank account that Sal Stropoli couldn't touch. Then he pictured himself as shark food after Stropoli caught up with him. "It's cool to cut The Strap in," he decided out loud. "That way he'll lend us some support troops. He'll also pay us wholesale value on the coke – we won't have to stick our necks out trying to hook up with some other distributor who might rip us off. Nobody will come after us, either, knowing our asses are protected by Sal the Strap."

"Hey, that's the way it *used* to be," Bow Left scoffed. "The escoria don't fear anybody. The Mafia's like a gang of kindergarten kids compared to them. I'm leaving the country after we make our score, and if you don't do likewise I'm gonna be wondering if you've got anything besides a beat-up hockey puck rattling around in your skull."

As luck would have it, it was a moonlit night when Bones and Bow Left drove out to the Root Doctor's farm in Bones's shiny silver Cadillac. "He likes the full moon," Bow Left explained. "Says the moonlight ain't dangerous but *safe* for the dope drops. Helps him work his spells so he doesn't get nabbed by the Customs Service. He claims technology is no match for voodoo – the smugglers' plane won't even show up on Coast Guard radar if he doesn't want it to."

"You believe that crap?" Bones asked.

"Hey, all I know is he's never been arrested," Bow Left replied.

"He's so magic, why are we going up against him?"

"For the bread. The bread's worth the risk. Anyway, his magic isn't gonna stop a bullet. Maybe a puny little .22, but not my .357 Magnum."

"Wouldn't stop a .22 either," said Bones. "And I sure hope you're kidding when you say it might, 'cause I don't like the idea of risking my ass alongside a partner whose head isn't screwed on straight."

"Hey, of course I'm kidding," said Bow Left. "I'm not like the superstitious jerks who come out here and make the Root Doctor rich. I swear, I don't know why he's into dope running at all, he's got such a good scam going without it – and it's a scam the law can't even touch, unless the IRS nabs him."

"He's greedy like the rest of us," said Bones. He was hoping his own greed wasn't going to somehow backfire on him tonight and make him wind up dead. The plan was for him and Bow Left to arrive in the middle of one of the Root

Doctor's voodoo ceremonies, being late on purpose, so they wouldn't come under too much scrutiny from the Root Doctor and the other three guys, besides Bow Left, who lived on the farm and doubled as chauffeurs, handymen, and bodyguards. All of them would have to be taken by surprise and put on waivers for the caper to go down smoothly. After the ceremony, the other guests would leave, while Ernie Bones would hang around under the pretense of wanting his pal Bow Left to introduce him to the Root Doctor. Then the fireworks would start.

"Slow down, Bones, you're gonna miss the turnoff!" Bow Left said. "Right here, on the left!"

Bones was right on top of it, and had to squeal the tires or else he'd have shot right on by. It was a narrow dirt road almost totally obscured by weeds growing wild and high. The Cadillac bounced along for at least a mile till the going got a little smoother. Then they came up on a barn, a chicken coop, and the Root Doctor's big yellow-brick ranch-style house. The gravel driveway was overcrowded with expensive vehicles: a Jaguar, a Mercedes, and a Caddy like Bones's, only a different color, dark green instead of silver. Just as they parked behind it, its headlights were killed, the doors opened, and people started getting out, having pulled in just ahead of Bones and Bow Left.

"They got their nerve being late," Bow Left joked. He slammed his door. Under his breath, he said, "We have everybody hemmed in for the time being. But we can let them out after they've had their kicks, and they'll be long gone before we swing into the main event of the evening."

Reciting mundane details like that seemed to reassure Bow Left that the caper would come off smoothly, as if his ability to martial trivial facts proved that he had the whole ball of wax under control. He and Bones ogled the other latecomers as they got out of their Caddy: two handsome black couples in tuxedoes and evening gowns, the men helping the women by offering their arms, very suave and elegant and out of place out here in the middle of nowhere, reminding Bones of characters in a bizarre foreign movie he had once seen by Michelangelo somebody.

Bow Left chuckled. "See what I mean when I tell you some pretty classy people show up here?" He talked loudly on purpose, so the objects of his compliment could bask in it and be charmed by him, thinking he was an okay guy.

"Why, thank you!" one of the women called out in a melodiously cheerful voice.

Bones mumbled something half affable, warily patting the pistol and silencer under his suit jacket as he and Bow Left hung back, letting the two black couples proceed ahead of them along the walkway to the Root Doctor's porch amid tinkles of feminine laughter, low masculine murmurs, and flashes of expensive jewelry.

"All here for the crazy-ass services," Bow Left whispered. "Remember what I told you about the barn and the chicken coop? The animals ain't for eating, man."

Bones grunted, psyching himself up for the part he was supposed to play during the "crazy-ass services." Bow Left had told the Root Doctor that Bones was a rich guy he had bumped into in Braxton Beach who was hooked on voodoo. For tonight, Bones was going to call himself "Mr. Gorman" and pretend he was hot to see some animal sacrifices and willing to shell out big bucks for the privilege. It occurred to him that Gorman was a good alias because he was going to deliver the gore, much more of it and of a different sort than the Root Doctor was figuring on.

One of the tuxedoed black men pressed a button and waited while someone checked him out through a peephole.

Bones scoped two hand-lettered signs on the porch pillars: one said DO NOT OPEN THIS DOOR WITHOUT PERMISSION, and the other said NO CHILDREN ALLOWED. The front door swung open and admission was granted by a big, burly, scar-faced black man with a shaven head. From Bow Left's description, Bones recognized the doorman as Drake "The Dragon" Mantee, one of the thugs who would have to be put on waivers before the night wore on too much further. Mantee stood aside with a grin that was more like a scowl as the two black couples filed past him. Bow Left stopped to introduce Bones as "my friend, Mr. Gorman man, that I told you about." Mantee lessened the intensity of his scowl and briefly shook Bones's hand, his way of acting nice toward someone he thought was a fresh mark for the voodoo scam.

Off the foyer was a long hall with polished wooden benches, like church pews, lining both walls. A second thug, with a drooping mustachio and a shaggy, unkempt Afro, was sitting at the end of a bench, a green metal strongbox open in his lap. He closed the lid on the wad of bills he had just taken from the people in gowns and tuxedoes. "Garrett Davis, meet my friend, Mr. Gorman," Bow Left said. Bones and Davis shook hands, and Bow Left told Bones to pay Davis a hundred dollars for his admission to the services. Once the two crisp fifties were safely in the strongbox, Davis opened a heavy sound-proofed door at the end of the hall, and a high, keening, primitive sound struck Bones's ears: the first – and last, he hoped – Creole chant he had ever heard in his life. Somehow it was more chilling than the rabid screams of fifteen thousand hostile fans reverberating in a domed hockey arena at an away game.

The Root Doctor was doing the chanting. Glassy-eyed, an intense, trancelike look on his lined, pockmarked face, he was a small, wiry, yellowish-brown man in dirty denim trousers and a wrinkled, faded plaid shirt, surrounded by flickering candlelight and burning incense. Bones knew that his real name was Ernest Blount, and his neighbors, the few that there were around here, considered him a devil worshiper. But he called himself a houngan, a practitioner of white magic. White magic that carried a heavy price tag. But not as heavy as the cocaine he smuggled on the side.

The two formally attired black couples and five other well-dressed guests, black and white, were sitting around raptly watching the Root Doctor and listening to him wail. His candlelit "temple" looked like a large but ordinary living room as far as most of its furnishings were concerned, except that there was a strange altar against the wall by the fireplace. Bones stared in that direction as Bow Left led him to a sofa where they both sat down. A fallen-away Catholic, he had no trouble recognizing the statues of Saint Joseph and the Virgin Mary that stood at each end of the long altar. There was a crucifix above it, too. But the plaster garments of the Holy Family were covered with strange symbols that appeared to be painted in blood. And they were surrounded by pagan icons, beings half animal and half man – the voodoo "gods" that Bow Left had told Bones about when they were laying their plans.

Suddenly the Root Doctor stopped wailing, and there was an eerie, hushed silence. Then the soundproofed door opened, and Garrett Davis dragged a leashed goat into the room. The animal bleated and defecated on the carpet, but Davis kept on dragging it along. The stink of the goat feces wasn't apparent because of the incense.

The Root Doctor picked up a long, gleaming knife and started chanting again, louder and more high-pitched than ever. Davis dragged the goat to the altar, picked it up and forced it down on its side, then pulled its head back by the horns, exposing its throat. The Root Doctor sliced with the knife, and blood gushed out in a powerful stream, splattering the altar, the statues, and the patches of white wall in between.

Thrilled, almost sexual gasps were emitted by some of the women watching the ceremony. The men were mostly silent, except for a couple of grunts, a cough, and a low, rumbling laugh.

As the goat's heart slowed and stopped beating, the blood gush lessened and the dying stream was collected by the Root Doctor in a silver chalice. Then he drank from it. And passed it around for others to drink. Bones damn near threw up when the chalice was handed to him. But he had to take a sip, and pretend to like it. He felt his face flush hot and sweaty as his own blood came to a boil.

He wasn't a conscienceless killer. Up till now, he had only killed three men, one of them (the cokehead with the cue stick) in such a fit of extreme anger that he wasn't required to go through any thought processes about it beforehand. The other two times he had had to steel himself, and to dream up rationalizations for why he was ending a human life. Now he had his reason handed to him in a silver chalice. As far as he was concerned, people who got their kicks out of torturing innocent animals deserved to suffer and die. The crazy perverts didn't even eat the goats, chickens, and calves that they sacrificed to their bloodthirsty whims. According to Bow Left, they merely tossed the carcasses into the fields to become buzzard feed after they removed the testicles, the skulls, the hearts, and the brains to make voodoo potions and charms.

It was almost ten o'clock when the ceremony ended. The dead goat was dragged out, the candles were extinguished, the regular living-room lamps were turned on, and the goat feces was cleaned up. Still trying not to gag over the sticky-sweet taste of blood in his mouth, Bones was introduced to the Root Doctor, who smiled affably as he mingled with his "congregation," then went into his study to meet with some of them one at a time as they were ushered in by Drake Mantee. Bow Left had told Bones that Garrett Davis would be in the study hovering over the strongbox, scarfing up money the people paid for potions, herbs, and "mojos" – little paper pouches tied up with string, containing animal bones, dried organs, and cemetery dirt – purported to bring good luck, ward off sickness, and combat evil intentions.

"You want to buy a mojo from him too?" Bow Left joked under his breath in a corner of the living room. "You may as well, Bones. You're gonna get all your bread back anyway, after he goes on waivers."

"Not so loud!" Bones warned in a hoarse whisper.

Just then one of the black men in a tuxedo came up to Bones, smiled pleasantly, and said, "Would you mind moving your car? You have me hemmed in, remember?"

"Sure," said Bones. "You ready to go?"

"Soon as I gather up all my friends."

Bones waited by the front door till all the people in gowns and tuxedoes were together in a bunch. On the way out, their driver said, "Don't I know you from somewhere? Aren't you buddies with Sal the Strap? I think I've seen you with him at Hialeah – right?"

"Sal who?" Bones said gruffly and threateningly.

"Hey, maybe I shouldn't have said anything. Sorry."

"It's okay," Bones barked. But he knew that he couldn't just let the incident slide. If the police ever questioned the black man about anything that went down here tonight, his memory might be jogged, pointing the way to Sal the Strap and Ernie Bones.

Behind the wheel of his Caddy, Bones quickly screwed the silencer onto his .38. By that time, one black couple was already in the back seat of their car and the driver was closing the door on the passenger side after helping his date slide in. It was a shame what Bones was going to have to do to her; she was the youngest and prettiest of the two women, and he had admired the way she looked in her emerald gown.

When the driver turned around, Bones shot him in the face. Before the man had time to fall or to even stop looking startled, Bones fired straight through the windshield, pumping two slugs into the breasts of the girl in the emerald gown. Her face was twisted and ugly in its death agony, even though he had avoided shooting her there so as not to destroy her beauty. He hadn't heard her dying screams, but he didn't know if his mind had blocked the sounds out or the glass and steel of the Cadillac had helped lock them in.

That left the two in the back seat. They were ducking and cowering, trying to cover their heads with their hands. The chick even tried to pull a little car pillow over her face. What did she think it was? Bulletproof? Bones ripped the door open, leaned in, and fired three times at point-blank range. The slugs blasted right through hands and fingers and the little car pillow, puffs of white stuffing flying everywhere. The man and woman sagged sideways, their high-classed clothes streaked with blood. "Try drinking some of that!" Bones said.

He ran back to his own car and rummaged in the glove compartment. He pulled out a box of .38 cartridges and hurriedly reloaded his revolver. He put a handful of bullets in his pants pocket. Then, because it wouldn't fit in the shoulder holster with the silencer on, he jammed the revolver under his belt, buttoned his suit jacket, and went back into the house.

Bow Left was standing out in the hall, bullshitting with The Dragon, keeping him off guard. They both glanced at Bones as he entered. He waited till Mantee was turned back around, then shot him between the shoulder blades. He fell like a limp, heavy sack, his bald head scraping the wall on the way down, leaving a thin red track. Bones slammed the dead bolt shut on the front door to keep anybody from getting away. He hissed at Bow Left, who already had his Magnum out, "Round up everybody in the living room. I'll take care of things in here!" He yanked open the padded door to the Root Doctor's study, spied Garrett Davis in a big red leather chair, and drilled him. The strongbox fell with a loud clatter, greenbacks spilling all over the carpet, but Davis never even got his gun out. The Root Doctor tried. He was reaching into his desk drawer as Bones shot him. The slug hit him in the mouth, splintering his teeth and tearing out the back of his skull, splattering half his brains on a big map of Haiti that was hanging above him. The fat frizzy-haired woman he had been talking to jumped up and wouldn't stop screaming even when Bones ordered her to by yelling in her face. She clutched her mojo and screamed, holding her hands over her ears as if she couldn't stand her own shrillness, so Bones sidestepped around her and pumped a bullet into the back of her head. She pitched

166

forward and sprawled facedown. Her body was so pudgy and soft it barely made a sound when it hit the floor.

Sweating and breathing hard, Bones jumped over Dragon Mantee's body and ran into the living room, where Bow Left had everybody covered with his Magnum. Looking nervous, he said, "What're we gonna do with them, Bones?"

"Which one's the other one who lives here?"

"That one," said Bow Left, pointing at a tall muscular black man in a white cashmere sweater. "Dwight Sparrow's his name. He thinks he's so handsome he should be in the movies."

Sparrow took a step toward Bow Left, snarling. "I don't know what you think you're up to, but your life ain't gonna be worth dog shit after today."

Bones shot Sparrow in the chest twice. He died with a surprised look on his pretty face. A slim blond white woman threw herself on him, sobbing hysterically. A black woman covered her eyes with her hands. A short little white guy stared at Bones with a strangely calm expression. And two big, chubby black guys, both in black pinstripe suits, kept licking their lips and trying to stop shaking. None of these five people was supposed to die, if things had gone according to the original plan.

"Keep them covered, Bow," Bones said. "I gotta reload." He hoped the people wouldn't get it in their heads that now was the best time for them to charge en masse and try to bust out of the room. He could've tried to fake it, not letting them know he had shot all six chambers. But he thought it was better not to leave himself vulnerable and to load up again right now, while they were in shock. He did it in just a few seconds, spilling the empty cartridges onto the floor, inserting fresh ones into the cylinder and snapping it shut.

"What're we gonna do with them?" Bow Left asked again, sounding even more shook up than before.

"Let's lock 'em in the bathroom," said Bones.

Hearing this, the captives visibly relaxed. The blonde pulled herself away from the dead Dwight Sparrow, her white blouse covered with his blood. The two chubby black guys shook a little less, but still kept licking their lips. The black woman and the little white guy with the calm face did as they were told and so did everybody else as Bones and Bow Left herded them into the large bathroom. "Now kneel on the floor," said Bones, "facing the shower stall." They all crowded and jostled each other as they struggled to comply.

"Now, shoot!" Bones said to Bow Left. He was already squeezing his own trigger, and he looked out of the corner of his eye to make sure his partner was following suit, both of them standing by the doorway, blasting away. The noise from Bow Left's big unsilenced Magnum was deafening. In less than twenty seconds, all of the people in the bathroom were dead. Then Bones and Bow Left backed away, and Bones shut the door. His ears were ringing. "We had to put them all on waivers," he said. "One of the ones outside recognized me. Tough luck. I didn't want it to go down like this, man."

"Hey, you're right, man. We had to," said Bow Left. He was breathing hard and he looked half sick. But he had a weird grin on his face, too, as if a part of him had gotten great unexpected enjoyment out of being an executioner. It was, Bones knew, not too far removed from the mean, nasty, lowdown, and yet exhilarating feeling they both used to get out of slamming people against the boards of the hockey rink, making their bones rattle and knocking the fillings out of their teeth.

The backup guys supplied by Sal the Strap arrived at the Root Doctor's house on schedule, at eleven-thirty PM. There were six of them: one black, four white, and one Cuban. A rainbow coalition. Bones thought it was evidence of how fragmented and chaotic the crime scene had become, thanks to the escoria and the drug wars. It used to be that a guy like Sal the Strap would only hire guys with Italian names. Now he had to use pistoleros of every stripe and color. "Use the commode in the powder room or piss outside," Bones told them. "Don't use the bathroom. It's a little crowded." None of them asked why. The Cuban smiled knowingly, but the others kept their deductions to themselves.

The moonlight was so bright that they didn't need flashlights when Bow Left led the way out to the unplowed field where the cocaine plane would land. "It'll be on schedule, right about midnight," he explained. "I helped unload three other planes in the past four months, and they were always on schedule, like clockwork. Just two guys in the cockpit, but they'll be armed with shotguns and Uzis."

"Christ!" Bones said. "You didn't tell me they'd be carrying anything that heavy!"

"What'd you expect? The thing is, they know me, they won't be expecting to get hit. They might not even take their weapons down from the plane."

"They won't," said Bones, "because we won't let them. We'll pick them off soon as they kill the engine."

"They never shut it off," said Bow Left. "They keep the prop turning in case a customs plane tails them down to the ground – so they can take off again in a big hurry."

"We'll hit them when the plane stops rolling, then," Said Bones. "That's where the night scopes will come in handy."

The six backup men were all carrying U. S. Army M-21 sniper rifles with telescopic infrared-sensitive sights, and were supposed to be expert marksmen with those weapons. Bones instructed them to spread out and find cover on both sides of the strip where the plane was expected to land. "Me and Bow Left will start toward the plane as soon as it touches down, making it look like a normal dope pickup. I want all six of you to zero in on the pilot and copilot, soon as they stop rolling. Draw a bead and fire – three of you from this side, the other three from over there. That way, you're not all six gonna single out the same target. Bow Left says the windows on the Cessna will give you plenty of glass to see through. These guys won't be figuring on an ambush. They think their usual worry is customs guys who never just blast away at them without giving a warning and a call to surrender."

At the edge of the field, waiting for the plane, Bow Left reached in his hip pocket for a flask of bourbon, unscrewed the cap, and took a long slug. He offered some to Bones, but Bones shook his head no because he didn't approve of drinking before a tense gig like this. He kept going over his tactics in his mind, and he couldn't think of anything he should do differently. All the bases seemed to be covered. The ambush seemed a cinch to pull off. Almost too much of a cinch. There had to be a hole somewhere, but Bones couldn't find it. The thing that made him so uneasy was that it didn't seem the dope drop could be as casual as Bow Left said. Just two guys in a plane. Where was the backup? Where was the insurance against the possibility that the pilot and copilot would just fly somewhere else and keep the $8,000,000 worth of coke for themselves?

On the other hand, Bones knew that the dope traffic was so enormously profitable that smugglers barely gave a damn if they lost one planeload out of three. Figure it out, he thought to himself. A Cessna cost about $150,000. Eight hundred pounds of coke could be bought for $1,000,000 in Colombia. So, if you lost one planeload and safely landed two, you'd be ahead to the tune of almost $15,000,000. Bones tried to feel $15,000,000 safer after doing the calculations in his head. He told himself the big numbers explained why the plane was coming in as carefree as a butterfly. But he still couldn't shake a nagging feeling that there was a spider lurking somewhere. Maybe it was just the Root Doctor's phony magic preying on his mind.

"There it is out there!" said Bow Left. "See the flashing lights?"

Bones grunted. Bow Left took a big gulp of bourbon and dropped the empty flask on the ground.

The flashing lights circled, up high. Then the drone of the props got louder, and Bones felt the wind as the plane passed overhead, then swooped and turned, heading at him, coming in low, touching down. In the roar of the props, he and Bow Left started across the field. The engine noise diminished, and the props slowed to an idle. The big black tires stopped rolling.

Right on cue, the fusillade began. Six snipers blasting away with M-21's. Glass shattering. High-velocity rounds whistling and ricocheting. Bones saw both the guys in the cockpit get hit. But one was still moving somehow. Suddenly the engines revved up and the plane started to taxi. It lifted into the air. Then it slammed down and flopped on its side.

"Don't fire!" Bones yelled. "The fuel tanks!"

Too late. The explosion rocked Bones, adding force to his dive to the ground, knocking the wind out of him. Some of the groans he heard weren't his own. Twisting his head sideways, he saw Bow Left sitting down clutching his throat. Shrapnel. Blood pumping like a small geyser through Bow Left's fingers. He gave a silly laugh and slumped sideways.

Suddenly Bones heard propellers again. Impossible. It couldn't be the Cessna. Nothing left of it now but a ball of flames.

Bones looked up and saw a huge black helicopter coming down out of the moon-lit sky. His luck was going from bad to worse. It had to be a Customs Service chopper.

"Fuck 'em! Shoot!" Bones yelled. And the guys with the sniper rifles started blasting. Bones drew his revolver and fired wildly. He still hurt all over from having the wind knocked out of him. He knew the dope was incinerated, his big score up in smoke. All he had left was his freedom, and he sure as hell was going to fight for it. He crawled painfully, trying to find a rock or a shrub or a hole to give him a bit of protection.

The bay of the chopper opened, and a dozen armed men – and women – started coming out. They weren't wearing any kind of uniforms. And they moved stiffly, in a kind of slow motion.

Piece of cake, Bones thought, and he squeezed off two shots at them. None of them was hit. He couldn't believe it. Even as shaky and hurt as he was, he thought he had to have hit one of them, because they weren't fanned out, they weren't crouched – they were all in a tight bunch, the easiest possible target.

The chopper was in the air again, circling and strafing, hovering over Bones's men one at a time and gunning them down with a tarret-mounted gun. Three of the snipers were down, and the other three were all in a pack, huddled behind a boulder, blasting away at the slow-moving squad of men and women who were attacking on the ground. None of the attackers seemed to have normal battle fear or self-preservation instincts. They just kept coming into the hail of bullets. Bones couldn't believe his eyes. They gotta be hopped up on dope, he told himself. They were armed with shotguns – no good at long range, but couldn't miss from up close – which would explain why none of them had squeezed off a shot yet.

Some of the attackers appeared to be hit, reeling back from the force of the slugs, but then they recovered and came forward again. Two of them fell and rolled, and it seemed they were down for the count, but they slowly arose and kept on coming in a shuffling, shambling gait, lackadaisically cradling their shotguns.

"Shoot for their heads!" Bones yelled. "They got bullet-proof vests on!"

The attack squad was almost on top of the guys behind the boulder now. The chopper was hovering about fifty feet above, not firing its machine gun – obviously out of fear of hitting the ground troops. From behind a bush, Bones got up on his knees, held his revolver steady in both hands, and shot one of the attackers in the head. It was a woman with long blond pigtails, wearing of all things a paisley house dress. Bones saw his bullet send brains and blood flying from the back of her skull. She went down like a ton of bricks. But then she got back up, stared soulfully at Bones in the moonlight, and slowly, as if she found the weapon almost too heavy to manage, she swung her shotgun in his direction.

He lept up and ran just as the shotgun went off. He heard the roar of the double barrels and felt pellets tearing into his right leg. Somehow he managed not to fall. Sheer terror brought back some of the speed he used to have on the hockey rink, before he got his whiskey nose and his beer belly. He slipped in Bow Left's puddle of blood, stumbled over Bow Left's body, and took a lucky tumble just as the shotgun roared again. He heard the pellets whispering over his head. He got back up, running for all he was worth, and made it to the cover of a patch of woods. Ignoring the pain in his right leg, he hurtled through weeds and brambles, trying to make it back to the Root Doctor's house. That's where his Caddy was, his means of escape – if he could only reach it and peel out to the main road without being machine-gunned.

CHAPTER 15

Hiding in some tall weeds, Vince Dawson pushed his sunglasses back on top of his head and squinted through the eyepiece of his camera. Luckily all the buttons were in the grip and could be operated with one hand, the tape compartment resting on his right shoulder for balance as he zoomed past the picket fence to a medium-wide shot that took in most of the front porch. He was running videotape surveillance on a man who had filed a claim for workman's compensation on the basis of a whiplash sustained in a car accident, the injury supposedly rendering him incapable of performing his job as a warehouseman for a large department store. The store had hired Vince to disprove the claim. One cripple working against another? Or a cripple against a fake?

In the three years since Chango had crippled Vince Dawson, he had adjusted with some bitterness to his handicap. His left arm was damn near useless, hanging at his side like a dead piece of meat, the fingers refusing to work individually, all clumped together like a claw. The right arm, the one that had been torn out of its shoulder socket by Chango's bullwhip, had recovered fully. But the left one, broken in three places when Vince was hurled against a tombstone, had had a key nerve severed, pinched between two jagged ends of splintered bone. Microsurgery to reconnect the delicate nerve fibers wasn't successful; they were no longer carrying messages from the fingers to the brain.

Several times in the past couple of years, new medical procedures had inspired hope that the function of the left hand could be improved, and Vince had gone back into the hospital for observation and tests, but in the end the hope had always flickered out. The latest time was three days ago, when all he had gotten for his trouble was a horrible nightmare. And the doctor's report that the nerve fibers were too unresponsive to be helped.

Vince was now a private eye, a damned snoop in his own estimation, making half his living by prying into peoples lives and the other half by cashing disability checks from the City of Braxton Beach. He could've stayed on the police force; his particular kind of injury did not appreciably interfere with detective work. But he had taken the opportunity to bail out. Sometimes he was sorry and sometimes he wasn't.

The front door opened, and the "suspect" came out onto the porch, a short, stocky, baldheaded guy named John Morris. He wasn't wearing his neck brace. He was carrying a chain saw, cradling it in his bulging forearms. It took a lot of muscle to push merchandise around in the warehouse, and according to his job history Morris had been at it for fifteen years. A tough gig. Not surprising that he would seize on a chance to take early retirement, even if he had to fake it a little.

Yesterday, when Vince had scouted Morris's house, he had noticed a big cypress tree that had apparently been struck by lightning, its trunk splintered, the top half of it lying sideways across the yard. The heavy leafy top branches had narrowly missed the corner of the roof, but had smashed down a good portion of the picket fence on that side of the house. Vince had figured that the tree would have to be sawed up and hauled away, and maybe he'd be able to catch Morris doing the job himself. Now he congratulated himself for being on the scene with videotape gear. Turning on his camera, he got good coverage of Morris wielding the chain saw, making the sawdust fly, not wearing the aforementioned neck brace, and certainly not giving the appearance of being incapacitated in any way. The telephoto lens captured him lugging a heavy load of logs around back to a shed, and Vince grinned inwardly at the thought of the great evidence he was amassing – in his old job he didn't usually get to catch "perps" red-handed.

Wiping sweat from his brow, Morris went into the house, probably for lemonade or a cold beer, so Vince flipped his sunglasses back down to the bridge of his nose and started putting away his camera. He looked up when he heard a door slam. Morris stared at him from the porch, then charged at him, stooping on his way to pick up a short stout piece of freshly sawed timber. Vince didn't want to get hit on his bad arm. He figured that because he was wearing sunglasses Morris wouldn't hit him in the face, so he didn't yank out his .38 as a precautionary measure. With a scornful snort, Morris swung his club and Vince tried to block it with the camera case, but instead his good arm took the blow and went completely numb. The camera case somehow didn't drop. The club did, which at first seemed like a break. But then Morris shot a roundhouse right at him, and Vince couldn't raise either arm to block it. The fist thudded into Vince's face, shattering the left lens of his yellow aviator's "shatterproof" sunglasses and driving glass into his eye.

He rolled with the punch, landing flat on his back and staying put. His fingers were no longer clutched around the handle of the camera case, and they seemed to be working a little now. But he still didn't go for his gun. No use shooting somebody when diplomacy might suffice. He pretended to be unconscious. To his amazement, his assailant knelt over him and started wailing, "Oh God, oh God, I'm sorry . . .I hope I haven't blinded you. . ."

When Vince began to believe that Morris probably wasn't going to hit him again, he opened his left eye slowly, peeking through the half-numb fingers of his right hand. He could see the blue sky and white clouds, but his eyeball felt jaggy. Morris said, in a mournful voice, "I'm going in and get an ice pack for you, then I'll drive you to the hospital. I guess you're gonna sue me. That's all I need."

Vince wondered why his life seemed to have degenerated from a mild tragedy to a tragicomedy after he left the police force. Maybe it happened to all private eyes, gumshoes, shamuses. . . . Were there any nicknames for what he was doing now that weren't silly or pejorative?

While Morris was gone, Vince grabbed his tripod and camera, hoofed it to his car, and drove to the hospital himself – refusing to allow Morris the penance of driving him there. In the heat of the moment, he really was determined to sue, and he figured it would be better for him when the case came to court if he didn't have to admit that Morris had shown any contrition.

His aversion to hospitals made him feel twice as ill as he was. He couldn't believe he had only managed to stay out of one for three days. With an eye injury, he couldn't see how he could possibly be treated as an outpatient, but to his amazement he turned out to be wrong. After waiting long enough in the emergency room to have become a doctor himself or at least an intern if he had used the time to study medical texts, an intern swabbed and bathed his left eye with an antiseptic solution and sent him to see a Dr. Feingold in his office, two blocks from the hospital. This time he didn't have to wait long. Feingold, an ophthalmologist, had apparently been notified that Vince was coming, and was ready for him. He used local anaesthetic to operate on the injured eye under a fluoroscope, extracting tiny slivers of glass that he said could eventually produce blindness if they were left in there.

"Even so," he added, "your left eye might gradually lose its ability to see, due to glaucoma initiated by the injury, in which case the other eye will probably follow suit, in a sympathetic reaction."

"Doesn't sound very sympathetic to me," Vince said.

The doctor chuckled. He said, "In two weeks, when the bandages are removed, we'll have a pretty good idea as to whether or not you're going to be blind."

"Hey, I only have one good arm to tap a cane and hang on to a seeing-eye dog," Vince said.

Feingold chuckled again.

During the next two weeks, Vince got a chance to learn what it would be like to lose his left eye. No peripheral vision on the left side, and no depth perception. He kept bumping into doorways and stumbling over furniture, and he had to leave his car parked, because if he tried to drive he might run over pedestrians and slam into vehicles the way he was bouncing off of other things when he was on foot. He couldn't take on any of the three potential new cases that came his way, so his bank account fell to near zero. But he didn't try to fatten it by suing John Morris. He couldn't stand the thought of haggling with lawyers.

Finally Dr. Feingold removed the bandages from the left eye, examined it with all kinds of instruments, and said, "It appears to be healthy and out of danger. I don't think I'm going to ask you to wear a patch over it. I must warn you, though: no more fistfights. You were lucky this time. One of those slivers of glass narrowly missed the cornea. You wouldn't like to be blind the rest of your life, now would you?"

Vince stepped out onto the street, feeling if not brand new at least rejuvenated. The good news had come as such a relief it made him realize how badly he had been worried and how hard he had tried to blot his fears out of his mind. It was a hot, muggy August day, but he didn't mind walking the seven blocks to his apartment because it was refreshing to be able to do it without bumping into anything. He walked with his left hand in his pocket, the dead arm hanging there like ballast while the other one swung freely, so that walking cost him more energy than it used to. His long-sleeved shirt was all sweated up by the time he got to the block where he lived.

His apartment was above Enrico's Pizzeria. The good smells often seduced him, so that he ate a lot of pizza, spaghetti, and calzone. Still, he had managed not to put back on the forty pounds he had lost in the hospital three years before, and he didn't have such a big belly anymore. It was as if his injuries and his uphill fight to survive had drastically changed his metabolism.

He noticed a silver Cadillac parked in front of the pizzeria. As he got closer, the driver's door opened and a guy he recognized got out: Ernie Bonino, alias "Ernie Bones," an ex-hockey player who was now a muscle man for Sal "The Strap" Stropoli, widely known to be a Mafia kingpin even though no law enforcement agency had ever been able to come up with hard proof. Back when he was a real cop, Vince Dawson would've loved to have been able to put Sal the Strap on ice.

Speak of the devil. There he was, getting out of the passenger side of the silver Cadillac and joining Bones on the sidewalk. The Strap was wearing a light-blue suit and a flowery shirt, open at the neck. He had a dapper little black mustache, and his wiry hair was all black too – probably dyed. He was in his late fifties, but he still looked spry and spunky. He had a small brown paper bag in his hand, and he glanced at it as if the contents were valuable. Dawson didn't think there could be coke in there, though; The Strap was surely smart enough to stay away from his own poison. But on the other hand, it was hard to tell what a man might be driven to when he was under duress. The grapevine had it that The Strap's empire was crumbling a bit of late. The escoria were worming into his illegal enterprises, taking a bite out of crime, so to speak, and getting fat on it, same way they were getting fat off of all the honest citizens.

Ernie Bones said, "Good afternoon, Dawson. Me and the boss want to talk with you if you can spare the time." The implication was that only a fool would be reluctant to make time for Sal the Strap.

Dawson said, "I was having a pretty good day up till now."

"We didn't come here to fight," The Strap said soothingly. "I have a business proposition for you." Again he glanced at his paper bag as if whatever was in there held considerable significance.

"Your kind of proposition doesn't interest me.

"Why are you so rude to me, Dawson? You're a peeper now, not a homicide dick. We shouldn't be enemies anymore, right?"

"I still belong to the part of our society that's basically honest. You don't."

181

"Well, I have something I want you to do," The Strap said with a thin smile. "Something perfectly legal, even admirable. And I'm prepared to pay you a million dollars for it. Are you interested?"

"You better hear what the boss has to say," Bones said.

"Shut up, Bones," said Sal the Strap. "Come on, Dawson. Your pad is air-conditioned, right? Let's talk where it's comfortable. Even if you decide not to go for my offer, I promise you you'll get some useful information. Info that'll help your fellow lawmen protect that tiny little honest segment of the population that you mentioned."

"Come on up," Vince said wearily. "Spoil my day."

He led the way up the metal stairs at the side of the pizzeria, unlocked the door on the landing, and ushered Bones and The Strap inside. The place wasn't cool, it was stifling hot. "I forgot to mention I don't have central air conditioning," Dawson said with unconcealed malice. "You're gonna have to sweat a while longer." He went from living room to bedroom to kitchen, turning on small window units. By that time, Ernie Bones and Sal the Strap had sat down on the narrow, threadbare red sofa, behind a dinky coffee table with rings in the varnish from numerous uncoastered glasses and cups. One of the cups was still there, half full of rank, oily-looking black coffee. Sal the Strap leaned forward and delicately set down the little brown paper bag he was carrying.

"Got anything cold?" Bones piped up and asked. "Damn, man, how the hell you live in this dump?"

"Don't insult the man," said Sal the Strap.

"I have some beer. No hard stuff," said Dawson.

"That'll be fine," said The Strap.

"Yeah," said Bones

Dawson fetched three cans of Coors, without glasses. They all popped the caps. Dawson took a sip, sitting in his cracked vinyl armchair. The pizza smells from downstairs wafted into the apartment now that the air was circulating.

"Smells good in here now," Ernie Bones admitted

Dawson told himself the smells probably would have made him hungry if he were in better company. He had skipped his breakfast this morning because he was so nervous over what Dr. Feingold was going to say.

After a long silence obviously intended to be dramatic, The Strap said, "How'd you like a chance to get even with the guy who made yon a cripple?"

Dawson swallowed hard, holding in his emotions, because he wasn't even sure what the emotions would be if he let them out. His apartment was so small the window units were rapidly sucking out stale air and cooling the place off, but new perspiration oozed out of his pores anyway, beading his face. Finally he said, "Chango's dead. My ex-partner, Clint Jones, put a bullet in his brain."

The Strap said, "If Chango was dead, how'd he escape from the hospital?"

"Well, maybe he *wasn't* dead. Either way, one of his crazy followers must've sneaked in and carried his body out. Then he would've had to die. The doctors assured me there was no way he could last for more than a few minutes once he was taken off the life-support system."

Ernie Bones emitted a gruff, sarcastic chortle. Then he upended his can of beer and downed what was left of it in a gulp.

The Strap said, "I have proof that Chango is alive and well. I wish I didn't. I wish he was dead, because he's causing me more grief than all the button men and mustache Petes I ever went up against." He leaned forward, picked up the brown paper bag, and tapped it with his fingers. "In here I got a wineglass our topic of discussion drank out of just last week. His fingerprints are on it, and I'm willing to bet you a thousand to one the prints will match the ones the medical examiner took off of Chango's corpse three years ago."

"Corpse?" said Dawson. "Why do you say 'corpse' if you're trying to tell me he never died?"

"Because he did," said The Strap. His voice was hushed, almost funereal. He took a sip of Coors. Then he went on. "I believe it now. This guy is supernatural. He and his six henchmen were *all* dead when you first found them washed up on the beach. He's calling himself 'Hector Chanfray' now.

Vince got a chill. "That's Chango's real name," he said. "Didn't you know that?"

"Yeah, yeah. He has a big, fancy palace – a temple, he calls it – north of Miami. He even has a cult of rich bitches and movie stars. They believe he's the reincarnation of some kind of ancient god that can communicate with spirits and see into the past and future. Maybe it's true, I don't know. From what I've seen with my own eyes, I'm tempted to believe damn near anything about this guy. I can't handle him, and that's damned hard for me to admit, Dawson. My guys are being blown away by what seems like honest-to-god sorcery. And the State Department and the CIA are protecting him! They arranged for him to acquire a visa and citizenship papers because he supposedly aided in the overthrow of Baby Doc Duvalier – you know, the ex-dictator of Haiti? There's no way Chanfray is ever gonna be prosecuted and deported unless somebody nails him down with something so damn strong the government can't sweep it under a rug."

Sal the Strap stopped talking suddenly, as if he had run out of energy. All the stuff he said was buzzing in Vince Dawson's head like a theorem based on a mixed bag of fallacies. But in a crazy way the sum of it made sense, even if the pieces didn't.

Ernie Bones cleared his throat and leaned back on the sofa. He slowly licked his lips. When he started talking, it was like he was recounting a dream. "Chango's guys ambushed us . . . eight of us and maybe a dozen of them. Not such heavy odds. The fight should've been almost an even match, even though they had the drop on us. Christ sake, some of them were women! At first I thought they were wearing bulletproof vests – but I swear I shot one in the friggin' head and she still kept comin'. It was nighttime, but there was a *moon* – I could see the bullet hole, the brains flying out the back of the skull. But she was still able to shotgun me – my leg was gimpy for a month. I was lucky to get the hell away. I almost think they wanted me to, so I'd spread the word about how *bad* they were. All the rest of my guys were dead."

"Things have been going against me," lamented Sal the Strap. "I set up a meeting with Chanfray on neutral turf, both of us with our muscle guys present. I was willing to make some kind of pact, even cut him in on a piece of my turf, in the interest of stopping the bloodshed between us. But he just acted so damn cool and smug, it was sickening. I had to hold my anger in. He's not satisfied with being like a *capo* down here. He wants the whole shebang. The big black son of a bitch thinks he's gonna be the *capo di tutti capi* – the boss of all bosses!"

The Strap's face was red with rage and indignation. He waved his arms in the air, almost hitting Bones with the paper bag. He calmed himself a bit and muttered, "Over my dead body he'll be a capo."

"Capo of all Florida?" Dawson said somewhat incredulously.

"Of the whole goddamn United States!" The Strap shouted, leaping to his feet. "For all I know, he wants to take over the whole fucking world! I lowered myself to talk to him as if we were equals, and he didn't give me the sweat off his balls! He sashayed out of the restaurant like it was his own palace and he was the high muckety-muck, and I felt like some kind of groupie, a souvenir hunter, snitching his stinking wineglass. But it'll prove he's who I say he is. You've got his prints on file yet, right?"

"The police department should," said Dawson.

"Well, I want you to check," said The Strap. "Your buddy Jones is still on the force. My idea is that you can go undercover, working with your old police contacts, and find some way of doing Chango in. First, check out the prints on this glass. You'll find out that what Bones and I are telling you is the God's truth. I don't even see how you can have a chance against this guy, but I'm hoping and praying you do. I admit I'm desperate, Dawson. If I don't get him soon, I know he's gonna get *me*. It's just a matter of time. Hell! There ain't no ordinary *man* that can stand up to Sal the Strap, but we're not talking about *ordinary* – we're talking about some weird shit I don't even pretend to understand."

The Strap sat back down, looking surprisingly small and pitiful. Vince Dawson was disturbed to find himself actually feeling a little sorry for the guy. Did human empathy have any rational bounds? It was what defense attorneys constantly manipulated, constantly banked on, in order to talk the good citizenry into setting muggers, dopers, murderers, and rapists free. The phenomenon used to make Dawson sick. Now was it working on *him*?

"Tell the truth," Sal the Strap said. "Won't it give you back some dignity and self-respect to be doing something besides snooping on regular people? Think of the irony! A guy like me hiring you to put an archcriminal on ice."

"Because you're too scared to take care of him yourself," said Dawson.

The Strap winced. He took a deep breath, then said, "The usual tactics are useless against this guy. I know. I tried. And I'm not stupid. If I can't blow him away, I have to go some other route, find his Achilles heel. All I know is you defeated him once and put him in the hospital. I think you actually killed him, or close to it – and somehow he came back. Why were you able to put some bad hurt on him when I can't? It doesn't make sense, but it's a fact. Maybe he'll still be scared of you, maybe you've got some kind of hex on him."

While he was talking, The Strap reached under his flowery shirt, dug out a little gold horn dangling on a gold chain around his neck, and fingered it like a rosary. Dawson noticed that Ernie Bones was wearing one, too: an Italian charm against the *mal och* – the evil eye.

"Dawson, I'm prepared to give you all the help I can," The Strap said. "I'll be on the side of the law for a change – and you'll make a million bucks. I'm not kidding. I'm offering to make you rich. If you've got the guts to take me up on it."

"You're trying to hire me to be a hit man for you," said Dawson.

"Hey," said The Strap. "The law works with criminals and informers all the time, plea bargains with them and gets them to turn state's evidence, or puts them in a witness-protection program. What I'm asking you to do isn't so much different. Desperadoes like me, from the old school, have a system of honor. The escoria don't. Neither does Chanfray – and he's got this weird, incredible power. I'm offering the law a chance to get him now, before he's totally out of reach, if he isn't already. Afterward I'll take my chances like I always have, let the chips fall where they may. I've always been fair game – you know that, Dawson. Believe me, I hope you pull this gig off somehow and you and I both live to see your million-dollar payday."

CHAPTER 16

After Bones and The Strap left, Dawson took two Darvon capsules to dull the constant ache in his left arm, swilling the pills down with the dregs of his warm beer, wondering why an arm that didn't work right as far as transmitting any useful signals could still manage to transmit so much pain.

Not wanting the Darvon to go to work on an empty stomach, he went downstairs to Enrico's and ordered two slices of pizza with mushrooms and anchovies, a tossed salad, and a small pitcher of beer. He sat in a booth and ate by himself while he thought over The Strap's offer. He had brought along the brown paper bag supposedly containing Chango's wineglass, and like an evil omen it sat on the tabletop, next to the napkin dispenser.

What could he do with a million bucks? Pay off the $15,000 he still owed a finance company for loans he had taken to help pay his kids' way through college? Buy himself a new car, a decent house? All that would take less than $200,000. The rest he'd probably piss away drinking and gambling. Having too much money all at once would probably kill him. Being poor had one advantage: his binges had to stop when he ran out of cash. In the absence of financial restraint, he might go completely over the edge.

Maybe he could protect a chunk of the cash against his bad habits. Even though they didn't seem to care about him anymore, he could set up trust funds of $100,000 apiece for his ex-wife and his two kids. Maybe it'd teach them he wasn't such a bad guy after all. Maybe if money couldn't buy love, it could at least buy a modicum of respect. Peg and Timmy and Janie had come to see him only once when he was in the hospital three years ago. He had entertained some vague hopes that his almost dying would bring him and his family back together, but it hadn't worked out that way. Peg was remarried now, to a computer repairman. Timmy, at twenty-two, was working in Greensboro, North Carolina, as a claims adjuster, and Janie was a twenty-one-year-old college dropout living with whoever would keep her in cocaine. Dawson wondered if it was his fault she had turned out that way. He tried to keep up with her ever-changing addresses, through Peg, and wrote her long letters in hopes of talking some sense into her, but the letters went unanswered.

If he ever got hold of a pile of money, the smart thing would be to invest it and live off the interest. Maybe instead of killing him it actually would furnish enough incentive to get off the ponies and the booze. He had just proved he could stay sober for two weeks, on Dr. Feingold's orders. He had kept only beer in the fridge and hadn't gone out for any hard stuff to dull the anxiety over the chance of going blind. True, he had spent a lot of time at the track, getting there by taxi. But a couple of ponies had been good to him, so he had only dropped a couple of hundred bucks since the punch in the eye.

He was getting too old to put himself in that kind of jeopardy. Being a one-armed detective was bad enough, but how would he have hacked it one-armed and blind? A no-eye private eye. The odds of his drinking himself to death if he ever found himself in that kind of condition would be better than a thousand to one.

It would be better to be rich and not have to take crazy chances anymore. But to become a millionaire he'd have to take the craziest chance of all, if Sal the Strap's theory somehow turned out to be a fact. Which wasn't going to happen. Checking out the wineglass would put the whole cockeyed notion to rest.

Dawson got his green seven-year-old Chevy Celebrity out of the parking lot behind the pizzeria and told himself how lucky he was that the air conditioning was working and so were both his eyes, as he drove across town to the municipal building. He hadn't seen Clint Jones in about three months. For a while after he quit the force he used to still hang out in the bars where cops drank, but he soon got tired of the looks they gave him, whether real or imagined, the kind of looks that said he was a quitter, a boozer, and a degenerate gambler on a fast track downhill. He hadn't even let Clint know about the eye injury. Nowadays the only time he saw his ex-partner was when he needed access to something a private eye couldn't get except by prying open a back door into official channels, but using Clint that way always made him feel guilty as hell. He always made promises to get in touch soon and not just for business reasons, but somehow he never quite found time for a friendly call.

So much of his life had been wound up in his image of himself as a cop that he always got strange vibes when he stepped inside police headquarters. He half hoped that Clint wouldn't even be there. But the desk sergeant said that he was. Dawson found his ex-partner in the old office that they both used to share. The office looked the same as ever, and so did Clint, as if three years hadn't changed anything or anybody but Dawson.

"You're looking good," Clint said. "Why didn't you come around earlier and spring for lunch?"

"I was tied up on a potential case that may turn out to be nonsense. Wait'll I tell you about it. You won't believe it. How's Deronne?"

"Fine. She'd like to cook dinner for you someday, if you'll let her."

"Sure. One of these days."

"I've heard that one before, pard."

Dawson let it pass. Sitting in front of Jones's desk, he lit up a Kool, his first one of the day, and sucked the smoke in deep. He was trying to cut down, mainly to save money, not years of life expectancy, and had succeeded somewhat, whereas Clint had stopped altogether, thanks to the urging of his new wife, Deronne, who was a health nut. Dawson thought that his ex-partner had a pretty good life right now, a life so much better than his own that he had to warn himself not to be envious. Clint didn't seem to age. He still looked boyishly handsome, still had the full use of his limbs, and on top of it he had a beautiful young wife. Out of the terrible tragedy three years ago, Clint had been the only one to reap something of value. Deronne Beck had come down from Brooklyn to claim the bodies of Paul and Shelly, her murdered brother and sister-in-law, and Deronne and Clint had fallen in love. Dawson had been a gimp-armed best man at the wedding, fumbling to hand over the ring – luckily the groom had caught it before it hit the floor.

Dawson told Jones about the visit from Ernie Bones and Sal the Strap, and Jones got several laughs out of the story as it unwound. At the end of it he said, "Yeah, sure, man, Chango's still alive. What's more, the magic's in the bullet. Let's prove it scientifically. I'll shoot a slug from my .38 into The Strap's brain and we'll wait around and see if he rises up and walks."

"Just for laughs, let's check the fingerprints on the wineglass," Dawson said.

Using a kit from Jones's desk, they dusted the wineglass, making prints and smudges stand out crisp and clear. Then Jones telephoned the Records and Identification Section for Chango's fingerprint card from three years ago. In a little while the intercom buzzed. Jones frowned as he took the message from R & I. When he put the receiver down there was a puzzled look on his face. "Strange," he said. "We never sent those prints back to Haiti, did we?"

"Not as I recall," said Dawson. "Anyhow, we'd have sent a copy. The originals should still be here."

"Well, they're not," said Jones. "They're gone . . . unless they're lost someplace else in the file."

"We'll never find them," Dawson said with a disgusted sigh. "Things keep disappearing from that case and never turn up anymore. Chango's body. His goddamn fingerprints. That composite corpse he made by stitching together body parts. It disappeared from the morgue, for Christ's sake, remember?"

"Sure do," said Jones.

"Voodoo schmoodoo," Dawson said, lighting up another Kool. "Want one?" He jerked a cigarette out of the pack, but Clint shook his head no. "Shit," said Dawson. "I almost had myself talked into going after that million bucks, dirty money or not."

"Nothing to hold you back on that score, pard."

"What do you mean?"

"No way can this Hector Chanfray that The Strap told you about be the Chango that we all know and love. But if The Strap is so shook up about him that he's even willing to side with the law for a change, maybe he'll fuck up royally once we get this deal going, and we can make them both

193

take a heavy fall. As far as the million bucks, you'll never collect one way or the other. He's probably already got it in his head to bump you off after he gets you to do his dirty work."

"Hey, I'm not figuring on doing it alone," said Dawson. "That's why I'm here. I'm going to need support from you and the rest of the department. For one thing, I want you to know what I'm up to. I'll have to worm my way into Chanfray's organization, and once I'm on the inside I could be arrested and prosecuted as a criminal, right? Unless somebody in authority knows I'm actually working for the law."

"If you're gonna be working for the law, you can't keep the money," Jones said. "You've gotta turn it over as evidence for the district attorney."

"Not if it isn't being paid to me for illegal purposes," Dawson pointed out. "If The Strap was paying me to kill Chanfray, I'd have to get proof of that, through a wire recording, a videotape, or whatever. Then I'd have to turn the money over to the proper authorities, along with the other evidence. But if he only pays me to infiltrate and investigate, I can legally accept the cash, as long as I pay taxes on it." Dawson grinned. "That's one advantage of being a private eye instead of a public servant, Clint. I don't have to turn down this kind of windfall. But I'm not just interested in the bread. I want to try to kill two birds with one stone. I'm talking about a sting operation."

"You mean, go undercover like Sal the Strap says, but turn the tables on him – nail him and Chanfray both on drug dealing and conspiracy charges?"

"Yeah. It'll be tricky, but I might need to get something on both of them in order to get out of the deal in one piece."

"In one piece is the right way to put it if this guy copies Chango down to the machete," Jones said.

"Hah!" Dawson pounced. "The machete! Isn't it still in the evidence room? The drum and bullwhip, too. There could be prints on that stuff, right? Why don't we check?"

"No use," said Jones. "It was all dusted and photographed three years ago, then wiped clean. The photographed fingerprints were put in the same file as the ones from the dead bodies. They're all gone, Vince."

"What the hell's going on?" Dawson said with disgust. "Is somebody snitching the stuff right under our noses – a goddamn voodoo freak right in our own police department? Are you sure the machete, the drum, and the whip are still where they're supposed to be?"

"I can check."

"I wish you would. Also, what about an exhumation order?"

"On who?"

"The other six bodies. Chango's henchmen. Find out if they're still under the ground."

"Naw, either way it wouldn't make any difference, Vince. Even if those bodies have disappeared, like Chango's, the most plausible explanation would be that they were taken by grave robbers. You're not starting to believe they crawled out of the ground alive, are you?"

"Well, remember Dr. Martha Lewis? What she said about Zombie Cucumber?"

"All right, if the six were drugged, there's a faint possibility they could have survived, like Indian fakirs that bury themselves and go into some kind of trance. But no way could Chango be still walking around with half his brain destroyed by a bullet."

"Could the doctors have made a mistake?" Dawson wondered. "Could the bullet have merely grazed him?"

"Shit, no," said Jones. "That sucker is dead as a doornail."

***

That night, Dawson fell off the wagon. It started innocently enough, with a carafe of wine at the Golden Pier restaurant, owned by Sal the Strap. Feeling lonely, Dawson had decided to treat himself to a fine seafood dinner. He told himself he would cheer himself up by celebrating the good news he had gotten this morning from Dr. Feingold. As he ate his conch soup, his crablegs supreme, and linguine al fredo, he kept washing the meal down with chianti, not giving a damn if only white wine was supposed to go with seafood. Skipping dessert, he went to the bar and switched to straight bourbon. He told himself he was saving money by staying here instead of going to the racetrack – after all, how could he be expected to subdue more than one bad habit at a time? He half realized that his dive into the bottle had something to do with his envy of Clint Jones's wedded bliss, his fear of what he might be getting himself into with Sal the Strap, and his tendency to panic at the idea of all the money that was being dangled in front of his nose. Since he didn't deserve it, it was sure to turn against him. Somehow he'd never claim it. He'd probably wind up on a cold slab in the morgue.

The drunker he got, the more he kept wanting to hang around, hoping The Strap would walk in. He was known to frequent his own restaurant; the customers loved the mystique of dining at a "Mafia hangout." At one point, Dawson thought that if The Strap showed up he'd tell him to shove his million bucks where the sun doesn't shine. But after the alcohol had sufficiently dulled his scruples and his memory of what it used to be like being a cop, he figured he might as well tell The Strap to count him in on the caper, and damn the consequences.

He didn't stagger out of the Golden Pier till two in the morning. Somehow he managed to drive home, but he passed out before he could turn on the little air-conditioning units in the windows. He woke up at five AM drenched in sweat, his head pounding like a voodoo drum, his tongue as furry and foul as a dust mop, his gimp arm throbbing as though it was pinned under a boxcar. When he sat up to turn on the air conditioning he got so dizzy he fell back down to the living room floor, which was what made him realize that he had never even made it into his bed. Luckily, he hadn't puked all over himself. He must have thrown up in the commode, but he couldn't remember doing it. Good thing he hadn't been visited by the DT's, because they would have made his nightmare in the hospital seem like a session with the Sugar Plum Fairy.

Opening the fridge, he washed down two Darvons with twelve ounces of Coors followed by a pint of tomato juice, both straight from the can. He took an ice-cold shower while he waited for hot water to drip through his Mr. Coffee machine. Then he drank the whole pot, sitting naked in his dismal little kitchen, thinking about Dr. Martha Lewis.

Taking on the Chanfray case would be an excuse to get in touch with her again. He hadn't seen her in almost three years; the last time was when she had visited him in the hospital. He had never bothered to audit any of the courses she taught at Braxton State College, even though she had invited him to do so. He had thought about her often, but had never phoned to ask her for a date. Clint Jones had tried to push him to do it, but he had never admitted to Clint, and had barely admitted to himself, that he was afraid to ask any woman to go out with a cripple.

To his amazement, when he lay down on his bed he conked out and slept for three hours, even with all that coffee in him. The thing that woke him was having to get up and piss it out. Still thinking of Martha Lewis, he found her old number in his book and worked up the nerve to dial. But the feminine voice that answered wasn't hers – and at first he thought she must've moved.

"Who is this?" the voice asked. Wary and keyed up. Expecting bad news?

"Vince Dawson."

"Oh, Lieutenant Dawson!" the voice said, shedding some of the apprehension. "This is Susan – Susan Crandall. Martha's daughter? Remember?"

"Yes, how are you?"

"Fine. Well. . . not so hot, actually, but thanks for asking. I'm living with Mother now. But she's not home."

"Will she be back soon?"

"Not for another week or so, I'm afraid. She's in Haiti. I begged her not to go. She's down there with a team of scientists, helping them study the AIDS virus, although God knows what that has to do with anthropology. Mother wouldn't say much about it. I might as well tell you . . .I had a nervous breakdown. She keeps things from me now, treats me like a child because I've had to move back in with her. But I'm only going to stay till I can start earning some money. I'm getting myself back together, I really am."

"That's really good to hear, Susan," Dawson said. He wondered how Barry Crandall figured in all this, if at all, but he didn't think he should pry.

Encouraged by his sympathetic comment, Susan rambled on. "I have a daughter to think of now. I can't afford to let myself go to pieces anymore. Clara and I are doing fine with Mother gone. It was for her sake I was worried, not my own. Honestly, that's why I didn't want her to go, but she thought I just couldn't stand to be alone."

"A lot happened to all of us three years ago," Dawson said consolingly. "It's perfectly understandable that all of us should need some time to learn how to cope."

"It's more than what happened three years ago," Susan said sadly. "It's what has happened since then, too. Please give Mother another call, in a week or so. She'll be happy to hear from you; she really will. I've gotta go now. I have to get Clara her lunch. Good-bye, Lieutenant. Keep in touch."

"I will," he promised. "I will for sure this time."

Hanging up the phone, he wondered if he really would. Or if it was one more of the empty promises he usually made when he was hungover and contrite. But as the day wore on, Martha Lewis stayed on his mind. He kept worrying about her and wondering what the hell had possessed her to go back to Haiti, which had become an extremely dangerous place since the overthrow of Baby Doc.

CHAPTER 17

Half drunk at eight o'clock in the morning, Captain Armando Raphael was lamenting the murderous riots that had taken place after the President-for-Life fled to Paris. "It was terrible, Dr. Lewis, absolutely barbarous. You would not believe such widespread violence could erupt in this peace-loving country. But the common people hated the Tontons Macoutes much more than we realized. They burned their houses down, butchered them in the streets with machetes, chopped them up in little pieces, and set fire to their remains, as if they were werewolves. In Haiti, unfortunately, calling someone *loup-garou* is often a justification for murder. Franz Midi, a respected man, a powerful man, was driving in his Mercedes with his beautiful young wife, Chantal, and their little boy who three years ago had narrowly been saved from Chango, the cannibalistic bokor who you say fled to America."

"He did," Martha Lewis said. "There is no doubt, Captain. I told you that he murdered some people that I dearly loved."

"You have my deepest sympathy," said the captain. "It is only that there is no proof that the murderer you speak of and the one called Chango were one and the same."

Martha saw it would be futile to pursue the issue, so she let it rest. She was riding in a black stretch limousine with bulletproof glass. There were three seats, each one like a luxurious leather couch, the back two facing each other, and in between them a small cocktail table, a television set, a car phone, and a bar. The chauffeur, a young corporal in a

200

brown uniform, sat up front by himself, behind a plexiglass divider. Martha sat in the rear seat with Dr. Paul Strauss, a serologist from the Centers for Disease Control in Atlanta, Georgia. Facing them, Captain Armando Raphael was sipping the second glass of neat bourbon he had poured for himself since climbing into the car. Next to the captain was Martha's old friend from the Albert Schweitzer Memorial Hospital in Deschabelle, Dr. Felix Metraux, who was acting as liaison between the American scientists and the Haitian medical establishment.

Captain Raphael smacked his lips and continued his narrative. "The riots were just breaking out, so Franz Midi was caught unaware. The mob swarmed all over his car, forcing it to stop. Then they broke the windows with bricks and dragged out his wife and son. Before he could do anything, their heads were hacked off – he barely managed to get hold of the ignition key to unlock the glove compartment and grab for his automatic pistol. Then he started firing into the blood-crazed mob, killing as many as he could. But he saved the last bullet for himself, putting the barrel of the gun in his mouth and pulling the trigger."

"Enough!" Dr. Metraux protested with an agitated wave of his hand. "All of us know pretty much what happened – we don't need to hear about it in lurid detail!"

"I am a man who believes in knowing the facts and facing them squarely," the police chief said slurringly. "It is a habit that has kept me alive in a dangerous occupation."

Martha Lewis didn't believe that Captain Raphael was as brave as he claimed. She also knew that the ruthlessness with which he ran his police department was only a shade less severe than that of the Tontons Macoutes. She had followed the newspaper reports of the past two years, hoping that true freedom would come to Haiti in the aftermath of the Duvaliers' reign. But elections had not taken place as promised by the present ruler, General Namphy. Instead, people who attempted to go to the polls were massacred by the army and the renegade Tontons Macoutes who wished to gain back their power.

"Everything is under control now," said Captain Raphael. "Namphy doesn't tolerate a show of force from anybody. You Americans criticize him for it, but he knows that he must establish firm authority among all the political factions before the people will be ready to handle democratic reforms."

He tossed down another slug of bourbon. Martha didn't argue with him, because in the present situation it was necessary to treat him with tact. Captain Raphael was taking her and Dr. Strauss and Dr. Metraux to a meeting with Claude Etienne, patriarch of a wealthy family of houngans who owned most of the town of Gonaives, thirty miles north of the capital. The Centers for Disease Control were investigating the theory that the rapid spread of the AIDS virus among heterosexual as well as homosexual Haitians might be due to the prevalence of voodoo practices, which often involved the ingesting of potions containing human blood, corpse powder, and cemetery dirt – ingredients quite likely to be a prime source of deadly contamination. The only reason that the Haitian authorities were cooperating with the group of scientists was that they hoped to recapture millions of dollars in American aid that had been denied ever since the elections were canceled. They did not like to help prove that Haiti was a major culprit in the spread of AIDS, but their lust for the money was stronger than their wish to avoid this blemish on their country's reputation.

It was almost like being in a time warp, traveling in a shiny black limo over rutted jungle roads, passing groups of peasants gracefully balancing baskets of fruit on their heads who were walking to Saturday market like countless other peasants had done before them on countless Saturdays in bygone centuries. The peculiar nature of Martha's mission added to the eerie, anachronistic feeling.

The Centers for Disease Control had asked her to help them gain access to the potions that needed to be tested, and if a sufficient number of the tests were positive, to then prepare a report on ways to curb the voodoo practices that could be responsible for the spread of AIDS. It wouldn't be an easy task. The Haitian populace would have to be reeducated, almost brainwashed, into giving up beliefs that had filled their lives with awe and wonder and magic dating back to the earliest origins of primitive religion in Africa. Martha felt considerable guilt over her proposed part in this. Anthropologists were supposed to study the world's cultures, not destroy them. Ironically, the battle against AIDs might finally wrench Haiti into the twentieth century. And a way of life would die in the process.

As the limousine entered Gonaives, a village of some two thousand inhabitants, the feeling of being in a time warp disintegrated somewhat. Many of the clapboard houses had TV antennas. A few old, rusty cars were parked in the dusty streets. And there were many beggars, some so feeble and gaunt that they could barely lift their heads out of the dirt to watch the limousine pass by. They were clearly dying of "slim" – the name that the peasants bestowed on AIDS before the rest of the world had a name for it, when its evil spirit first started possessing them and stealing the meat from their bones.

The driver parked the limousine in the town square and got out, slinging a rifle over his shoulder and briskly moving from one side of the vehicle to the other to hold the doors open for his passengers. In addition to the automatic rifle, the corporal also wore a holstered pistol. So did Captain Raphael. These weapons captured the attention of the peasants in the square, drawing gazes of awe and appreciation that seemed to outweigh the impression made by the long dust-coated limousine. Two groups of men sitting on benches in front of the town's only saloon watched the official-looking party approaching, their eyes fastening mostly on the rifle and sidearms.

"Don't let their stares upset you," Captain Raphael said loudly enough to be heard by all. "Their lives are so free of modern embellishments that they are childishly fascinated by any fine piece of equipment."

Still, Martha felt uneasy being stared at. She said good morning to the men on the benches and got barely a mutter in reply, and this did not jibe with her former knowledge of the warmth and friendliness of the Haitian peasantry.

The saloon appeared dark inside, and the door did not give when Captain Raphael tugged on it. It was one of the many establishments in Gonaives owned by Claude Etienne's family. He was to meet the scientists here at nine AM and introduce them to some of the houngans in the village who might discuss the ingredients in their potions and allow samples to be taken for analysis. The police chief pounded on the door, and still it did not open.

"Evidently he's going to be punctual," said Dr. Metraux, glancing at his pocket watch. "We have a quarter of an hour to kill. I'm going to see if that shoe store across the way is open yet. I need to buy a nice pair of high-top boots if we're going to be visiting some of the jungle villages later on in the week."

Feeling butterflies in her stomach for some reason, Martha watched her friend tuck his watch into his vest, then start back across the square. She almost said, "Ask the corporal to go with you," but she held the words in, trying to stifle her jumpiness, telling herself it was unwarranted. Yet Dr. Metraux appeared suddenly very vulnerable to her, a man of sixty-odd years, gray and stoop-shouldered, with a halting, unenergetic gait.

The morning air was unusually damp and there was a heavy fog hovering over the hills surrounding the town. Maybe, Martha thought, it was only the weather having an effect on her nerves. She glanced around the square. Groups of peasants in brightly colored shirts and print dresses were standing in front of the various shops, waiting for them to open. Others were trickling in from the dirt road, taking their baskets of produce down from their heads and sitting on the sidewalks to rest for a while. None of this activity seemed unusual for a Haitian village on market day. But usually the people would be talking and laughing loudly. Today they were hushed and sullen. Perhaps the violence of past months had irrevocably altered their frame of mind.

Suddenly one of the bench-sitters spoke up, loudly addressing Captain Raphael. "Sir, if you are seeking Claude Etienne, look for him in the general store. It is still too early for the saloon to open."

"Let's go," said the captain, leading the way toward the side of the square opposite the shoe store.

Martha glanced at Felix Metraux, who was looking at the shoes in the window. She almost said that she would wait here for him, but then she followed the captain. She glanced back at the central fountain and watering trough, and suddenly made a very strange observation: no dogs or farm animals were lapping at the water; the people had not brought any pets with them, or any livestock to be sold at the market. And many of the men were wearing long coats, when the weather did not oblige them to. Could they be hiding something?

Seven or eight long-coated young men were loafing outside the general store. They eyed Martha's group coldly, not bothering to show the usual deference due to the police captain. All of a sudden the front door of the store opened and a big, beefy black man barged out calling, "Good morning, Captain Raphael! Come inside early before I open! My father gave me the package you ordered from Cap Haitien!"

"What package?" said the captain.

"Ho! Ho! Don't pretend!" the big, beefy man said. But his joviality seemed forced, and Martha noticed that he was perspiring heavily as he spread his arms, enfolding her and the rest of the group and practically forcing them into the general store. Then he hurriedly rebolted the heavy front door.

"Andre! What's the matter?" Captain Raphael blurted. "Is your father all right?"

"Shhh!" said Andre. His eyes darted from the pistol Captain Raphael was wearing to the rifle and pistol worn by the young corporal. "Excellent! You are already armed! Maybe we stand a slim chance of getting out of this alive."

More alarmed than ever, Martha said, "Dr. Metraux is on the other side of the square, at the shoe store."

"Oh, my God, is he without a weapon?" Andre said, gasping.

"Of course! What *is* all this?" Captain Raphael demanded.

But Andre was looking past him, at the clock on the back wall. And a banging of fists on the front door had started, with cries of, "Open up, boss! It's almost nine o'clock!"

"It's too late to save Metraux," Andre said. "You do have plenty of ammunition?" Without waiting for a reply, he grabbed boxes of shells from a counter and shoved them into the hands of the captain and the corporal. Then he gave rifles and ammunition to Martha Lewis and Paul Strauss, spouting off an explanation of the situation as the pounding on the front door continued. "The Christian church is telling the people that their belief in voodoo is the source of all their misery, making them the slaves of ruthless dictators like Papa Doc and bringing the wrath of God down upon them. The preachers have used the pulpit to turn the peasants against their houngans. My father and mother were butchered last night at their plantation, but the dirty killers did not know my daughter was staying there, and she escaped. She had to make her way on foot through the jungle, and barely got here in time to warn me. If it weren't for Alita, I would've innocently opened my door as usual and the mob would've made corpses of us all."

"Which they may yet," said Captain Raphael, pulling his .45 from its holster.

The men outside were pounding and chanting. "Open up, boss! Open up, boss! What's the matter? It's time now! Market day is starting!"

Andre's daughter Alita, about seventeen years old, scratches all over her face and arms from her recent ordeal, ran downstairs into the store, carrying two rifles. She handed one to her father. "Mother will shoot from upstairs down into the street," she whispered breathlessly.

"Everybody get to the side windows!" Andre snapped. "From here we have a field of fire that takes in most of the square and the front of the store. Hide. Don't let them see you till they start something."

Alita planted a hasty kiss on her father's cheek, then hurried to a window.

"I've never used a gun before," Dr. Strauss said shakily. "I . . . I won't be any good with this thing. I'm not even capable of pointing it at another human being."

"You'd better!" barked the captain. "Or else those things you dignify with the title of human being will chop your head off!" He gave the meek middle-aged serologist a hard shove, propelling him toward a window at the end of an aisle stocked with canned goods.

"My brothers will be firing from the pharmacy across the square," Andre Etienne said. "Let's hope they will pick off the attackers we can't draw a bead on, like the ones right in front of our door. And we must return the favor, you hear?"

Consumed with terror, Martha Lewis said, "Is there any way we can call out to Dr. Metraux – maybe from the upstairs?"

Andre said, "Even if he heard you, it would do no good. The butchers won't let him come inside with us now. But look, why don't you go upstairs with my wife? Delia is a good shot, but she can use your company up there."

Dr. Strauss gazed forlornly at Martha from his position by a side window. She shrugged resignedly, then crossed the store and climbed the stairs as the pounding and the cries of "Open up, boss!" continued and got louder.

On the landing, Martha stepped into a surprisingly luxurious living room. Delia Etienne, plump and not as pretty as her daughter, was crouched by a front window, cradling a rifle that looked to be the same kind as Martha's. Boxes of ammunition and a stack of spare clips were lying beside her. With a tense expression, she handed two of the clips, heavy because they were already loaded, to Martha, and said, "Over there, but don't let them get a peek at you."

Martha crouched beside the other front window. The pounding and shouting downstairs had changed to a frenzied chant of "Open up, boss! Open up, boss! We need some werewolf blood for our mojos! Some *loup-garou* blood for our mojos!"

The insane chant made Martha shudder. It was as if an entire culture that she had studied and found charming had suddenly turned against her, personally, with a hateful vengeance, a murderous mockery of her calling. Clutching the rifle, though she doubted her ability to hit anything with it, she sneaked a look out over the square. The distant fog had lifted and the sun was very bright now. Squinting, she could make out Dr. Metraux crossing from the shoe store, a package under his arm. Three long-coated men came off the sidewalk, hastening to catch up with him. He didn't even glance back over his shoulder.

The chanting outside stopped, and the pounding on the door increased in ferocity.

The men sneaking after Dr. Metraux drew gleaming machetes from under their long coats.

With a short, anguished scream, Martha poked the barrel of her rifle under the window sash and began firing desperately. Metraux was running for the limousine with the men chasing him, and even if he could reach the vehicle the keys were in the corporal's pocket and all the doors were probably locked. Martha took aim as best she could at one of the attackers and squeezed the trigger, and to her horror she saw Metraux sprawl to the pavement. Did he trip and fall or did her shot go wild and hit him? She fired again and shot one of the men, and his machete went flying. Two more shots – from Delia Etienne or somebody downstairs – brought down the other two butchers. But more were coming.

Gunfire had erupted all around the square. Men with machetes were hacking at the door of the pharmacy, and others were dragging victims out of the shoe store. Martha's ears were ringing from all the shots being fired upstairs and downstairs in the general store.

She saw Metraux drag himself to his feet and limp to the limousine, trying to pull the back door open. Three terrorists charged toward him, and Martha fired frantically but missed every one. They leapt upon the aged doctor, swinging their heavy, sharp machetes like meat cleavers. Several more joined in the butchery, and Martha fired at them again and again, but she couldn't kill them all before they hacked Metraux to ribbons, using the fenders and hood of the limousine as a chopping block.

Martha's first clip was empty. She grabbed another one, but didn't know how to load it. Delia Etienne crawled toward her, grabbed the rifle, ejected the spent clip, and jammed in the fresh one.

When Martha was ready to fire again, she poked the barrel out the window, but the onslaught seemed suddenly to have diminished in intensity. The firing downstairs was lessening, and the chanting and pounding didn't seem quite so loud. Squinting into the bright sun, Martha saw that the attackers were running away from the pharmacy and the general store, which were more staunchly defended than most of the other homes and businesses, thanks to Alita's warning. The terrorists were choosing easier pickings. From parts of the village away from the square, Martha could hear the agonized screams of people being dragged from their homes and butchered.

Finally it seemed that the siege might be ending. Many attackers lay dead in the square. Others were running away, their machetes dripping blood. Some carried goods from the houses and stores with them as they ran. Shots rang out from downstairs, and some of the pillagers fell dead, sprawling in the sunlit street, their booty strewn beneath and beside them.

Martha did not take part in the last of the killing. Instead, she cowered against the wall by the window, sobbing violently, her face streaked with tears. Delia Etienne, who was also crying, came and hugged Martha, gently and silently stroking her hair.

PART THREE

THE CHANNEL

A man can no more possess a private religion then he can possess a private sun or moon.

– K. Chesterton

You never love people for their virtues. It's their shortcomings that make you lose control.

– Lawrence Sanders

CHAPTER 18

A week after his phone conversation with Susan Crandall, Vince Dawson rang Martha Lewis's number again. Perhaps the fact that he had been sober for seven days gave him courage. Now that the strategy of going after Hector Chanfray had been set up, Dawson had a mission in life, and its initial effect was to change his outlook for the better. He was more worried and afraid than he had been for a long time, but at least he wasn't thinking too much of his own misfortunes and drowning in misery and self-pity.

In order to be able to accept The Strap's million-dollar deal, Dawson had to remain a private investigator working in liaison with the Braxton Beach police force. As far as the public knew, Dawson had been rehired and placed on the narcotics squad. In order to get the chief to go along with using a private eye as part of an undercover sting operation, Dawson and Jones had had to convince the chief of the strong possibility that Hector Chanfray was behind the flood of narcotics pouring into Braxton Beach. The plan was for Dawson to try to insinuate himself into Chanfray's illegal operations by offering to take bribes. As a narc, Dawson could offer to feed Chanfray important info to help him avoid drug busts and other police traps.

Point two of the plan was for Ernie Bonino to pretend to turn against The Strap and join up with Chanfray. That way, Bones could work with Dawson from the inside of the organization they were hoping to bring down.

It was Dawson's idea, reluctantly approved by The Strap and Clint Jones, to try to enlist the aid of Dr. Martha

Lewis, whose anthropological knowledge had proven so valuable in anticipating Chango's actions three years ago and defeating him in the cemetery. Even if the current Hector Chanfray and the old one weren't one and the same, which Dawson believed and hoped to be the case, he still might make good use of Dr. Lewis's insights into the minds of demagogues who used fanatical religion or any other type of mumbo-jumbo to manipulate and control people.

He also wanted to see Martha again. He finally frankly admitted it to himself. And he would've been ashamed to confront her if he hadn't been "clean" of drinking and gambling for a decent interval.

It was a Saturday afternoon when he called her. Just like before, Susan Crandall answered the phone, but this time he recognized her voice. And she knew it was he right away, so why did she sound so upset? Was she wishing she hadn't encouraged him to call back? She certainly stammered a lot.

"Uh . . . I . . . hold on . . .I'll ask Mother if she can come to the phone."

"I can try again later if she's taking a bath or something," Dawson offered.

"No . . .it's uh . . .nothing like that. Hold on."

He could hear her mumbling through her hand over the receiver. Then Martha got on the line. "Hello, Lieutenant Dawson. I'm sorry if I don't sound like myself. Actually, I'm quite startled to hear from you after all this time."

"Didn't Susan tell you I called a week ago, when you were in Haiti?"

"Yes, she did. I would have returned your call, but I wasn't sure I could handle it. You see, something happened down there to bring it all back to life . . . all the memories I thought were deadened enough for me to cope with them, even if I went back to where that monster was born."

Unable to make heads or tails out of all this, Dawson said, "Would it help for the two of us to talk about it? It's my fault, I know, but we've never done that. Maybe we could sort of be each other's therapists." He chuckled nervously. "Maybe we should've tried it long before now."

He was surprised at the things he was saying to her. It was because he was afraid she was simply going to turn him off. Being on the phone helped. He wouldn't have spoken to her this way if he had had to look her in the eyes.

She said, "I'm sorry to have to say this, but I'm not sure whether seeing you again will be healthy or unhealthy for me right at this moment."

"Please," he said. "I have to talk with you. I don't want to give you the details over the phone, but they're very important."

"To whom?"

"To me. And possibly to you, too, Martha." He didn't sound convincing, even to himself.

"All right," she said doubtfully. "All right. . . where?"

"At your place?"

"Fine."

"Can we be alone there?"

"Susan is usually here. And the baby. Why don't we use my office at the college?"

"Can you meet me there at three, this afternoon?" Dawson pressed, not wanting to give her time to change her mind.

"Three-thirty would be better," she said.

He had two hours to kill without a drink, and somehow he made it, even though he was scared to face her without something to fortify him. She hadn't exactly made him feel welcome. But she managed a faint smile when he walked into her office in the Arts and Sciences Building at Braxton State College. It always amazed him that professors allowed their employers to stash them in cold, unadorned cubicles, not much different from his office at the police station, as if places like this could be conducive to intellectual and academic pursuits loaded with wit and nuance. It didn't take him long to suggest that they go somewhere for coffee, and they ended up at the student union, which contained only a sprinkling of students now that the college was in summer session.

He thought he could feel her making a point of not looking at his gimp arm. She was as attractive as ever, her ash-blonde hair shortened into a wavy bob, her figure trim in a white, ruffled blouse and powder-blue slacks. Every time she looked at him, her eyes blinked too much. She seemed to be fighting back tears.

"Spit it out, Martha," he said angrily. "Why does it bother you so much just to be sitting across from me? You didn't act like this last time I saw you, when I was still in the hospital and the whole damn mess was fresh in our minds."

"I'm sorry," she said, and the tears started to flow. Her crying was soundless, but that didn't make it any less pitiful. Perturbed at herself for not being able to control it, she hurriedly dabbed at her eyes with a Kleenex, same as she had done in his office three years ago.

She told him what had happened in Haiti, and he reached out and took her hand. The full realization hit him of how close he had come to losing her – and at the same time he reminded himself that she was never his to lose. He made up his mind not to ask her to become involved too deeply with his case. He had never wanted to put her in danger, and now he was determined not to risk even the slightest possibility of it. So he didn't tell her what he was really up to. He just said that he was back on the police force, and he might need her advice on something, and would it be okay to call on her from time to time?

"I'm not sure," she said. "What's it involve?"

He told her about the drug dealer who was also passing himself off as a "channel to the spirit world." He did not mention the names Chango or Hector Chanfray. But he did say that this channel's spiel was spiced with voodooistic jargon and doctrine. "I've got to worm my way into this guy's confidence, make him trust me so I can gather enough evidence to collar him. I don't know yet exactly how I might be able to use your kind of knowledge, Martha. I only know it helped a lot before."

"My so-called knowledge keeps getting people killed," Martha said, the tears flowing anew. "Dr. Metraux wouldn't have been there if it weren't for me, and Silvio and Jean might have survived if I hadn't brought them over here."

Dawson leaned toward her, squeezing her hand more tightly. "It's not you," he said intensely. "It's not your knowledge that's to blame, it's *their* ignorance – the ignorance and superstition that warps people's minds and makes them do horrendous things to each other in the name of religion or politics or . . . or belief in pagan gods that never existed. Your kind of knowledge is precious, Martha, because it helps us understand the primitive devils lurking in all of us – devils that can be brought to life by those who are clever and evil enough to prey upon our gullibility and our fear."

They left their cold coffee on the table, and he didn't try anymore to persuade her of anything. As they left the student union, on their way to the parking lot, he asked if he could call her later in the week. To his surprise, she said yes.

"I guess I'll try to help you," she added, averting her eyes. "I only hope your case isn't the kind to put you in extreme danger, but from what you say I'll be hoping in vain. Good luck, Lieutenant."

She shook his hand, her fingers long and slender and strong. Then she got in her car, which was a silver Buick instead of the red Mustang of three years ago. Standing beside his green Celebrity with the doors open so it would cool off a little, he waved good-bye to her as she pulled out, and she waved sadly back.

Driving to Enrico's for a calzone, he thought of how esoteric and geographically remote her particular area of study used to be, and how it had suddenly become terribly meaningful and pertinent to what was going on right here and now. Florida newspapers and tabloids were full of stories about skulls and other body parts stolen from graves by voodoo practitioners from Haiti and Cuba. And the religion was rapidly spreading among American teenagers, heavy metal groups, and assorted whackos – a widening demographic conglomeration of dabblers in the occult.

He managed to stay sober for two more days. And he did not go to the track.

On Monday morning he had an appointment with his lawyer. The lawyer had in his possession a $500,000 cashier's check, and did not know that it had come from Salvatore Stropoli, and did not inquire. All he had to know was that it was made out to Vincent M. Dawson. Vince instructed him to deposit $100,000 chunks of it in separate trust funds for Timothy Dawson, Jane Dawson, Martha Lewis, and Clinton Jones. The lawyer was executor of

Janie's money, and her receiving it was contingent upon her staying drug-free for three years.

Dawson was keeping the other $100,000 for himself. He had considered giving it to his ex-wife, but had decided against it. Her new husband had taken vows to support her in sickness and in health, for richer or for poorer, so let the vows be put to the test.

Vince would worry about the other $500,000 if and when he ever claimed it. The Strap had agreed to half of the million bucks in advance, but had refused to guarantee payment of the balance to Dawson's estate if Dawson got killed trying to pull the job off.

CHAPTER 19

That same week, on a Saturday at eight o'clock in the evening, Captain Armando Raphael stepped off an airplane at Miami International Airport. He was wearing a six-hundred-dollar silk suit exquisitely tailored to hide his growing paunch. On his wrist was a glittering diamond and platinum watch which he had appropriated for himself from among Franz Midi's personal possessions during his investigation of Franz's murder. The investigation hadn't amounted to much, since the corpse had never been found – only a greasy pile of roasted bones where kerosene had presumably been poured over the cut-up remains of Franz and Chantal and their baby boy. But Captain Raphael had taken it upon himself to break into Franz's house in search of evidence. He had beaten the looters, and had claimed the estate for the Haitian government, except for the watch and a few other valuables that he had filched for himself.

The captain had come to Miami on what he regarded as a patriotic mission. Before the overthrow of Baby Doc, Haiti was getting a hundred million dollars a year in American aid. So far, two years had gone by under General Namphy, and the aid had not been restored. The American State Department said that the restoration of support was contingent upon the establishment of free elections in Haiti. But that prospect was not imminent, under Namphy or anybody else. So, Captain Raphael had to help implement an alternative plan for bringing a great influx of American dollars into his country and preventing it from sinking into poverty and starvation. In the process, he intended to make sure that his own bank account was amply rewarded.

Woozy from the effects of ten or twelve little bottles of vodka that he had imbibed on the plane, he blinked his eyes, trying to clear his head, as he entered the deplaning area. The airport terminal was a muddle of squawking loudspeaker announcements in many languages and people of every stripe and color. But at last he spotted the man who was to meet him – Henri Blanc – a dapper little man in a white suit with a pink carnation. "Blanc," which in French means "white," was a misnomer, for Henri wasn't that color at all, except for his suit. His skin was the color of slate, his fuzzy fringe of hair the color of coal. His teeth were not white but yellowish brown. An ex-Haitian, he welcomed Captain Raphael in Creole French, calling him "Monsieur Benet," which was the alias they had agreed upon in advance.

Henri Blanc helped the captain to claim his baggage and carry it to Blanc's car, a two-year-old Dodge Aries. "I own a Mercedes and a Rolls," he said, "but I thought it best to leave them at home. Ostentation can sometimes attract prying eyes and pointy ears."

When they were in the car, safe from any intrusion on their privacy, Captain Raphael asked, "When will I be able to meet with your boss?"

"First you must tell me everything," Blanc said. "If I like your proposal, if I think it has sufficient merit, then I will recommend the meeting that you seek. But I warn you that the details, especially the financial ones, must be exceptionally enticing in order to command our interest. So it behooves you to – as the Americans say – sweeten the pie as much as you can for us, right at the outset. We do not believe in haggling, for we have no need to. There are others who will be all too glad to meet our needs in the proper way, if you should prove unwilling or uncooperative."

"That sounds like a threat," the captain said indignantly. "Don't forget I am an emissary of the Haitian government. These others that you mention are not likely to be in such a high position, and therefore they will not be able to deliver what they promise. All they can do is talk."

"Aha!" said Blanc with a thin smirk. "In Haiti, high positions become low ones overnight. It is not very much of a sure thing that either Namphy or you will still be in power by the time your return flight takes off from the airport."

A beautiful red sunset took the captain's breath away as the little Aries sped along Biscayne Bay, headed for downtown Miami. Within a few miles, the traffic thickened into a jam, and the sun was replaced by glittering neon. The skyline of the city, which the captain had admired from the air, was yet more impressive from the ground. Skyscrapers of glass and steel cast their shimmering reflections in the harbor, where hundreds of huge, fancy yachts were tied up at wooden docks.

They went to a restaurant near the water's edge. To the captain's surprise, Haitian food was on the menu. Miffed, he said, "Why did we come here? I can get this at home, and it would probably be better prepared."

Henri Blanc gave his thin smirk. "I doubt it, Monsieur Benet," he said knowingly. "I urge you to allow me to order for you."

The captain shrugged and set aside his menu. He took a big sip of bourbon. The waitress, a redheaded gum-chewing American wench, did not heighten his anticipation of actually getting good Haitian food in this place. But, to his amazement, she didn't flinch when Henri Blanc ordered *griots*, a staple of the Haitian diet, which consisted of deep-fried curls of piglet served with rice and beans.

As the waitress walked away, the captain said, "The griots will never taste good here. Even in Haiti they don't taste good anymore, ever since our pigs were replaced by the big, ugly American pigs."

He was referring to the scandal of the *cochon planche*, the mass extermination of native Haitian pigs that took place several years ago, in what was now looked upon by many people as a CIA plot.

Captain Raphael finished his first bourbon and was half-way through another when a loud bubble-gum pop interrupted the rundown of the latest developments in Haiti that he was giving to Henri Blanc: the riots and the killings of the Tontons Macoutes by the peasants, and the killings of the peasants who tried to vote by the army and the remnants of the Tontons Macoutes. The popping bubble gum signaled the arrival of the waitress with two huge, covered platters, which she proceeded to unveil. Henri Blanc grinned as she did so.

"*Cochon planche*!" the captain exclaimed. "Where did you ever—?"

"Do you believe now that my boss is a powerful man?" said Henri Blanc. "He owns this restaurant. And he rescued the food of the loas to be bred and raised secretly here in America."

They dug in and heartily enjoyed their very special meal, with barely a word of conversation. Afterward, when they were having cigars and wine, Captain Raphael outlined his business proposition. Working with "a gentleman in a very high position" in General Namphy's government, he was prepared to offer secluded Haitian plantations to be turned to the growing and processing of cocaine for wholesaling and retailing in America. Haitian importers and exporters, working under the protection of bribed government officials, would launder the profits of this drug operation, which should be worth a billion dollars or more annually. Captain Raphael and his partners wanted only twenty percent of the yearly take, half of which they would take for their own commission, channeling the other half into the Haitian treasury, to make up for the cutoff of American aid. "Henri," the captain concluded lugubriously, "you are a former citizen of Haiti. I am sure you will agree that it is our patriotic duty to rescue our country in its hour of crisis. And I am confident that you will be able to persuade your boss that this is truly a meritorious enterprise."

"No doubt," said Blanc. "But of course we have had similar offers from others."

"Others from Haiti?" the captain said with surprise.

"Yes. Not only from political factions that rival yours in Haiti, but from other Central American countries, such as Panama. I will present your proposal. It will be honestly and thoroughly appraised. And I will get back in touch with you as expediently as possible. Now, let me take you to a place where you may choose from an amazing selection of delectable wenches whose sole aim in life will be to show you a pleasurable time to take your mind off the rigors of your long airplane trip."

***

Mournfully he told himself that he had been right: the *cochon planche* was too good to be true. Something was wrong with it, for he was becoming quite ill. And it was a terrible time for it to happen, now that he was with a beautiful young woman whom he did not wish to disappoint.

She looked to be no more than nineteen. And she bore a striking resemblance to Chantal Midi, Franz's wife, who always had excited a secret lust in the captain's heart, up to the day she died. Now here she was, or the spitting image of her was here, in a smoky, noisy bistro in a section of Miami known as "Little Haiti."

Driving here, Henri Blanc had explained that there was also a Little Havana, a Little Nicaragua, and a Little El Salvador. "Each wave of new immigrants has set up its own fiefdom, with its own rules and customs, like a country within a country, or, rather, a little piece of a country within a great city. And all of these fiefdoms are awash in cocaine – you really wouldn't believe how much of it, tons and tons actually – and some people are too dumb to take advantage of the huge profits to be made. Why, the former president of Nicaragua lives in a hovel with his wife and nephew. A man who was a top minister in the Sandinista government is now a parking attendant at a nightclub. But his former adversaries, the Contras, know how to smell a good thing – they smuggle narcotics like everyone else and use the profits to buy arms and grease their own pockets."

Feeling on top of the world during the drive, with the bourbon and the griots in his stomach, Captain Raphael enjoyed hearing Blanc's spiel and dreaming of the portion of the vast wealth that he would soon claim for himself and for Haiti. His exuberance reached its peak when the girl who resembled Chantal Midi sat in his lap. Another young one sat in Henri Blanc's lap, laughing and cracking boisterous jokes and urging "Monsieur Benet" to order champagne.

He immediately complied. Glancing at himself in the murky mirror to the right of the table, he thought that a man of his depth, his experience, truly deserved a young woman like the one he was going to have tonight. After all, he was a hardened combat veteran and a patriot. He could be justifiably proud of the way he handled criminals and traitors. He had been in many close scrapes, like the one in the general store in Gonaives, and he had seen much suffering and death. When he made eye contact with himself in the mirror, he could see that his world-weary experiences had given his broad, fleshy face a new dimension of what people called "mystery" or "character."

But suddenly, as his young lady leaned toward him and kissed him full on the lips, his stomach churned and his vision blurred. He thought he would have to throw up right that second. He had to desperately fight down the impulse and pretend that everything was fine. He broke out in a profuse sweat. As if she did not notice his plight at all, the girl gave a tinkly little sexy laugh and let her hand rest on his groin. She was sitting beside him now instead of in his lap. He blinked his eyes and grabbed onto the table to steady himself, and when he gazed into her lovely face somehow he did not feel ill anymore, and he said, "I do not even know your name. Please don't tell it to me. Do you mind if I call you Chantal?"

Her laugh burst forth, more tinkly and sexy than ever. "Of course, for you I will be Chantal. Who is she? A girlfriend from back home?"

"Yes," he murmured. "Believe it or not, she looks very much like you." But as he said it, he saw that the resemblance was truly more superficial than he had thought. This girl's face was more cold, less expressive, and

228

there didn't seem to be quite so much vibrancy in her flashing black eyes.

All of a sudden there was music, Haitian music, and she grabbed his hand, tugging him onto the dance floor. On the stage there were five musicians, men and women dressed in ordinary peasant garb. At first, they were beating drums, playing bamboo flutes, and shaking tambourines. But as soon as "Chantal" pulled the captain to the center of the floor, the musicians laid down their flutes and tambourines and the drum rhythms changed, becoming wilder and more primitive. Captain Raphael's vision became blurry again as he looked up toward the stage. Voodoo instruments were now in the musicians' hands: an *asson*, or rattle, made of a calabash beaded with snake vertebrae; an iron bell and clapper, called an *ogan*; and a horn made out of a conch shell. These instruments, in and of themselves, did not alarm the captain; he had attended numerous ceremonies wherein they were used. But the way they were being played! The staccato speed of the drum riffs, the dizzying highs and lows of the bell tones, the screech and lament of the conch horn! Blends and clashes of sound that seemed to exceed anything that could be accomplished by musicians of ordinary talents and virtuosity!

Chantal spun away from the captain, her voluptuous body writhing and twirling in patterns that were just as fantastic as the music she was dancing to. His stomach was no longer upset. Somehow, without his realizing it, his nausea had been transmuted into an intense euphoria, a glow of wellbeing. He was transfixed by the pumping of Chantal's hips, the jiggle of her nipples under her sheer blouse, the rhythmic invitation of her lush, energetic thighs. She was the only one dancing now. He was alone with her on the dance floor. They were encircled by dozens of others who had stopped dancing and were merely clapping hands. Even Henri Blanc and his woman of the evening were watching and clapping.

The music was shrill and dazzling and all-encompassing.

Streamers of light burst through the dark, smoky bistro, bouncing from murky mirror to murky mirror, making Chantal's movements look spasmodic, almost grotesque, but still unbelievably sexual and enticing. There must be a bevy of strobe lights concealed somewhere, but the captain couldn't tell where.

Scanning the black depths of the bistro for the enigmatic light source, he saw Franz Midi gliding among the throng, and his heart jumped up to his throat. He told himself it couldn't be Midi, it had to be someone else. He was hallucinating. Perhaps he had been drugged. What the hell was in that *cochon planche*?

Chantal was naked now, and she pulled him down to the floor. She tugged at his belt, and it came undone. Other people leaned in and grabbed his jacket sleeves, his necktie, his diamond-and-platinum watch. Within seconds, he was as naked as Chantal. Cupping her own breasts and furiously rubbing the nipples, she lowered herself astride him and his iron-hard penis rose to penetrate her. Immediately he orgasmed. But so did she. She screamed and laughed all at the same time, the two contradictory sounds blending together, becoming one and the same, one and the same. . .

He opened his eyes.

The flesh was peeling from her face.

Her nipples were squirming and turning as white as wriggling maggots. Then clumps of maggots dropped from her split-open breasts, issuing from there as if they were being born. He clawed at his own loins, his hands mushy from maggots. He tore into them with his fingernails and squashed them between his fingers.

Franz Midi was hugging his wife now, his diamond-and-platinum watch on his thick black wrist. A strobing stream of light shot from his dead-looking eyes, and his head burst into flames.

Chantal was burning too. Her half-decayed bones began sliding out of her as she collapsed in flames atop the captain, still being hugged by her husband, so that the captain was weighted down by them, forced to become the base of the funeral pyre. Then his own body caught fire, the clumps of maggots glowing and igniting, adding fuel to the conflagration.

All the while, the asson and the ogan and the conch horn kept wailing over the mad pounding of the petra drums.

Henri Blanc looked on approvingly, showing everybody his thin smirk.

The throng of voodoo worshipers shrieked and chanted and clapped their hands till Chantal and Franz and Captain Armando Raphael were nothing but a large, black, greasy smudge on the hardwood floor.

Then, with a loud, ululating hiss that sounded like an eerie inhuman laugh, the curling, strobing beams of light disappeared into the darkness of the bistro as if they were reentering the bowels of hell.

CHAPTER 20

Clara was screaming, and Susan was spanking the table. "Bad table! Bad table! It shouldn't have done that to you!"

Susan cried as her hand smacked the table top.

"What happened? Is she all right?" Martha called out, not allowing herself to be overly alarmed, because she knew that in all probability nothing was seriously wrong. Spoiled rotten by Susan, little Clara would wail her head off over the slightest mishap, and Susan would comfort her as if the sky had fallen on her. Hearing the commotion from her bedroom, Martha finished applying her lipstick before even coming out to look.

"Bad table!" said Susan. "Clara was playing under it with Raggedy Ann, and when she stood up it bumped her head."

Clara looked up at Martha and gave a couple of unconvincing whimpers, trying for sympathy from someone new. But she didn't try hard, because she already realized that her grandmother didn't pamper her like her mother did.

"You shouldn't blame the kitchen table," said Martha. "Teach her to be careful so she won't hurt herself the next time. If you teach her that inanimate objects are responsible for her problems, she'll never learn the proper relationship between cause and effect."

"Oh, Mother, don't play scientist with me! You sound like Barry!" Susan snapped.

"Well, raising a child is to a large extent a scientific process," said Martha. "There are logical guidelines that tend to make everything turn out okay."

"What about love and caring?" Susan said in the midst of planting kisses on Clara's forehead.

"Too much of it applied in the wrong way can be utterly disastrous. If you—"

"Yikes! The stew is burning!"

Susan jumped up and ran to the stove, grabbed a wooden spoon, and frantically stirred the pot. Her bump on the head utterly forgotten, the baby tugged at her mother's dress and yelled, "Pick me up! Pick me up!" She wanted to get a look at the burning stew, a new and wonderful experience to her. But it wasn't burning, of course. Susan tended to perceive emergencies where none existed. "Go ahead. Don't worry, I can handle this," she said with a show of staunchness. "Enjoy your date, Mother. Don't worry about us."

"I'll be home early, I think," Martha said. She stooped to hug and kiss her granddaughter, her heart overflowing with love for Clara even though the child was spoiled. Then she went and kissed her daughter on the forehead, thinking how nice it would be if all of life's pain could be lessened that way, a parental peck on each booboo.

The doorbell rang, and Susan said, "That must be him now. Have a nice time."

"I'm going to bring him in to see Clara."

"Oh, I look a mess! Don't bring him in the kitchen! Take Clara out to the living room!"

"Nonsense. You look perfectly fine."

It was true. A very attractive young woman, Susan had put on makeup and a nice blouse and slacks, knowing she might have to be seen by her mother's company. But she still felt uncomfortable about herself. She was scared to meet people anymore. All she did was stick around the house and cater to Clara, making the child the center of the universe.

Martha opened the front door, and there was Albert Scanlon, when she had expected Vince Dawson.

"Hello, Martha," he said. "I just thought I'd stop by. Oh! Are you getting ready to go out?"

"Yes, but Susan's here. Would you like to have some leftover stew with her and Clara?"

"Thank you, I'd love to."

He was the other prime collaborator in the spoiling of Martha's granddaughter. Sometimes Martha wondered why they were usurping her role. Grandma was traditionally supposed to be the spoiler of children. But instead, she was the only one fighting for a shred of discipline, and it was a losing battle. Susan tried to make up too much for the absence of the child's father, and Albert came around and lavished on Clara – and Susan too, for that matter – all the kindness and affection that would have gone to his own daughter, Mary Ann, if she were still alive.

The doorbell rang again, and this time it was Dawson. He looked as shy as a teenager picking up a blind date for the prom. Martha reintroduced him to Albert and Susan while Clara ran away to hide.

"Don't you go under that table!" Susan yelled.

"She's cute," Dawson said.

"How can you tell? You barely saw her," said Martha.

"I caught a glimpse," he said. "Don't forget, detectives have sharp eyes."

"Clara's sharp as a whip herself," Albert said, chuckling dotingly. "She's a rascal. You have to be quick on your feet to keep up with her."

Susan came back, holding Clara, who hugged her tightly and pulled at her hair. "Turn around and let the lieutenant get a good look at you," Susan said. But Clara kept her blond curls toward Dawson, her plump cheek pressed against her mother's face and neck.

Vince noticed that Susan was looking rather thin and drawn, but still one wouldn't suspect that she had suffered the nervous breakdown she had mentioned on the phone a few weeks ago. Maybe she really was getting herself back together, as she had claimed.

"Don't let us keep you. Have a good time, you two," Albert Scanlon said.

"Enjoy your dinner, Mother," said Susan.

"Don't go, Grandma!" Clara wailed, and burst into tears. Ignoring her shrieking, Martha pivoted sharply and allowed Vince to hold the door open for her as they both said their good-byes over the din.

On the way to Clint Jones's house, Martha filled Vince in on how her life had been for the past three years. "Albert and I did our best to console each other," she said. "I almost married him for sure at one point. First I had lost my husband, and then he lost Mary Ann, and it seemed that we were going to keep being thrown together by grief, so we may as well make it permanent. But somehow we both realized that mutual bereavement wasn't a healthy basis for a marriage. We care deeply for each other, but I think at last we both know that it will always be platonic."

Dawson was glad to hear it was that way between Martha and Albert, and hoped she was saying it partly to encourage his advances, which so far had been more mental than overt. In addition to keeping himself sober and staying away from the racetrack, he had also quit smoking – hadn't had a puff for two and a half days. If he was going to pursue Martha, he had to do his best to feel worthy of her. Asking her to accept a man with a crippled arm was hard enough; he couldn't ask her to also buy into handicaps he brought on himself.

"I was getting along okay," she told him. "Not wildly happy, by any means, but content to immerse myself in my work. Then, when Susan had the baby, things picked up a little. I guess I was ready to be a grandmother but didn't want to admit it. But when I went up to New York to see them, I could tell Barry and Susan weren't getting along. They had decided to have a child for that old, trite, perfectly wrong reason: to keep their marriage together. But Barry didn't want to be a father; he never had any real desire to give birth to anything but his own business enterprise. He felt chained down, and started taking it out on Susan for having a child to command her attention instead of being able to work full-time to help him get ahead."

"Taking it out in what way?" Dawson asked.

"At first it was only what the divorce courts call 'mental cruelty.' But then it became physical, too. She never breathed a word about it to me, though. I had no idea he was beating her up. Till one day when she showed up on my doorstep with her mouth puffed up and her eyes black and blue."

"Was that when she moved in with you?"

"No, it took her another year and a half to divorce Barry. She tried going back to him a couple of times, but he'd never keep his promises. He'd end up brutalizing her again. And poor little Clara was starting to show the effects – nervousness, hyperactivity, and so on. That's what finally gave Susan the gumption to split. Then Barry wouldn't leave her alone. He fought her tooth and nail to keep Clara

– he wanted to *win* the divorce, and that meant keeping all his possessions, including his baby daughter. That's when Susan had the nervous breakdown, and it gave Barry ammunition to use against her. He called her an unfit mother, and was almost awarded custody of Clara, even though I testified about how he had beat my daughter up – and who could guarantee that he wouldn't do it to my granddaughter, too? He totally destroyed Susan's sense of self-worth. She's having an incredibly rough time starting to believe in herself again."

Dawson thought that, despite their differences, Barry and Susan might have grown old together if it weren't for the murders. The bad side of Barry's personality might never have been pushed to the surface. He and Susan would've gone into business with the Becks and the Morellis. Chances are, it would've worked out for the best. Instead, it all came crashing down on them in the most horrible way imaginable. Homicide always wreaked its destruction on the survivors as well as the victims. And what Chango had done was far worse than "ordinary" homicide – a word that almost seemed too mild to describe his atrocities. Barry and Susan had to endure the trauma of discovering their four closest friends dead and dismembered. A heavy burden of self-blame probably went along with it. It would be tough to forget that they were the ones who had invited their friends down here to be butchered.

"You're keeping something from me, aren't you?" Martha said, jarring Dawson out of his macabre reverie.

"What do you mean?" he asked. But he figured he already had a pretty good idea.

"The case you want me to help with. There's something more about it than what you told me."

He supposed he ought to be glad she was so perceptive. Ever since leaving her office the other day, he had wished he had just told her about Chanfray and gotten it over with all at once. All day today, he had been trying to think of a way to break it to her, because he knew it ought to be done before they arrived at Clint Jones's house for dinner. The case was sure to be discussed there, and Dawson hadn't warned Clint to keep his mouth shut about certain details. So in a way it was a relief that somehow Martha had seen through him and had opened the subject on her own. He only hoped that when she heard the whole works she didn't ask him to turn around and drive her home.

He told her everything, starting with the visit from Ernie Bones and Sal the Strap. She didn't look at him. She just stared straight ahead through the windshield. When he was done talking, he could feel her holding her breath. She let it out in a tremulous sigh. "Chanfray?" she murmured. "Chango? How can it be?" Her voice was timid and soft, and he wished he could hold her in his arms, because she sounded like a scared, puzzled child.

He told her, "That's what I'm hoping to find out. I'm going to one of his séances, or whatever he calls them, this weekend."

"I want to go with you. If it's him and he recognizes you, you'll never get out alive."

"It can't be him. He's dead."

"Then I'm going with you. I want to see for myself."

"No way. I'm not letting you put yourself in danger again."

"There's no danger if it can't be him."

"Maybe somehow it *can* be. A lot of things happened three years ago that I would've said were impossible. Besides, there *is* danger, even if he's somebody else using

238

Hector Chanfray's name. He's a crook and a drug dealer, probably even a killer. This is a police operation, and you shouldn't be part of it."

"I'm part of it already, because you asked me to be."

"I didn't ask you to be on the front line."

They both fell silent. Both angry. He thought it was weird that he had worried about her wanting out once she knew the whole truth, and instead knowing it had made her push to get in even deeper. And now he had to try to keep her out.

He said, "When I make my play, I'm going to have a hard time convincing him I really want to come over to his side. If you 're hanging on my arm, forget it. I might as well go in there waving a red flag."

"He's not going to recognize either one of us from three years ago if he's not Chango. And he can't be."

"I don't know about that," said Dawson. "And I'm not hinting at anything supernatural. Ordinary people sometimes get shot in the head and survive. About six years ago, I had a case where a young man and his girlfriend were taken hostage in a liquor-store robbery, and the robber plugged both of them in the back of the head. She died, but he lived. He managed to crawl out to the highway, and a motorist drove him to the hospital. Same hospital Chango and I were in, right here in Braxton Beach. The guy is still alive, still walking around, and he's damn near normal. The only lingering effect of the bullet in his brain is a little numbness in the side of his face. The human brain, even when it's damaged, is pretty adaptable. People have strokes and they're severely disabled, but little by little they recover when another part of the brain takes over for the part that can't function anymore."

"So," said Martha, "you think Chango could have been carried out of the intensive-care unit and nursed back to health?"

"I don't know what happened. But I think I have to try to find out."

Clint and Deronne Jones didn't bring up a thing about the case. This surprised Dawson at first, but then he realized what was afoot. The Joneses were resolved to devote all their energy to serving a marvelous meal and hosting a lovely, sociable evening. No unpleasant topics were to mar the occasion. Their goal was to help Dawson charm Martha. A large part of him appreciated this. He knew that a woman's path to falling in love with a man could be made smoother by his friends. No woman enjoyed the idea of falling for a loner – and everything was being done tonight to disguise the fact that for years a loner was exactly what Dawson had been. Wanting Martha made him ready to change, but his habits were so ingrained that he wondered if he could make the change anything but a veneer.

It was a pleasant September evening, not too cool and not too hot. Not too muggy, either. They had pre-dinner cocktails on the patio, in the orange glow of half a dozen tiki lanterns. Halfway across the yard, at the end of a long extension cable, there was the bluish glow of an electronic bug zapper. It kept zapping and fizzing, burning up lots of mosquitoes.

"You know," Dawson said, "that thing makes you think it's really efficient because it keeps killing bugs. But it also attracts all the bugs from your neighbors' yards, so it helps them more than it helps us. If you turned it off, we probably wouldn't be any worse off."

"I get a kick out of seeing the little bastards getting electrocuted," said Clint.

"All you cops dig capital punishment," said Deronne.

"Right on!" said Clint. "I wish we had a big zapper to use on our two-legged pests. How 'bout it, Vince?"

"I guess I'm glad it's not our job to exterminate them, just put them behind bars," he said. In front of Martha he knew that if he and Clint were alone he would have gotten a big horselaugh out of Clint's comment and would've heartily agreed with it.

"Mind helping me serve the meal?" Deronne said to Martha, and they both disappeared behind the sliding glass door.

Leaning confidentially toward Dawson, Clint lowered his voice and said, "I checked the whip, drum, and machete out of the evidence room. They were still there. But I don't want to take the chance that somebody might make them disappear, so I have them hidden in my garage. Don't wanna let Deronne know – those weapons killed her brother and sister-in-law. She'd go bananas if she knew they were on the premises. But you should know, in ease something happens to me."

"You want me to keep the stuff so you won't have to worry about having it around?"

"Naw, it's okay where it is. In my spare toolbox, under the workbench. Deronne never looks in there, and anyway it's locked. The key is on a little nail, under the far left corner of the bench, so you'll know where to look if you ever need to."

He hushed suddenly, as the sliding glass door came open. Deronne and Martha brought out a platter of roast beef, a bowl of mashed potatoes, hot homemade bread, and all the side dishes. Clint carved the pink, juicy roast while

Dawson got fresh drinks for everybody. It was exactly the kind of meal he liked to have when he was a guest at somebody's home, as opposed to eating in a restaurant, and he was glad that Deronne had remembered and had taken the trouble to please him. It wasn't fancy. It wasn't rich. It was just good plain home-cooked American food – the kind that a bachelor seldom had access to and never bothered to cook for himself.

They all dug in and ate heartily. At some point Clint turned off the bug zapper. At another point Clint and Deronne cuddled together on a chaise longue, and Martha sat beside Vince on a wicker sofa and held his hand. It was his good hand, not the useless one, so he didn't flinch when she touched it. The conversation, down through the nightcap of apple pie and coffee, was about movies and music and trivial pursuits, just as if there wasn't a wicked world out there waiting to claim their attention.

CHAPTER 21

On a Sunday afternoon, with butterflies in his stomach, Vince Dawson walked into the coffee shop of the Hotel Lamont in Fort Lauderdale and looked around for Henri Blanc. "He's a bald little guy as black as a coal mine," Ernie Bones had said the day before from a pay phone. "He'll be wearing a white suit and a pink carnation. It's his favorite getup. He looks like a flashy little harmless punk, but don't kid yourself, Dawson, he's anything but harmless. He'll put you on waivers as soon as look at you." Replayed in Dawson's mind, Bones's spiel sounded like bad dialogue from a B movie, adding to the unreality of being here in a hotel trying to make contact with a man who supposedly could put him in touch with another man who was supposed to be dead.

Bones had already "gone over" to the other side, first making contact with Blanc and using him to set up a meeting with Chanfray. Bones's pitch had been that he could now see that Sal the Strap was sinking fast, doomed to go under, so he wanted to jump ship while the jumping was good. To show Blanc and Chanfray he was on the level, he came across with inside info that enabled them to hijack some heavy dope shipments to a couple of Sal the Strap's crack houses in El Escoria. He also told them he could set them up with a Braxton Beach narc who was hot to latch on to some big cash under the table. He said he had been cultivating this turncoat cop for The Strap, but he could guarantee that the cop would just as soon have his

243

palms greased by someone who stood to be around after The Strap was pushing up daisies.

Failing to spot the man in the white suit and pink carnation, the turncoat cop sat at the counter, ordered a black coffee, and nervously took a couple of sips, burning his tongue. He was wearing a short-sleeved shirt, and his gimp arm, hanging limp and somewhat withered, was visible from the entrance, so it would help identify him to his contact. He wished he could buy a pack of cigarettes and light one up, but instead he told himself that if he could get through this case without taking a puff, he'd be able to stay off the habit after that, come hell or high water.

He got two more sips out of his coffee before Henri Blanc showed up, laid two dollars on top of the check, and said, "Let's go. The channeling session is about to begin, and Hector doesn't want you to miss any of it. You see, it is the best way for him to really get to know you, heart to heart, spirit to spirit."

This kind of talk increased Dawson's nervousness. He left his almost full cup of coffee on the counter and followed the little man in the white suit with the pink carnation through the lobby and into an elevator. They rode up to a conference room on the fourteenth floor. One of the double doors was closed and the other was open, but to get in you had to go through Ernie Bones, who was standing there with his arms folded across his chest, reminding Dawson of a blond, curly-headed gorilla in a powder-blue suit. The only way to get past him was to pay $500 cash to another big blond guy seated at a card table. A couple dozen people were lined up for the privilege. Dawson was amazed by the steep price tag, but there it was on a standee to the right of the card table: MEET HECTOR

CHANFRAY, CHANNEL FOR OSHUN, BABALU, AND OBATALLA. $500 ADMISSION.

"Hey," Dawson said to Henri Blanc, following him toward the door. "I hope you realize I'm not here to shell out."

"When you are with me, you don't have to," said Henri as Bones stood aside automatically and let them pass. Dawson and Bones acted as if they didn't know each other. It was best not to give anybody who didn't need to know the slightest glimmer of what might be going down. You never could tell what kind of prying eyes might be around, ready to make a big deal out of seeing an off-duty cop fraternizing with known or suspected criminals. The FBI, the Customs Service, or the state police might have some undercover guys here checking out Chanfray, and if so they probably wouldn't know Dawson from Adam. But he had a story ready anyhow, in case he was ever asked any embarrassing questions. He would say that he had come here to follow up a lead on a narcotics investigation, but the lead didn't go anywhere.

The conference room was pretty well packed. Dawson estimated about two hundred people, and at five hundred bucks a head the take would be $100,000. Not bad. Especially when you considered that this scam was being worked at least twice a month, moving from city to city. That added up to a yearly gross of better than $2,000,000. And other than the cost of renting a room, there wasn't much in the way of operating expenses and production costs. It didn't cost much to manufacture a ghost – or even two or three of them, as claimed on Chanfray's poster – and once he channeled them here they probably worked for free.

Dawson realized that he was using flippancy as a shield against his fear that maybe, just *maybe*, all this malarkey might turn out to be something more than malarkey.

Most of the paying customers were already seated on folding chairs, but quite a few were still milling around. "I will see you later," Blanc said in his French Creole accent. "Go and find a place to sit down." As he worked his way through the fringes of the crowd, heading toward the podium, people's eyes followed him. The ones who were still standing hustled to their seats, and a hush fell over all. Obviously they recognized the dapper little man in the white suit and pink carnation from past channeling sessions and knew that his entrance was a sign that the festivities were getting underway. Confirming this, Ernie Bones and the other blond gorilla came in and locked the double doors, then stood there as if to bar the way of anybody who took a notion to flee.

That notion crossed Dawson's mind, and he rejected it, but not with perfect ease. He'd be lying if he told himself he didn't feel a bit edgy as he took an aisle seat in the back of the room. Was Chango really going to step out here in a little while, reincarnated? Was The Strap right? Was the bokor somehow still alive and kicking? Even if somebody else was impersonating him and wanted to *be* like him, that idea alone was enough to send chills up a spine.

Behind the podium, Henri Blanc turned the microphone on and got a boom of loud mewling feedback. But after that the P.A. system worked fine. Tape-recorded voodoo music underscored Blanc's low-pitched melodious accent as he welcomed everyone to the session and told them they were about to witness the calling forth of the ancient voodoo gods Oshun, Babalu, and Obatalla. These gods were more venerable than any other gods known or worshipped by any religion. They were with mankind, ruling over him, when the first creatures that could be called human were born in the heart of Africa many eons ago. They knew all the secrets of the ages. All power and knowledge and wisdom resided within them. Blanc said, "Oshun is the god of love and money. If he favors you, he can ensure that you will marry well and that you will be rich in spirit and in material goods. If you displease him, you will live and die in poverty.

"Babalu is the god who can guarantee that you will be sensuous and fertile. He is capable of curing abdominal afflictions and cancer. But if angered he can cause leprosy, gangrene, and heart failure.

"Obatalla, the father of Babalu, is the god of hysterics. If his curse falls on you, you will be blind or paralyzed or deformed. But if he blesses you, you will gain wisdom, energy, and purity."

"Hector Chanfray, the greatest of the houngans, is the channel for Oshun, Babalu, and Obatalla. And for you he is ready to summon them so that the veil of the centuries will be washed away and they will speak to you here and now, mind to mind, heart to heart, spirit to spirit, conferring upon you all that they have learned through the murky eons of man's time on earth, thereby enriching all your daily affairs and giving you ready access to wealth and happiness."

"Ladies and gentlemen, here is the man through whom the true and ancient gods impart their wisdom! Here is their channel, their earthly voice! Here is the venerable Hector Chanfray!"

All the people leapt to their feet in a standing ovation as a side door opened and Chanfray walked briskly to the podium. Henri Blanc retreated to a seat in the front row. Smiling, wearing a black silk jumpsuit, Chanfray basked in the outpouring of admiration and awe and even love that came from his true believers. In his hand was a cordless microphone, but the way that he held it up and waved it around majestically, it could have been a scepter.

He raised both his arms and clasped his hands together in a prayerlike attitude, the mike pressed between his palms. The room fell incredibly, instantly silent. There was a sense that all the people were waiting for golden words, enchanting god-like melodies, to flutter forth from Chanfray's lips.

Dawson's stomach was queasy and his forehead was beaded with sweat. His eyes were riveted on Chanfray. Seven feet tall and built like a Russian weightlifter, the Hector Chanfray standing behind the podium looked exactly like the one that Dawson had fought to the death three years ago. His head was shaved bald; gone was the tangle of black braids with dangling voodoo emblems. But all his other features were the same. He had the same broad nose and flaring nostrils, the same wide lips and flashing white teeth, the same burning black eyes. The same serpent tattoos on his cheeks. But there was no sign of a scar on the side of his head. No indentation. No evidence that the shaven head had ever been shattered or even creased by a bullet.

Plastic surgery, Dawson said to himself, groping for an explanation. But wait – what the hell was he giving in to? Was he allowing his own thoughts, his perceptions, his common sense, to be usurped by primitive superstition? Was he at bottom no better than some savage hiding under a rainy bush, cowering from ignorant terror of the "gods" of thunder and lightning? If there was no evidence of a gunshot wound to the head, didn't that prove this guy *wasn't* Chango? And shouldn't Dawson just accept that proof with a sigh of relief? Why try to think of ways to convince himself that his nightmares had come to life – or had always *been* alive because the creature that inhabited them was refusing to stay dead?

Feeling a pair of eyes boring into his skull, Dawson turned around and saw that he was being stared at by Ernie Bones, who was still guarding the door. Their gazes interlocked with such force there could almost have been a discharge of static electricity. *See*? Bones seemed to say telepathically. *Don't you see now that I was right? And what are you going to do about it, Dawson? Are you going to stay and keep your end of the bargain, even though your bowels are turning to water? Or are you going to cut and run?* Not wanting to answer the silent question, Dawson turned back around. He told himself to be calm. And he fished a handkerchief out of his pocket and mopped his face.

Chanfray still hadn't uttered a word. And the rest of the people in the room were still so unbelievably quiet that a sleeping baby would have made more noise. They all seemed hypnotized by the soft but insistently throbbing rhythms of the tape-recorded voodoo music. So mundane, Dawson told himself. A drab conference room in an ordinary hotel. Not even a live voodoo band, just a tape recorder jacked into a P.A. system. Tacky and mundane. So mundane that no miracles, no magic, no sorcery could be about to happen here. But then, the Mount of Olives was an ordinary, mundane place, too. Till Jesus Christ preached a sermon there blessing the meek and the humble and feeding thousands of people on five fishes and two loaves of bread.

Suddenly the music got louder, and Chanfray began to chant, swinging his head from side to side. It was the weirdest, eeriest sound imaginable – it sounded Creole or

African or . . . or Dawson didn't know what. It didn't seem like human vocal cords could make noises like that.

Then Dawson saw something he didn't notice before, and it took his breath away. The necklace. Chanfray was wearing a leather thong and pouch that previously had been indiscernible against the shiny black silk of his jumpsuit. Now it was clearly visible, dangling and twirling as he chanted and swung his head back and forth, back and forth. What the hell was in the pouch? Dear God, don't let it be a child's finger! But Dawson had no way of knowing. And the uncertainty was almost as bad as knowing the worst. He and Clint Jones had forgotten about the pouch. They had talked about the drum, the whip, and the machete, but had left the pouch out of their discussions. Maybe it had always been around Chango's neck, even as he was being taken to the hospital.

Chanfray's eerie chant stopped suddenly, as if it had been cut off with a knife. He fell to the floor as if both his legs had been chopped out from under him at the same time. The audience gasped. Chanfray did not get up. The voodoo music continued to wail. Dawson couldn't see over people's heads, but the ones in front were staring toward the floor, giving the impression that Chanfray must be conked out up there, in some kind of trance.

The audience emitted a murmur of pleasure and approval.

Chango pulled himself to his feet. But he was leaning sideways, as if crippled. And then he began to walk in circles, around and around the podium, hobbling as if he was on a crutch.

Henri Blanc stepped up behind the podium. Leaning into a mike, he said, "Papa Legba! See the crutch! Papa

Legba is here, smoothing the path through the spirit world for Oshun, Babalu, and Obatalla!"

Dawson remembered that Martha Lewis had told him that Papa Legba was the patron of all magic. Without his presence no other spirits could be summoned, no other magic could take place.

Blanc sat back down. Chanfray hobbled back and forth across the front of the audience, "possessed" for a time by Papa Legba. Then his whole body rejuvenated in a burst of energy, and he stood tall, tossing away his crutch. Dawson could almost see the thing flying through the air and crashing against the far wall, even though it was only an imaginary object. Chanfray's acting was so superb, his every gesture imbued with such verve and passion, that even a skeptic could be turned into a convert.

Or *was* it acting?

Did the man truly believe in himself?

He picked up the cordless mike, which had been dropped while he was "crippled." In a rich, booming, bass voice he announced, "We are here! We extend our greetings across the centuries! Three gods in one person! Three holy loas! Oshun, Babalu, and Obatalla now reside in the earthly body and the eternal spirit of Hector Chanfray!"

Once having announced this, he became quite "normal." He started sauntering down the rows and between the aisles, having a good time saying hello to all the people. After some general prattle about the weather and how nice it was being in the twentieth century, he started singling out people to talk to. He laughed and chatted almost like a regular person, which was all the more unnerving and awe-inspiring because of his special charisma. He exuded raw power. Despite the ordinariness of his conversation, he had such a strong animal magnetism that somehow it didn't seem entirely farfetched that three primitive gods resided within this seven-foot giant with coiled serpents tattooed on his cheeks.

Abruptly his tone became more serious as he took a young woman by the hand, pulling her to her feet, turning her to face the audience. The first thing Dawson noticed was her amazing beauty, apparent despite her shawl and dark glasses. Then he realized that he had seen her before – on television. She was Helene Price, star of a wildly popular crime show filmed in Miami. A murmur of celebrity fever rippled through the room. Yet it was clear that among this crowd a TV personality didn't carry as much weight as Oshun, Babalu, and Obatalla. Now all three were to speak to Helene with one voice issuing from one earthly presence.

Standing close to her and putting his arm around her, Chanfray held the mike so they both would be picked up by it. He said, "Helene, we know that you have come to see us about a special concern, a special problem. Tell us, how may we be of help to you?"

Suddenly the beautiful lady's face crumbled, and she was in tears. Sobbing violently, she said, "You have helped me so much already! You've given me a marvelously successful career. . .But I'd give up all that I have if my father could get his health back. He has prostate cancer. . . the doctors say he only has six months to live."

Cuddling her and stroking her shoulder, Chanfray said, "There is no need to give up what we have already bestowed upon you. Go to your father's house. Give him a necklace of white beads, paying homage to Babalu. In his front yard, kill and bury a white pigeon. And in each room put a glass of seawater with seven pennies in each glass. Your father will get well bye and bye."

"Oh, thank you! Thank you!" Helene wailed. She kissed Chanfray on one of his serpented cheeks. Then she sank back down onto her chair, her shoulders slumped in humility and anguish tinged with hope.

About fifteen rows in front of Dawson, a short obese man shot to his feet, gave a gurgling scream, and hit the floor like a ton of bricks. Nobody rushed to his aid. He writhed and gurgled on the floor, clutching his throat. Dawson got halfway up, mentally rehearsing the steps of the Heimlich maneuver. But Chanfray raised a hand, signaling Dawson to stay put. Even though he really believed the fat man was choking to death or perhaps having a heart attack, Dawson obediently sat back down, amazed that someone could make him be so docile, and wondering if perhaps a large part of him yearned to be told to relax and let someone else take over, instead of always having to be brave and decisive in crisis situations.

Chanfray stood over the fat man, watching him clawing at his throat in a convulsive fit. With utter calm, Chanfray said, "In a previous lifetime, five hundred years ago, you were a serf in the fiefdom of a feudal lord. He was cruel and he punished you for a minor infraction by cutting your tongue out. Ever since then, in all your reincarnations, you have been a meek and timid soul, afraid to speak up for your rights, and clothing your body in folds of fat to hide its natural beauty. You must learn to be bolder, to stand up and tell others what you really think. Your ideas are good, but you have a bad habit of keeping them to yourself. That is why you are gagging. You are choking on your own stifled wisdom. Open up your mind. Find your true voice. And at last, in this lifetime and all future lifetimes, you will be free."

Even before Chanfray's spiel was over, the fat man quit spluttering and rolling on the floor. A beatific look on his face, tears streaming down his pudgy, rosy cheeks, he got to his knees. He reached out to touch Chanfray, but his shaky finger touched only air. Chanfray was already gone. He was striding down the aisle toward Dawson, the leather necklace and thong bobbing against his massive chest.

Dawson fought the irrational urge to get up and head for the exit. He had to act calm and collected if he was going to get in good with Chanfray and try to get to the bottom of this. He couldn't charge the door like some jerk pretending he had to all of a sudden go to the men's room. Anyway, Ernie Bones probably wouldn't let him out. It wouldn't look good for Bones if he seemed too accommodating to a turncoat cop turned chicken.

All this nonsense tumbled through Dawson's mind in the few seconds it took Chanfray to stride down the aisle and take him by the hand. His gimp hand. If the nerves were still working, a shudder would've run from his fingers to the brain. But he managed to control himself and stand on rubbery knees.

Gazing deeply into his eyes, Chanfray said, "You are afraid of us. Do not fear the presence of the ancient loas. Oshun, Babalu, and Obatalla wish you no harm, as long as you earnestly wish to revere and honor us. Only false worshipers feel our wrath. Only they must live in mortal terror."

Dawson couldn't really think straight. In the kaleidoscope of his fears and anxieties, one clear thought shimmered and faded, shimmered and faded: If Chanfray was ripe to buy into him as a turncoat cop, why was he putting him in needless jeopardy by calling undue attention to him and possibly blowing his cover? Was that sort of petty concern far beneath the channel and the gods that he summoned to protect himself and those who would do his bidding?

Chanfray said, "We can see that words fail you in our presence. We are here to tell you that we know you have sinned against us in the past. You have been our enemy. But your sins are forgiven. As long as you now swear your allegiance."

"I swear," said Dawson. His voice was barely audible. His throat was dry as sand. He wasn't sure how many levels of meaning could be read into Chanfray's words. Were the loas forgiving him for his misspent days of being an honest cop? Or were they also forgiving him for trying to kill Chango three years ago?

"We will make a new beginning," Chanfray said with an enigmatic smile. "Obatalla will give you a sign that this is so. Our intentions where you are concerned will be kind and benevolent. Your damaged arm will be healed, providing you do as we say. Praying to Obatalla and pledging to worship him forever, you must kill and drink the blood of a red rooster. Do this tonight, in the light of the quarter moon. Then wear a bracelet of red and white beads on the wasted arm. Wear it for one month, burning incense and red and white candles in your bedroom at night. You will see the strength of the damaged limb improve gradually day by day, until at last it will be made whole."

Dawson was so choked up he couldn't talk. His legs were so weak that Chanfray had to put an arm around his waist to hold him up. He hoped that Ernie Bones wasn't seeing him go to pieces. But he knew that Bones was.

Then Chanfray pulled Dawson's useless claw of a hand toward the pouch. The pouch dangling on the leather necklace. Dawson recoiled inwardly, all his synapses overloaded with horror and revulsion. He was thoroughly convinced now that the pouch contained a child's shriveled finger. But he was powerless to make his withered arm pull his hand back. Chanfray opened the nerve-dead fingers, then closed them, folding them around the pouch.

He said, "By this mojo, this holy charm, the cure is begun. It is up to you to ensure its efficiency by performing the rituals and sacrifices we have described. Oshun, Babalu, and Obatalla have befriended you anew and have conferred upon you their eternal wisdom."

Chanfray's fierce black eyes burned into Dawson's brain, almost making him think – and even wish – that the ugly little ceremony would somehow succeed where modern medicine had failed.

CHAPTER 22

Martha was in bed when the phone rang at two o'clock in the morning, jolting her out of a fitful sleep. She sat up, half woozy and half scared. More bad news? Dawson? The two thoughts crossed each other like a short circuit, zapping her. All through her waking hours on Sunday he had been on her mind. She didn't know where he was, and since he had played it cagey, saying merely that he wouldn't be seeing her, she was sure he was in danger, out somewhere working on his case, meeting . . .

She tried to break the thought off before the name of the person Vince was supposed to meet even entered her mind, but of course she was unsuccessful. The phone rang two more times. She knew Susan wouldn't answer it, even if Susan was awake, lying in her own bed, listening to the rings. Martha's daughter was even more afraid of bad news than Martha was. And sometimes it seemed that was all they had had for the past three years.

Martha plucked up the receiver, said hello, and held her breath. Nothing on the other end of the line. Not even a dial tone. "Hello!" she cried frantically. Then she heard the heavy breathing, and almost slammed the receiver down. But just in time, the slurred voice stopped her.

"It's me."

"Vince?"

"Uh . . .yeah . . .I have to talk to you. Please . . .can you come over?"

"Are you okay? You sound . . ."

"I know. I've been drinking. I'm sorry."

"You're a grown man. You're entitled to tie one on now and then," she said, managing a mild chuckle.

There was a long pause before he spoke again.

"Please . . . will you come over?"

"Is it about the case?"

"Yes and no. It's about the case, but it's also about me, Martha. I. . .uh. . .know I shouldn't be waking you at this hour . . .but . . ."

She heard the desperation, even through his slurred words. And it panicked her. But she tried not to show the panic. He gave her directions, and she didn't even mention that she had an eight o'clock class to teach Monday morning. She said she'd be at his place in about twenty minutes.

She left a note for Susan before she went out the door, shutting it softly, knowing that Susan would panic if she heard her leaving. Susan was already even more on edge than usual, because Barry was flying into Braxton Beach tomorrow for his first annual vacation visitation with Clara. He'd be around for a week, showing up each morning to take his daughter to the zoo or the beach or wherever. Susan dreaded the confrontations. In a lot of ways she was still under her ex-husband's spell. With merely a disdainful look, a hard probing stare, he could bring back all her old insecurities, making her feel like a miserable failure, as if the collapse of her marriage and everything that led up to it was purely her own fault.

As Martha pulled up to the curb, she thought she saw something moving in the muted neon burglar lights of Enrico's Pizzeria. Could it have been a dog? She had only caught a glimpse of it going around the side of the building.

Suddenly a rooster darted at her, squawking like crazy. She jumped back, letting out an angry, startled gasp. Beak and talons pecking and clawing, the rooster got her on the legs a bunch of times, and it hurt even though she was wearing jeans. She kicked hard and managed to connect. The rooster squawked and scrabbled and flapped, its combed head jerking spastically as it ran along the sidewalk. It stopped twenty feet down the street and turned around, ready to attack again. But Martha wasn't about to stick around.

She scampered quickly up the metal stairs to Dawson's apartment, holding on to the railing so she wouldn't fall. She noticed that the gate to the little yard behind the pizzeria was open, and figured there must be a chicken coop back there from which the rooster had escaped.

She rang the bell, and Dawson yelled, "Come in!" To her it didn't seem smart that he was working on a dangerous case and would still leave his door unlocked in the wee hours of the morning. Letting herself in, she opened her mouth to tell him about it, but then she froze.

From the darkened kitchen she saw him sitting in the living room, surrounded by glowing red and white candles. The whole place was smoky and smelled of incense. "Here's to Oshun, Babalu, and Obatalla," he said slurringly, giving her a sly, lopsided grin and tossing down whiskey from a big water glass. "Hair of the dog," he explained. "That's all I'm gonna have, I promise, 'cause that's all there is, there ain't no more."

"Do you do this sort of thing often?" she asked, hurt and angry and trying not to show it.

"Yep. 'Fraid so."

"Is that why you wanted me to come over here at this hour? So I could see you at your worst, get a good dose of it and see if I can take it?"

"Maybe you should. . .before you make the mistake of getting too heavily involved."

She almost asked him what made him think she was even considering making such a mistake. But she held the question. She could always ask it when he was sober. Briskly she stepped into the tiny living room, turned on a battered old floor lamp, and went around snuffing the candles, blowing them out or licking her fingers and squeezing the wicks. Twice she got burnt with hot wax. The candles were everywhere, at least two dozen of them dripping globs of wax onto the coffee table, the bookcase, the top of the TV.

She took the ashtray containing the burning incense into the kitchen and ran tap water on it. When she was sure it wouldn't start a fire, she dropped it into the garbage pail, on top of the empty bottle of whiskey.

She sat down beside Dawson, sinking into the faded red sofa. He didn't look directly at her. Through the smoky haze, she studied him. He leaned forward and tried to pick something up from the coffee table. It was stuck in a glob of hardening wax, and he had to grab at it twice to free it. "Didn't go through with it," he said, holding it up – a red and white bead bracelet. "You're the expert. That's partly why I called you. It wouldn't work anyway, right? No. You don't have to even tell me. I know the answer. At least, I think so. But I almost want to believe otherwise."

"What wouldn't have worked?" she asked him. But she already thought she knew. And it gave her a chill. Dawson was surrounded by the trappings of voodoo. And she knew from her anthropological studies that even the intelligent were susceptible.

She let him talk. A distant look in his eyes, he told her everything about the channeling session, down to the

260

moment when Chanfray had made him hold the leather pouch as if it were a holy relic. "Something snapped inside of me. I knew it was bullshit, but it made me clutch at a straw, I guess. It kept preying on my mind, and I kept drinking. I want you to know that up to today I'd been pretty straight, but then. . .the whole thing at the hotel knocked me for a loop and I couldn't handle it."

"It's understandable," Martha said. She reached out and took his hand, which was moist and hot, and she thought she felt a slight tremor in it.

"I don't know what got into me. I started acting like a whacko. The only excuse is by then I was bombed out of my mind. I don't even remember buying the damn rooster. I came home with it in the back of the car, squawking its fool head off and shitting all over the upholstery."

She laughed, and he gave her an angry look – but then he saw the humor in it and burst out laughing too. "I had a shopping bag full of candles," he said, shaking his head, "and this goddamn chintzy bracelet. Oh, and incense – let's not forget the incense. I had a hell of a time chasing the rooster around and getting it by the neck. I only had one good arm to work with, and I got pecked and scratched so much I think I wanted the arm to get better first so I could kill the rooster. Finally I got it all trussed up with a ball of twine, and I was gonna slit its throat in the bathtub. I even had my whiskey glass there for drinking the blood. But I couldn't go through with it. Somehow I came to my senses, took the damn rooster out to the yard, and used the knife to cut it loose from the twine. It damn near pecked my eyes out for good measure before it went screeching and flapping away like a bat outta hell."

"You didn't close the gate right," Martha said with a wry grin. "It got loose and attacked me a while ago when I pulled up and parked."

"Oh, gee, I'm sorry. Don't be too mad at me," said Dawson, giving her hand a tender, pleading squeeze.

"Are you kidding? I don't have any room for anger right now. I'm just thankful you're okay."

"I'm not. My head hurts. I must be sobering up."

Martha nodded in agreement. She had already noticed his words weren't so slurred. Reliving his meeting with Chanfray had burnt the alcohol out of his brain cells, and the void was about to be filled with a massive hangover.

"Black coffee?" she asked. "Can I make it for you?"

"Mr. Coffee machine . . . in the kitchen. All the stuff is on the shelf right above."

She made up her mind to stay with him, which meant she'd have to call in sick in the morning. The students wouldn't mind if her eight-o'clock class was canceled, but the college administrators would. Their attitude would be that if she was going to get sick or something, she had had all weekend to figure it out in time for them to hire a substitute teacher. In the morning, she'd also have to call Susan. She hoped that a seven-in-the-morning phone call from a forty-six-year-old grandmother who was supposed to be in her room asleep, instead of out cavorting all night, wouldn't utterly blow Susan's mind.

***

The air conditioner cleared the smoke out of the living room, so that part was okay. But the treacly strong smell of the incense persisted beyond all reason. And it was tough to get comfortable on the saggy couch. She ended up crawling into bed next to Dawson. He slept like a lump for the most part, except once when he woke her, moaning, having some kind of nightmare. She told herself that in the morning she would try to let him forget it completely instead of asking for the gory details.

She probably slept for about two a half and of the four hours that she lay there. But once she made the phone calls to the college and to Susan – who look it, surprisingly, rather cheerfully – she promptly conked out and slept for three more hours. Dawson was still snoring when she crawled out of bed.

Taking a shower was uppermost in her mind, but when she slid open the plastic curtain she got a shocking verification of his story about the rooster. The bathtub was splotched and streaked with mud – or worse. Also blood and feathers. Since the rooster's throat hadn't been slit in the end, the blood must've been Dawson's, from being pecked and scratched.

Martha got cleanser from under the sink and started with the tub and shower stall. Then she did the sink. And once she got going, there was no stopping her. Normally she was not enamored of housework, but this morning she kept on dusting, vacuuming, scrubbing, and scouring. It took her only a couple of hours to do the entire apartment – anyway, it was only three tiny rooms. She got a great deal of pleasure out of making it look and smell good for him. For herself, too. For she was turning it into a suitable love nest. Or at least acceptable.

He awoke to the smell of coffee and eggs, toast and bacon. When he saw how the apartment looked, he was so amazed that he kissed her. His breath was lousy, but she knew it would be and didn't let it bother her. They ate first, then they brushed their teeth and showered together. By that time, they were more than ready, and it was easy to make love. It wasn't the best that it could ever be, for they didn't know each other's bodies, each other's needs, well enough yet. But they were making a good start. And for the time being it was fine. And with practice it would get better. And better.

Afterward he said, "You acted like it didn't bother you."

"It didn't," she said, knowing that he meant his injured arm. To prove the point, she leaned over, took the hand at the end of the arm in question, and gave it a nice kiss.

For a long moment he was silent, just looking at her, thinking. Then he smiled. She kissed him and stroked his cheek, his forehead, his brown, thinning hair.

He said, "You know, I didn't get laid all the time I spent in the hospital. Nurses are supposed to be easy lays, not anthropologists."

"They both should be," she said. "They both know a lot about human needs and functions, physical and emotional."

"I was just joking, of course. Being too damn flippant, probably. It's my nature. I'm glad you didn't take it the wrong way."

"Uh-uh. But I'm not an easy lay, just so you keep your facts straight. There've only been a few, besides my husband. None during him and only one, besides you, after him."

"Albert Scanlon?"

"Yes, since you're so nosy. But the last time with him was about a year ago. I've been celibate since then . . . and I don't even fully understand why."

"I'm not going to tell you I was celibate," he said. "But the ones I was with didn't mean much to me, and I guess I didn't mean much to them. And there weren't many of them, either."

They kissed and cuddled for a while. Then they got in another round of practice. Martha was amazed at the zest and endurance they were bringing to it. Two middle-aged people acting like teenagers. Horny teenagers. Doing it in his small, modest apartment was almost like doing it in a motel. It was if Susan was the stay-at-home parent and Martha was the gallivanting youth, having to find a place to have sex away from the parent's disapproval. She didn't really know to what extent Susan would disapprove, if Susan knew, but the fact that Susan might think that way made the act deliciously naughty and almost adolescently wild.

Then they rested for a longer time than before. And Vince became more troubled, more anxious to talk and to have her listen. She was patient and obliging. He started telling her what went on at the hotel after Chanfray/Obatalla gave him the voodoo prescription for his damaged arm . . .

The rest of the channeling session had gone by in a blur. Somehow Dawson became aware that the music had ended, jarring him out of some kind of crazy mental jumble that he couldn't even begin to describe. He looked up and saw Hector Chanfray's black jumpsuit disappearing through the side door. Henri Blanc was at the podium again, thanking all of the people for attending, on behalf of Oshun, Babalu, and Obatalla. "Those of you who were physically touched by the loas today, please stay. All the rest of you are dismissed."

With a shock, it dawned on Dawson that having been singled out before, now he was to be part of a select group. He wanted to go home. Or to a bar. He needed a drink more badly than he had ever needed one. But his mission obligated him to stay.

In a surprisingly short time the conference room emptied, and Henri Blanc led the "special ones" through the side door where Chanfray had gone. Ernie Bones and the other blond gorilla followed. The side door led to a long hallway in the hotel, a corridor of guest rooms where one wouldn't expect guest rooms to be. Henri Blanc unlocked the door to one of these rooms and beckoned everyone inside, and they found themselves in the plush living room of an elegant suite, obviously high-priced and, like the others in the corridor, reserved for very special, very rich customers.

Blanc said, "Relax, everyone. Help yourselves to cocktails and hors d'ouevres." He pivoted and went into another room, closing the door behind him.

Bones and the other gorilla went behind the palette-shaped glass-topped bar and did the honors for themselves. Then they started doing the honors for everyone else. Dawson tried to hold back, but his mouth watered when he saw the beautiful actress Helene Price being handed a very dry, very large vodka martini. He decided to have one to steady his nerves. Bones flashed a wry twisted leer as he served up the cold, wet tumbler full of hundred-proof Stolichnaya diluted just a bit with ice cubes and vermouth.

Dawson went and sat by himself and gulped it. It went straight to his head, which was where he wanted it. He was desperate for something to help him relax.

There were about a dozen and a half people in the suite, and the only one who wasn't drinking or eating was the chubby young fellow who had thrown a fit on the floor of the conference room, gagging and clutching his throat. He seemed to be taking his first steps toward a leaner, more self-confident self, because in addition to abstaining from calories he kept smiling insipidly at everyone. At one point, still smiling, he took out a leather check portfolio and a ballpoint pen, and scribbled. His eyes gleamed with generosity as he eyed the numbers he had written, ripped the check out, folded it, and held it in his hand. Later, after he was ushered in to a private audience with Chanfray, he didn't have the check anymore.

That seemed to be the pattern. It wasn't always checks, though. Sometimes it was stock certificates or deeds to various kinds of property. Dawson knew this because some of the true believers were given to boasting, trying to impress each other with how much they were willing to sacrifice for Oshun, Babalu, Obatalla. He overheard one fellow saying that he had inherited a stable of racehorses that he had immediately turned over to Chanfray. A peroxided over-the-hill-hippie-type chick said something about a seat on the board of directors of a computer company that she allowed the spirit channel to hold for her, along with her proxy and power of attorney. And a little gray-haired man with an air of degenerate wealth about him hinted that his will would provide seven-figure clout for the loas.

One by one, the special guests were led in for their private audience with Hector Chanfray, and afterward they left the suite without being told to do so. Apparently they understood that this was the protocol.

Dawson's turn didn't come till last. By that time, he had slurped up two more Stolichnaya martinis, each one tasting better than the one before. Helene Price's turn had been just ahead of his, and she had stayed in the room with Chanfray for quite a long time. It was the master bedroom of the suite, and the smell of sex was obvious when Dawson entered. Chanfray didn't mind that he knew, either. In fact, the man was smiling smugly, and they both knew what the smile meant. It couldn't have been clearer if he had gotten up and given the rumpled bed a satisfied pat. Instead he made a gesture for Dawson to sit on the edge of it, while he sat in a big leather chair. There were two other chairs, but they were occupied by Henri Blanc and a much bigger black man, both of them busy counting money from a strongbox and putting it into a hotel safe.

Dawson wondered how Chanfray had convinced the actress to screw him with two of his men present. Perhaps he exerted such control over her mind that he was able to prevent their presence from registering. Or perhaps two lookers-on didn't mean much when you were already doing it with three loas at the same time.

Although the bed was rumpled and otherwise defiled, Chanfray's personal grooming was intact. The black silk jumpsuit didn't show any wrinkles or stains. He was still wearing the leather necklace. His feet were bare, though, and with a jolt Dawson saw that they bore the same tattoos, or at least similar ones, that he remembered being on the feet of Chango. Too bad the fingerprints and the police file photos were gone; it would have been nice to do a comparison.

"Of course I know who you are," Chanfray said bemusedly. "I remember you from three years ago."

Dawson's skin went prickly and chills shot up his spine. He didn't trust himself to pipe up with any sort of denial.

"You and your friends killed my brother," said Chanfray. "I was in Haiti at the time, but naturally I read about the episode in the newspapers. The authorities kept printing stories about it for more than a year afterward. And even now there is still considerable coverage, considerable rehashing. There is a strong need in some people to prove beyond a shadow of a doubt that Chango is dead. When of course he isn't. And can never be."

"What. . .what do you mean?" Dawson managed. He wished he hadn't killed the dregs of his martini just when it came his turn for a private audience.

"My twin is dead. But I am not dead. And I am the true Chango. He was merely the usurper who stole my name. Chango is the lord of the loas. That is why I am able to be the channel for Oshun, Babalu, and Obatalla. I can call forth any loa that I wish. But those three are the ones who can do the people the most good. They are able to provide material and spiritual wealth, and that is what my followers are most interest in."

Dawson said nothing. His mind went groping, trying to digest all this and make some kind of sense out of it.

Chanfray flashed his bemused smile. "You are afraid of me. And you do not fully trust me. But I am sure we can do business together. I do not blame you for what you did to my brother. In fact, I respect and praise you for it. It was precisely what I ought to have done myself."

Encouraged by those unexpected sentiments, Dawson said, "You say your brother is dead. I think so, too, but I have no real proof. Only my memories, my impressions, of what happened in the cemetery, when I was under extreme duress or unconscious, half dead myself. I don't know anymore if my recollections are real or unreal."

Chanfray didn't speak right away. He mulled Dawson's statement over for a long time. Then he said, "I can tell you for certain that Victor is dead but the only proof I can give you is what you already held in your hand." So saying, he took off the leather necklace, opened the pouch, and shook the severed finger out into his hand. He held it toward Dawson. "If Victor were alive, he would never part with this. The fact that I took it from him means that he is dead. I cannot tell you any more than that. But you have my word it is true."

Was he indicating that he had killed his own brother? Dawson decided to press farther and get all the cards out on the table at once. "Some say you are the one who was shot in the cemetery. You are Chango, the only Chango. And somehow you walked out of the hospital with a bullet hole in your head."

Chanfray laughed delightedly, deliciously, a deep resonant baritone laugh. "The killer of three years ago was not the true Chango, Hector Chanfray, but was my brother Victor. All my life I suffered blame for his crimes, his sacrilegious devouring of human flesh. Many times the Tontons Macoutes came after me, calling me loup-garou, ready to chop me up instead of him. We were twins. In vodoun – what you ignorant Yankees call voodoo – everything that happens has a dual significance – that of the real event, and that of the symbolic meaning that underlies reality. Therefore, identical twins are especially revered, since they are regarded not simply as two children born at the same time but as the physical expression of man's dual nature, half human and half divine. In fact, so indivisibly are they thought of as two parts of a single soul that every effort is made to arrange for all their important activities, such as baptism, confirmation, marriage, and all the rituals and sacraments, both Catholic and pagan, to take place simultaneously. So it came to pass in the natural order of things that Victor and I experienced everything together. We were both initiated as hunsis, spiritual apprentices, on the same day, in the same hour. We both took the name of Chango, the most powerful of the loas. But like Eve in the Garden of Eden, Victor was perverted by the Devil. I

270

became a houngan, a good priest, serving mankind; but my twin became a bokor, a dark and evil sorcerer. A murderer and cannibal, the scourge of innocent men, women, and children. Now I can forgive and even thank you for your part in killing Victor, because as a result all his powers reside within me, and I am more superb, more holy and invincible than I ever was before. And furthermore, Victor is not really dead, not in the truest, deepest sense. No longer fighting me, no longer adultering or usurping my spirituality, he lives on in me, you see – he and I are immortal."

"That gives me the shivers!" said Martha.

"It wasn't the best news I ever got either," said Dawson. "I had a notion of asking him how, if he wasn't the scourge of good innocent folks, like his brother was, how he could traffic in narcotics. But I figured I'd better not press my luck. So far he hasn't admitted anything like that to me. We're still feeling each other out. And who knows? Maybe Bones and The Strap aren't giving it to us straight. Or maybe they can't know the whole truth about Chanfray. Maybe his only scam is the spirit-channeling thing."

"Is there any way to find out if he really had a twin brother?" asked Martha.

"I don't know. We can try to check with the authorities in Haiti. But things are pretty much in a scramble there, right? I mean, the government, the whole bureaucracy is a shambles. And they were never known for being competent and professional and keeping scrupulous records – fingerprints, birth certificates, and so on – even in the best of times."

"I can tell you I never heard or read of Chango having a twin brother when I was down there," said Martha. "Did

Chanfray say that his having a twin was common knowledge?"

"No, he said his mother gave birth alone, out in the jungle. She never told anyone she had twins. She just gave the two babies over to the houngan who was their mentor. As they matured, they both led reclusive lives. Each had separate small groups of followers, and myths and legends grew around the two of them, sometimes confusing their exploits, whether good or bad, even adding to their reputation for magic as far as the peasants were concerned, because they seemed able to be in two places at once."

"The *ti-bon-ange* and the *gros-bon-ange*," Martha murmured.

"The what?" said Dawson. "Come on, clue me in, shed some light on the subject. I wanted you here for your anthropological expertise, not your expertise in the sack, lady."

Playfully punching him on his good arm, she said, "Chango was talking about the vodoun belief that each human soul is conceived in the form of two spirits, the ti-bon-ange and the gros-bon-ange, the 'little good angel' and the 'big good angel.' One is sort of like a conscience, and the other is the sum of an individual's personality, intellect, and worldly experience. Usually they complement each other, they behave harmoniously, making one complete person. But sometimes they war with each other, wreaking havoc and spiritual misery."

"Sounds like a rip-roaring good time," said Dawson.

Ignoring him, Martha said, "Sometimes when twins are born, neither one is spiritually complete. In effect, one gets the ti-bon-ange and the other gets the gros-bon-ange. Their hatred for each other is all-consuming, and even though they may be genetically identical, they become opposites in all other important respects. Neither can be complete and at peace until one of them is killed. Then the ti-bon-ange joins the gros-bon-ange, creating a powerful single harmonious entity."

"Shit!" said Dawson. "Are you telling me we've put ourselves in double jeopardy?"

His wisecrack was intended to relieve the tension that he and Martha both felt. But neither one of them laughed.

PART FOUR

LIVING THINGS

It may be that our role on this planet is not to worship God
but to create him.

— Arthur C. Clarke

Really we create nothing. We merely plagiarize nature.

— Jean Baitaillon

CHAPTER 23

Bones was riding in the cockpit of the helicopter with Dennis Lapidus, the pilot who had flown the chopper that gunned down Bones's men the night of the raid at the Root Doctor's place. This wasn't that chopper, which had been a combat chopper. This one was lighter and sleeker, red instead of black, a gay little machine for transporting civilians in style and comfort. But it made Bones feel weird, frolicking through the clouds with the man who had once tried to machine-gun him. Funny thing was, other than that, Bones liked Dennis and hoped they'd eventually become real pals. They looked almost like brothers anyhow, both big and burly and blond. If they each dumped twenty pounds and ten years, they'd be real diggers and bone-busters on the hockey rink. Except Dennis wasn't a skater. Raised down here, he grew up on a surfboard instead. Used to be pretty good at it, he claimed, but now he had a big gut like Bones.

Bones knew he couldn't get carried away with wanting to get too close to Dennis too fast. That would look suspicious, even though no harm was meant. So Bones had to tread lightly. He couldn't forget that the main reason Henri Blanc had teamed him up with Dennis was so Dennis could keep an eye on him, maybe even bump him off if he made a wrong move.

"Hey, man, don't look so shook up," Dennis said. "Did you have a big fear-of-flying thing going for you the whole time you flew with the hockey team?"

"It's not that, it's my stomach," said Bones. "Gotta buy some more Maalox. I forgot to get some in the hotel in Lauderdale."

"Well, I'm glad to hear it's your stomach and not my flying," said Dennis, "because one thing's for sure, Bones – I'm a crack pilot!"

He guffawed at his own pun, and Bones chuckled goodheartedly, hoping he wasn't overdoing it. He really liked Dennis's macho sense of humor. Crack pilot! That was a hot one! Much of Dennis's flying involved delivering loads of coke and crack from Hector Chanfray's cutting and processing labs to snort shops and crack houses all over Florida. Today he wasn't a "crack" pilot, though. There wasn't any dope aboard. No "dopes" either.

"Dopes" or "things" is what Bones and Dennis called the half-dead semi-human type of creatures that came out of that other chopper the night Bones and Bow Left tried to hijack the Root Doctor's coke shipment. By now, Bones had seen a good many of the things up close. And he didn't like being near them. No, sir. They gave him the heebie-jeebies.

Sometimes he wondered if all the weird stuff that was going on was making him lose his ability to keep his head on straight. Or was it the crack? He had been smoking a lot of crack lately – it was so damned easy to come by, always lying around like potato chips. Just dip your hand in the bowl. Today wasn't a good day for dipping, though. He didn't want Chanfray or Blanc to catch him turning on.

But, Christ, he could really use a hit! When he toked on that good shit, he didn't feel so unsure of himself. He felt powerful, more in control. Being stoned was as right and natural for him as it was natural for a fish to be wet. When he was straight, he went around scared he might slip up and say or do something that might make Dennis realize who was behind the fiasco that had sent an eight-million-dollar load of cocaine up in flames. He kept wondering when his luck was going to run out. His stomach was in a helluva big knot all the time. He couldn't tell if he was really making the right impression with Chanfray and his troops, or if they were just stringing him along for what they could get out of him. And they had gotten plenty! A damn sight more than Bones had ever planned on giving them.

Going in, the plan was that to avoid being put on waivers, Bones would keep spoon feeding them pieces of The Strap that The Strap didn't mind sacrificing – a low-profit crack house here, a bit of a dope haul there – puny stuff, nothing too important. And if he was lucky, he and Dawson would stumble on a way to knock Chanfray off before The Strap became the poorest capo this side of Sicily.

But Bones soon saw that he couldn't stop with the easy shit. The writing was on the wall. He had to take the acting out of his Benedict Arnold act. Hey, he had no choice. No choice at all. Do unto your enemies before they do unto you. His one consolation was that he was absolutely sure that The Strap would have seen it the same way and made the same move if the shoe was on the other foot. Dawson was a horse of another color. He'd have kept galloping down the center of the track as if he had blinders on. Yeah, the copper would've remained true blue. But Bones wasn't cut out to stand still and take a hockey puck in the mouth even if the puck was swatted by his own team.

Dennis Lapidus took the helicopter in low over the orange groves. Under the thick, orange-heavy foliage, where they couldn't be spotted from the sky, the things were probably down there working, watched over by an overseer with a whip. Bones imagined that if this was a plantation in Haiti they probably would be chopping sugarcane. But how the hell would the dopes use machetes without cutting off their own arms and legs? At least here in the orange groves all they had to do was reach up and pull, and drop the fruit into a burlap sack.

When Bones first saw all those doped-up slaves, he damn near flipped. Bingo! The way to nail Chango. Get the law to stage a raid and nab him for kidnapping, detaining people against their will, entrapment, prostitution, whatever. But when Bones learned more about the things and how they got that way, he knew the game was up. That's when he decided to defect to Chanfray for real. No way could the man be beaten. Bones had caught his first glimmer of the truth on the night of the Root Doctor massacre. Now he could see it crystal clear. If he didn't want to be put on waivers immediately – or worse, to be made into one of those goddamn creepy things – his days as a counterspy had to come to a crashing halt. Dawson and The Strap and all the people on their side were doomed. But not Ernie Bonino. Bones still had a chance. A slim chance or a fat chance, he wasn't sure. But he wouldn't have a snowball's chance in hell if he hadn't fessed up. So he became a straight skater. He told Chanfray and Blanc everything. The whole truth and nothing but the truth. Swore it on a stack of Bibles.

Coming down low over the orange groves, the helicopter circled above the mansion, just to check things out and make sure there were no intruders, more than to give the passengers a chance to appreciate the beauty of the place from the air. It was a big, sprawling, Spanish-style affair – a hacienda. It sat on a beautifully sculpted lawn the size of a football field, separated from the pastures and the orange groves by a high chain-link fence. In fact, there was an inner and an outer fence, exactly the same height, one inside the other, about three feet apart – forming a track for the Rottweilers to patrol. Even if somebody cut through the outer fence, the dogs would chew him up and spit out his eyeglasses, shirt buttons, and false teeth before he ever got a chance to cut himself a second wormhole.

The chopper landed on the asphalt tennis court. It was all it was used for. Nobody around here played tennis. As he cut the engine, Dennis said, "Hey, I know what we should do, Bones – get a couple of the dopes out here and give 'em racquets. We could bet on 'em. See which ones could learn to hit the ball over the net."

"None of 'em," said Bones. "They're too spastic."

"How'd you like to be one?" said Dennis. "You wouldn't have no worries anymore, Bones. Long as they do what they're told, they get fed and taken care of, right on schedule."

"Whaddaya mean, long as they do what they're told? They got no choice, do they?"

"Hell no."

They got down from the chopper, opened the bay door for the passengers, and lowered the steps. Chanfray and Blanc came out first, followed by the three guests: the actress Helene Price and two guys in almost identical gray suits, except one suit had pink pinstripes and one didn't. Both guys had black-and-red-striped ties with Windsor knots. Vests. Brown leather Gucci briefcases. And plain black shoes with laces, like military-style shoes. One guy wore eyeglasses and one didn't. Both had mousey brown hair and looked to be in their mid-forties. Neither one looked as if he had had a good piece of ass or a good horselaugh for the past twenty years.

Bones's mind was on a good piece of ass because he and Dennis were scoping on Helene Price, undressing her with their eyes. They gave each other lewd winks as they followed behind the entourage of VIPs. Bones got a rush of nostalgia thinking back on how he had had his pick of prime meat like Helene in the good old days when he was playing hockey. All his teammates were white, too. He didn't have to worry about heavy competition from a lot of black studs, like the white guys on the pro football squads had to do. He wondered if their dicks were really longer than whites'. Probably they were, he decided, watching Helene strut and wiggle on her way up the steps to the mansion. She was wearing a yellow one-piece jumper, almost like a flight suit, but with short sleeves and short pants. As Dennis had commented back at the hotel in Lauderdale, she had "legs clear up to her ass." The ass was a winner, too – what Bow Left used to call a "boss pooper."

Thinking about Bow Left made Bones's stomach churn, tossing harsh acid into the back of his throat. He swallowed hard, remembering the shrapnel in Bow's neck, his carotid artery pumping blood like a geyser. The memory killed off the horny thoughts Bones had for the actress. It would be suicide to try to get next to her anyway. She belonged only to Chango. When he was done with her, done pumping her full of coke and voodoo, he'd probably turn her into one of those things out back working in the orange grove. But first he'd probably let them have a go at her. They could still screw. Bones knew it firsthand. He had seen it one day when he was helping Dennis carry a bucket of gruel down to the grove to feed them. A half-dozen of them all at once went wild and sexually attacked each other, going at it like dogs in heat, not giving a fuck who was watching and sure as hell not wanting to stop, till the overseer took the whip to them. Bones remembered his own surprise at seeing that the dopes screwed just like normal people. Except the look in their eyes was more vacant, more mind-blown, even when they weren't yet close to reaching orgasm.

Inside the hacienda, Bones and Dennis had to become bartenders serving all the VIPs. Then they were allowed to help themselves. There were bowls of coke and crack around, too. Helene Price was the only one who took any. No sooner did she spy it than she laid out three long lines on the glass-topped bar and snorted it up through a thin, engraved, gold tube, a very delicate instrument that she used quite noisily, sucking it up like a fiend. Then her pretty little upturned nose got the coke drips. She kept sniffing and going through a ton of Kleenex from her purse, which really laid waste to her sex appeal. Bones knew that if she kept that up, before long she'd be just one more scrawny little bummed-out groupie. A fallen star. A tragedy.

But it was one thing for him to clearly see that she should stop doing the dope, and yet another thing for him to get a handle on his own problem. He got all itchy and twitchy and jangled trying not to dip into the free goodies. But he had to wait till the VIPs took their drinks down the long corridor into the wing of the hacienda that held the humfo. He watched them going, not envying what they were going to see behind the locked steel door with the painting of Damballah the Serpent God on it. Bones had been taken behind that awful door only once, as a warning. And he sure as hell didn't want to be invited back. Sometimes people who were invited in came back out in the same shape as the things working in the orange grove. In the humfo, the freaking temple, was where the things were created.

Bones sucked on a pipe full of crack, and before it hit him he laid down three lines of coke, but when he leaned his nose toward it a mad irrepressible giggle burst out of him and blew it all to powder – about two hundred dollars' worth. No matter. He laid down three more lines. He looked at Dennis, and Dennis smiled, and it seemed to Bones that his pal must be reading his mind, knowing exactly what he was thinking. It was just too damn funny. A real side-splitter of a joke on Dawson and The Strap. But Bones forced himself to keep a straight face this time while he snorted his toot. Then he allowed himself to laugh hilariously. Because, as wild and wacky and weird as the things in the grove were, there were some other kinds being made at the end of that corridor, things lying in the humfo in their formative stages, that were going to be some rootin' tootin' humdingers for Dawson and The Strap to have to deal with.

Hector Chanfray was about to show the "humdingers" to Mr. Specter and Mr. Trance, the CIA gentleman and the gentleman from NASA. They weren't creative fellows, so they probably hadn't invented their own code names, which were quite appropriate and wryly amusing. Helene and Henri had gotten a big kick out of it when Hector told them about it. He had to tell them this morning before they were introduced to Specter and Trance. Otherwise, they'd have had a hard time not laughing in the faces of the two gentlemen. Sometimes Chango himself had a hard time treating them seriously.

Politics certainly did make strange bedfellows. It was utterly amazing, the extent to which the United States government would go to ingratiate itself with those who rightfully ought to be, and were, its enemies. After the Second World War, many Nazi war criminals were protected and smuggled across the ocean to live in peace, well rewarded, as long as they were willing to turn over to America the scientific and technological knowledge they had originally acquired for Hitler. Also protected were Japanese concentration-camp doctors and scientists who had learned much about biological warfare by injecting fatal diseases into the bodies of American prisoners. Bureaucrats and high-ranking army officers decided that it was better to profit from their former enemies' ill-gotten expertise than to stick like foolish diehards to a policy of making them pay for their evil deeds.

Hector Chanfray was one of the more recent beneficiaries of this pragmatic rationale. Certain key officials in the American government knew who he really was. They knew that he was guilty of a string of murders three years ago, and that he had committed even more murders and more varied types of crimes since then. Furthermore, they knew that he had no intention of reforming or restricting his illegal activities. Yet they were willing to look the other way, because he had helped instigate the violence in Haiti against the Tontons Macoutes, which had led to the overthrow of Baby Doc, and because he had special knowledge coveted by the American military and scientific establishments.

NASA scientists were extremely interested in tetrodotoxin and Zombie Cucumber. They wanted to analyze and learn everything about the ingredients of Chango's potions, so they could mix their own concoctions for highly specialized purposes. To travel to distant planets in vehicles that might have to journey for many years, many lifetimes, through outer space, it was going to be necessary to place astronauts in some kind of suspended animation, some kind of trance, similar to what Chango already was achieving with his magic. The creatures out in the orange grove didn't age rapidly, and didn't readily succumb to disease – distinct advantages during a lengthy space trip. But unfortunately, they weren't too bright; in the trancelike state their intelligence quotient was drastically diminished, and so was their motor coordination, so that they were unsuitable for any but the most elementary, unreasoning tasks. A way had to be found around these difficulties.

But what was a deficiency for NASA was a plus for the CIA. There were many applications for the technology of turning people into automatons. Making whole populations vote a certain way, for instance. Or making them fight whoever you wanted them to. Or making them stop fighting and remain docile. If used properly, this kind of thing would give a whole new meaning to the phrase "puppet government."

These were the heady dreams and ambitions that were shared by Mr. Trance and Mr. Specter. They had no idea that Hector Chanfray was stringing them along, milking millions of research dollars from them, spoon-feeding them insignificant dribs and drabs of arcane knowledge, with no real intention of ever letting them in on his deepest, darkest secrets.

Flanked by Helene Price and Henri Blanc, the bokor led Trance and Specter down the wide corridor behind the steel door. The walls on each side were hung with weapons over which Chango had prayed, blessing them and making them more formidable. There were rifles, pistols, machine guns, shotguns. Machetes and swords and daggers. Bombs and grenades and incendiary devices. All were powerful weapons made even more powerful by chants and mojos. But Chango wished he had the old drum and whip and machete. These were his mightiest talismans, his vevers. And he had lost them three years ago. Weakened to a certain extent by the loss, he had been unable to work the right magic to regain them. They had been locked up in the police station in Braxton Beach, and the janitor, one of Chango's worshipers, who was able to remove the photos and the fingerprints, hadn't been able to get at the other things. But in his trance at the hotel, when Chango stared into Vince Dawson's eyes, Papa Legba had told him who had his vevers now. And he intended soon to reclaim them. He could get along without them before, but now he'd need them for his final triumphs against his enemies.

The corridor opened into a huge bay that was lined with twenty-four glass coffins, a dozen against each of the two long, opposing walls. The walls were festooned with voodoo emblems and paintings of all the ancient loas. The occupants of the coffins were all casualties of the Florida drug wars, members of gangs rivaling Chango's, rivals either extinct now or soon doomed to extinction. Trance and Specter and their superiors had decided that they didn't mind letting Chango kill off these unsavory types. No doubt their intention was to let the bokor perform his good deeds for America, thereby salving their own consciences, and to wind up really feeling good about themselves by killing Chango off in the end, when they were finished with him. But he wasn't about to let them succeed in this. Oh, no. He had other plans.

"How long have these ones been like this?" asked Mr. Trance, waving his arm in a gesture that encompassed all the bodies in the glass coffins.

"One for three days, one for six days, the others anywhere from a month to forty-five days," said Chango.

"You can see that they are all looking healthy. I can revive them anytime I please."

"Yes, but will they retain their mental faculties?" asked Mr. Specter.

"I believe that some will," said Chango. "I believe I have the proper mixture this time. In fact, I varied the mixture, so we will see which ones are more viable for your purposes once they are revived. Henri will send you all of the data as soon as we have it."

Inwardly Chango was quite amused by all this. It was nothing but a charade. NASA and the CIA were out to discover the scientific properties behind Chango's potions. They didn't acknowledge the fact that there was legitimate sorcery involved. They didn't know that he wasn't merely putting people into trances and then reviving them. He was killing them and bringing them back as the walking dead. Some, like the six disciples who had drowned with him when the boat sank on its way to America, he would cause to be reborn, reincarnated, into a second life, unmarred by death, and blessed with all of their lifelike faculties. He could do this when they weren't dead for long, providing he desired to give their reincarnation his full blessing. But there were others for whom death would be permanent. And still others who would be brought back in a diminished state, transformed into zombies or into an even worse condition.

Lord Chango, the King of the Loas, could create monsters if he wished, by using dead human clay and molding it in his hands, in his mind, sculpting it to whatever image he envisioned. His satanic powers rivaled those of Jehovah in this regard

Soon everybody who was against Chango would be dead – or else bewitched, transformed into his familiars, his ogres, his cretinous slaves. They couldn't stop him. They hadn't even stopped him when they had put a bullet in his brain. He had walked out of the hospital. His kindred loas had not let him die. Three days before that, they had brought him back from a watery grave and an earthen grave. And then they had let him walk out of the hospital, rejuvenated. Made whole. Soon his six disciples had joined him, thanks to his sorcery, and around this nucleus he had gathered his flock. As he had realized even before he left Haiti, there were many true believers in America nowadays.

Henri Blanc was one of the first to acknowledge Chango as his lord. And Blanc introduced him to influential politicians and businessmen, people who helped him secure visas and passports. Some eventually came to realize the full truth about him. Others wanted to believe that he wasn't Hector Chanfray but Hector's twin brother, Victor, or that Victor was the one killed by the policemen's bullets. To these fools, it was impossible for anyone shot in the body and head to still be alive. But it was Victor who was dead. Before leaving Haiti, the bokor had beheaded the houngan and feasted on his flesh, then cut him up in little pieces and burned the remains. His archenemy was no more. The ti-bon-ange and gros-bon-ange were joined in vengeance and might. Likewise, all of Chango's enemies would soon perish. For he knew that each time he killed and each time he ate the flesh of a victim, he acquired the heart, the mind, the spiritual force of the vanquished, growing stronger and more invincible day by day.

"They certainly look dead," said Mr. Trance, gazing at a beautiful young brunette in her glass coffin. "Are you sure there isn't any formaldehyde in their veins?"

The question was so absurd that Chango didn't deign to answer it. Instead he smiled his enigmatic smile and said, "She is lovely, isn't she? But unfortunately she was the girlfriend of a cocaine importer. A stubborn cocaine importer who wouldn't do business with me."

"Please . . . we don't want to know those kinds of details," Mr. Trance said, fidgeting nervously.

"We're only interested in specific kinds of results," said Mr. Specter. "How you arrive at them is none of our concern."

"Ah, yes, the end justifies the means," Henri Blanc intoned in his deep, melodious voice. "We are every bit as patriotic as you gentlemen are. Right, Helene?"

Stoned out of her skull, she gave Chango's hand a tender, loving squeeze. His power, his formidability, was the thing that really turned her on. But not so much lately. She was losing her sex drive because of doing too much dope, and of course Chango knew it. But he wasn't about to stop her. She would soon be dead, and by the terms of her will he would have all that was left of her estate. Her father's cancer would not get better, and therefore he would not be around to file a motion to overturn the will. Little did Helene know that it was a cancer that Chango's magic had induced. But since her days on earth were numbered, let her believe for a little while in the false cure given her by Babalu.

Specter and Trance were ready to leave. They never stayed long. Just long enough to file a report that would justify an expense-paid trip to fun-loving Florida.

"Go with Henri," Chango said to Helene. "I have some things to do here. By myself. Good day, gentlemen. Your company has been a pure pleasure, as usual. I will have the helicopter take you to Miami International Airport."

The CIA man and the NASA man said their good-byes and headed down the corridor, escorted by Henri Blanc and Helene Price. Chango waited till he heard the self-locking door slam shut. Then he pivoted and unlocked an adjoining room that was his personal chapel, his own private, inviolate humfo. His shrine to Chango, Oshun, Babalu, Obatalla, the entire pantheon of loas.

In this room there were six more glass coffins. And in the coffins were six corpses, three handsome young men and three beautiful young women, all of whom had been dead for more than a year. But they were not decayed. There was no foul smell coming from them.

But strips of flesh had been sliced from various parts of their anatomy. This was flesh that Chango had dined on, and had offered to the other loas. Succulent strips from the inside of the thighs and arms, the calves, and the palms of the hands. Among the Yoruba Indians in the Haitian jungles, fresh, meaty human palms were always regarded as a prime delicacy. The bokor had found that the delicacy especially suited his own palate, which was why meat had been carved from the hands of all of these corpses.

The six dead ones were ready to come back to life at Chango's bidding. Each ex-human had an emblem of a voodoo god – an animal spirit or loa – branded onto its forehead. They were ready to transform and arise, as soon as they were summoned to destroy Vince Dawson and Salvatore Stropoli.

Above the array of fat multicolored candles on the altar of Chango's private humfo was an eight-foot-tall crucifix. The magic for the transformation resided within the crucified figure. Hanging on the cross was the life-size voodoo doll that Chango had created three years ago out of severed human body parts. Looking up at the composite creation and praying to Papa Legba, he remembered the delicious joy of taking the head of Paul Beck, the torso of Mary Ann Scanlon, and the arms and legs of Silvio Narbonne, Shelly Beck, and Dan and Lisa Morelli.

CHAPTER 24

Ernie Bones set up a meeting with Vince Dawson at Pang's Cantonese Restaurant on a strip of lonely road halfway between Braxton Beach and Fort Lauderdale. A few months ago, Pang's was a saloon and billiard parlor called Yutzy's. Not too many people had caught on yet that there was now good Chinese food in the whitewashed concrete block building, so the place didn't have much of a clientele, and with not too many cars parked in the gravel lot, there was not much chance of unfriendly eyes spying Dawson and Bones together.

Over the pay phone, Bones had told Dawson he had to see him in person because something big was going down. He had a hot packet he had to hand over, too. Something that looked as if it might help nail Hector Chanfray. Dawson bit on it all right. He sounded a little leery, which was only natural, but he said he'd be at Pang's at seven PM. "On the dot, now," Bones said gruffly. "If you're late, it'll be like putting my head under the ax. Or maybe I should say under the machete. I can't flit away from the mansion for too long without them looking at me when I get back like they're measuring me up for a coffin."

A glass coffin in the freaking humfo, Bones thought to himself. The proverbial fate worse than death. He'd rather be put in a regular pine box in a regular cemetery. Once he was dead, he'd be perfectly willing to call it quits. He didn't want to be one of those corpses in the glass coffins, getting up and walking around now and then, and still doing Chango's dirty work.

Following his orders to a T, he got to Pang's fifteen minutes early and took a booth in a dimly lit corner. He was the only customer, so the slender little Chinese waitress was thrilled to wait on him, smiling like mad and bustling around like a ball of pure nervous energy. She laid down menus and silverware and brought a pot of tea. Bones ordered wonton soup and egg rolls for himself and his guest, even though the guest wasn't here yet. When the waitress went to fill the order, he poured himself a cup of tea, took a plastic vial out of his pants pocket, and dumped half the potion that Chango had given him into the teapot.

The soup and egg rolls came, and Bones dumped the other half of the potion into Dawson's bowl of wontons. Then he called the waitress back and told her to take away the two glasses of ice water. He didn't want there to be anything on the table to drink except soup broth and tea. He didn't have to worry about Dawson's ordering booze; the Chinese restaurant didn't serve any.

Dawson arrived right on time, while the soup was still hot. Bones almost laughed, knowing that Dawson was toeing the mark because he thought that if he screwed up it could mean Bones's life. The joke was that Dawson's habit of toeing the mark like a true-blue cop was going to lead to his own downfall.

To Bones's satisfaction, Dawson had two cups of tea with his soup and egg rolls. "Delicious," he said. "I shouldn't be eating; I already had pizza at Enrico's. I thought this'd be all business tonight."

Little did he know that it *was* all business, even the eating and drinking. Chango had said the potion would be odorless and tasteless, and that apparently was the case. Dawson hadn't noticed a thing. The bokor had said, "Once he drinks this, it will relieve you of the necessity of convincing him of anything. He will do exactly what you ask. He will have no other choice. This is much better, much more effective, than sodium pentothal and other truth serums used by the CIA, because their concoctions rely only on chemicals, whereas mine depend on the power of the ancient loas."

After enjoying the little snack, Dawson did indeed seem more relaxed, more mentally pliable and receptive. For him, the situation seemed to have lost most of its tenseness. It was as if he was stoned, without outwardly losing control of himself. But he did suddenly take a lot of interest in the flashy colors of the Chinese paintings, lanterns, and silk screens. He seemed at peace, leaning back with a half-smile, ogling the gaudy birds, trees, flowers, and dragons.

Somewhat envious of the groovy state that Dawson's mind must be in, Bones excused himself, went to the men's room, locked himself in a stall, and snorted some coke. Dawson came in just as he finished, so to make it look good Bones hit the flush handle. He washed his hands while Dawson pissed. In a little while they were both back at the booth, ready to talk.

Bones took a fat white envelope out of his inside jacket pocket and handed it across the table. "This is the first important stuff I've been able to snatch. It's a list of names and dates for payoffs. You'll be surprised when you see who's on there – city councilmen, mayors, law enforcement people – some right at the top. I think it goes all the way to the governor's mansion, but I don't have anything concrete on that yet."

Hefting the envelope, Dawson said, "I can see why you didn't want to hang on to this."

"Yeah, I could've tried to hide it, but if they catch me my ass is grass. I didn't wanna be seen dropping it in the mail either. The best way was to get it to you in person. I think we better work out something safer, though. Like maybe a dead drop – the way the real spies do it."

Dawson grinned.

"What's so damn funny?" Bones snapped.

"What do you know about real spies, Bones?"

"Only what I see on TV. But I saw this really authentic-looking movie once on HBO, and that's where I learned about dead drops. It's like a prearranged place I'd try to get to whenever I could, and tuck away whatever I have – it can be in a fork of a tree even, in some out-of-the-way spot – and you know to come by and check once a week or something. In case you didn't know, that's what a dead drop is, Dawson."

"I'm impressed."

"Well, you oughta be. I'm no dummy. Just 'cause I was a hockey player don't mean I got a hockey puck for a brain."

"Easy, Bones. I never thought you were stupid. Look, let's not waste time arguing. You said you didn't want to take the chance of sticking around the restaurant too long. I don't blame you, man. So why don't you just tell me what you need to get across."

"Chanfray is buying your act. He wants a meeting with you."

"You know that for sure?"

Bones solemnly shook his head yes.

"It'll be on the level? No trap?"

Dawson's probing questions didn't surprise Bones. He had been told that the potion wouldn't alter a person's normal reservations, normal suspicions, about a tricky or dangerous situation. Dawson would be as wary as usual, and his self-preservation instincts would appear to be functioning normally, even to himself. But in the end those instincts would be put in abeyance. He would find himself complying with Chango's wishes without really knowing why.

"He wants you to come to his mansion on Saturday," said Bones. "He's arranging a big powwow and – dig this – this will knock your socks off. The Strap is gonna be there, too. Chanfray wants to form a combine, like in the Capone days. He's gonna hold out the olive branch – he might even kiss The Strap on both cheeks. He wants them both to join forces instead of fighting each other. They'll both be capos, sharing power equally and jointly running all the Florida operations – for ten years. Then, after that, Chanfray wants to be numero uno."

Dawson said, "Why does Chanfray think The Strap might go for a deal like that? It's not in his nature to agree to a loss of power, even if it doesn't go into effect till ten years down the line."

"Hey, The Strap was ready to make a deal before, remember? This one is better than he expects. In ten years he'll be set to retire anyhow. The reason Chanfray is ready to deal is he's making more money on his spirit-channel scam than he can make on the other stuff – and the law can't touch him. His line of shit is protected just like any other religion. Also, he's putting in to become a naturalized American citizen. I guess he doesn't want to screw it up by being in open warfare with The Strap. It'd be a pretty good deal for The Strap, actually. He might live out his last days in a nursing home with all the other old duffers down here, if he agrees not to go up against Chanfray anymore."

"I thought we were all in this together to put Chanfray on ice," said Dawson. "What happened to the big game plan, Bones?"

"Still in effect."

"What do you mean? I don't see it."

"That's 'cause you don't know the whole scoop yet." Bones flashed a smug, triumphant smile. "Dig this, Dawson. The Strap is gonna go in wired. Then he and I will turn state's evidence, with your testimony backing us up. But we don't turn over anything that incriminates ourselves. We take the Fifth Amendment on any of that crap. Chanfray is the only one who takes the fall. Then everything keeps clipping along same as before, with the law's job that much easier and The Strap back in the driver's seat on the other side of the law."

"Why can't I wear the wire?" said Dawson.

"That'd be stupid. They're gonna search you. But they can't search The Strap. It'd be a big loss of face as far as the Sicilian code of honor is concerned. They've got to act like they trust him going in. And besides, who the hell'd figure that he'd be recording himself in an act of criminal conspiracy? Chanfray's guard'll be down on that score."

"Makes sense," Dawson agreed.

"Right," said Bones. "The sting is on."

***

Two hours later, Bones met with The Strap in the same Chinese restaurant. The meeting went as smooth as the one with Dawson, thanks to the vial of potion that Bones dumped into his ex-boss's tea and wonton soup. The Strap fell for Bones's assurances that Chanfray was serious about the gang-land truce.

"But he wants proof of *your* sincerity," Bones said to The Strap. "He wants you to personally pull the trigger on Dawson."

"He knows Dawson's not on the level?"

"Yeah. He didn't buy the turncoat-cop act. Dawson is an alkie, too jittery. My grandma could see through him."

"But I'm no cop killer, Bones. Besides, it's my rule never to get my own hands dirty. It's how I've managed to stay out of jail all these years."

Yeah, you can say that again, Bones thought. Guys like me get our hands dirty. Then we take the fall for guys like you. So it serves you right, what's gonna happen to you, big shot.

"Hell, maybe I've gotta be flexible in this situation," The Strap said. "After all, I didn't get where I am by shying away from the big risks."

"Right on," Bones said. "Think of all the grief Dawson caused you in years past. You're gonna enjoy puttin' him on waivers. Chanfray will dispose of the body. You gotta admit it takes balls, him lettin' you do it at his own pad. But he wants to *see* you do it, so he knows the bargain is sealed. Believe me, he has ways of taking care of corpses that you never heard of, boss. The authorities won't never get their hands on the corpus delecti. No corpus delecti, no murder, right?"

The Strap thought it over, but he didn't think long, because the potion was helping him make his mind up. He said, "I hate to see Dawson bite the dust, since I was the one who got him into this in the first place. But hey, I'm a practical man. This accomplishes everything I want, and it saves me half a million bucks."

"Now you're talking, boss," Bones said.

"The shamus thinks I'll be wearing a wire?" The Strap said with an amused look on his face.

Bones nodded, grinning from ear to ear.

The Strap laughed out loud. "Hey, Bones, that's a hot one, ain't it? Sal the Strap turning state's evidence! Never happen! If Dawson fell for a thing like that, he's too dumb to live."

CHAPTER 25

Dinner at Martha Lewis's house on Saturday evening was full of tension. She had done her best to cook a scrumptious meal of southern fried chicken, green beans, and black-eyed peas over rice, and had coaxed Susan into baking an apple pie. But as good-tasting as the food was, it didn't go down well for anybody. Vince Dawson was nervous about having to leave for his meeting with Hector Chanfray. Martha was worried about what might happen to Vince. And Susan was uptight about the fact that Barry was supposed to be bringing Clara back home in a couple of hours.

"Relax. You can't deny him some time with his own kid," Martha said as she served the pie and coffee.

"I know," said Susan. "But I don't trust him. If you ask me, Barry's exactly the type of man who would kidnap her out of spite and take her someplace where I'd never see her again."

"He won't do anything of the sort," said Martha. "He's far too selfish. You and Clara were burdens to Barry's career, and he's glad to be rid of you both."

"Well, thanks a lot, Mother!"

"I didn't mean he was right about it. I was just trying to ease your fears by pointing out why they're psychologically unsound."

"I'll have you know," Susan snapped, "that my mind is much sounder than you think it is, even if I did have a nervous breakdown six months ago."

"Of course you're of sound mind," Martha said, exasperated. "I wasn't implying anything different. I was talking about understanding Barry's psychology, not yours, Susan."

"Is mine so unfathomable to you?"

"Oh, forget it! Eat your pie and coffee!"

"Don't order me around as if I were a child!" Susan shouted. "I'll have my dessert after you're gone! Maybe then I can enjoy it!" She got up from the table and stormed down the hall to her room.

Martha muttered, "I swear, I don't remember her being this tough to deal with when she was a teenager."

"Delicious apple pie," Vince said. The non sequitur was his way of telling Martha that he didn't want to be drawn into her feud with Susan. He didn't feel like a full-fledged member of the family yet, even though he wanted to be. It was important to him to gain acceptance not only from Martha but from her daughter and granddaughter. For that matter, he had no objections to trying to get along with Barry Crandall, too, as long as Barry didn't set up insurmountable roadblocks.

"I didn't bake the pie. Susan did," Martha said. "I don't know why her crust comes out flakier than mine when I was the one who taught her, and she claims she still follows my recipe."

Voodoo, Dawson thought. But he didn't say it, because it mightn't have gotten a laugh. It wasn't a word that they joked about anymore. Clearing his throat, he said, "Martha, do you believe in reincarnation?"

She chewed and swallowed a bite of pie. "No, I don't think that people are literally born again. Therefore, I don't believe in spirit channels like Hector Chanfray. To me, a person's soul is not a ghost that flits around in the hereafter or gets born from one body into another. It dies when the person dies, because the soul is really the aura, the force field, the glow of thought energy and cell-binding energy emanating from a living person. Its fundamental source is probably the human mind. The person makes the soul live, not the other way around."

"Then what about people who are regressed by hypnotists and seem to remember past lives? Channels like Chanfray say that deep-seated emotional problems can have their origin in our previous lifetimes."

"I don't believe those kinds of hang-ups go back any further than early childhood," Martha said. "Hypnotic regression can produce some dramatic cures when it helps a person face a problem that he's unaware of because he's blocked it out of his memory."

"What about the guy I told you about who was choking and gagging on the floor?"

"Chanfray was the one who attributed the problem to a previous lifetime, but the poor man's low self-esteem probably originated in his youth – some trauma that he doesn't fully remember or acknowledge. If he faces the problem and does something about it, there may be some beneficial results. But those results will probably be short-lived if he continues to delude himself. It'll be like cripples who are cured by faith healers and actually stand up and walk without their crutches. Then they get home and the spiritual fervor wears off and they fall down and break a hip or something."

"But," said Dawson, "why couldn't they keep walking if they could continue to believe they were cured?"

"Do you mind if I use your crippled arm as an example?"

"No."

"Well, it's possible that one of these so-called healers could psyche you up and make you believe you could use the arm. And in the grip of intense passion, an intense *need* to believe, your mind might put out some unusually strong signals, making certain nerves do a job that they don't normally do, even taking over the functions of the useless nerves, so that the fingers can move, and so on. But you can't stay in that kind of mental state all the time – you can only sustain it for a couple of minutes. So, in that sense, the cure is an illusion, it's like a kite that seems to be flying on its own till the wind dies down and sends it crashing to the earth."

Dawson sipped his coffee. Even though he was totally open to this kind of talk with Martha, having to think about his own handicap and the futility of its ever being cured wasn't as easy as he thought it should be.

"Now, there are some interesting pseudoscientific theories about how memories of past lives *could* be real," Martha said. "One theory is that ESP, extrasensory perception, is involved. In other words, perhaps extraordinarily clairvoyant people are able to pick up vibrations of past times. I tend to think that there may be something to ESP, but I don't know about that degree of clairvoyancy. I'd have to see some pretty convincing proof before I'd go for it, and so far all the famous cases that we've had, going all the way back to Bridey Murphy in the fifties, have finally been shown to be people who were unconsciously recalling pieces of stories they'd been told or things they'd read when they were very, very young."

"What else? You said there was more than one theory," Dawson said.

"Well, the other one I find sort of intriguing is the notion that maybe memories can be transmitted genetically, just like physical traits are. If that were so, a person could be living with memories of things that were actually experienced by his or her ancestors."

Dawson grimaced and drew in a deep breath. "It's not really too different from Chanfray's claim, is it? Maybe the spirits of the ancient loas aren't inhabiting his body. Perhaps their memories of long ago are inhabiting his mind."

"In order for it to be even remotely logical," Martha said, "the loas would have to be his direct ancestors, his kin. He'd have to be connected to them by blood."

"And of course," said Dawson, "that's exactly what he claims."

They heard a door click open down the hall, and Susan came out of her room, looking sheepish. She leaned toward Martha and gave her a peck on the forehead. "I'm sorry, Mother. I shouldn't have blown up at you. I guess I just took what you said the wrong way."

"That's all right, dear," said Martha. "You're under a strain. I know it's not easy to face up to Barry again, after what he put you through. But I really don't think he'd harm Clara."

"It's just that. . ."

"What?"

"I've had the funniest feeling all day long. Like something is going to happen, and I don't know what, but it's not going to be good."

"We're all on edge, that's all."

But the truth was that Martha believed in premonitions; it was part of her tentative belief in ESP. On that Thursday five years ago when her husband finally passed away after his long battle with multiple sclerosis, she had somehow known even before she walked into the hospital that it would be his last day. And today, even though she had tried to downplay Susan's uneasiness, she was afraid that somehow those feelings of dread might be rooted in fact – maybe something bad was going to happen, not to Clara but to Vince Dawson.

"To make up for my childish behavior, I'll do the dishes," Susan offered. "You two can get an early start."

To avoid putting any additional stress on her, Martha hadn't told Susan where Vince was actually going tonight, so she was under the impression that both Martha and Vince were going to a movie with Clint and Deronne Jones. But only Martha was going to the movie with the Joneses. Vince would drop her off at their house, then drive himself to the meeting with Hector Chanfray.

"I still have time," Martha said. "I'll wash and you dry."

"No, it's okay, really," said Susan. "I don't have anything to do but wait for Barry and Clara. I might as well be busy. I'm too jittery to read or try to watch TV. I guess you're right, it's silly of me, but I can't help it. I wish they'd just get here.

"Well, they're due at eight-thirty," said Martha, glancing at the kitchen clock.

"Yeah, only another hour and a half to sweat it out, Susan," said Dawson with a mild chuckle, trying to cheer her up.

"If they're not late," said Susan, refusing to be consoled.

"God, Susan, take a Valium, will you?" Martha said, at the risk of provoking another argument. She thought that at this rate she might need a couple of Valiums herself.

"Tell you the truth, I already took two," said Susan. "And it didn't help."

CHAPTER 26

At nine o'clock, while Martha was at the movie theater with Clint and Deronne, and Dawson was making an eighty-mile drive to Hector Chanfray's mansion north of Miami, Albert Scanlon pulled up in front of Martha Lewis's house. Good. The lights were on. He hoped that little Clara was still up and he'd get to see her, play with her a little and kiss her good night.

A Saturday night, and Albert was a lonesome bachelor. He knew that he ought to try to make new friends, even maybe become romantically involved with someone, but instead he'd been wallowing in a desperate kind of inertia ever since Mary Ann was murdered three years ago. He still drove his silver Jaguar and wore flashy smoking jackets and ascots, outwardly as flamboyant and debonair as ever, but inwardly very much a beaten man. He clung to Martha and Susan and Clara. They were his surrogate family.

Stepping up onto the front stoop, he went to ring the doorbell, and noticed that the door was ajar. He pressed the bell button anyway. He would've been welcome to walk right in, but he was finicky about not wanting to catch anyone off guard, half undressed maybe, or in some other kind of private moment.

Two more presses of the bell button, and no one came to the door.

Hearing voices inside the house, Albert decided to enter. Susan must be on the phone or in the middle of something with the baby. But then why didn't she call out "just a minute" or something?

He opened the door and stepped into the foyer, calling, "Martha? Susan?"

No answer. He still heard voices, but he recognized them now as coming from the television. Actors in a familiar TV sitcom. He headed toward those sounds, calling out, "Susan! It's Albert!"

No one was in the living room. The TV was playing to the couch and the chairs. Albert was starting to be worried. Had something awful happened to Clara? Maybe Susan had to rush the baby to the hospital, leaving the front door open in her haste.

Moving much more briskly, he went into the kitchen – then stopped in his tracks, his heart pounding, the blood draining from his head so fast he almost swooned.

Barry Crandall was sitting at the kitchen table. His throat was slit. From his neck to his lap, he was wearing a bright, bloody bib. His face was ash-white. Gone were all vestiges of the sunlamp tan he had sported when he first came down here for his vacation.

Albert wanted to cry out, "Susan! Clara!" – but the words wouldn't come from his throat. In his mind, Barry's face changed to that of Mary Ann, and back again, both faces gashed open at the throat, horribly deformed. His feet were rooted, his legs wobbly. He couldn't make them move. His hands went to his face, covering his eyes, but the visions of death persisted. Barry . . . Mary Ann . . . Barry. . . Mary Ann . . .Mary Ann . . .Mary Ann . . . Mary Ann . . .

He felt himself losing consciousness, blacking out, and the dread of hitting that kitchen floor and lying there next to Barry's corpse made him fight to regain partial alertness.

Suddenly he heard Clara's muffled voice. Then her terrified scream as she ran toward him –

"Uncle Albert!"

He whirled around.

Then came a heavy blow, a hard punch between the shoulder blades, as the bloody butcher knife plunged into his back.

CHAPTER 27

Martha didn't really enjoy the movie, even though it was an excellent comedy, *Raising Arizona.* The scenes went by her in a blur. A slow blur, because she couldn't wait for them to be over. At about the time that the movie *was* over, Vince would be having his meeting with Chanfray. So Martha's worrying would have to go on – for how long she didn't know. Vince had promised to phone her at Clint's as soon as he could to let her know he was okay. If she didn't hear from him by midnight, she was to go home. Then wait for the phone call in the middle of the night, hoping it was the right kind of news

He was such a strong, brave, and yet vulnerable man, possessing those three qualities in about the same proportions as her husband. Except in Dawson they were amplified. Perhaps this was because, although the policeman and the anthropologist both had to cope with the human condition in some of its strangest variations, those variations were most likely to be life-threatening for the policeman. Being with Dr. Morgan Lewis was safe and comfortable and sometimes pretty exciting, and being with Lieutenant Vince Dawson was all those things, with an extra ingredient of danger – which she hoped would be diminished to an acceptable level once this business with Chanfray was over.

On the way to their house, Clint and Deronne chattered about the movie, and it was obvious that they had been able to enjoy it. Of course, they were worried about Dawson, but they didn't have as much at stake as Martha did. They would miss him if something bad happened to him, but losing a friend wasn't the same as losing a lover,

Martha didn't know yet if she was in love with Vince. She was trying to keep any decisions about that emotion at bay till their relationship was reasonably free of external stress. In wartime, lots of people thrown together during bombing raids became lovers in a sexual and even a compassionate sense; but the deeper, truer kind of love had to be there in order for two people to stick together through the longer, calmer times that would come after all the fear and excitement was over.

Vince hadn't told Martha that he loved her when he kissed her good-bye on Clint and Deronne's front porch. She hadn't spoken up either. Now she wished that she had, even if the sentiment might be doomed to flake away at some later time, in a more placid future.

It was nine-thirty when they pulled into the driveway, and Dawson was scheduled to arrive at Chanfray's house at ten. It was roughly a two-hour drive from Braxton Beach, and by now he had been on the road for an hour and a half – unless, God forbid, he had been ambushed on the way, Martha thought, with a rush of panic that she worked hard to fight down.

While Clint fixed cocktails and Deronne freshened up in the powder room, Martha dialed her home phone number, just to make sure that Barry and Clara had arrived okay and that Susan's anxieties were relieved. Six rings, and no one answered. But there was always a chance that Susan was giving Clara her bath or something and couldn't come to the phone right away. Ten more rings. No answer. Puzzled and upset, Martha reluctantly hung up, determined to try again in the next fifteen minutes.

She came out through the sliding glass door onto the patio. Citronella candles were burning on the picnic table and lounge table, and Clint and Deronne were already sprawled in lawn chairs, sipping gin and tonics. They were all in comfy slacks and short-sleeved shirts, but Clint was wearing a beeper in case the police department had to get in touch with him.

"I'm a little worried," Martha said. "Nobody answered the phone at home. Susan wouldn't go anyplace with the baby at this hour." She glanced at the beeper on Clint's belt as if it might go off and confirm her worst fears even as she was trying hard to stifle them.

"Maybe Barry's playing the loving father and dutiful ex-husband," said Clint.

"What do you mean?"

"Tomorrow's his last day in town, right? Susan would probably go along with him and keep Clara up a little later than usual, if he wanted to take them out for ice cream sodas or something. It's a perfect night for it."

"If the bugs would only stop biting," said Deronne, swatting her arm with a loud smack. "Those candles aren't keeping them away like they're supposed to."

"If we can't keep 'em away, we gotta burn 'em," said Clint. He got up, went out to the middle of the lawn, and turned on the bug zapper. Looking back over his shoulder, he said, "Your drink's on the picnic table, Martha."

That's when he saw Ernie Bones. The gate at the side of the house squeaked open, and Bones came into the yard. Clint's first thought was, Uh-oh, why in the devil is *he* here? Something must've happened to Dawson.

Bones was walking stiffly, almost limping, and as he sidestepped onto the patio the glow of the citronella candles showed an agonized expression on his face. Martha gasped.

Clint started toward Bones, thinking he must be wounded, about to collapse – but there didn't appear to be any blood on his clothes.

Then Bones grabbed Deronne by the throat. But he stumbled over the chaise longue, crashing it to the flagstone pavement. Deronne was struggling to get up, but she was crushed under the tangle of webbed aluminum and Bones's oafish body.

Clint got halfway to Deronne when five more people came into the yard, blocking his way, pushing him back. He fell, tripping over the cord to the bug zapper. He could hear Deronne's choked-off screams, but his view of what was happening to his wife was blocked. In the glow of the bug zapper he saw the glazed dope-fiend eyes of the five attackers who were coming at him. But, no – it wasn't dope, not ordinary dope anyway, the kind that Clint had seen turn many people into near zombies. It was something worse this time. It was the glaze of death, which Clint had seen many times also, in the course of his homicide investigations.

All this went through his mind in a matter of seconds, while events around him moved in nightmarish slow motion. As if they were halfway in the throes of rigor mortis, the attackers lumbered toward him. It all came back to Clint in a rush – how Bones had told Dawson that the beings who worked for Hector Chanfray couldn't be killed because they were already dead.

Desperately, Clint tried to scramble and juke around the five who were hemming him in, but they spread out and pressed him back, toward the redwood fence. Even though they walked stiffly and slowly, just like Bones, Clint was finding it weirdly impossible to outmaneuver and elude them. Were his perceptions out of whack? Were they more agile than he thought? Or was it that their aura of unspeakable menace weakened him psychologically and slowed him down, making *them* seem faster than they were?

They were toying with him, pushing him back, closing in. He couldn't get to Deronne. He couldn't even see what was happening to her. Was she dead or alive? Glass shattered. And Bones grunted. Clint hoped Deronne had hit the oaf over the head with a citronella candle.

He caught a glimpse of Martha. She was frozen. It didn't look as if she was going to be any help. Yet he remembered Dawson telling him she was brave. But when a guy is in love with a chick, it warps his judgment. Bad luck all around.

The five attackers were almost on top of him now, reaching out for him with fiendish smiles on their dead-looking faces. He felt utterly weak and powerless. He had no idea how he could possibly defeat them. His revolver was in the house – and according to what Bones had said, it wouldn't be any use even if he could get to it. But he didn't quite believe that yet, even though Bones seemed to have become one of the dreadful bulletproof beings that he had described.

Suddenly Martha screamed, flew at one of the attackers, and smashed a lawn chair across his back – which seemed to make all of them angry. They growled and hissed like hellish creatures thwarted in their quest for human souls. Three of them – two big men and one skinny little woman – continued to come at Clint. And the other two – both burly middle-aged men – pummeled Martha down to the ground and started kicking her, singlemindedly and fanatically trying to kick her to death.

Clint reared back and punched the skinny little womanish zombie as hard as he could in the face. She let out a tiny croak, like a scream trying to be formed on half-dead lips, and reeled backward and fell. As if surprised by this turn of events, the two males watched her crawl around and start to get back up. But they didn't retreat. Clint tried to bull his way through them, but the shortest, stockiest male dived for his feet and tackled him, and he fell hard, hitting his head against the bug zapper.

The attackers jumped on him, punching and clawing. A set of razor-sharp fingernails raked his face. He flailed and kicked and cursed. "Damn you! Damn – you – fucking – dead – things!" Each word punctuated a blow from his feet or his fists against the slow-moving but yet awesome, undefeatable creatures who had him pinned. They kept punching him, choking him, and trying to gouge his eyes.

Martha rolled on the grass, trying to avoid having her ribs kicked in. The kicking feet shuffled and shambled after her. She managed to clamber to her hands and knees, then threw her body against an attacker's shins – as she had seen in football games on television. The wind was knocked out of her by the man's weight and momentum. She groaned as he flew over her head first and sprawled in a three-point landing.

The other one dived at her and missed as she got up and ran. She made it to the aluminum lawn shed at one corner of the redwood fence. Thank God the door wasn't locked! She yanked it open, her hand plunging and groping inside, getting hold of something – a rake. Spinning around, she saw that the two burly zombies were almost on her, and she swung the rake. The prongs buried themselves in the front one's face. He emitted a hissing, angry groan and plucked the rake out of her hands, tossing it away. But she didn't stand still to watch it land. Again she reached into the shed and came out with a pick. She swung it hard, embedding it in the other zombie's chest. He gave an inhuman cry of anguish, thudding to the earth, clawing at the pick. He pulled it out of his chest and got up. The wound was bloodless. There was a gaping hole in the front of his shirt, but nothing red around it, nothing gushing forth. He grabbed the pick and swung it at Martha, but she dashed past as the weapon whooshed through the air.

She was headed toward the patio. She remembered where Clint's gun was. While she had been dialing her home earlier, she had seen the holstered weapon on the dining-room buffet.

Meanwhile, Clint was still pinned on the ground, fighting with three zombies. He got both arms free, reached back and grabbed the bug zapper, and smashed it over the head of the zombie who was sitting on his chest. There was a zap and fizz and smell of roasting hair and flesh. The zombie gave a yell that was almost human as he toppled and rolled on the grass. The other two zombies backed away snarling, as Clint scrambled to his feet, brandishing the bug zapper, hoping their intelligence was diminished enough that they wouldn't think of yanking the cord.

Ernie Bones had his big paws around Deronne's throat, choking her to death, as Martha dodged past them – glass from a broken candle bottle crunching under her sneakers – and ripped open the sliding glass door. She got the gun from the buffet, yanked it out of its holster, and ran back out the door. She placed the muzzle right against Bones's temple and pulled the trigger. There was a horrendous roar – and gray matter went flying. Bones was knocked backward as if he had been hit with a truck. Deronne crawled out from under him, holding her throat. He got back up, and Martha shot him in the chest at point-blank range. It stopped him only momentarily. He growled at her and kept coming, reaching for the gun.

Clint whirled around, still using the bug zapper to hold the three zombies off. The one he had hit over the head had a burned-up face – and his skin and hair were still smoldering. But he wasn't electrocuted. He wasn't dead. Or rather, he *was* dead, so he couldn't be killed again. But he feared the effects of fire and electricity anyway. So did the other two. They all made menacing gestures at Clint, but they didn't try to come closer.

Clint's beeper went off, making him jump. How ironic! Someone at the police station was trying to reach him on an emergency, probably a homicide, not realizing that three of them were about to happen right here and now. Could the beeper have something to do with Dawson? Well, whoever it was would have to fend for himself.

Gaping holes in his head and chest, Ernie Bones – or what was left of him – barred the entrance to the house by standing in front of the sliding glass door. Again Martha fired the gun at him, the force of the heavy-caliber slug knocking him back a step or two.

"Come on!" Deronne yelled, her voice hoarse from having had her larynx nearly crushed. She grabbed Martha's hand and pulled her toward the garage.

Clint saw where the two women were heading. He whirled around and around with the bug zapper, making the three zombies hesitate. Then he crashed through them, bowling the skinny woman and one of the men over, and followed Deronne and Martha through the side door of the garage. He slammed the door shut and bolted it while his wife flipped the lights on.

His eyes were scanning the place for weapons even as all six zombies started pounding on the garage doors. "Too bad the car's not in here!" Clint yelled. His eyes met Deronne's. "How are you, honey?" he said. She gave him a scared, sorrowful look and said her throat hurt pretty badly but she'd be okay.

"Unless they get in here," said Martha. "Here, Clint." She handed him the revolver. "It won't kill them, but it slows them up a little. I think there are only a couple of shots left."

He flipped out the cylinder, looked, and said, "Three." Then he thought of the voodoo stuff in the toolbox under his workbench. He grabbed the key from the nail and unlocked the box, then pulled out the machete and the whip. "This might be what they're after!" he said. "Here! Take this!" He handed Martha the machete, while he kept the whip and the gun. Then he gave Deronne a chisel and an axe.

"What am I gonna do with this?" she said, holding up the chisel.

"Use it like a dagger. Sorry, it's the best I can do."

"Can we make it to the car?" Martha asked.

"I doubt it, it's—"

His beeper started going again and wouldn't quit.

"Something bad is goin' on somewhere," he said. "But it can't be any worse than what's goin' on here."

Crash! The zombies used their fists to break the glass out of the big garage door in front. Their arms were lacerated but didn't drip blood. They kept clawing and pounding, trying to break in somehow. The ones at the side door kept pounding too.

Martha ran to the front and used the machete to hack at the grasping arms. Swinging with all her might, she

318

chopped one off at the elbow – and to her surprise real blood gushed out. And the zombie screamed a really human-sounding scream. A bright geyser of arterial blood spurted from his arm stump, and he dropped from view. The other zombies stopped clawing and pounding and fell back.

Clint and Martha stared at the machete. He said, "Maybe we got ourselves some powerful magic here."

Just then the side door crashed in. Clint pulled the trigger on the first zombie through, shooting him in the face. All it did was slow the advance a little.

Deronne screamed in terror. The axe and chisel fell out of her hands. She backed away, covering her eyes.

Martha stepped up and stabbed the machete like a sword into the first zombie's chest. As it went in, he seized the blade in both hands, almost pulling it away from her – but instead several of his fingers were sliced off. He quickly died, his body crumbling to paper-thin flesh barely covering his bones, so that the blade came free easily when Martha pulled it out by the hilt. Even as she did so, the dead zombie's body was decomposing to a heap of smoldering ash.

Clint and Deronne and Martha had no time to be astounded by this phenomenon. Two more zombies were upon them. One was Ernie Bones, smiling savagely, despite the fact that his chest was riddled and a chunk of his head was missing. "Die, damn you!" Martha yelled. As hard as she could, she whacked him in the throat, nearly decapitating him. For the first time, he bled – a torrent of it gushing out as he fell – and Martha jumped back so she wouldn't get drenched.

Clint had looped a coil of the whip around the neck of the other – the skinny zombie woman – and he used it to garrote her to death. She kicked and gurgled and clawed at the noose – but her struggle was soon over. Like Bones, she died "normally" – and the thought crossed Martha's mind that perhaps this was because they had only recently been turned into the undead – maybe just the older creatures would decompose and crumble to ash.

"Let's let the last two in," Clint suggested. Deronne backed away fearfully, while Martha and Clint positioned themselves on either side of the doorjamb. In a little while the two zombies came through, spotting Deronne immediately and heading right for her. But Martha hacked with the machete and Clint used the garrote. Both zombies died rather easily, one of them falling in a heap of bone and flesh that rapidly decayed, bubbling and igniting, as if being consumed in the sulphurous flames of Dante's Hell.

Clint's beeper was still going.

He ran outside and looked around, trying to satisfy himself that all the creatures had been vanquished. Suddenly a shot rang out, and he dived, hitting the turf. With a loud screech of tires, a black van peeled out – it must have been the vehicle that transported the zombies. From a kneeling position, Clint aimed his revolver and squeezed off his last two rounds.

The van kept going. He wasn't sure he had hit it with any of his shots. He had no chance to get the license number. It made a squealing left turn down a side street and was gone.

Suddenly incredibly weary, Clint walked wobbily back to the garage. He hugged and kissed Deronne, then hugged and kissed Martha. Arms around each other, they went into the house. They felt compelled to go around making sure all the doors and windows were locked. Then Clint went to the phone and dialed police headquarters.

The desk sergeant answered, and with manufactured nonchalance Clint said, "You beeped?"

"That you, Lieutenant Jones?"

"It ain't the archbishop."

He was still breathing hard, still pretty shook up, but trying his foolish best not to show it. He liked to show the other men on the force that he could remain flippant and cool, even under duress. It was his way of facing fear and tragedy and pain. He told himself that any news he got now couldn't be worse than what he had just been through.

But when the sergeant gave him the scoop, his flippancy evaporated. He looked at Deronne and Martha, who were holding and comforting each other, and he could almost feel them shudder when they saw the grim look on his face. And he wondered if they would be strong enough to take yet another hard blow.

CHAPTER 28

The floodlights around the tennis court were on, making a nicely illuminated landing area for Dennis Lapidus as he dropped down out of the sky. He parked the big black assault chopper next to the bright red civilian helicopter. Then he killed the motor and climbed out of the cockpit, a .45 automatic stuck in his belt.

Chanfray and Blanc were already coming across the yard. The bay of the chopper opened and two men jumped down, then dragged out two trussed-up human bundles and lowered them to the asphalt. Both men had Uzi machine guns slung over their shoulders, and one had a cat-o'-nine-tails in his hand.

Dennis Lapidus stood by looking up into the bay, the interior light revealing an array of hulking, silent figures who were sitting on benches, not making a move. "Come on out, dopes!" Dennis called. "Home sweet home!" The creatures moaned and stirred just a little, as if they weren't anxious to comply.

But Chanfray shouted something at them in Creole. Then they started to come down the metal steps, stiffly and awkwardly, as usual. "Take them to their shed," Chanfray said. "Use the whip on them if you have to."

Both of the men with the Uzis looked sheepish, their eyes averted from Blanc and Chanfray. But Chanfray wasn't taking notice. He was smiling at Susan Crandall and her baby daughter, both bound and gagged, lying at his feet like trussed-up chunks of meat. Susan moaned and squirmed a little, and Clara was softly crying, as if most of her tears had already been spent. Chanfray laughed, a soft rumbling self-satisfied chortle.

"There was a screw-up," said Dennis. "One of the vans never showed up at the rendezvous point. We lost two guys – and six dopes – I mean, transformed beings. I waited as long as I could. I don't know what happened to them."

Anxious to escape Chango's wrath, the man with the whip and an Uzi herded the zombies toward the shed, flogging them viciously to hurry them up.

"Your part of the mission was a complete success?" Henri Blanc asked the other man with an Uzi.

"Yes," he said. "We killed a young man and an old one, and as you can see we captured the young woman and the child."

"What might have happened to your comrades?" Blanc asked.

"I don't know. Maybe they weren't able to work as fast as we hoped. But perhaps they will still get their part of the assignment done. If so, they'd have to drive all the way here in the van, which would take them a while yet."

"They had better show up here with Lord Chango's vevers, or not show up at all," said Blanc. "If they have already failed, they know we will be extremely displeased, so they are running away, trying to avoid punishment. But we will catch up with them. They cannot hide from us for long. So they might as well slit their own throats."

Chango purposely made no comment on the partial failure of today's mission. He did not wish to convey a true impression of just how important his vevers were to him. It would be unwise to let the people around him know how vulnerable he might be to whoever should come into possession of his drum, whip, and machete.

He knew that someone must have discovered the power of the vevers. It would have been impossible for any part of tonight's plan to fail unless his own sacred artifacts were being used against him.

"Quickly!" he said. "Take the woman and the child into the humfo. We don't want them out here where they can be spotted by our other guests, who are soon due to arrive."

***

Following Bones's directions, Dawson had exited the interstate a half hour ago onto a two-lane blacktop. By the odometer, he clocked nine and two-tenths miles, then started looking for the narrow left turn onto a one-lane bridge. He almost shot by it, but managed to spot it out of the corner of his eye, squealed on the brakes, backed up, and made the turn. After that it was cake. The bridge put him on a narrow dirt road through a patch of woods, and he only had to drive five more miles till he got on the private road to Chanfray's estate.

It was odd coming off the public road made of dirt to the private road, which was paved; one would normally expect the reverse. It was a long private road, too, about three quarters of a mile, totally isolated from civilization, in an area that the developers hadn't gotten to yet. Chanfray must either have his own generator, or else the power lines were underground, because there weren't any poles. Maybe he had some means of getting free electricity – for instance through sorcery, Dawson joked to himself.

The mansion was a two-story pink stucco hacienda. The way it was all lit up, by means of flood lamps hidden behind shrubbery, reminded Dawson of the Lincoln Memorial on display at night in the nation's capital for the admiration of tourists. But the Lincoln Memorial wasn't barricaded behind concentric six-foot-high chain-link fences topped with barbed wire and patrolled by slavering Rottweilers.

The dogs were barking and snarling, throwing themselves madly against the fence at the mere approach of Dawson's car. "Hey, don't tear my throat out just 'cause I'm driving an old clunker," he muttered to himself, fighting off his dread of arriving here – a dread that he had felt all week in one part of his mind, while another part kept overriding it, almost as if some external force was pulling him along. Well, at least he was glad he could stop driving. His right arm was tired and his gimp arm ached like hell at the shoulder, the only part where he had any movement or feeling. He was basically a one-armed driver, the right hand having to do all the steering with the useless hand resting like a claw at the bottom of the wheel while he tried to make it pitch in by manipulating it from the shoulder. Doing this for two hours wasn't exactly a laugh.

He could hear the full fury of the Rottweilers when he stopped his battered green Chevy in front of the closed security gate and wound down the window. He could have bought a new car with Sal the Strap's half-million-dollar down payment on his services, but then he would've looked like a cop who didn't need to be on the take, which might've tipped his hand to Chanfray.

Two short, lanky black guys in black T-shirts, with Lugers in their hands, came out of the booth by the gate and checked him over. With their eyes. They didn't make him get out and frisk him. If they had, they would've found his .38 in the clip-on holster under his jacket. Bones hadn't told him to come here unarmed, and off-duty policemen were required to carry their weapons anyway.

"I'm Vince Dawson," he said to the scowling black guys with Lugers. "I've been invited." They didn't say anything, but apparently they believed him or else recognized him from somebody's description. They went back into the booth, and the gate swung open. Through sorcery or electricity, Dawson wasn't sure.

***

"If I'm gonna plug the pig, I wanna do it right away," Sal the Strap said. "Let's just get it over with, no pussy-footing around. Now that I've had time to think about it, I kinda like the idea of icing that copper. He and his partner Jones have put me through lots of hard times."

Henri Blanc delicately swirled his cognac around in the snifter, then sipped, enjoying the bouquet. He and The Strap and The Strap's three cohorts, subcapos of his crime empire, were gathered around the bar in the living room, where there was a bank of television monitors tied in to the hidden cameras that were trained on the front gate and various segments of the security fence. They had arrived fifteen minutes ahead of Dawson, and were now observing his arrival with engrossed looks on their faces, as though they were watching an episode of *Miami Vice* and they might spot themselves as bit players.

"I think it would be grossly impolite not to at least welcome Lieutenant Dawson and offer him a cocktail before he dies," said Henri Blanc. "He has had a long drive, and he must be looking forward to some pleasant conversation."

Blanc was of course toying with The Strap and getting his rocks off doing it. By interrogating Ernie Bones under torture before he was changed into his nonhuman form,

326

Blanc and Chanfray had learned all the details of the conspiracy against them. They knew that The Strap, not realizing that the beans were already spilled, would want to shoot Dawson right away, with a view toward preventing him from spilling them.

"Why don't I do it soon as he steps outta his car?" The Strap recommended with solemn enthusiasm. "Then all you gotta do is cart away his remains and hose off your driveway. What are you gonna use on the corpus delecti, quicklime?"

"Lord Chango has his special methods. In all things. That is why we must wait."

"Well, don't try any funny stuff. Once we shake hands, we got a deal. But till then, I ain't no pushover. We're armed, you know – me and my boys. By the way, where's my man – I mean my ex-man, Bones? I got a yen to scope on his big ugly face – for old times' sake."

"He is on a special mission tonight. He may be here later."

"Then where the hell's Chanfray?"

"In his private chapel, his humfo, down at the end of that corridor. Before all great undertakings, he must pray to the ancient loas."

The Strap didn't like that word "undertakings." It sounded too much like what went on in a funeral parlor, and he didn't want to be lumped in that category. His boys had insisted on packing their pieces, and he didn't object if it made them feel better. But privately he knew that his bluster about being armed didn't mean a damned thing. If all hell broke out, bullets wouldn't faze Chanfray's troops.

Despite his nagging misgivings, he had persuaded his top men to go along with tonight's deal. But his reasoning didn't sound too cogent, even to himself. Ever since that meeting with Bones in the Chinese restaurant, The Strap had been unable to concentrate, unable to focus sharply on his affairs. Maybe it would all straighten out once he got through tonight and knew for sure that Chanfray wasn't playing him for some kind of sucker.

The doorbell rang.

And Henri Blanc said, "Excuse me, gentlemen," and went to welcome Dawson.

***

The blades of the Blackhawk helicopter were already whirring as Clint Jones held out his hand to pull Martha Lewis up into the cockpit. They buckled themselves in next to the blond, boyish-looking pilot, Jack Mills, of the U.S. Drug Enforcement Administration. Immediately the copter lifted off.

Another DEA copter was already in the air ahead of them. Each machine carried twenty men in the bay, armed with automatic rifles, shotguns, and machine guns. Also on board were grenades and flame throwers. The incendiary devices were used for burning down fields of opium and marijuana. Clint and Martha still had the whip and the machete, but he was also thinking that grenades and flamethrowers might come in handy against zombies – although he hadn't dared mention that word to Jack Mills for fear that Mills would write him off as a lunatic, a cop gone mad from the stress of the job.

Mills wasn't as boyish as he looked. He was thirty-two years old, chief of the DEA branch that patrolled South Florida, working out of the Braxton Beach airport. When he realized the kind of hell that Dawson was unwittingly headed for, Clint knew that the Braxton Beach police department couldn't handle it. They'd never get to Chango's place in time. They didn't have choppers, just patrol cars. The only thing to do was phone the DEA and make them scramble. To his great relief, Jack Mills had jumped at the chance to put Hector Chanfray and Salvatore Stropoli away in one fell swoop. But to gain Mills's avid cooperation, Clint had had to lie a little. He told Mills that Ernie Bones was killed by Chanfray's men for informing on a ten-million-dollar cocaine buy that was scheduled for tonight at Chanfray's estate. The deal was going down between Chanfray and Sal the Strap. Lieutenant Dawson was on the inside, working undercover for the narc squad, but the crooks knew he was wearing a wire and were going to rub him out. For good measure, they were trying to wipe out everybody close to Dawson. That was the reason behind the attack at Clint Jones's place. It was also why Albert Scanlon and Barry Crandall were dead and Susan and Clara Crandall were missing.

"Oh, God, it's almost eleven o'clock already!" Martha said, looking at her wristwatch. We'll never get there in time."

"Don't be negative," Clint said. "Keep your hopes up."

His words sounded flimsy, even to him. But where there was life there was hope. After all, when Bones and the other hellish creatures had come at them earlier, he didn't think they had a snowball's chance, but they had lucked through. Afterward, Deronne was a wreck, though. She had begged Clint to stay home, saying, "I don't want to lose you, honey – isn't it enough that I already lost Paul and Shelly?" But Clint had told her he couldn't ever look at his own face in the mirror if he let Dawson die. Meekly, Deronne had backed away from him. "If you come back, I'll be here waiting," she had said, crying softly.

He had promised her that he'd come back, but his promise was a wish put into words, and what he was heading into was a harsh, cruel nightmare turned into bloodcurdling reality.

***

Chango's eerie chant reverberated inside the humfo, amplified by the bare walls of the room, which had been emptied of the glass coffins. The crucifix was no longer above the altar. But stretched out beneath the place where the effigy used to be was the limp body of Clara Crandall. The tiny child was asleep, drugged. Her blond ringlets tumbled down around her cherubic face. She looked innocent, peaceful, off on a delightfully pleasant adventure somewhere in her dreams.

She would never awake.

Beside her was the sacrificial knife. Later tonight, when his triumph was complete, Lord Chango would feast on her tender flesh. By this holy sacrament, his supernatural powers would be increased, and the loas would rejoice.

***

Martha tried to hear nothing but the drone of the helicopter. She didn't want to hear her own thoughts. She wanted to drown them out. Drown out her fears. Drown out her hopes. Drown out her grief.

According to the pilot, they were about forty minutes away from Hector Chanfray's estate. Forty minutes away from trying to rescue Vince Dawson. If he was still alive. Forty minutes from trying to rescue Susan and Clara. If they were even there.

But it seemed that they *had* to be. It was the only logical deduction. If voodoo had a logic. Martha rued the day she had ever started studying it and trying to uncover its mysteries, its archaic traditions, rituals, and hidden meanings. If she hadn't gone to Haiti in search of this knowledge, she would never have met Silvio and Jean. She would never have brought them to America. And the chain of murders, even if it had still happened, might have happened to someone else, leaving her untouched.

Clint Jones looked at her as if reading her despair, and reached out and held her hand. "It's not your fault," he said. "Don't go blaming yourself. The evil people in the world will always try to have their way, and sometimes succeed. Their successes are made that much sweeter if they can make *us* feel guilt for their actions."

"Guilt and grief," Martha said. "When will it ever end, Clint?"

"We're gonna make a large part of it end tonight," he told her, trying to sound confident.

Maybe if she believed what he was saying, it would come true. She had to find a way to be brave. For Vince and Susan and Clara. She had to try to get to them – and hope that all three of them were at Chanfray's place, still alive. She couldn't just let the killing go on. First Silvio and Jean, then Albert and Barry. She had to do something to stop the horrible losses. It would be better to die trying than to be a lone, wretched survivor.

***

Groggily, Dawson tried to open his eyes, but a heavy coating of mucus had them glued shut. His back ached, and his gimp arm was throbbing like mad. He remembered the two Darvons he had swallowed with bourbon at Chanfray's bar. It must've knocked him out. Ow! He went to rub the small of his back and his fingers touched cold steel. Then he rubbed furiously at his eyes, making them water, washing away some of the mucous crust. His vision was blurry. He smelled dog shit. And it dawned on him that he wasn't in the house. He was inside the double fence, lying on the grassless track, the grass worn to dirt by the pacing of the Rottweilers.

That thought made him jump up. Immediately the five dogs charged, yiping and yowling. He whirled, his heart jumping into his throat. But the dogs weren't inside the fence. They were chained nearby, outside the compound, throwing themselves against their leashes, trying to break loose and tear Dawson to shreds.

He shuddered, and adrenaline coursed through him, jarring him into a greater state of awareness. Was it morning? No. The entire area was floodlit, powerful lights beaming down from surrounding trees. He felt for his .38, but of course it was gone, and so was the clip-on holster.

Down along the track, about fifty feet from him, he saw four other prisoners. One of them turned toward him, and he recognized Sal the Strap. The Strap and his boys. All of them caged like dogs. Just like Dawson. He heard someone crying, and looked to his left. It was Susan Crandall! She was caged, too – and she was totally nude, sobbing, clinging to the fence, her body sagging against it. Leering at her, the two gate guards stepped up and prodded her with their Lugers, making obscene comments about where they'd like to put their barrels.

If Susan was here, where was Martha? And Clara? Were they dead? A jolt of panic shot through Dawson, overriding his concern for his own future. He started toward Susan to question her and give her whatever help he could. But then he saw that his section of the dog path was partitioned off from hers. And there was yet another partition between him and Sal the Strap. When Chanfray was relying on the dogs to patrol the place, the partitions would ensure that the animals couldn't all be drawn to one place while somebody breached another part of the double fence.

Suddenly Sal the Strap screamed out, "Dawson! You fuck! You got us into this! If we get outta here, your ass is grass!"

Dawson couldn't think of a thing to say. He didn't quite understand how he was responsible for the predicament. He also couldn't see how The Strap thought he and his men might get out of it. No, all of them were stuck, just like he was, and it was easy to see that their biggest threat at the moment wasn't each other. But The Strap wasn't exactly a paragon of coolheaded logic. Why, the man even believed in zombies!

"Chango!" The Strap yelled at the top of his lungs. "Get your ass out here! I thought we had a deal!"

Just as Dawson was pondering the meaning behind those words, he heard music in the distance – weird music accompanied by chanting. Then a procession came around the side of the hacienda, which was still all lit up like a Christmas tree.

Chango was leading the congregation, dressed in his black jumpsuit. Directly behind him came Dennis Lapidus – whom Dawson recognized as the other blond gorilla, besides Bones, who had guarded the door and tended bar at the channeling session. The gorilla was carrying a huge crucifix, and when it got closer the figure suspended from it could be discerned – it was the composite "human body"

Chango had buried in the cemetery three years ago! It wasn't mummified; it wasn't decomposed. Its composite parts looked as fresh and recently dead as they had looked when Chango first sewed them together.

Behind the crucifix followed the voodoo musicians – the same ones who had played in the saloon when Captain Armando Raphael met his final fate – wailing on the ogun, the asson, the conch horn, and the petra drums. Henri Blanc and all the higher echelon of Chango's organization, about twenty of his henchmen and disciples, all followed the musicians, chanting in Creole.

Then came the undead, the ones newly arisen from the glass coffins. Twenty-four of them looked much like the beings who had made the attack at Clint Jones's house. But the six in front were different, for they had voodoo emblems burned into their foreheads. And the emblems were vevers of the ancient loas, the African animal gods. A snake. A ram. A leopard. A crocodile. A rhinoceros. And a bull. And on the cheeks of the creatures bearing these emblems were tattoos of Chango's lightning bolts and his whip and machete – which were here in spirit even if their physical presence was temporarily absent.

Dennis Lapidus set the base of the crucifix into a slot in a concrete pedestal embedded in the ground for that precise purpose, so that the effigy was held solidly upright. Then the entire congregation, the living and the undead, knelt around the crucifix, all except Chango. They stopped chanting, but he continued, his piercing wail carrying above the frenetic pulsing and throbbing of the music.

Hissing, ululating cries came from the lips of the undead as they began their own kind of chant, attempting to do it in unison. But their attempts at this were as ragged and awkward as their body movements.

Dawson's mouth gaped open as he stared at everything that was happening, horrified and yet riveted by its awful repugnancy. He now had no doubt that he was truly seeing the undead – the unkillable beings described by Ernie Bones and Sal the Strap. A deep sense of dread invaded and permeated his mind and body, a deeper, more gruesome fear than he had ever felt before, even in his first encounter with Chango, which had ended with them both in the hospital. He glanced to his right along the dog track – The Strap and his men were frozen, awestruck, wondering what it all portended and what was to be their fate. Dawson turned his head and saw Susan Crandall facing away from the spectacle, unable to watch.

Chango's chanting rose in pitch and fervor, his voice reverberating loudly and unnaturally. He had no microphone, no amplifier. This was the outdoors, and there were no hills, no natural barriers to produce an echo. But he seemed to possess a superhuman ability, an unearthly ability, to generate resonance and volume.

Then the bokor gestured to the crucified figure, calling it down from the cross. And it started to move! At first Dawson wasn't so sure that was what he really saw. But, yes! The hands and feet twitched. And twitched again.

Sparks burst from the effigy's eyes. And the macabre creation began to emit a phosphorescent glow.

Dennis Lapidus began to lead the twenty-four "ordinary" undead toward the part of the fence where Susan Crandall was. At the same time, Henri Blanc led the six special ones toward The Strap and his men. One of the men with a Luger went with Dennis, and the other went with Blanc. They made the prisoners step back while they unlocked the gates that were built into the inner fence so the Rottweilers could be let in and out.

The dogs certainly didn't want in this time. They were snuffling and mewling in the dirt, probably wishing they were even farther on the other side of the compound.

But the zombies were going in in place of the dogs. As they slowly entered, moving stiffly and awkwardly, hissing and groaning, the guards didn't need their Lugers to make the prisoners quickly back away.

The twenty-four zombies began to peel their clothes off. Those who had been living men and those who had been living women ogled Susan with dead but yet lustful eyes. They also lusted for each other. All of them were sexually aroused – but for them the drive to copulate and the killing instinct were intertwined, one and inseparable. They gave off a sulphurous smell, an effluvium, that carried on the night air, filling living nostrils with paralyzing revulsion and terror.

The human – or inhuman – effigy was down off the cross now, and was actually *walking*. All around it its greenish-yellow aura, its animating force, sparked and glowed. Lord Chango walked ahead of his creation, beckoning it onward as he continued his overpoweringly loud, reverberating voodoo chant.

The six special zombies seemed confused and somehow purposeless. For the time being, they were just milling around inside the dog gate – but The Strap and his men had run from them anyway, and were all cowering and huddling down at the far end. Then Dawson heard a clanging sound. And he saw that Henri Blanc had unlocked the partition and slammed it open. The six zombies were now free to come for Dawson or for The Strap and his men.

Susan Crandall was still the only human in her compartment. She had run as far as she could from the twenty-four lust-crazed zombies, and in pursuing her they had stumbled and fallen, all trying to pass at once down the three-foot-wide dog track. Some were clawing and biting and pounding at each other. Some were having sex in all its forms. And some were fighting and fornicating all at once. Susan stared at them, utterly horrified. Then she jumped up and started to climb the fence, even though if she made it to the top she would be lacerated, maybe disemboweled, by the barbed wire.

Chango stopped walking but kept chanting. The life-size voodoo doll stopped three feet away from the fence, making eye contact with the six special zombies with the emblems of the loas on their cheeks and foreheads. The effigy's eyes glowed bright yellow. Then radiant beams shot out from its eyes, a multiplicity of multicolored rays shooting from the effigy's eyes to the eyes of the six undead.

They began to transform into weirder, more frightening creatures than they already were – and the form that they took was dictated by the vevers burned and tattooed into their cheeks and foreheads. One of the creatures retained its human shape except for its eyes, which evolved into poisonous serpents jutting and coiling from its eye sockets. Another's arms became a whip and a machete made of elongated flesh and bone. Yet another developed a head that had human hair and skin but was otherwise that of a crocodile, with a crocodile's evil, beady yellow eyes and multitude of sharp, drooling teeth. Yet another of the hideous creatures resembled a leopard that happened to have dotted, pink, humanlike skin. The fifth had a rhino's horns and jaws. The sixth was still shaped like a man, but its whole body was transparent and sizzled and zapped and sparked like electricity.

Rays of reanimating energy kept spidering out from the eyes of the voodoo doll to these ugly, hellish creatures it had created. Chango looked on approvingly.

The thing with snakes for eyes and the thing with the whip and machete made of elongated flesh came at Dawson. And the others went after Sal the Strap and his band of merry men.

One of the merry men was screaming in mortal terror and trying to climb over the barbed wire, which was cutting him to pieces. The creature made of Chango's lightning touched the fence with its electrified hand, jolting the man with a jillion volts, frying him on the fence. In less than thirty seconds he was charred to half his size, like an overdone hamburger with all the fat cooked out, and in thirty seconds more he was a small lump of smoldering charcoal that smoked and stank and dropped in sizzling lumps to the ground.

The lightning creature transformed again. Now it was part ram and part man, with a ram's horns and an otherwise human shape.

Dawson whirled around to check on what might have happened to Susan. Luckily, she had not been electrocuted. She had stopped trying to climb to safety. Her hands weren't on the fence. She was backing away from two big, horny zombies, who were chasing her right down the center of the track.

The thing with a whip and machete for arms was heading for Dawson again, but the one with snakes for eyes had been distracted by the electrocution, then had turned toward one of The Strap's men. The snakes were coiling and striking, and a hideous laugh was pouring from the creature's mouth as the poor fellow tried to get away. He fell and didn't move a bit – possibly dead of a heart attack –

but the snake eyes struck at him anyway, sinking their fangs into his face and neck.

Dawson had about seventy-five feet in which to run. And run he did, the fleshy blade and whip hissing and snapping behind him as they sliced through the air.

He knew he was doomed. But he kept running anyway.

Then he felt the roaring wind in his face, and he looked up as the DEA helicopter touched down out of the sky. A second copter was right behind it, coming in for a landing in the front yard of the estate.

With a loud crack, the flesh whip snaked out and coiled around Dawson's neck, choking him, yanking him backward off his feet, sprawling him in the smelly dog track dirt.

"Vince!" Martha screamed, jumping down out of the cockpit, running toward Dawson with the machete in her hand.

She didn't see Susan because the sex-starved zombies had closed in on her and had her surrounded, blocked from view.

Chango laughed his macabre laugh as a burst of white-hot energy shot out from his corpse creature's eyes, searing a section of the fence, making the chain-link steel glow molten, then melting it away. The rainbow beams of light once more came from the creature's eyes, pulling the zombies away from Susan against their will, making them come out through the hole in the fence to attack the DEA men.

Chango came at Martha, but Clint Jones caught up with her first, making Chango's whip snap and crack, keeping the bokor away from her. Chango backed away in fear of his own vever, and the beams of light shooting from the corpse creature's eyes weakened somewhat, their power diminished.

The fleshy snakelike coil was strangling Dawson, dragging him along the dog track toward the machete made of skin and bone. With his good arm he grabbed on to the fence, temporarily saving himself from the upraised blade but making the whip tighten even more around his throat.

Martha stabbed at the creature through the fence, and it screeched and roared, and its coil came loose from Dawson's throat.

"Vince! Take this!" Martha yelled, handing Chango's machete to Dawson through the fence. At the same time the creature stabbed it's flesh machete at her, but she jumped back, saving herself. Dawson managed to grab the hilt of the weapon he had been handed just as the lash of flesh once more coiled around his throat, pulling him toward the creature's blade. But with a desperate blow he cut the coil away, and the creature screeched and hissed as its elongated arm gushed greenish blood. It backed up, swishing its flesh machete through the air, closing in for a duel.

But Clint Jones shot the creature in the head, distracting it. And Dawson plunged Chango's machete into its chest. It died instantly, its evil heart penetrated, and fell to the ground, its elongated arms quivering in their death throes.

The mere thought that some of his creatures could be defeated seemed to unnerve Chango. Clutching his mojo – his pouch with the severed finger – he backed away as Clint Jones came after him with his own whip.

At first the DEA men were shocked by the failure of their guns to dispatch the zombies. They killed the two gate guards who shot at them with their Lugers, but then none of the others would die. When they were shot, they got back up, even if pieces of them were blown away. Five DEA men were mobbed and torn apart by the undead.

But luckily one of the Blackhawks had stayed on the ground, and a squad of DEA men was able to arm themselves with flamethrowers. Others resorted to grenades. Explosions rocked the compound as groups of attacking zombies were blown to bits and others collapsed, their dead flesh afire.

Chango turned and ran toward the hacienda, trying to make his way there in the confusion. Henri Blanc and some of the other disciples had already made it into the corridor that led to the humfo, and were arming themselves with the consecrated weapons.

Dennis Lapidus and a half-dozen of the disciples were headed for the tennis court. He shot two DEA men dead with his .45, then climbed into the cockpit of the assault chopper as the rest of the disciples got into the bay. But Jack Mills was already in the air again, in his Blackhawk helicopter, and he fired a stream of incendiary cannon rounds into Dennis's craft. It exploded before it even got off the ground. All aboard perished in a ball of reddish-yellow flame.

Martha squinted. A young woman, totally nude, was wandering slowly toward her, obscured by smoke and flame. She was about to yell for Clint to help her, thinking one of the zombies had singled her out. But then she saw it was her own daughter. "Susan!" she shouted.

But Clint grabbed Martha and pulled her back. "Don't!" he yelled. "She might be—"

He didn't say the rest, but Martha knew what he meant: her own daughter might be an enemy now. Chango could have transformed her into one of his undead beings.

But Susan was crying, reaching out toward Martha, tears streaming down her cheeks. Clint backed up, aiming his revolver.

"Mother!" Susan cried.

They fell into each other's arms.

"Clara. . .oh dear God, Clara," Susan sobbed. "I don't know where she is, what he's done with her."

Clint shot the locks off the dog gate nearest Dawson, and he was a prisoner no more. He stepped out, wielding Chango's machete, and the corpse effigy backed away from him, its aura diminishing, changing from yellow to orange.

Martha yelled, "Watch out, Vince! See the life-giving aura! That's what animates all the other monsters!"

Dawson made a couple of slashes at the thing, driving it back. Its hissing anger made the aura glow brighter again, going from orange back to yellow.

Clint ran along the fence toward Sal the Strap and his men. Three of them were done for, poisoned by the snake-eye creature or torn apart by the other half-human undead beasts. Clint shot the lock off the dog gate at that end of the compound, giving the last of the prisoners a chance to escape, and also opening the way for Chango's hideously transformed creatures to come out into the yard. But two of them didn't come out right away. Sal the Strap and one of his men were trapped. The mutant crocodile and the mutant leopard closed in on them, pinning them against the other dog gate as Clint ran down there to shoot off the lock. But he didn't make it in time. The Strap was chomped in two by the human crocodile and the other man's throat was torn out by the fangs of the leopard made of human flesh.

Clint backed away in horror and revulsion. And with a sick, scared look on his face, one of the DEA men came up and blasted the two creatures with his flamethrower, destroying both of the beasts as well as the remains of their hapless victims.

Feeling now that Martha must be right – the corpse effigy must be the "mother" of all the zombies – Dawson plunged his machete into its womanish breast. He knew that this breast had come from Mary Ann Scanlon, the head from Paul Beck, and the limbs from the other victims of three years ago.

As the machete entered the stitched-together body, the blade sparked and sizzled, and Vince thought he would be struck dead, electrocuted by the effigy's force field. He tried to let go, but couldn't. His hair was standing on end, his teeth chattering, his whole body shaking from the tremendous surge of the creature's aura.

He managed to lift his gimp arm, using the feeble power that was left in his shoulder to get his clawlike fingers on the hilt, for whatever help they could contribute to the life-and-death struggle. The effigy's force field sizzled through that arm, making the dead nerves quiver.

For a moment it was almost as if life had returned to that damaged limb, restoring it to its former vigor.

Instead of trying to let go of Chango's machete, Vince plunged it in deeper, using both hands.

The "human" voodoo doll screeched and hissed – and began to die. Its stitches fell apart, its legs collapsed, and its body crumbled to dust in the yard.

Clint Jones snapped Chango's whip at the mutant leopard, driving it back. He had one shot left in his revolver, so he thought, what the hell, he might as well use it. He shot the thing with snakes for eyes in the head. And to his surprise, the writhing, hissing snakes pulled back into their sockets. The thing transformed back into human form, then its flesh began to sizzle and dissolve to greenish slime, dissipating into the earth.

The death of the effigy had weakened all the rest of Chango's hell creatures. Now they could be more easily dispatched. Ordinary weapons were effective against them. As Clint stuck his empty revolver in his belt and looked around, ready to plunge into some other part of the battle, he saw that the zombies were now keeling over from the effects of regular rifle fire.

Inside the hacienda, Henri Blanc and the rest of Chango's disciples burst out of the corridor that led to the humfo. All of them were heavily armed. They ran up the stairways. Taking up positions in the upper windows of the house, they began firing at the DEA men.

But both choppers were in the air now, hovering and strafing. And then incendiary cannon rounds were aimed at the house, and the upper story burst into flames.

"Clara!" Susan screamed. "If she's in there she's going to be killed!" Wearing only a field jacket that one of the DEA men had given her, she broke from her mother's arms and started running toward the hacienda.

"Find somebody with a walkie-talkie!" Dawson shouted at Martha. "They can radio the choppers, tell them a little girl is in there."

Jones and Dawson ran after Susan. She was headed for the side door to the wing of the house that held the humfo. It was the door through which the ghastly procession had exited earlier.

Dawson stopped a DEA man who was running and firing an automatic rifle up at the windows. "Come with me!" Dawson shouted. "We might need those grenades – a little child is being held hostage in there!"

Susan was already pulling on the handle to the side door as Dawson, Jones, and the DEA man ran around the side of the building. The door wouldn't budge. "Stand back, Susan!" Dawson yelled. The DEA man fired a couple of rounds into the lock. Then Dawson yanked the door open.

They found themselves in the corridor that led to the humfo. The walls were largely bare now, Blanc and his men having stripped them of weapons. Down at the end, the steel door painted with the image of Damballah the Serpent God was locked shut. The DEA man fired several rounds into it, but it didn't budge. So he pulled everybody back, then lofted a grenade. The explosion rocked them all back on their heels, and made their ears ring. But the steel door swung partially open. The DEA man prodded it with his rifle barrel, opening it the rest of the way. Cautiously they entered the humfo.

Nobody was around. The glass coffins, now empty, were back in place, lining the walls. The voodoo paintings and effigies hung down in evil, silent array.

Hearing the explosion, Chango hurried his prayers to the ancient loas. He needed to complete his ritual, his human sacrifice. He stared down at Clara's blond curls, her peacefully entranced face, and he knew that she was his only salvation. If he gave the loas this innocent child, they would come to his aid. United, he and his kindred spirits would prevail over his mortal enemies.

Dawson had found the door to Chango's private chapel. He yanked on the knob. But the door was locked.

Chango raised the sacrificial knife, about to plunge it into Clara's breast.

A grenade exploded, blowing the door inward. Dawson, Clint, and the DEA man burst into the room, followed by Susan.

Chango didn't even turn to look at them. He started the dagger on its downward flight.

At the same time, Dawson threw the machete.

He was standing fifteen feet away from the bokor when he let the blade fly, whipping it by the hilt as if it were a throwing knife. But it didn't have a throwing knife's heft and balance. And Dawson wasn't a skilled man at tossing any kind of knife.

But the machete had the bokor's magic in it. The magic was heightened when the weapon was turned against him. And so it could do nothing else but fly true to its target.

With a loud *thock* the point of the blade hit between Chango's shoulder blades. It kept on going, coming out through his chest, and impaling him on the wooden altar.

The altar had been meant to be the deathbed of little Clara Crandall, but now it served that function for the bokor himself. He kicked and thrashed, dropping the dagger. His arms flew behind his back, and his hands seized the hilt of the machete, trying vainly to pull it out. But the magic in his own vever was too much for him.

Shrieking and hissing like one of his own hell creatures, he began to die. His bones glowed, a reddish glow, like an X ray, through his skin. Then the flesh started to peel away, in ribbony layers, like the wrappings of a mummy. Underneath the wrappings, there was no flesh, no organs, only red glowing bones. . . .

But their glow was dimming . . . turning orange.

Dawson, Jones, Susan, and the DEA man had backed away, and were frozen, their faces ashen as they watched the death of the bokor.

The gigantic seven-foot-tall skeleton was now crumbling, its bones reduced to a dim silvery glow. The bones turned to powder, and then ash. And the ashes turned to smoke, which rapidly dissipated to nothingness beneath the demonic altar.

It was as if the bokor had never existed. Except that the results of his murderous ways, his evil legacy, would always remain in the hearts and minds of his living victims.

Vince Dawson realized suddenly that he had used both hands to throw the machete. His bad arm was working – somehow it had been made whole. He clenched and unclenched the fingers, knowing that the charge of energy from the effigy's aura had somehow worked a miracle. But how long would the miracle last? He didn't know. Perhaps the arm would revert to its former dysfunction in a few minutes, an hour, a few days. Well, even if he wasn't permanently cured, he was glad to be alive.

Clint helped Susan unshackle little Clara. She wasn't awake yet, but she stirred a bit and smiled, as if in her trance her dreams had suddenly turned pleasant.

Protecting them with his rifle, the DEA man led the way out of the humfo. The noise of the battle was lessening. It was almost over. Chango's disciples had run from the flames that were consuming the main part of the hacienda, and had charged outside firing their weapons. But they were no match for the helicopters, which had kept hovering and strafing.

Henri Blanc perished in a hail of machine gun fire. And within a few more minutes the last few of the disciples were killed, too. There were a few final volleys of mop-up fire. Then everything was quiet, except for the whirring of the helicopter blades.

The fire continued to consume the hacienda, affecting the electric-power supply. The floodlights all around the compound went out. But the sun was coming up now. And the world was lit anew.

Martha was waiting for Vince and Clint and Susan and Clara as they came out of the side door. The DEA man looked on, starting to smile, as she tried to enfold all her loved ones in her arms at once, hugging and kissing them. Then she hugged and kissed them each in turn. The DEA man got his own share of hugs and handshakes too.

And they emerged into the light of dawn, leaving the darkness of hell behind them.

ABOUT THE AUTHOR

With twenty books published internationally and nineteen feature movies in worldwide distribution, John Russo has been called a "living legend." He began by co-authoring the screenplay for NIGHT OF THE LIVING DEAD, which has become recognized as a "horror classic." His three books on the art and craft of movie making have become bibles of independent production, and one of them, SCARE TACTICS, won a national award for Superior Nonfiction. Quentin Tarantino and many other noted filmmakers have stated that Russo's books helped them launch their careers.

John Russo wants people to know he's "just a nice guy who likes to scare people" – and he's done it with novels and films such as RETURN OF THE LIVING DEAD, MIDNIGHT, THE MAJORETTES, THE AWAKENING and HEARTSTOPPER. He has had a long, rewarding career, and he shows no signs of slowing down. Recently his screenplay for ESCAPE OF THE LIVING DEAD was made into a five-part comic book released by Avatar to great acclaim; it made the Top Ten of Horror Comics nationally and spawned two graphic novels and ten sequels.

Russo's recent novel is THE HUNGRY DEAD, was published by Kensington Books. He is also slated to direct two movies: a remake of his cult hit, MIDNIGHT, and a brand new take on the "zombie phenomenon" entitled SPAWN OF THE DEAD.

Russo's latest novels DEALEY PLAZA, THE ACADEMY, THE AWAKENING, and LIVING THINGS are published by Burning Bulb Publishing. His short story CHANNEL 666 appears in THE BIG BOOK OF BIZARRO.

His popularity among genre fans remains at a high pitch. He appears at many movie conventions each year as a featured guest, and he considers his appearance at the Orion Festival, hosted by Kirk Hammett and METALLICA, one of the highlights of his career.

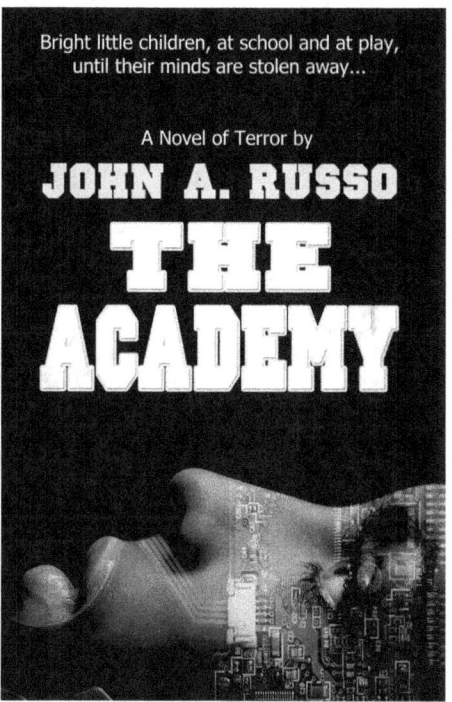

Bright little children, at school and at play, until their minds are stolen away...

A Novel of Terror by

JOHN A. RUSSO

THE ACADEMY

THE ACADEMY

The Academy. It's every parent's dream, turning their little darlings into geniuses, superachievers, perfect little children.

And if there's a problem, the Academy fixes that too. It's a simple operation. Just a little device. Then a teeny pink scar on a tender little skull . . .

One boy knows the secret. Now he wants his mind back. But it's much, much too late. Too late for anything but the ugly feelings. The bad feelings. The messy sexy feelings. The knife-cold hatred, the murderous rage, for total, screaming, blood-drenching revenge . . .

www.TheJohnRusso.com

Burning Bulb
PUBLISHING

THE AWAKENING

For two hundred years, he has rested. Now he rises. Now he will be satisfied. Nothing can stop him. No one can resist him.

Benjamin Latham is young and handsome, his eighteenth-century mind wakened to a bizarre twentieth-century world. And there is the need deep within . . . an animal need, frightening, murderous, unholy . . . a vital need that must be fed.

And with his need comes a power over men and women to do his bidding, to quiet his dark craving . . .

Until the murders begin. And the inquiries. All suggesting the same hideous truth.

Now Benjamin must find a sanctuary: a lover, a partner, a friend. Someone who can share his darkness. Someone he can lead to . . . The Awakening.

www.TheJohnRusso.com

THE BOOBY HATCH

With NIGHT OF THE LIVING DEAD, John Russo helped blaze a path in the horror genre that has never been equalled. In this hillarious erotic novel, he blazes a path through the wild, zany Sex Revolution of the 1970s.

Sweet, innocent Cherry Jankowski works for Joyful Novelties, where she tests sex toys ranging from the ridiculous to the sublime. But she can't find love or peace of mind and her efforts are hampered by a Peeping Tom, an exhibitionist, a cross-dressing boyfriend, a quack psychiatrist, and even her own product-testing partner, Marcello Fettucini, who can't get it up anymore and is scared of losing his job!

www.TheJohnRusso.com

Burning Bulb
PUBLISHING

DEALEY PLAZA

From legendary horror and suspense writer JOHN RUSSO comes a harrowing tale where no one is safe!

Dealey Plaza is one of the most notorious places in America, and when youthful conspiracy buffs go there in 1964 to stage their own reenactment of the Kennedy Assassination, four of them are brutally murdered ~ the first victims of a hate-filled legacy that continues for four more decades.

The survivors of that long-ago Dallas trip, each of them now icons of the American way of life, are about to be honored ~ or killed.

Who will live and who will die? Will it be country-western star Lori McCoy? Her loving husband? Her scheming ex-husband? Or the case-hardened FBI agent and longtime friend who risks his life trying to protect them?

www.DealeyPlazaBook.com

Burning Bulb
PUBLISHING

"A sense of infectious fun, straight from the author's pen."
– Nightmare Library

From Legendary Horror Writer
JOHN A. RUSSO
LIVING THINGS

"Russo carries his talent for the horrific neatly over into the novel form."
– West Coast Review of Books

LIVING THINGS

Beneath the shimmering Miami sun sprawls one of the Mafia's biggest empires, a glittering world of lavish beachfront mansions, neon-painted nightclubs, beautiful women, expensive cars—and absolute control over the state's billion-dollar drug trade. But, one by one, its ganglords and henchmen are falling prey to a new rival. His powers are fueled by monstrous ancient rituals; his hellish undead legions slaughter mobsters and innocent citizens alike, his unholy lust for power is virtually unstoppable.

Now a burned-out ex-detective and a brilliant anthropologist must enter a gruesome, nightmare world to fight this master of malevolence and illusion. Their time is short, their weapons few, and they face an ultimate, terrifying choice - annihilation or the loss of their souls to the eternal torment of those who never die. . .

www.TheJohnRusso.com

Burning Bulb
PUBLISHING

NIGHT OF THE LIVING DEAD

Why does **Night of the Living Dead** hit with such chilling impact?
Is it because everyday people in a commonplace house are suddenly the
victims of a monstrous invasion? Or is it because the ghouls who surround
the house with grasping claws were once ordinary people, too?

Decide for yourself as you read, and the horror grips you. All the
cannibalism, suspense and frenzy of the smash-hit move are here in the
novel.

www.TheJohnRusso.com

Burning Bulb
PUBLISHING

OTHER GREAT TITLES FROM

Burning Bulb

PUBLISHING

WWW.BURNINGBULBPUBLISHING.COM

ANTHOLOGIES
BIZARRO AND TRANSGRESSIVE FICTION

THE BIG BOOK OF BIZARRO

The Big Book of Bizarro brings together the peculiar prose of an international cast of the most grotesquely-gonzo, genre-grinding modern writers who ever put pen to paper (or mouse to pad), including:

NIGHT OF THE LIVING DEAD horror writers John Russo & George Kosana; HUSTLER MAGAZINE erotica contributors Eva Hore, Andrée Lachapelle, & J. Troy Seate and established Bizarro genre authors D. Harlan Wilson, William Pauley III, Wol-vriey, Laird Long, Richard Godwin and so many more!

From Alien abductions to Zombie sex, The Big Book of Bizarro contains OVER FIFTY STORIES of the most outrélandish transgressive fiction that you'll ever lay your capricious and curious hands upon!

WARNING: This book may be one of the most controversial and dangerous books you'll ever read.

WESTWARD HOES

Nine outlaw writers rode into town from obscurity to pen nine tantalizing tales of horror and fantasy, and leaving once they branded their own personal marks on the weird western genre and became living legends of the American Frontier experience.

Like drunken Indian scouts, the writers fervidly tracked down and captured the Western genre, tore off its fashionable veneer and ravished its exposed essence.

So belly up to the bar with your favorite soiled dove and enjoy perusing these thrilling tales of Old West debauchery, danger and desire; compiled by the publisher of The Big Book of Bizarro and featuring the bizarro novella *Big Trouble in Little Ass* by Wol-vriey.

Burning Bulb
PUBLISHING

ANTHOLOGIES
BIZARRO AND TRANSGRESSIVE FICTION

THE BIG BOOK OF BIZARRO SPECIAL KINDLE EDITIONS

OTHER AWESOME COLLECTIONS

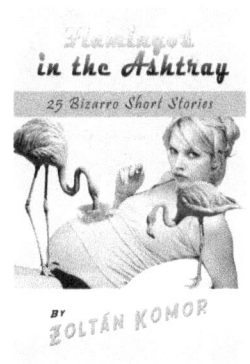

Burning Bulb
PUBLISHING

GARY LEE VINCENT'S
DARKENED
THE WEST VIRGINIA VAMPIRE SERIES

DARKENED HILLS

When evil descends on a small West Virginia town, who will survive?

Jonathan did not start out his life to become a rambler, it just worked out that way. William was a troubled youth with something to hide. Both were from Melas, a small town tucked away in the West Virginia hills... a town where disappearances are happening more and more frequently.

After the suicide of a wanted serial killer, the townsfolk thought the nightmare was over. But when a centuries-old vampire is discovered they find out the hard way it's just getting started. Dark secrets can only stay hidden for so long and when the devil comes to collect, there will be hell to pay. Can Jonathan and William find a way to stop the vampire before it's too late? Find out in *Darkened Hills*!

DARKENED HOLLOWS

In the heart-stopping sequel to the award-winning *Darkened Hills*, Jonathan and William must return to West Virginia to face possible criminal charges stemming from their last visit to the damned town of Melas, where both had narrowly escaped the clutches of a vampire seethe.

And as livestock start mysteriously getting murdered with all of their blood drained, worried farmers are searching for answers - leaving the local Sheriff and his deputy racing against time to learn the cause before a more violent crime is committed.

Burning Bulb
PUBLISHING

WWW.DARKENEDHILLS.COM

GARY LEE VINCENT'S
DARKENED
THE WEST VIRGINIA VAMPIRE SERIES

DARKENED WATERS

When the world goes to hell, the chosen must arise!

As Talman Cane orchestrates a flood of epic proportions in this third installment of the *Darkened* series the towns of Melas and Tarklin are caught completely off guard by the deluge. Hell-bent on finishing what they started, the evil brothers return to the lunatic asylum to take care of the witnesses and add to the ever-growing army of the undead.

Aided by Lucifer himself and the insane vampire demon Legion, the stage is set to channel all of the forces of hell to come forth. In an all-out race to survive, Jonathan, William, and Amanda soon discover they are up against impossible odds as Lucifer opens the Gateway to Hell, ushering in the zombie apocalypse and the End Times.

DARKENED SOULS

Melas and the Madison House are about to be rebuilt.
True evil is about to be reborne!

Young ex-priest and vampire-killer William is drawn back to the West Virginian town that almost killed him, where his vampire arch-enemy Victor Rothenstein still stalks the earth.

The town of Melas lies destroyed after the battle of the End of Days. But why is wealthy Jackie Nixon so eager to rebuild it using the bone dust of murdered souls?

Terrible evil has visited before, but the Gateway to Hell is about to be reopened in a horrific climax. And this time – it's personal.

WWW.DARKENEDHILLS.COM

Burning Bulb
PUBLISHING

WEST VIRGINIA-THEMED
HUMORROROTICA

BY RICH BOTTLES JR.

HELLHOLE WEST VIRGINIA

From the heights of Mothman's perch high atop the Silver Bridge in Point Pleasant to the depths of Hellhole Cavern in Pendleton County, evil lurks within the shadows as the sun sets upon the haunted hills and hollows of West Virginia.

Bizarro author Rich Bottles Jr. blows the coffin lid off horror genre clichés with this tour de force cast of Eco-friendly vampires, beach-yearning zombies and sex-starved she-devils.

LUMBERJACKED

If you are easily offended or do not possess a truly depraved sense of humor, this story may not be the light summer reading fare you desire. As for the four feisty female freshmen stranded on top of West Virginia's third highest mountain, they have no choice but to experience the sick, twisted debauchery and perverted mayhem described deep inside the tight unbroken bindings of this horrific missive.

Lumberjacked takes the reader to a nightmarish world where character development and aesthetic integrity are prematurely cut short by the swinging axes of maniacal lumberjacks, who are hell bent on death and destruction in the remote forests of Appalachia. And at the climax, when paranoia crosses over to the paranormal, Lumberjacked makes Deliverance look like a family raft trip down the Lower Gauley.

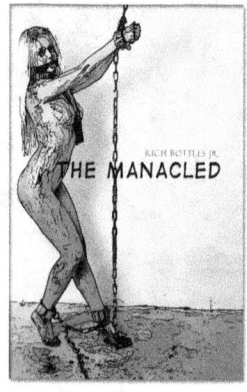

THE MANACLED

What happens when twin brothers lease out the former West Virginia State Penitentiary with the false purpose of filming a documentary on supernatural phenomena, but their true intention is to make a porno-graphic movie?

Chaos ensues as the disturbed spirits of murdered convicts, along with the reanimated dead from the neighboring Indian Burial Mound, take their vengeance on the unwary and undressed trespassers.

Zombies, ghosts, mobsters and porn collide in this bizarro tale from horror author Rich Bottles Jr.

Burning Bulb
PUBLISHING

WOL-VRIEY
BIZARRO AND TRANSGRESSIVE FICTION

Burning Bulb
PUBLISHING

BOSTON POSH

In 2028 AD, the USA is a nation ravaged by hungry dragons and dinosaurs. In Boston, Massachusetts, private eye Bud Malone is hired to rescue a kidnapped heiress. But nothing is as it seems. Malone works to unravel a tangled web involving Boston Chinatown, a 200-year-old woman with a 9-year-old body, white robots, a human-liver-eating psychopath, a golem, a porcelain dragon, and a snake goddess with a crush on him. There's also a woman obsessed with chicken sex. Then Malone meets Posh Lane, a gorgeous call girl who's desperate to quit her pimp. Romantic sparks ignite between Posh and Malone, but Posh's past suddenly catches up with her in a BIG way. To save Posh, Malone agrees to run a quest for Earth's new rulers, the Forks. But, Malone has no idea that agreeing to the Fork's odd request will send him on the weirdest trip he's ever been on in his life.

VEGAN VAMPIRE VAGINAS

The biggest bank heist in US history. And Tom Palmer can't remember pulling it off. And no, this isn't your standard case of amnesia. After a one-night-stand gone horribly wrong, Boston salesman Tom Palmer wakes up with a vagina implanted in his left hand. Then his day gets worse:

Tom is transported across space-time to a nightmare version of Boston, one where the Bizarro virus has transformed half the population into cannibals. Worst of all, Tom discovers that in this new Boston, he's the infamous gangster Pussypalm, wanted for robbing the Federal Reserve Bank of Boston a year ago. He also learns that the vagina in his hand is prophetic, i.e. it talks . . . after sex. With 130 people left dead during his bank heist and six billion dollars missing, Tom knows he's living on borrowed time. It is in his best interests not to remember anything. Because once he does . . .

VEGAN ZOMBIE APOCALYPSE

In the post-apocalypse worlderness, zombies rule the earth. They're allergic to meat, and brains literally make them explode. Zombies now eat blood potatoes, parasitic tubers grown in the flesh of humancows corralled in maximum security farms. Two fugitives meet in the ancient ruins of Texas. The first is Soil 15-f, a womancow who's escaped her farm a week before she's due to be killed and her blood potato crop harvested. The second fugitive is Able Kane, former head necros food technician, now sentenced to death for heresy. But Soil is no ordinary humancow. Unknown to herself, she's the vegan zombie agricultural revolution, and the zombies desperately want her back. And the necros equally desperately want Able Kane dead. He's fled with a forbidden discovery which will reshape the world for the worse if used. And Able is just hardheaded/misguided enough to use it.

MINOR CONFESSIONS OF AN ANGEL FALLING UPWARD

by Planner Forthright, as edited by Joey Madia

Confession. Revelation. Rant. *Minor Confessions of an Angel Falling Upward* is all of these... and more. Set in modern times and spiraling back to the swirl of Pre-Creation, this postmodern blend of genre-bending pop-prose and socio-political commentary is a classic tale of the (anti-)hero's quest for Reason and Redemption in a Universe gone mad.

Who is Planner Forthright? A fallen angel made Man. A once-winged evil with un-Divine purpose on this Plane. A cannibal prince chosen to inherit a castled landscape of destruction and despair. An Alchemist of sorts—a mental magician; a mortar-and-pestle wizard converting carbon lies to golden Truth, whose language is his own. A Vampire by nature and condition whose been walking the waters and thorny highways of our planet for over 40 years. And he's seeking a way out...

PASSAGEWAY

by Gary Lee Vincent with illustrations by Andy Hopp

When an archeological dig goes horribly wrong, the team is trapped in an alternate world where evil awaits them at every turn. Find out who will survive the *Passageway*!

From Gary Lee Vincent, the author of supernatural vampire thriller *Darkened Hills*, comes an unforgettable tale that spans four continents and takes the reader to the very realm of Hell itself.

Skeleton warriors, zombies, other undead beings and werewolves are allvery real inside the *Passageway*! In this Bizarro-genre tribute to H.P. Lovecraft and Indiana Jones, this deadly tale will keep you guessing and leave you breathless to the end!

THE TWELVE STEPS

by Zachary Crabtree

"A Man who Cannot Keep Awake Cannot Keep it Together." There is always something that pulls an alcoholic deeper into his unquenchable thirst – something degenerative to the human spirit. Indeed, there have been incidents in my life that carry tragic significance to me, yet I know they pale in comparison to the tragedies experienced by others.

When the jagged pieces of a disfigured past become a troubled, broken-up, glass-bottled mosaic in one's present life, all the innocent souls affected along the way become entangled in one's conscience; while the depression, pills, manic behavior and soul-searching coalesce in a series of twelve steps.

Alcohol affects the lives of hooligans, stubborn old fools, lovers, and families torn apart by drunk drivers – drunk drivers like me.

Burning Bulb
PUBLISHING

THE FALL OF TOMORROW

Hopelessness... How do you protect your loved ones when Hell
itself opens its insidious mouth?
Horror... Nightmarish Creatures invade your world and there is
nowhere to hide.
Blood... How long can you hold out before they come for you?
Pain... Where do you run to avoid being eaten alive by monsters
with a voracious appetite for your flesh?
Screams... While you selfishly run for your own life.
Questions... Who is to blame? Where did they come from? How
many people survived...and how does the human race find the
means to fight back?

THE FALL OF TOMORROW is man's last tale of desperation
told by those that are striving to salvage some hope against a
ravenous bastion of evil beasts bent on ruling our world.

*"David Fairhead writes compelling stories that offer very human characters
and very inhuman monsters. There is no subtlety in Fairhead's imagination -
he is simply dying to scare the hell out of you."*
- Nelson W Pyles - author of DEMONS, DOLLS AND MILKSHAKES

Burning Bulb
PUBLISHING

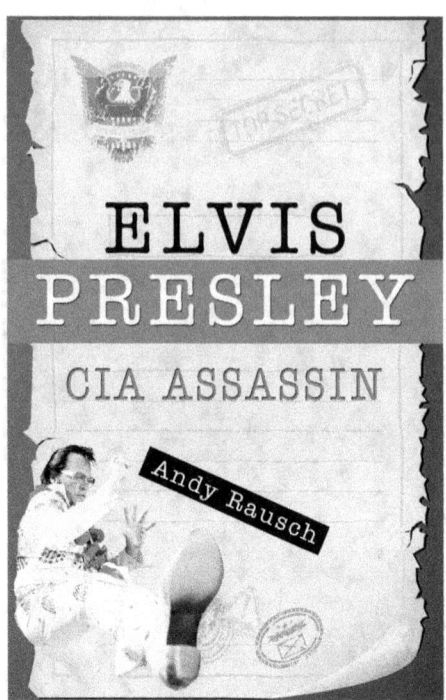

ELVIS PRESLEY, CIA ASSASSIN

"I can guarantee you. Read this book and you'll never look at Elvis the same way again!"
~ Douglas Brode, author of ELVIS CINEMA AND POPULAR CULTURE

SOON TO BE A MAJOR MOTION PICTURE

In 1970, singer Elvis Presley secretly met with President Richard Nixon. This new comedic novel imagines that Presley became a Central Intelligence Agency operative, eventually moving up through the ranks to become a skilled assassin.

Presented in an oral history fashion, the book tells us about Presley's secret transformation by the people who knew him best.

Did he fake his death in 1977? Was Presley involved with the Watergate scandal? The Iran hostage crisis? Communicating with aliens?

Read this book to find out the answers to these and many more questions.

Burning Bulb
PUBLISHING